One Remarkable Year

I0741108

Meredith Resce

One Remarkable Year

Melrose is not just a place.

Meredith Resce

One Remarkable Year

Golden Grain Publishing

PO Box 880, Unley SA 5061

The National Library of Australia Cataloguing-in-Publication information:

Resce, Meredith, 1963- .
One remarkable year.

ISBN 0 9585523 7 1

1. Title.

A823.3

This is a work of fiction. Some of the stories are based on fact, however names, characters and incidents are either the product of the author's imagination or are used fictitiously. Permission has been gained for the use of actual names and basic information.

2nd printing 2016
First printing April 2003

Australian Rural Life;
Cover Photographs: Front cover – Nott Street Melrose, The World War One Monument, Jim Bishop, Jack Dickson, Geoff Arthur and Graham Leske. Back Cover – The Trotts at Melrose Show, The Mount Creek in flood, The 1988 Fire, The Brewery Paddock, Stuart Street Melrose.

This book is dedicated to the people of Melrose,
Past and Present

ACKNOWLEDGMENTS

To put a book like this together takes the dedication of a great team of people.

Thanks must go to the research and review team: Lorrie Lellow, Peter Abbott, Jim Bishop, Sue Hoffmann, Jayne Dick, Lyall Arthur, Janice Moulton, Peter and Carol Bamman.

Special mention must go to Jennette Bishop who has spent literally hours and hours of transcribing, phone calling, chasing up and reviewing.

Thanks to the team of editors: Pat Mayfield, Ed Darwood, Elisa Resce, Margaret Wigg and Judy Headley.

Thanks to the team of artists:

Dan Chattaway (cover), Peter Heaven (text) and Matthew Holmes (map).

A special thanks to all of those people who sat and told their stories and who were such good sports allowing us to use them.

I must pay special tribute to Mrs Vera Fuller, who not only inspired me as one of her music students, but whose stories simply sparked with humour and life. May God bless you in your 93rd year.

Lastly, thank you to my family, Nick, Elisa, David and Michael, who have never lived at Melrose, but by virtue of the fact that I live there in my imagination half the time, are members of the community by association. Thank you for your patience.

God bless you all
Meredith Resce

INTRODUCTION

Forty-four years ago I came, as a bride, to Melrose. It was when Clarrie, if he had truly lived, would have had his escapades. This small country town was unique, yet mirrored life in other towns around Australia.

In those days, instead of watching TV, we listened to the wireless. Everyone knew the country hour followed by "Blue Hills". We cared for the home and the children and helped on the land.

Life had a certain structure. Early morning rise to milk the cows, and feed the fowls, before the children went to school. Tuesdays and Fridays we went to town. That was when the bread was baked, the doctor visited, and meetings were held. Then, after an ever so slow process, I realised things had changed in Melrose. Life was different.

We shopped in other distant places, wives worked off the farm and once thriving businesses had gone. Old familiar faces were gone. We were losing some of the character of our town.

Although we have an excellent history book "Child of the Mountain", the town's own character, and the story of its people were not recorded fully.

So when the 150th year celebration was announced, "One Remarkable Year" was born, but not without some struggle.

It is our wish that in this work of biographical fiction you will see your town and mine. A place where even today it's safe to leave your car unlocked, where you know almost everyone you meet on the street and where the people share your joy and your pain. A place where people truly care, and where a child like Clarrie could, and in some cases still does, live.

"One Remarkable Year" is about the child that had to leave the country; it's about the battlers of the bush, their individual personality and good humour, and it is about the spirit and moral fibre of every country town. But mostly it is about our beloved town Melrose – not just a place.

by **Jennette Bishop**

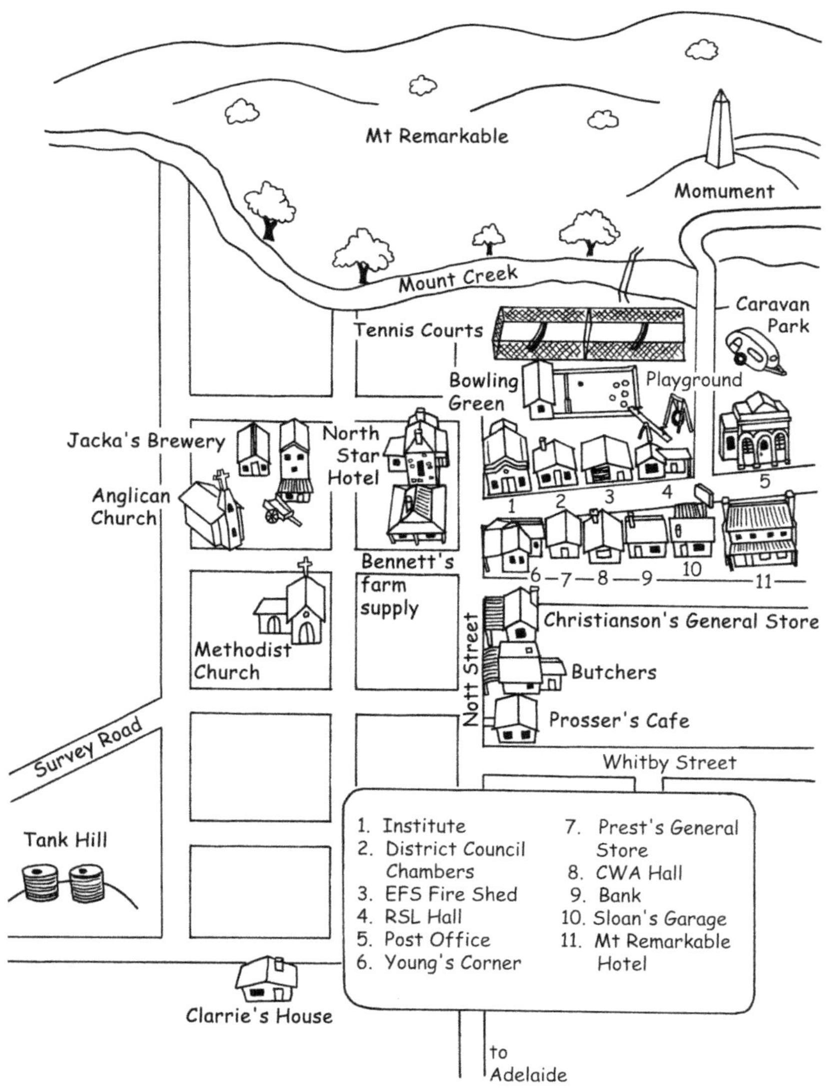

Mt Remarkable
Momument
Mount Creek
Tennis Courts
Caravan Park
Bowling Green
Playground
Jacka's Brewery
North Star Hotel
Anglican Church
1
2
3
4
5
Bennett's farm supply
6 — 7 — 8 — 9
10
11
Methodist Church
Nott Street
Christianson's General Store
Butchers
Prosser's Cafe
Survey Road
Whitby Street
Tank Hill
1. Institute
2. District Council Chambers
3. EFS Fire Shed
4. RSL Hall
5. Post Office
6. Young's Corner
7. Prest's General Store
8. CWA Hall
9. Bank
10. Sloan's Garage
11. Mt Remarkable Hotel
Clarrie's House
to Adelaide

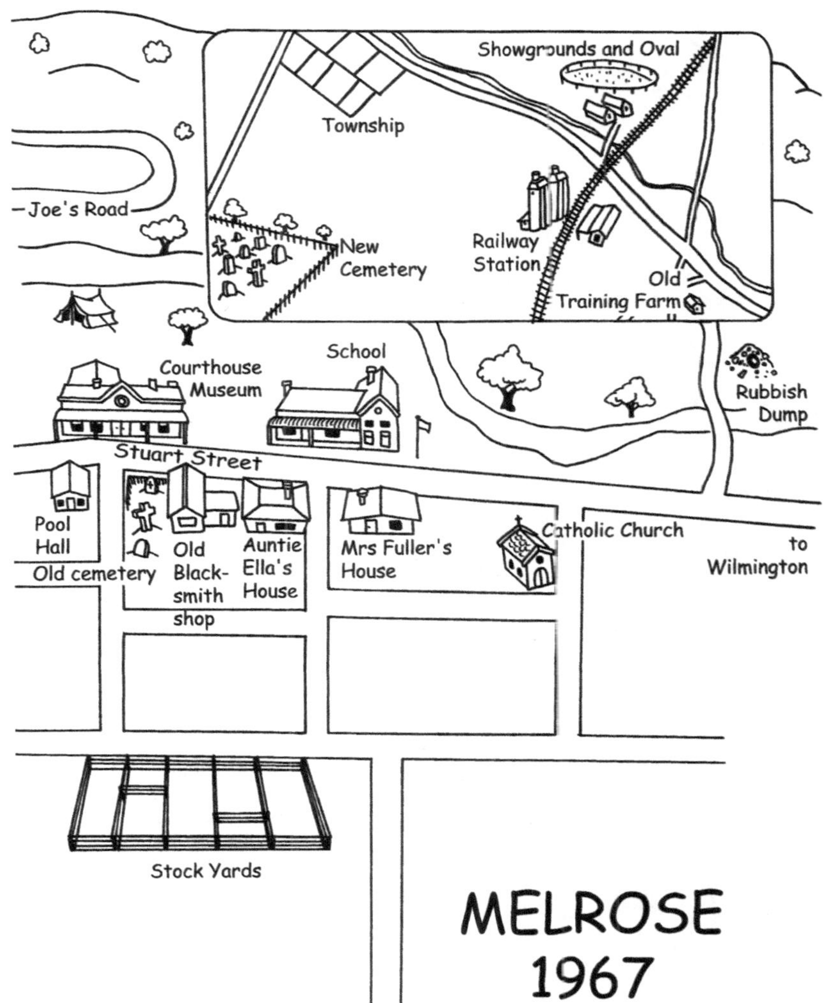

Showgrounds and Oval
Township
Joe's Road
New Cemetery
Railway Station
Old Training Farm
School
Courthouse Museum
Rubbish Dump
Stuart Street
Pool Hall
Old cemetery
Old Blacksmith shop
Auntie Ella's House
Mrs Fuller's House
Catholic Church
to Wilmington
Stock Yards
MELROSE
1967

Prologue

Clarrie could see that they were in trouble. The creek-bed was full of reeds and undergrowth, not to mention the dry fallen branches and the trees that grew thickly along the banks. With the fire rushing their way, it was like sitting on a powder keg. If only there had been water in the creek. As it was, it was the middle of summer, the temperatures soaring into the forties, and there was no water anywhere near that would save them from the inferno that was threatening.

He was with one of the local volunteers, Peter Bamman, and a bulldozer driver. They were out the back of the mountain, Peter trying to guide the process of grading a firebreak and Clarrie along as an extra driver. A major bushfire was raging through the Mount Remarkable National Park and they'd hoped to contain it there, and not allow it to burn south into the foothills where there were farms and grazing land.

But they had been caught. Clarrie could hear the rush of flames whooshing through leafy branches, jumping from tree to tree, coming more quickly than even he had imagined. They were virtually stranded in the bottom of this dry creek-bed, surrounded by tinder-dry fuel. The bank they'd descended was far too steep to try and get back out that way, and there was only a steep hill in front of them. It was not a good option, considering the propensity of fire to burn up hill rapidly, but it seemed to be their only one.

They decided to try it, but it quickly became obvious that Peter's ute was not going to be able to make the steep grade.

"I'll grade a track up to that flat spot up there," the dozer driver yelled

above the roar. Clarrie stood with Peter knowing that all they could do was stand and watch, monitoring the billowing smoke and the approaching flames. With a rough track graded the dozer returned to the bottom.

"Now, I'll have to give the ute a bit a of nudge up the hill." It was like these volunteers to speak calmly, even in the face of danger.

A bit of a nudge was not as easy as it sounded. The traction was almost none, and even the dozer, bearing the weight of the utility, had its tracks spinning around and round until it hit rock and took grip. Still nothing was being achieved. The tension rising with each passing second, Peter decided to start the engine of his vehicle to give that extra horsepower to the exercise. What followed was a series of small advances, followed by the ute rolling back into the blade of the dozer, making a noise like a rear-end collision. Clarrie, who was riding with Peter, could almost feel the vehicle getting shorter by inches but even though he felt for Peter, having his vehicle so badly damaged it was easily dismissed as a minor concern when compared to what was coming.

Eventually, they made the small piece of flat ground.

"We'll go back and get the other bus," Peter yelled. Clarrie didn't object. Though it was the vehicle that he'd been driving, he knew that he didn't have the experience of negotiating such difficult conditions that these men had. He waited with the ute already on the level rise.

But when he saw that the fire was now well over the top of the nearby hill and well on its destructive way toward them he felt a rise of panic in his stomach. He realised that Peter had seen it too as he heard Peter's voice calling from the other truck at the bottom of the hill, coming over the CB radio in this ute.

"Melrose Base, this is Melrose 21, over." Clarrie heard Peter make the call several times with no response. They were out the back of the hills and the communication often had to be relayed back to the main base. Peter's call came again, and this time got a response from another CB unit not far away.

"We're trapped," he called into the mike. "The fire's surrounded us now. I can't see a way out. Over."

Clarrie wondered what really could be achieved by communicating this piece of news. The situation seemed hopeless now. He'd seen the bits of burning debris carried by the wind from off the mountain, fall and start spot fires, as if it had its own murderous intent to surround and attack. Below he watched as his companions wrestled with the other four-wheel-drive. They had made small progress when he saw the ute slip from the dozer blade and roll back to the bottom of the hill. There isn't time, *he thought to himself.* Just leave it! *But they returned to start the slow process all over again. Meanwhile the fire raged forward, the roaring of the flames increasing with every yard it moved closer.*

Desperately, Clarrie considered starting a back-burn to leave ground around himself free from fuel, but he knew he couldn't do that until the others were with him. Come on! Come on! *He mentally urged them along. It seemed like an age before they were finally on the small flat. Clarrie thought of a thousand things to say, but none of them seemed useful in the face of the oncoming menace. What advice was there to offer in such a situation? The driver didn't comment, but simply began to grade a break. But it was only one blade wide and the way the fire was approaching with such ferocity, Clarrie doubted it would stop a thing.*

There was no time left. The dozer-driver left his vehicle and jumped into the cab of the ute with Peter and Clarrie. The door was scarcely closed and they saw a twenty-foot wall of fire burst up in fury, right in front of them.

"God!" the driver exclaimed.

"We're finished!" Clarrie muttered under his breath.

The roaring blaze seemed to come right over the vehicles to consume them. The heat and the smoke was so intense, it was unbearable. It seemed that this would be the last few moments of their lives.

Chapter
One

January 1988

As soon as he saw the thick cloud of smoke, Clarrie Brown's mind was torn with conflicting emotions. It was like an alarm that triggered a rush of anxiety. His mind had been consumed with his own personal troubles ever since he'd left home some three hours earlier, but with the sight of the black and grey shroud that hung ominously in the air, his focus changed sharply.

Mt Remarkable was alight, and Melrose, the small town that nestled right at the foot of the mountain, was under threat.

At this point of time, the past and the future came crashing wildly in on top of each other. Melrose.

When his editor had said in a blasé manner that some little no-account place out in the sticks was threatened by bushfire, Clarrie hadn't thought much of it until his boss had said the name of the town. 'Melrose'.

"Melrose?" Clarrie had said sharply. "Mount Remarkable?"

"I dunno," his editor had replied, "and to be honest, I don't much care. It's not like there's any great number of people there, like when Mount Lofty was alight five years ago. But someone will have to go and be on hand in case something worth reporting happens."

"I'll go!" Clarrie had said without a second thought. The words had slipped out automatically. For eight years this little town had been his home. His mother had taken him and his sister there to live at the time his father had been killed in a forest accident in 1960.

His childhood memories were bound up in that place. How could he not offer to go?

"Well that was easy!" the editor had remarked. "And I thought I was going to have to pull rank to get someone to go!"

The volunteering had been the easy part, but when Clarrie had gone home to hurriedly throw some things in a suitcase, he met a very different response.

"You've got things you have to do here, Clarrie," Sue Brown had said in an agitated tone.

"It's my job, Sue," Clarrie had replied without looking up from his open bag.

"I don't care about your stupid job," she had screamed. "What about the kids? What about the fact that the bank is breathing down my neck and wants money? What am I supposed to tell them?"

Clarrie hadn't answered but zipped his bag shut and hoisted it off the bed with extra strength born of anger. He didn't have an answer to the problem. He'd just wanted to escape the constant pressure of troubles he couldn't fix and didn't want to face.

When he'd left home several hours ago Sue had been angry. "Don't bother to come back, Clarrie. We don't need you! We don't want you!"

That had cut deep and added to the hurt from arguments long since past, but still was not enough to make him turn back. There were too many things — troubles brought about by his own actions — that he didn't have any idea of where to begin to stem the flow of trouble.

But as soon as he saw the fire looming in front, the home crisis and all the things they had shouted at each other before he'd left seemed to take a back seat. Memories of years past seemed to rush back into his mind. Good memories. Times when he'd been settled and secure. They were probably the happiest years of his life. With all the faces and names of the past buzzing around in his mind, mixed with the sight of angry orange flames licking the landscape the closer he drove, fear — a real, cold, gut-wrenching fear - emerged. Clarrie seemed unable now to rehash the recent traumas when this rush of memories was intent upon swamping his thoughts. People who'd held a special place in his heart during those years were back in his mind's eye. He hadn't lived here for twenty years, and yet those times were easily recalled, as fresh as the day they'd happened.

By the time Clarrie approached the cemetery, about a mile and a half from town, he could easily see that a major catastrophe was upon this fondly remembered community. Alongside the road leading into the town limits, four-wheel-drives of all makes and models were pulled up, each one bearing the burden of fire fighting tanks and hoses. There were groups of men involved in animated discussions, waving arms and pointing, with looks of great concern on their faces. Clarrie's imagination told him what it was they must have been saying. It appeared that one was a supervisor of some sort and the rest were there listening as a plan and strategy were laid out.

He wanted to stop and listen and ask questions, but common sense, and previous experience of reporting crisis situations, told him that his investigation would not be welcome. He drove on along Nott Street, past the butcher shop and what had once been Christianson's General Store, making mental note that things had changed. The butcher's was closed up and was looking rather rundown, while Christianson's was now an antique shop. But Clarrie's mind was too distracted to really process these dramatic changes. By the time he'd come to the North Star Hotel, and turned right into Stuart Street, he could see that both main streets had cars and vehicles lined up on both sides. Clarrie was unable to remember a time when he'd seen so many cars in town at one time. But there didn't seem to be as many people as this amount of cars would warrant. Obviously a lot of volunteers were out battling the raging blaze.

Clarrie knew where the action centre was. The EFS shed; right opposite the now empty building that had been Young's Café. Things had changed so much here. The fire shed was now labelled CFS, the word 'Emergency' having been replaced with 'Country' Fire Service. There was nowhere to park in this general vicinity and Clarrie had to drive much farther up the street, past the Post Office, before he found a place to park his late model Holden. He saw that there was now a roadhouse, come general store, where the old pool hall had been, and decided then and there that it would be wise to buy himself something to eat. He'd been too upset when leaving home, and hadn't even thought of it since. He thought he'd better grab something now, and even book into the Mount Remarkable Pub to stay before trying to find out some details to fax back to the office.

He didn't see anybody he recognised in the shop as he ordered a salad roll and coke. Neither was the woman in the pub anybody he'd seen before, and yet this hotel was as familiar to him as his own house back in Adelaide. Twenty years ago, his mother had been a cook and domestic for the Mount Remarkable Hotel.

Clarrie didn't blame the women who served him for their seeming lack of friendliness. He could sense the tension they must have been feeling.

"I'm sorry for sounding short," the woman from the pub eventually said, as she handed Clarrie a key to one of the outside units. "The fact is we might all have to fly out of here at a moments notice. I've been busy all morning packing up all my valuables and taking them across to a friend's place in Booleroo."

"So there's a chance the fire could reach the town?" Clarrie asked, not just motivated by the need for a story, but also because this town had been like his whole backyard as a kid. Melrose sat right at the foot of this mighty mountain that was now alive with consuming destructive flames.

"It's so hot and the wind keeps changing. They reckon that nothing seems to be holding the fire. It keeps jumping firebreaks and roads. God knows what will be lost before it's all over."

Clarrie understood her depth of fear. He really did. They stood just outside the Mount Remarkable Hotel, one of the oldest buildings in the town, a landmark and a place that held a lot of memories and had seen a lot of things happen. To think that this place and many others like it in the town could be burned to the ground raised Clarrie's own anxiety. But what was there he could do to stop it?

1967

Clarrie played with the handle of his school satchel. Miss Jolly seemed intent on prolonging the dismissal, as if it gave her pleasure to see the children squirm. They could all read the school clock, and once the hand had passed the three thirty mark, they ceased to pay attention. Clarrie couldn't see why she just didn't let them go, but the power was in her hands and she would not yield, no matter how much they fidgeted.

Eventually, she allowed them to move quietly outside, and every one did move quietly. They all knew that if one person showed just an ounce of eagerness by too hurried a step, they would all be called back and lectured about respect and decorum. But once they were safely beyond the bounds of the cement steps, the laughing and shouting amongst themselves got full vent.

Now outside, Clarrie tossed several options around in his mind. Georgie Greenbank had some wild scheme of feeding bread on a string to Mr Ey's chooks. They'd done that before, and the unsuspecting fowls ended up tied to the school fence with the bread and string in their poultry stomachs. It was tempting, but then so was the offer to ride the school bus route. Mr Briggs offered this treat to Clarrie once in a while, when there were children away. Georgie thought it was a dull sort of treat, and certainly none of the children who rode the bus home every day, to their homes a way out from the town, could understand why Clarrie would want to make such a boring trip. Their little blue Morris bus that looked like a loaf of bread on wheels, putted around an eighteen-mile circuitous route morning and night. Clarrie, who lived in the town, and usually walked to and from school, saw the occasional ride as an amusement and distraction from the mundane.

But he didn't have time to take the ride this afternoon.

"I have to do a job for my mother," Clarrie told Mr Briggs when turning down the offer.

"Doesn't matter!" the bus driver returned. "Next time. You need to keep your mother happy, Clarrie!"

He hadn't actually lied to Mr Briggs, but he had just avoided telling the whole truth. He had his piano lesson scheduled and he knew that it was unavoidable. But this was certainly not something he was going to use as an excuse for not tormenting the chooks. Georgie would laugh himself silly. And he wasn't quite ready to entrust this particular secret to the bus driver either. He was sure Mr Briggs would probably be quite polite about it, but there was always the danger that he would let the information slip, and it could get into the wrong hands. Learning the piano was a secret that Clarrie was willing to take to the grave. He only did it to honour his father's memory, which was the clever stroke of genius his mother had used to get him to learn in the first place. Mr Vincent Brown had been quite a musician before his death, and though he only ever played at home, it was a legacy that his wife, Beth, wanted passed on. Clarrie's older sister had already shown her ineptitude when it came to things musical, and had been reprieved. Unfortunately, Clarrie had been unable to hide his ear for music, and the lot now fell to him.

He crossed the road from the schoolyard, and looked in over the fence to see if Auntie Ella was on her veranda watching the day's activities. Mrs Bishop wasn't really his aunt, but she was one of those characters that could have been anyone's auntie, and by virtue of the fact that Clarrie didn't have any extended family to speak of, she'd told him to call her Auntie Ella. She wasn't on the veranda today, and this was unusual, for that was where she usually sat of an afternoon about this time. She liked to watch the comings and goings of people, and going-home time was an interesting time of day. Clarrie hoped that she wasn't unwell.

"The Methodist Ladies Fellowship have a special meeting this afternoon, Clarrie," Mr Briggs called across the road to him, noticing his hesitation in front of the Bishops' house. "Mrs Bishop will likely be there, I'd guess."

That was good enough for Clarrie, and he hurried on along the street, only regretting the lost chance of being invited in for milk and those famous honey biscuits for a short time. He was sure to see Auntie Ella another day. He walked down the street past the old blacksmith shop, and, as was his usual habit, tried for all he was worth to see if he could see anything inside the dark window of the small dwelling next to it. He didn't loiter for long, as Auntie Ella had told him that Mrs Young didn't like nosey young people poking about in their premises. But he always wondered what went on in there. He just didn't accept the story that it was simply a closed up place, used only for storage. He was certain that something far more sinister was afoot.

And there was the story about the empty block of land next door to the old blacksmith, an abandoned cemetery: dead people everywhere, right in the middle of town, and not one gravestone to mark it. He wondered if that could possibly be true. But even Auntie Ella had confirmed that story. Apparently that empty block had been a cemetery when the town had first been settled. She hadn't given him much more detail than that, and the only thing left was to try and formulate some sort of theory from the actual facts known, and the many whispers of conjecture that went around the schoolyard. One thing was for certain, Clarrie didn't go wandering past the old cemetery or the old blacksmith shop after dark, - well, at least not when he was alone. Fact or fiction, there were all sorts of ghostly terrors when one's imagination was left to itself.

Clarrie could have turned off down Jacka Street, past the pool hall, and gone the back way to reach his house, but he elected to continue straight ahead along Stuart Street. The other way was a quiet, lonely route, and he was unlikely to see anyone of interest if he went that way. The only time that Jacka and Whitby Street offered more excitement than the main street was on market day, when all the farmers would come into town with stock, either to buy or to sell. That only happened once a month, and Clarrie usually went to sit on the stockyard fence and watch the auctioneer gabble away in his particular manner. He loved to observe the various farmers' responses. But market day was also the day that the ladies served afternoon tea up at the institute supper rooms. That was always something really special in the way of food, and if Georgie had any influence over his friend it was always in favour of the food. He couldn't understand Clarrie's odd habit of wanting to observe people. So on a market day Clarrie had to balance his schedule very carefully to make sure he got full benefit from both functions.

But today was just a dull, ordinary Monday, and all Clarrie had to look forward to was his piano lesson. He knew he had time to get home and get changed, and if he hurried, he would be able to stop in at 'Young's Corner' for a milkshake. There were two cafes in Melrose and Clarrie felt a responsibility to support both, turn about. He mentally calculated that the last milkshake he'd bought had been at Prosser's Deli, so today it was Young's turn. His five cents was hard earned, and he wanted to make sure that it was well spent. Only last year he'd been carrying sixpence but he'd found the conversion to decimal currency quite easy. His mother and other oldies in the town still insisted that the Dollar was a fool idea, and that the Pound had served them well enough. But Clarrie was not one to stand in the way of progress. He would have taken a dollar any day, but today, five cents would do.

As it turned out, Clarrie didn't have time to stop for anything, as he'd found the dog loose when he got home, and he'd had to scour the immediate area around their place to find him. He hated the thought that Scamp might have wandered down to the main road and got run over, or worse yet, that he'd gone after any of the sheep in the paddocks surrounding town. Not all the farmers could shake such an offence off with a careless laugh, and Clarrie feared that one day Scamp might run into the wrong end of a loaded gun. Eventually, Clarrie located Scamp lying happily on the veranda of the butcher shop.

"You're gonna run out of luck, one of these days," Clarrie scolded the small, mongrel. "I bet you've been begging a bone from Mr Arthur." He secured a piece of bailing twine through

Scamp's collar, tied the black dog to the veranda post, and then went inside the fly screen door of Sid Arthur's Butcher shop.

"Clarrie!" Sid greeted him cheerfully, as he was wrapping up Mrs Fry's meat order in butcher's paper. "Scamp has been living up to his name again!"

"I'm sorry, sir," Clarrie spoke respectfully. "Did you have to give him any meat to keep him here?"

"Only an old shin bone. That kept him quiet for half an hour or so."

"How much do I owe you for the bone?" Clarrie asked, looking sadly at his five cents, already bidding farewell to his promised milkshake.

"None of that. It was from Friday's kill anyway, Clarrie. I would've thrown it out in any case."

"Are you sure?" Clarrie brightened up, his taste buds alight again.

"If you stop by my house, Clarrie," Mrs Fry entered into the conversation, "I have an old roast bone that's of no use to me. You can take it home for Scamp."

"Thanks, Mrs Fry," Clarrie said gratefully, "Is it all right if I pick it up later, after I've been to Mrs Fuller's house?"

"That will be fine, Clarrie," Mrs Fry said kindly. "Are you taking piano lessons from Mrs Fuller?" she asked. Clarrie nodded in affirmation, but didn't show much enthusiasm. "It's a good opportunity, Clarrie, and we're lucky to have someone like Mrs Fuller in town to teach music to the young ones."

"Yes, ma'am." Clarrie nodded, but sounded unconvinced. "Well, I better hurry, or I'll be late." He turned to leave the butcher's shop.

"Wait a moment," Sid called.

Clarrie stopped and watched the butcher as he cut a thick slice of fritz from the bung he had hanging from one of his butcher's hooks on the bar overhead.

"You'll be as hungry as Scamp after all that running around, won't you?" Sid smiled as he handed the generous chunk of sausage to the young boy.

"Thanks, Mr Arthur," Clarrie said with a beaming smile, and

this time left the butcher's shop, untied his dog and began to run back along Nott street to his house.

"Mr Arthur spoils you," Clarrie spoke sternly to his dog. "It's no wonder you're always digging your way out of the back yard!"

Chapter Two

Clarrie put a pen in his shirt pocket and a small notebook in the back pocket of his jeans. He'd dressed casually, deciding that the normal office dress was too obvious a statement that he was from out of town. The landlady had told him there were a lot of strangers about, fire-fighters from other districts and reporters from various newspapers and radio and television stations. Clarrie had won just a little more acceptance from her by mentioning one or two local people, asking about them and showing he knew them well by the questions he asked.

"You'll likely run into Jenny Bishop and Carol Bamman at the fire shed," she'd told him. "Most of the men are out fighting. Poor blighters. It's been two days on full alert. They must be about ready to drop by now."

Clarrie had walked down the street, crossed over in front of the ANZ bank, and come to join the group of people milling outside the CFS shed. The large interior space that usually housed the large fire truck and smaller fire appliance was now set up with tables and chairs. The large sliding doors stood open, probably to allow some air to move inside the iron shed but also revealing all that was going on to those who would brave the blistering heat, standing and observing.

But Clarrie could see that the stifling weather conditions had no effect on those who were working feverishly to do their part in bringing the blaze under control. The shed interior had a number of women stationed about at various places, maps all over the walls and on tables, coloured pins inserted in various places, with little bits of paper tagging certain points. He could hear the cackle and static of the VHF radios, the women communicating with operators elsewhere, listening to their reports, making notes, and returning the necessary replies. It didn't take much to hear the tension that was in the voices of those transmitting, and the concern was quite evident on the base workers' faces.

Clarrie saw a couple of fellows who were very obviously colleagues from his own industry of news mongering, but they weren't being very subtle or sensitive. One had a camera, and another was barging his way forward, trying to talk to anyone who seemed likely to tell him something.

"Look, mate," an older male volunteer took the reporter to task with some authority, "now's not the time to be asking anything. The fire's out of control and these women have got all they can do to keep track of what man is where and just which way the fire's burning."

"I just want a statement for the evening news," the reporter pushed. "Surely, just a minute."

"Don't you understand? People's lives are at stake. It's their husbands and sons out there. Just let them be. You'll get your story if and when a supervisor is free and ready to make a statement."

Clarrie could see that the reporter was going to argue the point, and so he stepped in. "Let it go, Len," he said, for he recognised the other man now. "This is a life and death situation for these people."

"And the rest of the country have a right to know about it." Len turned angrily to the interferer.

"And I have a right to punch you in the nose if you don't let up. We'll get our story later." Clarrie's patience was gone, and Len could see it. He decided to retract.

"S'pose I could always use a beer," he said by way of consolation, "and it's on the station, so why not?"

"I might join you later," Clarrie said and watched the two newsmen drift back toward the main street. He turned back to keep observing the activity of the communications centre for a while.

"They've got no idea," the older man spoke to Clarrie as if he'd found an ally in his cause to shield the volunteers at the communication base.

"I'm a reporter too," Clarrie decided to confess, "but you needn't worry. I'll get the story when the time is right."

"Well, since you've decided to be sensible about it," the man said, "I don't suppose there's any harm in talking with me about what I know."

"Have you lived in Melrose long?" Clarrie asked. "You see I lived here twenty years ago, and I don't recognise you from then."

"Actually, I don't live here now. My son and daughter-in-law live here, and when we heard the fire was bad, my wife and I got in the car and came to see if there was anything we could do for them while they are giving everything they've got to fighting this thing."

"Would I know your kids?" Clarrie asked, interested.

"My daughter-in-law was a Bishop. Lee-Ann Bishop."

"One of Jim Bishop's daughters?" Clarrie asked, not really able to recall the name.

"Yes! Do you know Jim and Jenny?"

"Many years ago. I haven't seen them since I left when I was a kid."

"Jenny's working in the shed today," the man inclined his head in that general direction. "By the way, my name's Glen, Glen Malcolm."

"Pleased to meet you." Clarrie acknowledged the introduction by shaking hands. "Do you know how it started, Glen?" Clarrie asked, trying not to sound like a reporter, but as if he was genuinely interested.

"Lightning strike out behind the mount. In the National Park area back from Peter Blieschke's place, so I heard."

"That was two days ago?" Clarrie drew out his notebook ready to jot the answer.

"No! A few days before that, apparently the crews went out straight away and got it under control in a few hours."

"Then what happened?"

"The National Parks' people were left to watch it, and then two days ago, an ants' nest that was alight, came loose from the tree and rolled down the steep hill, into the dry grass, and up she went again. Now with the wind playing havoc with everything, and this hot weather, it's just the conditions to get that blaze raging."

Clarrie listened for a bit more, and jotted down a few notes before the gentleman excused himself and left. Clarrie remained, and continued to stand and watch the activity of the communications centre for a while. It didn't take him long to recognise Jenny Bishop and Carol Bamman. Of course they were twenty years older than when he'd last seen them, and had those extra burdens that years will add to one's appearance, but they were the two women he remembered. He decided that the lines of worry and tension that were etched into their faces didn't suit them. He'd hardly ever seen them in the past when they weren't laughing or chatting happily.

About half an hour later, another woman he recognised from the past, Flora Axford, and two other women, arrived, and it appeared that they were going to change shifts. Jenny packed a few bits and pieces into a basket and then began to make her way out of the shed.

"Mrs Bishop," Clarrie said in a low tone, laden with respect. At first he didn't know if she would stop as she looked very tired and obviously had the idea of going straight home. But she did stop and looked up at him with weary anxious eyes.

"I don't know if you remember me," Clarrie said quickly. "Clarrie Brown. My mother used to work in the hotel."

A light of recognition showed momentarily in her eyes. "Yes! I remember," she said with just a faint smile. "You've grown up since I last saw you."

Clarrie smiled. Thirty-two could be considered quite 'grown-up', but then he hadn't seen her since he was twelve.

"Things are bad just now," Jenny said, her burden settling again. "It's not a good time to visit."

"No," Clarrie agreed. "I know. I'm a reporter."

"Oh!" she didn't react much to the revelation.

"I'm sorry I can't stop to talk. I've got to get out home and pack up all our valuables and all my mother's things. We'll have to get them over to Booleroo."

"Then it's a real threat then?" Clarrie knew where the Bishop farm was, some two or three miles out from the mount on the plain.

"It's a real threat," she confirmed with a sigh.

"What about Auntie Ella?' Clarrie asked quickly, thinking of Jenny's mother-in-law.

"I'm sorry, Clarrie. She passed away about two years ago now."

This really struck Clarrie in a way he never thought it would. He hadn't thought for a moment that all of the townspeople who'd been so good to him as a child wouldn't still be here.

"And Mrs Fuller?" he had to ask.

"She's still in her house down the street," Jenny replied. "There's been some talk that she might move to Adelaide to be near her children, but for now she's still here."

" Do you think she should be evacuated to Booleroo as well?"

"I imagine somebody has helped her by now, but it wouldn't do any harm for you to go and see."

Clarrie let Jenny go. He would go and see if Mrs Fuller needed help to evacuate. He had to go. She and Auntie Ella had both been like grandmothers to him. Here was something constructive he could do.

"Clarrie! You must look at the music!"

Clarrie looked sheepishly at the cheery faced woman who sat on his right, a lead pencil in her hand, which she would use to tap out the timing, if only he would play in time.

"It's hopeless, Mrs Fuller," he said mournfully. "I aren't ever going to be a good pianist."

"I won't ever be a good pianist," Vera corrected his faulty grammar patiently.

"Oh, but you are a good pianist," Clarrie immediately exclaimed, taking her correction as literal. "I've heard you play at the strawberry fete, and the Friday night balls."

"No, no! Never mind." She decided to abandon that conversation, as it was only likely to get more tangled. "You have as good a chance as any, Clarrie, to play the piano very nicely, only you really must learn to read the music."

"But it's all just dots and lines on a page. I don't reckon anyone could possibly understand it!"

Vera laughed. She was one of those jovial characters, who never let frustration or bother get the better of her. It was probably the reason why she was firmly established as the district's most favoured piano teacher.

"Who taught you the piano?" Clarrie asked, not altogether innocently, as he knew that his piano teacher was a born storyteller, and would just as soon launch into a lengthy tale as get bogged down in dots and lines. Vera eyed him suspiciously, and for a moment, Clarrie thought she would second guess him and call him back to the lesson at hand, but the moment of decision passed, and he saw her visibly sigh before choosing the path of a tale over a lesson.

"When I was a girl, my father paid for lessons from a Miss Tonkin."

"Did you live here, in Melrose, when you were young?" Clarrie always had more questions than were entirely reasonable to answer in the one conversation.

"Yes, Clarrie. My father, Mr Thomas Slee, was the butcher here in Melrose, all those years ago…"

"Mr Sid Arthur is the butcher now, isn't he?" Clarrie added needlessly.

"Yes, he is now, but then it was my father who ran the butcher business, and we lived in a small house adjoining the butcher shop up near where Christianson's general store is now."

"And did you go to the Melrose Primary school as well?"

"Yes. I went there, just like you, only those years ago there were many, many more children than there are now. Somewhere near 120, if I remember clearly. And we had four teachers."

"Wow! How come so many kids…er, children? There aren't half so many now."

"At that time, it was just after the First World War had ended, and the government had set up and were running a training farm for returned soldiers."

"What? Here at Melrose?"

"In the general area, Clarrie. You know out at Gumville, where young Mr Jim Bishop lives now."

"I know Mr Bishop," Clarrie said knowledgeably. "He's the Sunday School superintendent, isn't he?"

"Yes, dear, and it seemed as if there were hundreds of soldiers that used to live out there on that property, all learning how to farm. Of course, there probably weren't any more than seventy or eighty at a time, but it seemed like a lot of people to me."

"How come?" Clarrie asked, his face a quizzical picture.

"How come what?" his piano teacher asked, amused.

"How come there were so many of them living out at Gumville? Where did the Bishops live?"

"That was before Mr Dick Bishop had bought the property, Clarrie. After the first War, there were hundreds of young men returned from Europe and North Africa, who'd gone away as boys to fight in the army, and come back years later with no trade, and didn't seem to know what they would do with themselves. The government of the time made the decision to set up this training farm to give them some education in the ways of agriculture, and a bit of a start for their future. Some of them had wives and young families, and that was why there were so many more children at the primary school than there are now."

"Does Mr Bishop still have some soldiers out there at Gumville?" Clarrie asked, his imagination suddenly alive with the prospect that there might well be some excitement still to be had.

"No, dear," Vera laughed. She could see the wheels of imagination turning in the child's mind. "The soldiers and their families left the district years ago. They weren't there for very long at all."

"That's a darn shame!" Clarrie said without thinking, and then decided to correct himself, seeing his teacher's look of disapproval at his choice of words. "I mean, I would love to have seen real live soldiers marching about on Mr Bishop's farm."

"I dare say you would."

"My friend, Geoff Arthur, is going to be a soldier, did you know that?" Clarrie's mind jumped from one subject to the next.

"Yes, I had heard from his mother. Now Clarrie, perhaps we should get back to our piano lesson."

"Just a minute. You didn't tell me about your piano teacher, and you said you would."

"I tell you what, if you work hard for the next ten minutes, and concentrate on this piece of music, I will tell you the story about Miss Tonkin after. All right?"

Clarrie realised that his attempt to distract her had come to an end and so he submitted quietly to his teacher's patient attempts to get him to read the notes on the page in front of him, and translate them into some acceptable form of musical interpretation.

Vera waved to her student from the veranda. "See you next week, Clarrie," she called cheerily, successfully hiding the frustration she must have been feeling. That one piece of music, 'Larkspur' it was called, sounded more like a prickly pear than a beautiful flower. Still Clarrie had enjoyed his time, though wild horses would not be able to drag a confession out of him in front of the boys at school.

He left the small, green house with the red roof, and walked back up the street towards the centre of town, passing the solemn, mysterious building on his left. Auntie Ella had told him it was the Masonic Lodge, but in finding out much at all about it he hadn't progressed very far, and that was not from lack of questions. By the time he was opposite the Post Office, Mr Keith Fuller was pulling up in his vehicle. Clarrie's fifteen year old sister, Sally, got out of the back of Mr Fuller's car, along with several other high school students. Mr Fuller often gave the older students a ride back into town. It was his job to pick up the mail from the train and take it to the post office every day. The railway line didn't run through town, as railways usually did, but ran some mile and a half north, right past the showgrounds, and then continued its way further on to Wilmington. The Melrose children who wished to continue their schooling locally, travelled by train across to Booleroo Centre High School, about twelve miles to the south east. The railway line ran right through Booleroo Centre, but nobody from Melrose was likely to draw attention to such an advantage in the rival town, when their own town lacked it. Clarrie might have been only eleven years old, but he knew how the wind blew when it came to comparing the two towns – you didn't mention it, unless you were prepared for an argument.

"Sally," he called, as he ran across the road. "Did you have a good day at school?"

"What d'you think?" Sally answered in an annoyed tone. She had no particular fondness for school, and her little brother often asked a lot of 'dumb' questions.

Clarrie sensed the usual hostility, and didn't bother to press her. He waited while Sally said goodbye to her friend. As usual, he admired their smart school uniform, the maroon box-pleat tunic with white shirt, maroon tie and jumper, and the neat woollen blazer that had the Booleroo Centre High School emblem embroidered on it. To him, the whole routine of walking down to the station in the morning, and riding the train to school, wearing that sharp uniform, was something of an adventure. His sister Sally saw it differently, so Clarrie didn't bother to share his thoughts with her.

"Did you go in and see Mum after school?" Sally asked.

"Not yet. I had to go to piano lesson."

"Did you learn anything yet?" Sally asked, perhaps a little unkindly.

"Actually, I learned all about how Mrs Fuller learned to play piano," Clarrie began. "You wouldn't believe it, Sal. A woman used to come by train to Melrose every week from Adelaide. Her name was Miss Tonkin, and she used to teach Mrs Fuller at the hotel, where Mum works."

He paused to see if his sister was still listening, and she gave the customary grunt that saved her from having to make any comment. Clarrie was usually satisfied enough to chatter away endlessly, so long as the listener made some noise every now and again.

"She was very strict, Mrs Fuller told me, and she taught that classical music. Not like the Beatles and Rolling Stones, or any of that stuff. Only those old boring songs by Balthoven and Bark."

"Beethoven and Bach." Sally couldn't help herself correcting this obvious error, but immediately retreated for fear of being drawn in too deeply.

"But Mrs Fuller began to like all the modern music. Not like our rock and roll but some stuff they had back then called pop music." Clarrie remembered how his teacher had described it to him, 'something with a bit more life in it', she had said.

"Mr Slee, her dad, was disappointed that after all her lessons, she couldn't play anything he could dance to. He'd taught himself to tap dance and was pretty good too."

Sally gave a perfunctory nod, hoping that it would be enough to satisfy her brother.

"When she turned sixteen, and had finished all her exams, her dad encouraged her to play this pop music for concerts and balls here in Melrose. They used to have a lot of concerts and dances back then, you know."

"We still do," Sally commented. "They play all of that slow waltz music. If it wasn't that there is nothing else to do on a Friday night, I wouldn't bother going."

"Well, anyway," Clarrie continued, unperturbed, "one day, Mrs Fuller, she was Miss Vera Slee then, was playing the piano during the supper while the band was taking a break, and was really enjoying herself, when she looked up, and to her horror, she saw her music teacher, Miss Tonkin, in a white fur cloak, standing in the doorway. She nearly had a fit, but Miss Tonkin didn't say anything at all. But the next time she went to lesson, her teacher was very cross, and told her she didn't ever want to hear her playing that type of rubbish again."

He looked across to his sister to gauge her reaction to his story, but was disappointed to see a blank look on her face. Sally's got no imagination, he lamented to himself, as he followed her along the footpath. But Mrs Fuller is sure good at telling stories, even if Sally can't see the good of them. He decided to leave his favourite part of the story: The row that Mr and Mrs Slee had

had when the sixteen-year-old Vera had told them what Miss Tonkin had said. Mr Slee was all for quitting the lessons there and then, but Mrs Slee insisted that Vera complete the term. Clarrie laughed to himself. He loved the way his piano teacher could make old stories seem so alive and funny.

"We'd better drop in on Mum, and see how long she's going to be tonight," Sally said as she stepped up to the veranda of the Mount Remarkable Hotel. Sally and Clarrie were used to going in the hotel, as their mother worked there as a cook and cleaner six days a week.

"We've got a bus load of people on their way up to Wilpena Pound coming in for tea," Beth Brown spoke in a tired voice. "I'll be working late tonight. Sal, you can cook those chops I left in the fridge for tea, all right?"

Sally nodded, her displeasure showing on her face. She would much sooner have spent the time down the street at Young's or Prosser's catching up with her school friends, rather than being home with her little brother having to cook his tea.

"I'll make it up to you, Sally." Beth could read her daughter's look, and knew exactly what it meant.

"Don't worry about it," Sally said breezily, and picked up her school bag ready to go home.

Once the two children were back on the footpath and heading up past Sloan's Garage and the bank, Sally began to talk.

"I'm going to stop in at Young's for half an hour. If you don't tell Mum, I'll buy you an ice cream."

"Ok!" Clarrie agreed. His sister's generosity was patchy at best, and he knew to take what he could when he could. When they got to Young's, Sally pushed the glass door open and they walked in to the sound of the small bell that rang in response. Sally immediately saw two of her friends and greeted them in a cheerful friendly way that made Clarrie wonder about personality transformations. But he was used to it, and knew he was about to score a Golden North ice cream, so he didn't dare make any comment drawing attention to the fact.

"Can I have the honey flavour?" he asked his sister, risking just a little by asking.

"All right," she hissed under her breath. She ordered the ice cream cone from Gilbert Young, who was serving behind the counter, and after she handed it to her brother, she ushered him outside.

"Go outside and eat your ice cream, and then keep out of trouble for half and hour."

Clarrie knew the shop would be closing in half an hour, as every business in Melrose shut up shop on the stroke of five o'clock, and he didn't have any intention of getting in to trouble in that small amount of time. Getting into trouble wasn't his usual style, but that didn't mean that trouble wouldn't be able to find him. Still, he sat on the stool out the front of the shop and attacked his honey-flavoured ice-cream with relish. He had worked his way methodically through the ice-cream, and around and round the cone, and he was nearly at the favourite crunch of the tip of the cone when he heard his name being called.

"Hey, Clarrie!"

He looked across the street to where the voice came from and beamed in response. It was Lyall Arthur and his brother Geoff, sitting in their Holden Ute.

"Come on," Lyall called. "You wanna go for a ride?"

Clarrie hesitated for a moment, considering the possibilities. The sun had already gone behind the mount and twilight was setting in. That always happened earlier in Melrose than any of the places on the plain, simply because the town was set right at the eastern foot of the huge old mountain, which cloaked the town in long shadows. Clarrie wasn't thinking so much of the geography as of whether it was a safe bet to join his older friends. "I reckon I should wait here for my sister," he called back across the road using a distinctly disappointed tone. "Where are you going, anyway?" he asked, full of curiosity. He loved hanging out with the Arthurs.

"We just have to move a bit of rubbish," Lyall answered in a beguiling tone.

"I better not," Clarrie answered. "I'd like to, but…"

"We're going to go out to Mr Bishop's house." Lyall continued to promote the scheme. "You like Mr Bishop, don't you?"

The fact that Clarrie liked his Sunday School teacher was not an issue, but the recent story about soldiers on his farm was still very much at the forefront of his mind. Quite suddenly, Clarrie's imagination was alive again with the story that Mrs Fuller had told him. He could not dismiss the possibility that there still must be at least one or two soldiers hiding somewhere out at Gumville, and here was just the opportunity that he needed to investigate.

"Ok!" Clarrie answered without any more thought, and looked both ways before crossing the quiet street and getting into the ute. He clambered across Geoff's knee and sat in the middle between the two of them.

Clarrie's imagination was alive with the thrill of a possible discovery, and he had no more questions to ask about Lyall's proposed job, but they were not too far out of town, coming up to the railway line, when Lyall decided to offer the information anyway.

"Actually, Clarrie, we're going to play a bit of a joke on Mr Bishop," Lyall confessed.

"Why?" Clarrie asked, rather resenting the interruption to his own mental plans.

"You know what day it is tomorrow, don't you?" Geoff asked knowingly.

"Tuesday," Clarrie answered without any enthusiasm.

"Clarrie!" Lyall sounded surprised, but also a little smug, as he proceeded to instruct his young protégé. "Tomorrow is April Fool's day. The first of April. You know!"

"Oh!" This fact had escaped Clarrie's notice, but now that it had been brought to his attention he began to see the possibilities. "Do you think Mr Bishop will mind you playing a joke on him?"

Both the older fellows laughed. "He won't mind," Geoff said, full of confidence.

"And besides," Lyall added quickly, "this joke is to pay him back for a trick he played on me."

Clarrie's mind boggled. To think that the Sunday School

Superintendent had played a trick on anybody was almost too much for his youthful loyalty to comprehend. "Did he really?" Clarrie asked doubtfully, and watched Lyall nod earnestly. "What did he do?" Clarrie asked.

"One day, we'd been helping Mr Bishop at a church working bee, clearing the weeds from the kindergarten yard, and he sent us down the street to buy some pies and pasties from Young's for our lunch. He gave us some money, and just as we were about to leave, he asked me to drop into the bank and ask Mr Cullen for a pad of verbal agreement forms."

Clarrie couldn't see the joke in it, nor why it deserved revenge.

"Don't worry about it, Clarrie," Geoff said evenly. "All you need to know is that Mr Cullen and two other people in the bank at the time had a good laugh at our expense."

"Anyway, now we've got all this rubbish in the back of our ute, and you can trust us when we say Mr Bishop's always good for a laugh."

"Oh!" Clarrie didn't seem to be inclined to object anymore. He didn't have much of an idea of playing a joke on anybody, but he did relish the opportunity of getting out to Gumville and having a look around.

The unlikely threesome took the Orroroo Road turn off at a speed that Clarrie's mother would definitely have disapproved of, but despite the clouds of dust billowing out behind, and the gravel that was raised as the ute took Cases Corner rather too quickly, they arrived at the ramp entrance of Gumville in very brisk time.

"It's still quite light," Geoff commented, slightly apprehensive. "Shouldn't we come back when it's completely dark?"

"Probably be a better plan, but Mum has ladies' hospital auxiliary meeting tonight in Booleroo, and Dad needs the ute to go to a show meeting. It's now or never!"

Geoff and Lyall jumped out of the ute with an energy that only comes from the tension of an awkward conscience, and Clarrie followed them with rather less enthusiasm, somewhat apprehensive at the likelihood of being found out. The two Arthur brothers began to unload the back of their ute, dumping boxes of rubbish, bits of old metal and two broken chairs into the ramp, making sure that they poked the smaller bits down between the great iron bars. The humble ramp, common at the main entrance of most farms, was designed as a great hole in the ground, with thick iron bars running crossways, parallel to one another. This enabled the cars to rumble over the hole with only a bit of a shudder to the passengers, but the animals were usually unable to negotiate the rounded bars with their cloven hoofs, and thus remained within the property. On this brisk autumn evening, as the light gradually gave way to the grey twilight, the Arthur boys felt wildly triumphant in clogging up this convenient entry with a whole load of household refuse. Nobody would be able to drive over this ramp until the rubbish had been removed. Lyall and Geoff laughed to themselves with the excitement of those who knew they could very well be caught at any moment. Just as they were about to hop back into the ute, they suddenly noticed that their young friend was missing.

"Hey! Where's Clarrie?" Geoff asked, suddenly alert to the fact that they were not going to make their clean get away.

"I dunno! Wasn't he with you?" Lyall asked lamely. "Come on! We'd better find him, or his Mum will kill us."

What they didn't know was that Clarrie had left them the moment they had arrived at the Gumville entrance, and started his search of the many stone sheds, acting with a method and precision usually found only in accountants. He worked his way through first one shed and the next, both full of a lot of old spiders' webs and with thick blankets of dust. He was troubled that the light was fading, and his ability to see in the dark corners was not as good as he really needed for a thorough investigation.

Clarrie's mind dismissed Lyall and Geoff's escapade the moment he entered the first old stone shed. He read on a flagstone the date, sometime from last century, and felt sure that this would be a likely place for soldiers from times past to hide. There was a lot of old junk stored in this shed, and the one next to it housed a tractor and some other bits of strange looking farm equipment. Clarrie wasn't really familiar with all the bits and pieces that a farmer might use. He searched carefully, squinting to try and make out the dark shapes in the dim light, staring intently in case anything moved. With his vivid imagination, he could see that some of the shapes could very well have been soldiers holding their breath and standing still, and he thought that if he stared long enough they would eventually have to move. But despite his determination to outstare them, nothing in the shed proved to be alive, and so Clarrie was forced to move along. Gumville was one of those farms that had a lot of sheds. Mrs Fuller had told him that there used to be even more, when the training farm was running, but not nearly as many now that it was just a private concern. Clarrie moved in and out of each one, checking carefully to make sure that he hadn't missed anything. Then he came to the Briggs' house. It had originally been built as the office block for the training farm, years ago, but now Mr Briggs and his wife lived there. Clarrie could see the Morris school bus parked around the side. As he approached, the Briggs' dogs started barking, which in turn alerted Mr Bishop's dog to the fact that there was an approaching visitor. Though Clarrie's conscience was clear, he did wonder if perhaps his two friends might not wish to remain undiscovered playing their April Fool's joke, so instead of going any further, he reluctantly decided that he'd better go back and see how they were getting along. He didn't let go of the idea that there still might be soldiers though, but did admit that it was probably getting too dark to find them in any case. He would come out another time, he decided.

As he turned back toward the ramp, he heard Mr Briggs open the front door, and saw him look out into the fading light. Since there was no sign of any car approaching, he turned and yelled at the dogs to keep quiet, and then went back inside. Clarrie realised that his friends had had a narrow escape, and then for the first time realised that he himself was probably in for trouble.

His sister had told him to wait outside Young's for half an hour. That seemed like an age ago, and he would be nowhere for her to find. The urgency of the situation gripped his mind, probably far too late to be of any use, but he decided he'd better run. In the grey twilight, he couldn't see all of the obstacles that lay about under the trees, and he stumbled in potholes and over stones, until one large tree trunk finally brought the retreating Clarrie ungracefully to the ground. He came down with a thud that knocked the wind out of him, and he'd put his arm out to break the fall. Even as he did it, he knew that something had gone very wrong in his forearm. Still, he got up quickly. He was not going to be a cry baby in front of his older friends, and so he continued on, quite a lot slower now, and eventually came upon them as they were searching for him around the first lot of sheds, calling his name softly, not wanting to alert the dogs to their presence.

"Clarrie! Where the dickens have you been? We've got to get out of here before we're found out!"

"Sorry!" That was all Clarrie could say. He was in some pain, and it quite overwhelmed him, but he was determined not to let Lyall or Geoff know. It would be too humiliating to admit that he'd fallen over a tree trunk, let alone that he'd hurt himself. He got quietly into the ute, wincing as Geoff shoved him across, obviously unaware that he was injured.

Lyall drove their ute back into town at the same speed as the trip out. Clarrie usually enjoyed the fun of this kind of ride, even when the vehicle tyres got caught in a build up of gravel on the side of the road, and the ute swung out in a precarious way. Of course his mother never drove like that, and he somehow suspected that the Arthurs probably shouldn't be either, but he never said a thing, especially now that his mind was totally absorbed with trying to keep a brave face. His arm throbbed with pain, but he refused to give any indication.

"I'll drop you home if you like, mate," Lyall offered, somewhat calmer now that the threat of discovery was past.

"Sally told me to wait outside Young's," Clarrie said weakly.

"Crikey, Clarrie! Sally will've had a pink fit when she found you were missing! Why didn't you tell us you were supposed to be waiting for her?"

Clarrie thought that he had tried to make those objections initially when the invitation was made, but he wasn't sure, and besides, now the pain was so great that his head had begun to spin, and he'd begun to feel nauseous. He couldn't think of any clear excuses or answers.

"You all right?" Geoff asked, suddenly aware that Clarrie was acting rather strangely. In the dim light he saw the way the young kid held his arm, as if trying to protect it. "Have you hurt yourself?" Geoff asked, his sensitive side instantly coming forward. Clarrie nodded earnestly.

"Why didn't you say something?" Lyall scolded. "Your mum isn't going to be very happy with us."

"We'd better take him to his house," Geoff suggested. "Sally will probably be back there by now."

Nothing further was said until they'd driven right through town and out to the other side, the last street on the right. Lyall's driving dramatically improved from that point, and he pulled up very sedately in the driveway. Both he and his brother were scrambling for excuses and apologies that they were certain to have to offer.

"Clarrie!" Sally shrieked when she saw him, as she had instantly responded to the sound of the car outside. "Where the heck have you been? I told you to wait for me outside Young's!"

"Sorry, Sal," Lyall spoke on Clarrie's behalf. "We talked him into coming for a ride. Didn't know he was supposed to be waiting for you. Is your mum cross?"

"She's not home yet, thank goodness, or I'd be dead. I wasn't supposed to be in Young's in the first place, so we're both in trouble – except she doesn't know."

"I think Clarrie's hurt his arm," Geoff offered, sorry to have to present another difficulty.

"Serves him right!" Sally said, a little callously. "He should have stayed put, and not gone off gadding about. Come on, Clarrie. If we hurry, we can eat tea, and clean up, and Mum won't be any the wiser."

Clarrie was determined that he was not going to cause any more difficulties, and so, despite the fact that his head spun, and his arm throbbed with excruciating pain, he followed his sister inside. He didn't look back to say goodbye to his friends, as it took all of his concentration and will power just to stay upright and quiet.

Chapter Three

It was like a blast from the past. Clarrie had wandered back to the CFS shed, and had got there in time to see a small fire appliance pull up outside. He stayed alert for any information, now fully aware that anything he was likely to learn officially would have to wait for the Supervisor's twice daily press release. Carol Bamman, after getting reacquainted, let him know that the volunteers had been given strict instructions to say absolutely nothing regarding the fire to the media. Clarrie accepted this easily, knowing that would probably be the case as it was the norm at most situations.

But as to gleaning his own impressions about what was happening, there was nobody who could stop that, and when he saw the four-wheel-drive pull up, he walked over to observe.

It was then that Clarrie saw him. Actually, it was his voice he recognised first. That slow easy tone that even in the excitement of a crisis, didn't show any alarm or distress.

Geoff Arthur, Clarrie thought to himself. I know it's him. He had to look two or three times to make sure, because twenty years had certainly told their story in his appearance. It seemed weird not to see his younger brother somewhere nearby. With him was another man that Clarrie recognised from the past, Malcolm McCallum. He couldn't really hear the details of the conversation, but it was enough to reveal that both were men in authority within the ranks of the Country Fire Service. When they'd finished talking Clarrie couldn't help himself. He had to say hello.

"Clarrie Brown!" Geoff said easily. "Carol told me you were back in town. It's been a while."

Clarrie nodded, speechless.

"Haven't got time to talk now," Geoff said matter-of-factly. "Do you think you could be any use pumping a knapsack?"

"You mean at the fire?" Clarrie asked. Suddenly he felt twelve years old again. This was just the sort of thing he would have got into as a kid, and it was often Geoff or Lyall who helped him into trouble.

"We need all the help we can get," Geoff answered. If Clarrie hadn't known from the reactions of everyone else, he would never have guessed there was anything urgent happening at all. Geoff's calm manner didn't provoke anxiety.

"If I can be of help, I will."

Without further comment, Geoff grabbed a hard hat, a spare pair of the bright yellow overalls that hung on the shed wall, and checked Clarrie's footwear to see if it was suitable.

"We've a few details to tidy up here," Geoff said. "Run over to Bennett's and grab a decent pair of boots your size. Tell them I'll fix them up later."

Clarrie could see there were other men eager to get back out to the fire, so he didn't waste any time seeing to the task he'd been given. As he walked across the road to Bennett's Farm Supplies store, he considered the commitment of the volunteers he'd seen. Just in the short time he'd been in the town he'd see numbers of them walk into the shed so exhausted they looked like zombies, hardly knowing what time of day it was, or even who they were. And yet they weren't looking to go home and rest. They were driven with a sense of responsibility to be back out at the front, fighting this monstrous blaze.

The woman who was looking after the business didn't ask a second question once Clarrie told her that Geoff Arthur had sent him to get boots. She quickly supplied his size and sent him on his way with a wish for good luck.

The crew headed out of Melrose, north along the main road to Wilmington. It was approaching late afternoon, but it was almost impossible to see where the sun was. The heavy layer of smoke was now being covered by gathering storm clouds. There was some talk that perhaps it might bring rain and relief to everyone. They'd been on full alert for three days, and the fire was burning out of control on many fronts. The manpower of the district was long past overtaxed, even with the volunteers from neighbouring districts. No wonder Geoff was willing to let someone he hadn't seen in twenty years come and add his strength to the cause.

Eventually, the driver turned the vehicle off the main road taking the Spring Creek track that headed right up into the dense bushland of Mount Remarkable. The smoke increased, and Clarrie could see flames as they approached. Suddenly he wondered if he really knew anything about fire fighting at all.

"We're trying to create a fire break by back burning this area before the main fire gets here," Geoff explained.

Clarrie was blowed if he could tell the difference between a back burn and a main fire. It was all hot, and it roared amongst the trees as it consumed the tinder dry fuel that lay in its path.

Already there were men, masks strapped over their mouths and noses, walking up and down the line of fire, squirting it with the knapsacks they had strapped to their backs. Clarrie saw that the main fire appliance from Melrose was there, and guessed that it would probably have to go back to a place where it could be refilled, and probably take some of these volunteers back to rest.

But suddenly, the situation changed, and no man was going to go anywhere. The fire seemed to have its own thoughts and decided to do a little attacking of its own.

Sally thought that she and Clarrie had got away with their little escapade, though Clarrie had not eaten any tea, and had taken himself straight off to bed. Sally had fussed a little. She was often mean to her little brother, but that didn't mean that she didn't really care for him. True enough, that depth of concern rarely showed itself, but on occasions such as this one, when

Clarrie was obviously not himself, and, Sally suspected, in quite a lot of pain, she allowed her real love for her brother to show.

"You OK, Clarrie," she asked, leaning over his bed, her brow furrowed with worry.

"My arm really hurts, Sal," Clarrie admitted. "But don't tell Mum. We'd both be in big trouble if she knew we hadn't come straight home."

"Yes, we would be in trouble, but we're going to have to tell her. Perhaps you've broken your arm. I did once, when I fell off one of Spen Fuller's horses, and it hurt really bad."

"It'll be all right. I'll just go to sleep, and in the morning it will be OK."

Sally was not absolutely convinced, but she had to admit that she wasn't in a terrible hurry to confess her negligence, so she cleaned up the tea dishes, probably better than she had ever done before, and she sat straight down to do her homework. Sometimes, now that they had a television set, she would sit down and watch the black and white ABC broadcasts to the country areas. It was certainly much more exciting than just listening to the wireless all the time. But tonight, Sally was too consumed with guilt to be able to concentrate on anything at all. It was hard enough getting her homework finished.

Clarrie slept fitfully. He wanted to toss and turn, but the pain in his arm kept him still, as each movement caused new waves of agony. He heard his mother come home, and when she came to look in on him, he lay very still, pretending to be asleep. But he hardly slept a wink. By the time dawn began to lighten his room, Clarrie had made up his mind. Trouble or no trouble, he had to tell his mother.

"How did you hurt your arm?" Beth asked, sounding tired, and as if she wished that Clarrie would just go back to bed.

"I tripped over when I was running, and put my arm out to break the fall."

"Why didn't you say something to Sally? She could have told me last night."

"I thought it would be better this morning," Clarrie said. He'd managed to withhold the incriminating details, and was still within the realms of being treated as if a normal accident had occurred.

"Well, it's lucky that it's Tuesday. Doctor Wheaton will be in town this afternoon. I'll take some time off work and take you to see him then."

Beth was one of those mothers who was far too busy, and she was always tired, simply unable to give the full amount of attention to family issues that arose.

"I don't know if I can go to school." Clarrie had to make his mother see the extent of the injury. "I feel sick and dizzy."

"Good heavens, Clarrie. It's just a bump on the arm, isn't it?"

"Sally thought I'd broken it maybe."

"So you did tell Sally?"

"I told her not to tell you. I thought I'd be better this morning."

Beth sighed in frustration. "All right," she said in a resigned way. "I'll call Auntie Ella and see if you can spend the day with her, until the doctor comes."

"Could we drive over to see the doctor this morning?" Clarrie was feeling rather desperate. Doctor Wheaton had his home and surgery in Booleroo Centre, but on Tuesdays and Fridays he drove to Wilmington and Melrose to hold surgery consultations in those towns. He used the RSL rooms opposite the bank to consult in Melrose. Clarrie had been to see him there plenty of times, but today, he felt so unwell that he wished his mother would drive him to Booleroo to see the doctor straight away, instead of waiting for his scheduled visit to Melrose.

"I can't really, Clarrie." Beth sounded frustrated. "I took the car in to Sloan's Garage yesterday, and Mr Sloan said that it needed a new radiator. He has it all in bits, and has ordered the new one to come in. We'll have to wait until this afternoon. I'm sure Auntie Ella won't mind coming to pick you up and watching you for the morning."

Clarrie knew very well that Auntie Ella would be on their doorstep five minutes after his mother called, and he didn't mind. She was one of his favourite people in the town.

He began to resign himself to the fact that he would not be able to see the doctor until later in the day.

Clarrie knew that Sally was worried, but whether she was worried about being found out, or whether her concern was for him, he wasn't quite sure, but still she hurried away to meet the other high school kids at the post office where they'd wait for the ride down to the station. Just as he'd predicted, Auntie Ella was quick to respond to the call for assistance, only she sent Mr Bishop to pick Clarrie up instead of coming herself. Dick Bishop, whose real name was Walter, but no one ever called him that, arrived in their brand new, green Chrysler sedan. It was a wonderful, posh car, with brown leather seats, and Clarrie wished that he could enjoy the luxury of the ride without the constant nagging pain.

"How'd you hurt yourself, Clarrie," Mr Bishop asked in his gruff way.

"I fell over a tree trunk." Clarrie wanted desperately to tell the whole story, but he knew that Mr Bishop would probably be going out to Gumville later, and that the obstruction in the ramp would soon be discovered, if it hadn't already. Clarrie wasn't quite sure, in the cold light of day, that he really wanted to be associated with the crime.

Clarrie watched the old farmer as he drove carefully back to his house opposite the school. He didn't look anything like his son, Jim. Rather, he was quite bald – this Clarrie knew from seeing him without his hat – and the few hairs that did remain as a band around his head were grey, and he was quite a rotund fellow. Clarrie liked him, even though he didn't say much to him. His main comment to Clarrie was likely to be, "you need to eat a few more bags of flour." Clarrie had heard this on more than one occasion in reference to the fact that he was small, and in need of some height. Though Dick Bishop was officially retired from farming, he still went to work every day, to help one of his sons on their farms.

They drove around behind the house and into the large car shed at the back. Clarrie saw the dog, Lassie, tied up to the post, waiting eagerly to greet him as he came through the back gate. He knew that Lassie would go with Mr Bishop in the back of the old Holden utility, when he left for the day.

"Clarrie!" Auntie Ella greeted him in a half-friendly, half-scolding way. "What have you been doing to yourself?"

"I hurt my arm when I fell over," he repeated again, and wondered how many more times he would have to say it before the whole story would come tumbling out.

"You come inside and sit down by the fire, and I'll get you something to eat."

That was the standard remedy of every good farmer's wife, and Auntie Ella's biscuits, scones and jam tarts did have a certain medicinal value, if only to revive a dented spirit.

Clarrie was rather sorry that he wasn't feeling well. Usually when he'd visited Auntie Ella, she'd have him helping to collect the eggs from their chook yard, or she'd get him to come with her across the way to Coad's place where she kept a milking cow, and she would let him try some milking. At other times she would get him to take the bacon rind out to feed to the kookaburras. She called them Jackasses, and Clarrie loved to watch them swoop down from the surrounding gum trees and take up the bacon rind from the fence post.

But today, Clarrie had to accept the fact that he would have to sit quietly by the fire and be fussed over.

"How do you like Miss Both, your new teacher?" Auntie Ella asked as she set a glass of milk and some biscuits down on a small table next to Clarrie.

"Miss Jolly is my teacher," Clarrie answered with much less enthusiasm than usual, but still with the expected politeness. "I'm in the big room now. Grade six, remember?"

"Grade six!" she exclaimed. "By jingoes, you're growing up quickly!"

This comment was one that most kids heard frequently from older relatives, but Clarrie only ever heard it from his adopted aunts and uncles like Auntie Ella and Mrs Fuller.

"Do you miss Miss Keller?"

Clarrie nodded solemnly. He didn't feel much like talking, but the truth was he did wish for the friendly, smiling face of his junior primary teacher. Not that he hadn't reason to think that the new junior room teacher, Miss Both, wasn't friendly and kind just as Miss Keller had been, it was rather the overpowering strict atmosphere that was set in the big room at school. Miss Jolly was a tall, silver haired woman who'd obviously been teaching school for a good many years. Unlike Miss Keller and Miss Both who were both young and dressed in all the modern, colourful clothes of the 1960's, Miss Jolly's appearance was as stern and rigid as she was. She had her grey hair in a bun, and usually appeared at school in a dark, box-pleated skirt, with a dull coloured cardigan over the top of a starched buttoned blouse. She always wore old fashioned, black lace-up duty shoes. Clarrie shuddered to think of her strict discipline. He didn't have the same appreciation of grammar and arithmetic that the older generation seemed to think was necessary. Miss Jolly's only saving grace in Clarrie's opinion was that she insisted on having a small band accompany the Monday morning assemblies and he had been chosen as the bass drum player. Together with the kettle drum and fife, the three instruments would set the rhythm while the school children would get into formation and march to their places beneath the flagpole. There they would space themselves at the required arms length from their neighbour, and they would soberly repeat the loyal oath, and sing 'God Save the Queen'. The honour of bearing the bass drum Clarrie owed to Miss Jolly. Generally it fell to the lot of one of the grade seven boys, but it appeared that Clarrie had a greater talent for rhythm than any of the other boys, and so despite his junior status he was given the responsibility.

Now I won't be able to drum for a long while, he lamented to himself, already accepting that the dreadful pain in his arm meant major trouble.

"It's a shame you don't have Miss Both for a teacher," Auntie Ella broke through his mental fog. "I find her to be a very nice person."

"Does she live here with you, like Miss Keller used to?" Clarrie asked, well aware that Auntie Ella had formerly boarded the other junior primary teacher.

"Yes! Her people are from Adelaide, and so she's staying here with Mr Bishop and myself. I like the company, but she doesn't eat nearly enough."

Clarrie understood that nobody would ever eat enough to satisfy Auntie Ella's notion of a proper meal.

"Well, I'd get you to come up to the top room with me and have a practice on the organ while I do some sewing, but I think you look a bit pale. You can lie down on the lounge for a bit if you like."

He was glad to rest, and only slightly disappointed at losing the opportunity to play the magnificent pump organ that Auntie Ella kept in her top room. She often let him play, pulling out all the different stops to change the deep bellowing sounds, while he pumped madly away at the foot pedals. Of course it sounded very different from her playing. Ella Bishop was the organist at the Melrose Methodist Church, and Clarrie was always amazed at how she could play all of those hymns just as the minister decreed.

Soon Clarrie went to sleep. His fitful, restless night had caught up with him, and despite the pain, he managed to sleep the entire morning away, and woke up only when Miss Both came in at lunchtime. She sometimes came across from the school to her boarding house for the hot dinner that her landlady cooked for her, but it was always a hurried affair, as she had to take her turn on yard duty while the headmistress took her lunch break.

Clarrie stayed in the lounge under a blanket. He didn't feel much like eating, and though he appreciated Miss Both's kind enquiry after his health, he didn't feel much like talking either.

Finally, two o'clock approached and Beth Brown came to fetch Clarrie off to the doctor.

"You'll have to walk, Clarrie," she said plainly. "I'm afraid Mr Sloan still hasn't been able to get hold of that part for the car."

"Never mind walking," Auntie Ella interrupted. "Jump in the car, both of you, and I'll run you down the street."

"It's not too far to walk," Beth made an attempt to object.

"Clarrie's not really too well. I'll drive you down and be done with it."

Clarrie noticed his mother's reserve and guessed that she felt pretty bad about having to rely on other people's good will. But he didn't think about it too much. His main focus was his own aches and pains. Even though it was a mild day for the first day of April, Clarrie felt rather cold. When they stepped inside the small RSL clubrooms, he felt colder still. No one had put any heater on, and the hard, wooden chairs were uncomfortable, creaking affairs.

On other visits, Clarrie amused himself by reading the memorial plaques that listed the names of local servicemen. He recognised some names, but not others, and sometimes wondered about them. On the wall was the grand portrait of Queen Elizabeth II, which Clarrie always admired. She was such a beautiful lady, and he loved the robes and jewels that she wore. It always brought to mind the national anthem that they sang every Monday morning at school.

But today Clarrie was not in the mood to study the interesting pictures and plaques on the wall of the RSL rooms. He was impatient to see the doctor and have him make the pain go away. But already, Clarrie knew that he would have to wait. There were several other people in the waiting room before him, and he knew the routine. It was always first in first served at the Melrose consult surgery.

Clarrie wriggled about trying to find a position on the wooden chair that was less uncomfortable. There was a loll-about lounge on the far wall, with a patchwork quilt on it. Clarrie had a strong desire to lie down on it, but his understanding was that it was reserved for very sick people to rest on. He didn't consider that he quite fitted that description, so he remained sitting and uncomfortable.

He gradually became aware of other people waiting for their turn to see Doctor Wheaton. He noticed Mrs Jenny Bishop come into the waiting room carrying her baby, and ushering her two little girls in before her. He watched as she found a seat and arranged for all the children to sit down quietly, and then he was suddenly alert to her conversation.

"Hello, Jenny," Mrs Sybil Arthur greeted the young mother. Clarrie knew that this was Lyall and Geoff's mother. "I'm sorry about that business with your ramp," she said with real regret in her tone.

Clarrie wished he could sink through the floor. He felt as if there must be a red flashing light on his forehead proclaiming, "Over here. I'm guilty". He sat painfully still and listened to the conversation.

Jenny laughed. "Don't be too sorry," she said cheerfully. "Jim got them back already."

Clarrie was very keen to hear to the rest of the story, so was careful not to make any sudden movements that would draw attention to himself.

"Sorry to call you so late last night," Jenny apologised, "but Jim was going to be away for the day, and I wasn't able to manage the milking on my own."

"Don't mention it," Sybil said happily. "Those two boys deserve more than just to do a bit of milking for you."

"It was lucky that Jim discovered the prank on his way out to the show meeting last night, or Mr Briggs would have found it this morning when he had to go out on the bus run."

"They're a pair of rascals," Sybil remarked, determined to see the worst of it.

"It was just a bit of fun," Jenny laughed, "and even more so when they arrived out to help do the milking this morning and found the rubbish still in the ramp, and the gate carefully padlocked. Mr Briggs locked it for us after he left on the bus run."

Sybil laughed. "So they had to shift all the rubbish themselves, is that it?"

"Yes!" Jenny said quickly, "and they arrived up at the house with it all in the back of the ute. I asked them, since they were on the way to the dump, if they would load up a few other bits of rubbish that we had lying about the back of the shed."

The two women laughed, and Clarrie laughed under his breath. He wanted to laugh out loud, but he couldn't let anybody know that he'd actually been part of the escapade as well. Hearing about the outcome of last night's mischief had taken Clarrie's mind from his pain, and thinking it over further was enough to help the time pass more quickly.

Just as Jenny was called in by the Mothers' and Babies' sister, who held her clinic in the front room of the RSL hall, Clarrie became aware that Doctor Wheaton had also entered the waiting room from his back consult room, and was apparently waiting for him.

"Come along, Clarrie," said Beth impatiently. "The doctor hasn't got all day."

"Well, well, what have you done to yourself?" The tall, brown-haired doctor greeted Clarrie in a business-like tone, though Clarrie knew from other visits that his gruffness was only his manner, and that his genuine care and concern were quite evident once you got to know him a bit. As long as you weren't intimidated by his great height and high qualifications, everybody came to know Doctor Wheaton as everything a good country doctor should be.

"Clarrie took a fall yesterday," Beth spoke timidly. She was one of those who was always intimidated by important and educated people. "He's been complaining quite a lot of the pain in his arm."

"Well, then. Let me have a look."

Clarrie yielded his injured arm gingerly, allowing his apprehension to show on his face. The doctor gently prodded a couple of spots, saw Clarrie's immediate response to the pain and said without any hesitation:

"Better bring him over to the hospital and we'll do an x-ray. Call the hospital and tell them to book him in for 5.30 this evening. I should be back by then, and we'll see what comes of that."

Beth nodded, without voicing her concerns about how she would get Clarrie across to Booleroo Centre. Even though her car was still in pieces, she didn't feel able to confide her problem to the doctor.

"So what made you fall over?" Doctor Wheaton asked by way of conversation.

"I fell over a tree root that was sticking out." Clarrie answered honestly, hoping that the inquisition would end there.

"Whereabouts?" There. The question was out and Clarrie knew he could lie, but had taken very seriously his Sunday school lesson about lying.

"It was out at Mr Jim Bishop's farm," Clarrie said in a small voice, hoping that the doctor would be too busy writing his notes on his card to hear the answer. But unfortunately Beth heard him, and quite suddenly her nervousness disappeared in the light of this revelation.

"Mr Bishop's farm!" she repeated her voice filled with surprise. "When were you out at Mr Bishop's farm?"

"I went for a ride with the Arthurs," Clarrie confessed. "They were playing an April Fool's joke on Mr Bishop."

"Clarrie!" Beth had heard about the joke from the conversation in the waiting room, and was shocked to think that her young son had been a part of it. "How could you do such a thing?"

"Oh, I didn't. I just went for the ride so that I could look for the soldiers."

"This sounds like an intriguing tale." Doctor Wheaton said as he closed Clarrie's case notes and stood up.

"Mrs Fuller told me that soldiers used to live out at Mr Bishop's farm. I wanted to see if there were any still out there."

The doctor gave an almost imperceptible chuckle and stepped toward the door to let the pair out. "I'll see you later on this evening," he said evenly. "Don't go out hunting any more soldiers today. OK?"

Clarrie was mortified. The truth was out. The doctor was amused and his mother was horrified. He wondered if he would ever hear the end of it.

"Whatever are you thinking, Clarrie?" Beth Brown started on

her son once they'd left the RSL building. "What would Jenny Bishop be doing keeping soldiers out at her place, what with three little children to look after?"

Clarrie knew that Mr and Mrs Bishop wouldn't have been knowingly keeping any soldiers. He had entertained the idea that some had remained there after all the others had left, and were living secretly in the many sheds that were out at Gumville, but he couldn't admit that to his mother.

Once outside in the mild autumn afternoon, Beth instructed her eleven-year-old son to sit on the white, wrought-iron bench beneath the shady carob tree, just outside of the RSL room. "Wait here for me," she said in a tired, resigned tone. "I'll just go over to Sloan's and see if he's any closer to having the car fixed."

Clarrie sat patiently just back off the footpath and watched as his mother crossed Stuart Street to Sloan's Garage. He could just imagine Mr Doug Sloan or Mr Dick Keating, dressed in their mechanic's overalls, wiping their greasy hands on the rag that was conveniently stuffed in their pocket. Despite the pain in his arm, Clarrie was now feeling a great sense of remorse. He guessed that if he'd asked his mother's permission to go on the ride with the Arthurs there wouldn't be any reason to fuss. But because he'd gone without asking either Sally or his mother, he imagined that he was in trouble.

"Good afternoon, young Master Brown."

Clarrie was aroused from his state of misery by Georgie's mother. "Hello Mrs Greenbank," he replied as politely as he could.

"You look rather out of sorts. What's the matter with you today?" Mrs Mavis Greenbank was a forthright sort of woman who never minced words.

"I went on a ride without my mother's permission, and had an accident and I've hurt my arm."

"I daresay your mother is cross with you, then!" Mrs Greenbank stated firmly.

"Yes, and now she has to take me over to the hospital in Booleroo, and her car is not fixed, and I don't know how…"

"There, there. Don't worry yourself about it. If Mr Sloan hasn't managed to fix your mother's car, I'll take you over to the hospital." Georgie's mother was one of those women who saw a need and immediately took action to meet it. She saw it as her Christian duty. "You tell your mother to come and find me at Prests' if she needs me. I'll be there for half an hour or so as I have a good bit of shopping to do."

Mavis Greenbank left as quickly as she had appeared, crossing the road and going up the street a little way, before entering Prests' general store. Sitting on one of the white benches outside the RSL rooms Clarrie was in a good position to see the comings and goings of the townsfolk on a Tuesday afternoon. From there he got good view of just who came and went into the doctors' and Mothers' and Babies' sister; directly across the road was the ES&A bank, up the road to the right from there was Prests and a little further up was Young's Corner. Down the road to the right was Sloan's Garage, and right next door to that was the Mount Remarkable Hotel, where his mother worked. It was a Tuesday afternoon, so there was a reasonable amount of activity in town. School was out, Clarrie noticed as he began to see first one, then others of his own class mates walking down the street. Some of them stopped to ask why on earth he hadn't been at school, and Clarrie supplied them with the basic detail, leaving out the part about the soldier hunt. He didn't feel that anybody without imagination would understand that, and he wasn't prepared to leave himself open to further ridicule.

"Well, I don't know what to do!" Beth Brown's troubled voice broke into Clarrie's thoughts. "The car's still…"

"Mrs Greenbank has offered to take me to Booleroo. She's over at Prests' doing the shopping," Clarrie interrupted her.

"Clarrie Brown!" his mother cried. "You haven't been pouring out our troubles to the whole town, have you?"

"No!" Clarrie said quickly. "She asked me how I was. She said I wasn't looking well, and I told her about having to go for an x-ray and…"

"Never mind!" Beth cut him off. "I don't see that I have much choice, but I do hate having to rely on other people, Clarrie. It goes against my grain."

Clarrie knew that about his mother already, but didn't bother to say so. He knew that she worked herself to a frazzle trying for all she was worth to make ends meet on her own. She didn't want to be beholden to anybody, but the truth was, there were times when she simply couldn't manage all she had to do. Being both mother and father to two growing children was almost impossible. Sometimes she needed help, and there were people in the town like Auntie Ella and Mavis Greenbank who were quick to offer, and often insisted that she make no fuss about it. It was times like this that Beth Brown had no choice but to swallow her pride and gratefully accept the assistance.

Chapter Four

The main fire seemed to be not far away, roaring like an angry dragon intent on consuming everything in its path. The smoke was thick and choking. Clarrie had his mouth covered like all the other men. He'd done his best to work with the team to confine the back burn, and keep it heading towards the ravaging beast. He wondered how on earth these men had been battling at this level of intensity for days. He was almost spent and had only been at it for a couple of hours.

During the last few hours Clarrie had recognised several people from years ago, and had met some others for the first time, but it was not the time for pleasantries and the exchanging of histories. It was as Geoff had said; they needed every able man and woman to play their part in the conflict.

The front this team were supposed to be holding was some two hundred metres in length, and Clarrie knew that Geoff was working some distance away. With the worry of doing the job properly, Clarrie had not been watching out for anyone but himself and what he'd been told to do. When he took his empty knapsack over to the four-wheel-drive, he found a couple of the Melrose fellows communicating with Geoff by radio.

From the conversation that went back and forth, Clarrie gathered that Geoff had been about 150 metres away, and had picked up a lift with the Booleroo truck to come back to join his own unit. But somehow, they'd gone right past the Melrose truck. Clarrie wasn't too surprised. It was quite dark now, and the smoke was thick.

"What's that over there?" a man yelled. "It looks like a rescue chopper."

It was a flashing orange light that broke through the thick, dark night, and seemed to be ascending.

"It's not! It's the Booleroo truck. They've missed us completely."

The talk went back and forth on the radio. By now the Booleroo crew were well aware that they'd gone too far, and now they reported that they were on a narrow ascending track. It was little more than a rocky and overgrown fire track, and it was certain that there was nowhere for them to turn. They had no choice but to continue upward. Clarrie recognised Geoff's voice as the one communicating and noted again just how composed and unruffled he was.

"How the heck are they ever gonna turn on that sized trail up there?" someone asked. "It goes straight up to the top!"

"Tell them to get back now!" the other man yelled, his tone loud and suddenly full of panic. "Look over there! It'll get them for sure!"

Clarrie looked in the general direction indicated and could see for himself. It was the fire. He didn't know if it was the back burn or the main fire, but it didn't really matter. The way it was burning, it would do untold damage. Even Clarrie knew by now that fire burnt up hill, and rapidly. It was gathering ferocity at the bottom of the hill where the Booleroo truck was slowly making its way upward.

"The fire's coming your way," the agitated voice of the Melrose operator said.

"Melrose 4–3, this is Booleroo 4–2," Geoff's controlled tone came in reply, observing all radio protocol, despite the dire circumstances. "Ah, it would appear that we are in a spot of bother. Over."

The Melrose boys had completely abandoned procedure in their state of panic. "Get out! Get out!" The operator yelled back.

Clarrie's heart was in his mouth. The orange roaring blaze was mounting that hill in seconds, and he could see just where the Booleroo truck was by the evenly flashing light. There wasn't a thing any of them on the lower ground could do. He'd written and read enough to know that it was common to lose men during a bushfire. Clarrie's alarm increased when he considered that he'd only just been reacquainted with a good friend after twenty long years, and within a few hours of meeting, a horrible tragedy could end that friendship forever.

Mrs Greenbank had been more than happy to drive Clarrie across to the hospital, and had even insisted that Beth go back to her work.

"There's no use both of us going. You don't want to be losing pay when you could be working. I'll look after Clarrie and call you if there's anything serious to be attended to."

Clarrie felt badly having his mother lose money, and worse that she would always feel uncomfortable having to accept this kind of charity. But he didn't have a problem with accepting Mrs Greenbank's help. She treated him much like she treated her own son, and though Georgie often complained about her strict ways, Clarrie knew there was a good heart beneath the meticulous exterior. She was a funny lady, likely to scold him often, but just as quick to offer a stop at the shop to buy lollies.

The results of the x-ray showed that Clarrie had indeed broken a bone. Doctor Wheaton attended to it with a minimum of fuss, setting the arm in plaster, and recommending that Clarrie stay in the hospital overnight so that they could give him some strong painkillers.

But here Clarrie balked. He had never much liked the sterile environment of the hospital, ever since he'd been there to visit his father after the accident. He'd seen his father, and then after he left, he was told that his father had died. Clarrie's association with hospitals was that of loss and grief. He wasn't going to stay for any reason, even pain relief.

"There, there!" Mrs Greenbank said in her typical fashion. "There's no need to make a fuss. You needn't stay if you don't want to. He lasted all right last night," she spoke to the physician, "I dare say he will manage again, with a Disprin or two for help."

Doctor Wheaton seemed to think that the few benefits of staying were not worth the apparent distress that staying would cause, so he agreed to send the boy home again. He issued a number of instructions to Mrs Greenbank to pass along to Clarrie's mother, about care of the plaster and taking care of the arm. All in all, Clarrie was glad to leave with his life. He liked Doctor Wheaton all right, so long as he was in the relatively safe environment of the RSL consulting room.

Beth just sighed when she heard the instructions. Clarrie was to have the rest of the week off school, needed to keep relatively still, and needed to be given Disprin if pain persisted. Mrs Greenbank was at once alert.

"Don't you worry about it! I'll come along to your place as soon as Georgie's off to school, and see to the boy while you're at work."

Beth was grateful, but she did so hate imposing on people in this way. "Thank you, Mrs Greenbank," she said, injecting as much gratitude into her tone as she was able. "I'd like to be able to return the favour some time."

"Don't talk nonsense. When Clarrie is good and well, he can come and pull some weeds for me. All right, Clarrie?" she directed the proposal to the patient.

Clarrie nodded in return.

"And coming up on the weekend is Easter," Mrs Greenbank continued. "I've got a lot of cooking to be done for the Tennis Tournament. By Thursday, Clarrie might even be able to give me a hand with a thing or two."

And as the week progressed, the pain subsided. Other than the cumbersome plaster that made certain tasks difficult, Clarrie found that he felt well enough to do anything he normally did. However, Mrs Greenbank watched him like a hawk and wouldn't allow any nonsense like riding bikes, climbing any trees or anything that wasn't quiet and sedate. Clarrie almost felt that he was looking forward to going back to school. He didn't feel sick and this enforced quiet was almost more than he could bear.

Friday morning came around quickly enough, and Clarrie felt the excitement that all the kids felt at having a four-day long weekend. It was Good Friday and Clarrie had every intention of becoming part of the town's activities regardless of the plastered arm.

But first thing on this solemn religious morning, Clarrie was compelled to go along to the Good Friday service at the Methodist Church. Mr Bishop had rung the night before and asked if he was feeling up to coming along. Clarrie was up for anything. He had been restricted enough for the week, and so promised to go along if Mr Bishop would pick him up before nine o'clock.

"Don't you want to come?" Clarrie asked his mother as he finished off his breakfast. "It's an important time of the year for going to church."

"That may well be, Clarrie," Beth Brown answered tiredly, "but if I had the day off, which I don't, I would stay home and sleep. I'll come with you another time." She promised lightly.

"What about you, Sal?" Clarrie asked his sister, who was busily searching for her hairbrush.

"You say a prayer for both of us, Clarrie," she said without much thought. "I'm meeting some of the gang down at the tennis courts first thing."

Clarrie was a little disappointed. Not that he should have expected anything different. The Brown family had never been a church-going family, even when his father was alive. The only reason he went now was because Mr Bishop was such a good sort of fellow, and always offered to pick up the lonely lambs to bring them to church. After a few years of attending the Sunday School, hearing Mrs Curyer teach all about Jesus, and His love for children, and then later Mr Bishop teach more about how he should love others, Clarrie had begun to accept that going to church was an important part of life. He only wished that his mother and sister would share the experience with him.

Good Friday service was always a very sober affair. Clarrie remembered other Easter Fridays and knew exactly the story the minister would use this morning. There was no children's program this morning. All the church members, most of them regular and those who came only twice a year, settled quietly in the long wooden pews. Clarrie chose to sit with the Arthur family. Mrs Sybil Arthur, with her husband, Frank, and their three sons almost filled the pew, but there was enough space for one small eleven year-old boy. Clarrie just fitted on the aisle end. He carefully held the black hymnbook that old Mr Reg Arthur had handed him on the way in. He didn't want any of the adult worshippers thinking that he was not old enough or mature enough to find the hymn numbers on his own. They were displayed on the board above the organ, and Clarrie had already turned up the first hymn in anticipation.

As the service began, and the strains of the old pump organ echoed through the small church, Clarrie began to feel a sense of Good Friday spirit – a sense of having to pay serious attention. Auntie Ella played the introduction of the hymn number 180. The congregation all stood up as one, the sounds of shuffling feet on wooden floorboards echoing in the high ceilings. Clarrie stood as tall as he could next to Geoff, holding his hymn book open at the right page and began to sing, *'There is a green hill far away, without a city wall, Where the dear Lord was crucified, Who died to save us all'*.

As the tightly packed room of worshippers worked their way through this hymn, and others that drew attention to the crucified Christ, Clarrie imagined the whole story of that first Easter. He sat and listened to the Reverend Ian Anderson as he read the Scriptures telling of the betrayal of Jesus, the trial and then the awful crucifixion. Clarrie was an impressionable child, and he couldn't help but feel as if it was all happening again on this actual day, nearly two thousand years after the actual event. He didn't dare allow the real sorrow he felt to develop into tears, as he did have an emerging reputation to protect, but he felt all of the grief and trouble that the disciples and friends of Jesus must have felt.

"The peace of God which passeth all understanding, keep your hearts and minds in the knowledge and love of God, and His Son Jesus Christ our Lord," the minister began the benediction. Clarrie had heard this plenty of times before. He could almost recite it. As the sombre service came to its end, Clarrie whispered his own prayer of thanks that Sunday was coming. He hated to think that they were going to leave this church building with Christ dead and buried in the tomb. He knew enough to know that Sunday's service would have a whole different feel about it, and he looked forward to it in anticipation.

He filed down the aisle of the church, admiring the maroon pattern on the aisle carpet runner, which he had always thought very classy. The minister, as was his normal practice, waited at the door of the church for his parishioners to file past, shaking hands and offering a greeting to every one of them. Clarrie liked Mr Anderson. He always talked to him as if he were grown up. Sally always treated him like a child, and having the minister recognise him as a normal intelligent member of the congregation was something that Clarrie enjoyed.

"God bless you, Clarrie," Reverend Anderson smiled at him, while shaking his hand in a firm grip. "I see you've met with an accident." He said, alluding to the plastered arm.

"Yes, sir," Clarrie answered. "I tripped over and broke my arm."

"I hope it won't spoil your Easter plans. Were you entered into the junior tennis tournament?"

"No!" Clarrie couldn't help smiling. "I've had lots of tennis coaching with Mrs Blieschke, but I'm not very good."

"Well, I hope you have a good holiday weekend anyway." The minister released his grip and gave a final smile of farewell.

Clarrie moved into the porch and dutifully handed the hymnbook back to Reg Arthur, who carefully stacked it away in the porch cupboard. Mr Arthur never said much to anybody, child or adult alike. But he was very diligent about his role as steward. Clarrie stood on the top step of the church porch for a moment, surveying the gathered crowd below. As he looked, he saw two or three carloads of people who had just come from the Anglican Church service just down the road. They evidently had their Good Friday service at the same time. In one of the cars were Vic and Claire Blieschke, hurrying from church to the tennis tournament. Rex and Matilda Deekin were also getting into their car parked just across from the Methodist church.

Clarrie knew that these people wouldn't wait outside church for a chat as they were amongst the chief organisers of the famous Melrose Easter Tennis Tournament. It was a big affair in the town, and there was a lot of organization to be done. Clarrie wondered how much work they must have already done for them to be able to make the early service at all.

"Are you going down to the tennis?" Clarrie's thoughts were interrupted by Auntie Ella as she came out of the church behind him. She had obviously followed his gaze and drawn the same conclusion.

"Yes!" Clarrie answered without ceremony. "Mum said she didn't mind what I did over Easter, just so long as I didn't get into any more trouble." He held up his plastered arm meaningfully.

"If you want to wait for ten minutes, I'll give you a ride down to the tennis courts on my way home." Clarrie smiled his thanks, and then watched as she began to mingle with the people standing out the front of the church. He wasn't too surprised to see her stopping by her two daughters-in-law, and fussing over her little grandchildren. Clarrie didn't quite see the attraction that small children seemed to hold for their grandmothers, but he waited patiently while she cooed and chuckled, the children responding in a manner that, to his way of thinking, only encouraged further adult foolishness.

"Mr Bishop and I will be heading down to the bowls this afternoon," Auntie Ella said, by way of conversation, once they were eventually under way. "We might see you for afternoon tea, if you are still at the tennis then."

That was one of the things that Clarrie meant to make a priority. He had already worked out that he was not going to make a first rate tennis player, and doubted that he would ever enter the competition himself, but to the side attractions that were offered, especially the food, Clarrie had definitely committed himself. In fact, he knew just how he would be able to get the best opportunity for some great food. He'd learned from past years that the women in charge of the luncheons and afternoon teas would always welcome a reliable child who offered to help, and in return for being reliable, Clarrie had often scored a cake that wouldn't fit on a plate, or a sausage roll that had fallen apart, or a curried-egg sandwich with the filling oozed out. Clarrie wasn't necessarily concerned with the elegance of presentation of this 'cast-off' food. It tasted just as good as if he'd bought a proper plate.

Auntie Ella dropped him off at the corner by the post office, and it didn't take Clarrie two minutes to run down the hill towards the tennis courts. Already there were many cars pulled up under the shade of the numerous gum trees, some down behind the tennis club shed, and some over the creek and up on the bank on the other side. There was a whole area on the southern end of the shed that had been roped off, and a lot of long trestle tables had been set up.

"Do you want any help setting the tables?" Clarrie asked Mrs Claire Blieschke, the first woman he saw as he put his head through the door of the small, galvanized iron shed.

"Yes, please, Clarrie," Claire answered, without looking up from the chicken she was cutting up. "If you go and see Mr Deekin, he will be able to get the table cloths from the back of his car, and his two boys will be able to help you put them on the trestles."

Rex Deekin was registering players, and letting them know the draw for the competition, but he took a moment to give Clarrie directions for finding the tablecloths. "Round up some of the other kids to give you a hand, Clarrie," Rex said quickly, before turning his attention back to another player, this time a fellow from the city, who had come to register. Clarrie paused just a moment, intrigued by the stature and manner of this unfamiliar character.

"Oliver Printen," the tall young man gave his name.

"You ever played here at Melrose before?" Rex asked, his interest slightly aroused.

"No! Never. Didn't really think it'd be worth my while. Bit of a backwater, isn't it?"

Oliver obviously didn't realise that all tennis officials were long time Melrose residents, and likely to take such a comment badly. Still he blundered on, oblivious. "Won a lot of tournaments around the state. Of course, I've heard about this one, but never bothered before. Only came now because my father wanted me to play one more tournament before trying out for the state team."

"Is that right?" Clarrie thought he could detect an underlying antagonism in Mr Deekin's tone, but he wasn't sure. It might have been that he felt antagonistic himself. Mr Oliver Printen suddenly seemed likely to become the tournament's favourite challenger – the one that all locals were likely to side against. Just before Clarrie took off to get on with the job of the tablecloths, he quickly scanned the draw sheet and saw two names that he felt were promising against this citified up-start. *Our Rossy Miller and Keith Bowman will show this fellow a thing or two,* Clarrie thought to himself. *Fancy calling Melrose a backwater.*

Clarrie had already formed his opinion of Oliver Printen, and Mr Printen, who had arrived in a late model Mercedes, of all cars to drive out into the country, was even now making himself more obnoxious by dropping derogatory comments about the antiquated facilities, and the ramshackle state of the courts. Mr Printen was not making friends anywhere, not that that had been his intention in the first place, but even long-time rivals of the Melrose team, players from Orroroo and Wilmington, were taking offence at the unnecessary remarks about country towns. Melrose was one town amongst many represented on the draw card for this tournament, and a fierce parochial rivalry could always be expected, but suddenly, all country players alike, no matter on which side of the Whim Creek they lived, decided that of all players they wanted to see soundly beaten, it was this insufferably conceited fellow from the city.

The first round games were under way on the three courts. Carol Bamman was taking on one of the Orroroo girls on the top court. This was the newest of the three courts, just down the hill from the prestigious bowling green. There was a pleasant slope just above the court, and many spectators had placed their blankets and picnic chairs under the huge river red gum to watch the local girl do her best.

The two older courts were on the flat down lower, then there was the old tennis shed where the ladies prepared all the food, and directly behind ran the Mount Creek.

While the tennis competition started in earnest, the children of tennis players and organisers alike, hurried down to the creek behind the shed, where they amused themselves with all sorts of games. It was lucky for them that there had been some rain the week before, which had left several reasonable water holes where they could skim rocks and hunt for tadpoles. The Mount Creek, which meandered out onto the plain and was then called the Willochra Creek, was generally a dry, rock-lined water-course that only ran after very heavy rain. Still, despite its lack of water, with the picturesque line of river red gums guarding its length along the base of magnificent Mount Remarkable, it provided a very pleasant backdrop to the weekend's proceedings. Of course, as it was the Easter long week-end, there were many campers who had made the pilgrimage to the country, and had set up tents in the adjacent caravan park, as well as over the creek, and quite a way across the flat leading to the first major foothill. Melrose children were always fascinated by the sudden increase in their town's population. A small tent city always seemed to appear over the Easter weekend, and there was a huge increase in the number of cars and pedestrian traffic. The number of strangers he saw caught Clarrie's attention. Living in a little town like Melrose, children were used to seeing only people they knew, and saying a polite 'hello' to every one of them. This weekend was different.

Clarrie found the tablecloths without too much trouble, and Matilda Deekin helped by pressing her two older boys into service, much to their chagrin. Noel Ryan's twin girls offered kindly to help, and between the five of them they soon had the old, scarred wooden trestles covered in snowy white linen. Clarrie helped the Deekin boys set chairs at every place, while the Ryan twins placed the cutlery, carefully spacing the settings to make it look quite proper for an official luncheon.

Clarrie cast a few sideways glances at the Ryan girls. He knew them quite well as Mr Bishop often picked them up to take them to Sunday school, but he simply could never tell them apart. The whole phenomenon of identical twins was brought right to him as he watched the two girls work quietly and efficiently.

"Thank you, children," said Claire as she came out of the shed to see the job all but finished. "That looks very nice."
She had hardly finished speaking before the two boys took the opportunity to run off down to the creek to join their other friends. Clarrie knew he could have joined them, but felt that with just a little more effort he could probably gain something special in the way of reward for his efforts.

"Is there anything else I can do?" he asked, hoping that his ulterior motives were not too obvious.

"Yes," Claire answered immediately. "If you stay about here, I will call you if I need you to run any errands, and in the meantime, can you keep an eye on the tables. Sometimes gum leaves fall down and that doesn't really look very nice for paying customers. If you can just keep the table clear of gum leaves, I would really appreciate it."

Clarrie nodded his willingness to oblige, trying to hide his disappointment at not having been offered something to eat. He watched Mrs Blieschke return to the tennis shed, now positively humming with activity as quite a number of women stood inside about the tables, slicing salad vegetables and cold meats.

"You're a good lad, Clarrie!" Clarrie turned to see who had spoken and saw Peter Blieschke, Claire's son. He was dressed in long white trousers and a white jumper. "You're not going to play tennis dressed like that, are you?" Clarrie asked.

"No!" Peter laughed, "I'm no good at tennis. I'm one of the bowlers, you know."

Clarrie looked confused. "But bowling is for old people," he said tentatively.

Peter laughed again. "You'd better not let anyone else hear you say that. You know that they are all prodigiously proud of the sport, and the skill involved."

"But your mother is the tennis coach," Clarrie argued, not quite ready to accept that this young man had chosen a rival sport.

"Yes! She is," Peter agreed. "And she's a very good coach. But the trouble is, I don't really like tennis much."

"And you like bowls?" Clarrie sounded doubtful.

Peter laughed again at the obvious prejudice. "You know, I didn't think much of bowls either, when I was a young fellow like you. When they were talking about putting the bowling green in on the recreation reserve between the playground and the tennis courts, back in the fifties, I thought to myself, what a ridiculous thing. With all those old people chucking those heavy balls around, someone is going to get hit in the head."

This time Clarrie laughed. "I thought they rolled the balls along the grass," he chuckled.

"Oh, they do," Peter nodded, "but I didn't know that at the time. I thought they threw them through the air, or something."

"So have you come down to watch someone play tennis?" Clarrie asked.

"I've got quite a while before my match on the green, so I thought I'd come down and see Dex Fuller play that rich bloke who's been prancing about the place, flashing his fancy duds at everyone."

"Oliver Printen!" Clarrie didn't quite know whether to be excited or worried to hear that Dex Fuller had been first in the draw against the Printen fellow. He didn't want Oliver to win, but wasn't certain that Dex could do the job. He knew of Dex because Mrs Fuller often talked about him during his piano lesson. Clarrie knew that he was a good tennis player, of course, but also knew that there were others who could beat him.

"So, you didn't enter, Clarrie?" Peter asked by way of conversation.

Clarrie held up his plastered arm. "Can't play with a broken bone," he said, "and besides, you know I'm not very good."

"Wouldn't have hurt to try, if your arm had been all right," Peter offered. "My mother says that you are always at practice, and are always very reliable."

"I'm not very reliable when it comes to hitting the ball though." Clarrie's head drooped just a little.

"Ah, well!" Peter ruffled his hair. "Perhaps your talent runs in a different direction. Maybe bowls!"

"Your mother is a very good coach," Clarrie offered, quick to divert him away from the suggestion of taking up bowling.

"She loves to help the kids," Peter replied. "She's very patient."

"Has she ever played tennis?" Clarrie couldn't help the question coming out. Of course it seemed ridiculous asking if his own tennis coach had played tennis, but Mrs Claire Blieschke was different from most sporting coaches.

"You're curious about her leg?" The comment sounded almost accusing, but Peter's tone was quite understanding.

"Well," Clarrie said slowly, "I have wondered about that great big shoe she wears, and she limps about."

"That's a special built-up shoe. She's worn it for as long as I can remember."

"How come?" Clarrie asked, genuinely interested, and not aware that his question might be considered intrusive or rude.

"She told us that she'd had an accident when she was a little girl which had caused some damage. Apparently it stopped her leg from growing, and her left leg is now some three inches shorter than her right. That's why she wears the built up shoe, so that when she walks, it's sort of even."

Clarrie's face showed intense awe.

"And to your first question, yes. She did used to play tennis," Peter added.

"Even with the built up shoe?" Clarrie asked.

"Yes! And apparently she was very good."

"So she used to be able to run, then?"

"No! Dad told me that she was a very skilled hitter of the ball. She didn't have to run because she would place the ball in the most difficult positions, and would have her opponent running all over the court after the ball. That was the main weapon in her game."

Clarrie was clearly impressed. Just at that moment, as two young female tennis players passed by, a new question crossed his mind.

"What did the tennis players use to wear?" he asked. The question was prompted by the neat short skirts that he'd seen on the two girls going past, and his imagination was trying to fit it in with the now glorified image of his tennis coach. Peter laughed outright at the question, having seen the course of Clarrie's thoughts.

"When my mother used to play, the girls wore nice knee-length tennis dresses, not too much different to those girls over there, though a few inches longer."

Peter could see that Clarrie's mind was whirling almost out of control, his eyes as large as saucers, and decided to set him at ease. "But my mother always wore a long skirt to play in. Just a little different from the others, but then she was something special by way of a tennis player, wasn't she?"

"Yes!" Clarrie agreed.

"But did you know that the fellows used to wear long trousers instead of shorts?"

Clarrie's attention remained fixed.

"Yes! You know Mr Frank Fuller, Dex's dad?"

Clarrie nodded.

"He was quite a champion player a number of years back. I remember when I was about your age, he and his brother-in-law, Clem Slee, still held quite a high ranking in our Melrose Tennis club. I always thought they were very funny because they played in long trousers."

Clarrie's fertile imagination was quite exercised by Peter Blieschke's brief history lesson, and his attention was only broken when somebody called Peter's name.

"Good luck with your bowling!" Clarrie called out after Peter as he moved off to watch Dex Fuller face his first opponent, Oliver Printen. Clarrie wanted to watch this match as well, but it had been drawn for the top court, and that would mean that he would have to leave his duty of watching out for gum leaves. Clarrie was not the sort to shirk a responsibility, once it had been given him, so he contented himself with sitting down to watch the other match that was going on court two, just opposite where the luncheon was to be held. It was two out-of-towners.

One woman from Port Germein, and another from Wilmington. They were quite an evenly matched pair, and Clarrie watched them battle furiously for the right to progress to the next round.

The morning passed quickly. Peter Blieschke returned from the top court, his set face telling Clarrie all he needed to know. Oliver Printen was loud and arrogant, boasting openly of his prowess as a tennis player, and Peter quietly admitted to Clarrie that he had some grounds. Oliver had soundly beaten Dex, and Clarrie was not overly pleased to hear this. Of all the players entered, he fervently hoped that Oliver Printen would not be the one to take the tournament championship.

When the lunch hour came, Clarrie made himself useful helping to fill large jugs with rainwater.

"Make sure you strain the wrigglers out before you fill the jugs," Mrs Deekin had insisted to Clarrie as he stood with a bucket at the rainwater tank behind the shed. "It's not very pleasant pouring out a glass of water and having wrigglers swimming before your eyes."

Clarrie silently agreed that the prospect of drinking mosquito larvae was not particularly pleasant, but was at a loss as to how he was supposed to strain them out. He'd heard Jim Bishop skite about how he'd strained the sergeant major's tea with his pocket-handkerchief when he was in the National Service, and wondered if that was an altogether acceptable practice. His own pocket-handkerchief looked less than clean, having been used for a number of emergencies, including a quick polish of his shoes before church. Still, if no better option presented itself, he thought perhaps it would be better than wrigglers in official glasses.

Thankfully, Mrs Deekin provided a suitable solution before it came to that point, though Clarrie still wondered if it was any better. She produced a piece of old stocking and secured it over the tank faucet, the theory being that it would let the water through and catch the squirming larvae.

I hope that didn't come straight from her shoe, Clarrie thought, shuddering at the thought. But then remembered that his own idea would not have been much better.

"Here you are, Clarrie," Claire Blieschke held out a loaded plate of food to him.

"I don't have any money to pay for it," Clarrie spoke very quietly, a little ashamed of the fact.

"You don't have to pay for it. This is wages for all your work this morning. You've been a terrific help. Now you can take this along with the other children and sit down on the bank of the creek, if you like."

Clarrie took the plate and thanked his tennis coach politely. He had hoped to get some rejected leftovers, but the ladies had prepared a full plate of perfectly good food. There was a chicken drumstick, a slice of ham and a slice of corned-beef on one side of the plate. On the other side was a large lettuce leaf with slices of tomato and cucumber placed very decoratively next to a slice of cheese and a slice of beetroot. Clarrie made a mental note to hide the beetroot under a rock. This was not his favourite food. And then there was a rather interesting cube of jellied peas. He'd heard Auntie Ella speak in awed tones of Matilda Deekin's famous jellied peas, and had wondered. Jelly he had eaten, and peas, but never together in the same recipe. Still, it looked very 'official' and Clarrie decided he would try it at least, and thought that if it was too out of the ordinary, it could occupy the same place under the rock with the beetroot. With this he was given a complimentary slice of bread and butter. Altogether, Clarrie considered that he had done very well.

"Hi, Clarrie!" He heard his sister Sally's voice and rolled his eyes, wondering why she hadn't appeared all morning when there was work to be done, but suddenly found him when he'd just received a plate of food.

"Where'd you get the money to buy that?" she asked in an accusing tone.

"The ladies gave it to me for helping them all morning." Clarrie answered, holding his plate protectively to one side.

"You are such a goody-two shoes, Clarrie. Why don't you go down the creek with the others, and have some fun?"

Clarrie didn't think it was necessary to answer as he had his reward, and was happy with it. Besides, his broken arm was more conducive to quiet helping than to boisterous rough and tumble.

"Do you want to share any of that?" Sally asked, eyeing the chicken drumstick. Clarrie had already decided that she was welcome to the beetroot, and if she pressed, he was willing to give up the jellied peas, but when he made this offer, she turned up her nose.

"Yuck!" was her rather uncomplimentary response. "Doesn't matter anyway. I'll get one of the boys to buy me something better."

"You know that Mum said we shouldn't beg," Clarrie lectured.

"I'm not begging. There are plenty of boys who are begging me to have lunch with them."

Clarrie watched as his sister flounced away, calling out to a group of teenagers who were just coming down the hill from the main street. He was rather annoyed at his sister's careless attitude about boys. He didn't think it was quite the decent thing to be always flirting, and with a different boy every week. Still, he didn't feel as if he was in any position to make her mind her manners, and so he dismissed her from his mind quite easily.

He found an old log in a shady spot just on the side of the tennis shed and decided that he would eat his lunch there in peace, without the loud and jostling crowd of kids that he knew from school. He didn't like the fact that his sister had called him goody-two-shoes, but the taunt wasn't enough to make him run headlong into a crowd of mischief as a reaction to it.

He was just searching for a suitable rock to deposit his beetroot under, and had decided that the jellied peas were all right, though a little strange, when Lyall and Geoff came up to him.

"How's your arm, mate?" Lyall asked cheerily, settling himself down.

"Doesn't hurt much anymore," Clarrie answered easily.

"Can I have your beetroot?" Lyall asked. Clarrie handed it over without comment, and it was thus disposed of more easily than he had thought possible.

"Been watching the tennis?" Geoff asked, good-naturedly.

"Yeah!" Clarrie answered dejectedly.

"Why the long face?" Lyall asked.

"There's a real pain in the neck of a fellow who's entered, and already he's thrashed Dex Fuller. I don't like him. I hope he doesn't win."

"I reckon I just met him up the street," said Geoff. "Does he drive a Mercedes Benz?"

"Yeah!"

"And is he tall, and prances about like he's the bloomin' Prince of Wales?"

"Sounds like the one."

"Oh, you mean the bloke that was in the shop?" Lyall asked his brother.

"Yeah," Geoff answered. "Did you hear him? He waltzes in and makes all these loud comments, so that everyone in Young's can hear him, saying how you can't get a decent meal anywhere in this town."

"I just had a real good meal," Clarrie offered meekly. "He was one of the players. He was supposed to sit down to dinner with the rest of them."

"He's got a flamin' nerve," Lyall said hotly. "If he thinks he's too good to eat with our tennis boys, then he should flamin' well go home."

"Not until we've beaten him first," Clarrie said firmly.

"You fancy yourself a chance against him?" Geoff laughed, tapping Clarrie's plaster.

"Not me! But Rossy Miller might."

"Ross Miller isn't really a Melrose boy," Lyall said.

"He's married to Jeanette Mount, and she's a Melrose girl," his brother argued. "Close enough, if you ask me."

"Speaking of Melrose girls, did you hear how our cousin Carol went in her game?"

"No!" Clarrie answered. "I know she's already played, but I don't know if she won or not. But there's Peter Bamman over there. We could ask him."

Lyall, never shy about anything, called out to his cousin's husband, and Peter immediately walked over to meet them.

"Hey! Did your wife win her game?" Lyall asked.

"Yes, she did. And by the way, I've got a bone to pick with you."

"With me?" Lyall looked surprised and injured.

"Yes! What do you mean by pinching Cyril?"

"Cyril?" Lyall sounded confused.

"Lorna's garden gnome! You know the one!"

"Lorna's gnome?" Lyall cried. "What on earth are you talking about?"

Meanwhile, Geoff and Clarrie fell about laughing, seeing Peter's indignation and Lyall's outraged innocence.

"Someone's come in during the night and pinched my mother-in-law's garden gnome. She's very upset about it. You know how she is about her garden."

"Yes, I know, but I didn't go anywhere near Auntie Lorna's garden last night."

"Are you sure?" Peter looked stern, though Clarrie thought he could detect a mischievous twinkle.

"Of course not. Why would I risk Auntie Lorna's wrath to pinch her garden gnome?"

Peter relaxed and he laughed. "Well, I thought you were the obvious suspect."

"Oh!" Lyall feigned a sharp intake of breath and put on a wounded expression. "I'm crushed that you would even think such a thing, and me of all people."

The other three were laughing loudly at this point, and Lyall pretended to have been deeply offended

"I heard about your escapade out at Bishop's last week," Peter said.

"One mistake in life, and I'm a marked man!"

"What about the time you painted old Norman Smythe's cow," Peter reminded his cousin.

"Lyall played a joke on Mr Smythe," Geoff explained to Clarrie. "The cow was a black and white Friesian, and we…I mean, he, took a can of black paint and made it a totally black cow. You know old Mr Smythe used to get a bit confused sometimes, and he couldn't make out what had happened to his cow, and where on earth this black cow had come from."

"All right. But two jokes don't necessarily make me a criminal suspect," Lyall grumbled.

"And what about the New Year's Eve when Mr Brigg's garden gate disappeared, and mysteriously found its way into Geoff Slee's full wheat bin?"

"That wasn't me," Lyall denied hotly. "That was you." He pointed an accusing finger at his brother.

Geoff didn't deny it, only laughed, as the whole thing was a joke by now.

"Well, I suggest, that if there has been a kidnapping of Auntie Lorna's garden gnome, that the police must be informed." Lyall made this comment, and as Clarrie looked up, he knew why. He saw the police constable from Booleroo Centre driving his paddy wagon down the hill toward the tennis courts.

"If this had happened a couple of years ago, then we'd only have had to run up to the museum for Bernie Faraleigh to give us proper police attention," Peter commented, obviously not serious.

Clarrie had not been in the town when there was a police presence, but he knew that what was now the town museum used to be a police station. In fact, it was one of the reasons that Melrose had become a town in the first place. When white settlers had first come to the Mount Remarkable district, they had not understood the native inhabitants, and the aboriginals had not understood them or their ways. The white squatters had quickly called for an English law enforcement to be stationed there to deal with the problem of 'sheep-stealing' natives. Naturally, the natives had not understood that the animals that were now roaming their land were not free for all to hunt, and so there was the usual conflict of cultures. Clarrie had heard all about this when Miss Jolly had marched the children down to the museum for an educational excursion. He had wondered about how the natives felt at this rather sudden punishment that was meted out to them, without them knowing or understanding who the white settlers were, or what their strange laws were all about. But then Clarrie was one of those children who thought deeply beyond the surface presentation of facts.

All he knew now was that in the early sixties the township of Melrose had so little crime in it, just an odd cow being painted black and a stolen gate or so, that a police presence was no longer required. The old police station and courthouse building was duly turned into a museum, and now the Melrose people relied on the policeman from Booleroo Centre for their law enforcement needs, a situation that was not entirely acceptable considering the rivalry that existed between the two towns.

"There you go, Peter." Lyall's voice brought Clarrie back to the situation at hand. "There's Constable Thomas. Now's your chance to report the crime."

Constable L.B. Thomas pulled the police van up beside the group of four, as they stood chatting near the tennis shed.

"How's it all going?" he asked in a friendly tone.

"Mr Thomas. It's a good thing you've happened along," Lyall said with apparent seriousness. "We have a dreadful crime to report."

If it hadn't been for Clarrie's inability to keep a straight face, the poor policeman might have been quite worried.

"It appears our gnome has gone a-roaming," Peter put in. "If you should see him, be sure and send him home."

The policeman, a jovial sort of chap, gave an amused chuckle, and tipped his hat by way of salute. "I'll be sure and keep an eye out for him, Peter."

"Roaming gnome!" Lyall muttered in a disgusted tone under his breath.

"Say what you want," Peter responded. "Until Cyril is returned to his rightful place in Auntie Lorna's garden, you will always be a suspect."

"Now, that's a terrible thing to say!"

But before the two cousins could continue their silly argument, the small group was interrupted by the noise of a small Suzuki four-wheel-drive, roaring down the hill toward them.

"Joe Clucas!" Peter called out to the driver, as he skidded to a rather dangerous halt just in time to miss the group of four. "I thought you'd be up on the Bowling Green."

"Finished my match!" Joe said in a careless manner.

"Did you win?" Lyall couldn't help but ask.

"Nah!" Joe didn't sound as if it mattered one way or the other.

"I heard that you were one of the best bowlers in the team, Mr Clucas," Clarrie put in. "Was the competition really good?"

"Weren't that good!" Joe dismissed the idea easily. "Want to come for a test drive in my four-wheel-drive?" he asked.

"Where you going?" Peter asked. "We've got things to see to around here."

"Not goin' anywhere," Joe said. "Just gonna run her up and down the banks of the creek over behind the caravan park, see how good she is at steep slopes."

Peter's interest was aroused. "If Carol is looking for me, tell her I'm…"

"We'll tell her you'll be back soon," Lyall entered into the conspiracy as Peter stepped into the compact vehicle, ducking his head to avoid hitting the canvas roof.

"You know what happened at the bowls, don't you?" Geoff asked his brother.

"Yeah, I reckon," Lyall grinned.

"What?" Clarrie didn't like being on the outside of a secret. "What happened?"

"Joe Clucas is a sharp bowler, probably the best in the Melrose club, but the trouble is he's such a larrikin. Won't take anything seriously."

"I've heard Harry Bamman, Peter's dad, talk about it before," Geoff said knowingly.

"He's such a great draw as a bowler, gets his bowl closer to the jack than anyone, and in the first shot," Lyall explained.

"So why doesn't he win?" Clarrie asked.

"Ah, I don't know. He can't stand being serious about anything, and so in his very next shot he always drives his own bowl away from the jack. He's a sharp shooter when it comes to driving as well. He positively torments his team mates."

"Funny bloke, Joe Clucas," Geoff said in a thoughtful tone.

Clarrie would like to have explored Joe Clucas's psyche just a bit more, but their attention was captured by the loud roaring of the Suzuki's engine as it was apparently negotiating some steep incline. Then they heard Peter Bamman shouting, and weren't certain, but thought there was a burst of very colourful language from someone. Clarrie joined the Arthur boys as they ran towards the loud, revving engine, and noticed that quite a number of other tennis spectators followed as well.

When they finally arrived on the scene at the back of the Caravan Park, right up against the School fence, Clarrie couldn't believe his eyes. How Joe had got them into this fix was anyone's guess, but the Suzuki was perched halfway down a decidedly steep slope, and he had tried to turn it sideways to drive along to a less steep section, but it was so steep that the Suzuki had begun to tip sideways. Obviously, Peter's immediate response, since he was on the high side, was to stand up and lean out, holding onto the roof, a little like leaning out over the side of a yacht to prevent it from capsizing. And there they were, perched in this awkward state.

"I'll get my Nissan and hoist you out," some helpful fellow called from the crowd of gathered on-lookers.

"Be blowed you will," Joe yelled back. "I'm not having any Nissan pull me out!"

A number of the locals, who knew Joe's reputation, laughed, and waited to see just what he would do. Joe Clucas didn't have the reputation of dogged determination and raw courage for nothing. The amazed crowd of tennis fans watched tensely as Joe effected what could have been classed as a twenty-two point turn, manoeuvring back and forth and back and forth until he eventually got the vehicle to an angle where he could drive it safely back out of the creek again.

Clarrie joined with all the others as a spontaneous cheer and applause broke out.

"That's Joe Clucas for you," Lyall muttered as they watched him roar away.

Chapter Five

Clarrie arrived back at the fire shed with the crew that were supposed to be coming off shift. That they were all coming back alive and unscathed was something that Clarrie hadn't quite got his head around. For one awful moment, Clarrie and others that were with him, thought they were going to witness the Booleroo truck and crew being incinerated. But Dean Phillips had turned that truck on nothing. If it had been light, he probably wouldn't have had dared try it. But he had, and apparently had done it as quickly as it could be done, and considering the proximity of the angry, murderous fire, it was just in the nick of time.

The crew were supposed to change so many hours earlier, but Clarrie saw first hand how they all resisted coming in. To some extent he felt it as well. How could they leave the front and come and sleep? But eventually the fire had jumped the breaks they'd tried to create and had set off further north on its devastating path toward Wilmington. It was somewhat discouraging to know they had failed to stop it at this point, and Clarrie felt their low spirits. It was now about seven in the morning, and Clarrie was dead on his feet. He could only imagine what the others must have been feeling. They had been battling those flames for a full twenty-four hours. If they had not been directly ordered to come in for rest, he doubted they would.

On the way back to the fire shed he'd been in a vehicle, following Jim Bishop's unit as they'd made their way out from the fire area, travelling over rough terrain that went up and down. On the back of Jim's ute lay his youngest son as if he was dead. But Andrew Bishop wasn't so much dead as he was dead to the world – asleep. Clarrie wondered how on earth he stayed on the flat tray-top. Every time they ascended a slope he felt for sure Andrew would simply slide off under the wheels of the vehicle following.

Once back at the shed, Clarrie knew that he should go to the hotel that his paper was paying for, and sleep. But he felt he was like the other fighters now. They were all reluctant to leave, despite the fact that their shoulders sagged, their spirits slumped and their eyes drooped. Finally, the supervisor in charge ordered them all to go home, and Clarrie went as well. Before he went into the transportable unit set next to the hotel, he spoke to the landlady.

"Wake me if anything happens," he said. "That fire could burn up this whole town in seconds, and I don't want to be asleep if it comes."

She assured him that she would check all the units before she evacuated if it came to that.

Still Clarrie struggled to sleep. He could see the flames in his mind's eye. He could hear the roar, and could feel the rough choking feeling of smoke in his throat. He lay there thinking of Geoff, and how close he'd come to death, and then his thoughts went to his own family. What if he'd been killed? Would they have cared? Would they be better off without him? Those were searching questions, to which Clarrie found the answers most disturbing. He knew it was his fault they were at the point of bankruptcy. He'd gambled their life savings away on anything that had odds on, from the soccer pools to the scratchies. And when he lost more often than he won, he'd drink himself into oblivion. When Sue asked him for the weekly grocery money, he often didn't have it. She knew him enough by now to know that it was probably in the bottom of some poker machine, or the till behind the bar.

He could understand why she was angry, resentful, even bitter. He knew that he'd brought them to this point, where his two little girls had grown out of their school shoes, and all Sue could get for them was some scuffed hand-me-downs from her older sister's kids.

Today, when he'd stared death in the face, he suddenly wondered why on earth he'd thrown his life away on some flimsy hope of winning the lottery. Why hadn't he stood and faced the fire of his own addiction instead of being consumed by the fever of alcoholism in a pathetic attempt to escape responsibility. Somewhere in all this soul searching, Clarrie fell into a restless tormented sleep.

He sat bolt upright, sweat pouring from his body, when he heard the urgent pounding on his cabin door.

"Get up!" the landlady's voice penetrated, not waiting for him to respond. "It's coming our way. We've got to get out of here!"

Clarrie only stopped to throw an old t-shirt over his head, and then opened the door. From the step he could see the whole mountain alight in front of him. He could hear the roar of the flames. Between him and the creek there were only about two hundred metres. The Mount Creek, winding its way along the foot of the mountain, was like a line that separated the town from Mount Remarkable. Between him and the creek there was only the playground, the Bowling Green and the tennis courts.

The first thing on Saturday morning, Clarrie was back down at the tennis courts, ready for the second day's play. Day one had been a day of mixed emotions.

Oliver Printen was not only still very much in the running, but had bundled out every opponent with hardly any trouble at all, and had made this fact quite well known to anyone who cared to listen. He had been quite contemptuous in his remarks about the local competition, and this had irked most of the locals, including Clarrie.

"There's something on the umpire's seat, Clarrie." Rex had spoken to him when he'd come to offer to help. "Do you think you could get it and take it down? Don't want to ruffle any official feathers first thing in the morning, now do we?"

Clarrie was quick to comply, and saw which umpire's seat had a foreign object on it. He headed straight to court one, the tournament's centre court. As he approached the raised metal seat, fixed precariously to the high post, he was amused to see a garden gnome, seated ready to preside over the first match. But it appeared that he was a little late to retrieve Cyril as the players for the first game had already assembled at the post and were looking to the gnome for instructions.

Several onlookers laughed at the nonsense as both players made a joke of the situation, talking to it as if it really were the official umpire. Eventually the real umpire arrived, and the two players retreated to opposite ends of the court, ready to play. The umpire was looking at the score sheet, and didn't see what the others had been laughing at until he was ready to climb the post to be seated. Then he came face to face with the clay garden ornament. He looked startled for just a few moments, and those who'd been amused by it before broke into laughter again.

"Well, you could have let me know that I wasn't needed this morning," he said with a hint of humour. "I trust this isn't an indication of what you thought about yesterday's match." He reached out to take the usurper from the seat of authority.

"I'm sorry about that," Clarrie said shyly as he came forward to claim Cyril.

"Better take him home, son," the umpire said kindly. "Can't have him thinking he can run the show."

"Oh! He's not mine!" Clarrie said quickly.

But before ownership could be established, the game had begun, and so Clarrie quietly set Cyril up on one of the spectators' benches, as if to watch the match. He guessed that Peter or Carol Bamman would come along and claim him sooner or later.

Clarrie saw Claire Blieschke arrive, and she smiled and called out a cheery good morning to him. "Are you available to help us again today?" she asked. "You did such a good job yesterday, we would really appreciate it." Clarrie nodded happily. "There'll be a plate of food, or maybe two in it for you," she said with a smile.

Clarrie's spirits lifted another notch, and he moved across to help his tennis coach lift out plastic containers with salad ingredients, and a flat kind of suit-case that, he knew from experience, would have row upon row of the best tasting cream puffs you could ever imagine. He'd sampled one of them at yesterday's afternoon tea, and he decided that you'd have to go a long way to ever taste another quite like it.

He continued to make himself available to run whatever errands any of the ladies wanted, and watched with eager anticipation as each of the ladies brought in their various containers of cakes and sandwiches and sausage rolls. Being the deep thinker that he was, Clarrie was in awe of these ladies, who he assumed must have gone home from a full day at the tennis, to bake and prepare for the next day's luncheon and afternoon tea.

"There's only three locals left in the competition," Noel Ryan informed Clarrie in response to his enquiry. "Keith Bowman and Ross Miller in the men's and Lila Chalmers in the women's competition."

"Do you think one of our boys will beat Oliver Printen?" Clarrie could not conceal his anxiety over this issue.

"I hope so, Clarrie, but Mr Printen, for all his arrogance and pompous ways, is a good tennis player, if he's nothing else."

"I heard Mrs Greenbank say that he might become a Wimbledon Champion one day, and then that would be a feather in our cap to say that he'd once played at the Melrose Easter Tennis Tournament."

Noel laughed at the comment. "Well, it would at that, but I'm sort of hoping that one of our blokes will stop him in his tracks before he gets that far. Of course I'm not supposed to have a bias," he whispered conspiratorially, "so you won't tell anyone that I said that."

Clarrie gave a knowing nod and left the registration area, ready to help set the tables for Saturday's luncheon.

The day passed much like the Good Friday competition, except there had been no spectacular display from Joe Clucas, and Cyril was duly reunited with his grateful owner, who declared that from now on he would be safely locked away over the Easter weekend.

By the end of the day's play, Lila Chalmers had fallen victim to one of the Orroroo girl's superior play, and Keith Bowman, though he had put up a gallant effort and better performance than any seen so far, was still defeated by the obnoxious Oliver Printen. The only consolation for Clarrie was that Ross Miller remained undefeated, and that more than likely, he would eventually come face to face with this arrogant city challenger. Sunday's draw saw both of them facing other remaining challengers. If both Oliver and Ross made it through Sunday's play, they would very likely face each other in a final on Monday. This was something that Clarrie began to think would be really worth watching, but they had to get through Sunday first, and before Sunday, there were the Saturday night activities.

Easter Saturday night was always set aside for a dance. Sally had prattled on about the dance continuously for the last week. Clarrie didn't care much for dancing, since that usually meant close contact with girls. He didn't see the attraction, and for the life of him couldn't understand the boys that were always mooning over his rather vain and empty-headed sister. Still, he had decided that he would probably go. Most of the other kids his age would go, and they would find opportunity to slide on the wooden floor during the breaks in the dance. Clarrie was sorely tempted, but wondered if he would get away with such an activity, since his arm was in plaster. Still, he knew what could be expected by way of supper, and if nothing else, that was worth going for.

Beth Brown actually had Saturday evening off, but told her two children that she felt too tired to be bothered with dancing. She wondered aloud if Clarrie might not have had enough excitement for one weekend, but was met with such a convincing set of reasons why it would be good for him to go, that she agreed he might go along to the Saturday night Easter dance, just as long as he was home by ten o'clock.

Clarrie didn't bother with small details like time, just as long as he was given permission to join with all the other town folk.

Sally was furious that Beth had insisted she take Clarrie along with her, and that she be responsible for him for the whole evening. She complained about the burden of it all, and would have continued but then her mother began to reconsider the idea of either of them going at all, and Sally deemed it wiser to co-operate cheerfully or they would both be grounded for the night.

"Now, don't you go running off with those Arthur boys," Sally warned as they crossed the road in front of Bennett & Fisher Farm Supplies. "So help me, Clarrie, if you end up in any more mischief, I'll never take you with me again."

Clarrie nodded but wasn't really listening to his sister's threats, because he was more interested in the people who were coming out of the North Star Hotel, obviously ready to cross the road to the Melrose Institute.

"Howdy, Mr Clucas," Clarrie called across to Joe Clucas, who was heading out of the pub, now that it was closed, but instead of going across the road to the hall, he was heading in the other direction.

"G'day, young Clarrie," Joe replied cheerfully.

"Aren't you gonna come to the dance?" Clarrie asked, while Sally went on to the hall without him.

"Might come and have a look a bit later," Joe said non-committally.

"I liked your trick with the Suzuki," Clarrie said shyly before he turned to follow his sister.

"'Tweren't much. I reckon I could do better than that if I put my mind to it."

Clarrie laughed, sure that Joe must have been joking. Clarrie had a very cautious personality, and couldn't for the life of him think of anything more daring, or dangerous, than the stunt he'd seen yesterday.

"I'll see you a bit later then." Clarrie waved good-bye, and continued toward the Institute, mounting the large cement steps and going through the large wooden doors into the now crowded entrance hall. He passed the ladies' cloakroom on the right hand side and went straight to the ticket booth.

"Hello Clarrie!"

Clarrie peered through the glass to recognise Mr Don Bishop,

Jim's younger brother, seated in the ticket-seller's position. "Sally came through a few minutes ago. She paid for your ticket then, so you can go along inside."

"Thanks, Mr Bishop." Clarrie smiled as he turned away. He could see that the crowd was already spilling into the brightly lit hall, and he could hear that the band had begun to play some music. It was Jim Francis's band from Appila, which often played at the dances here and everywhere else. It certainly wasn't the Beatles or the Rolling Stones, but Clarrie knew he was not coming for the music. As he walked through the large brightly coloured doors, he noted many of the people already assembled. He saw his friend Georgie Greenbank with many others he knew from school. Rex Deekin's boys, Bruce McCallum's boys, the Clarke girls, Clair Prosser's boys, the Dickson girls, Laurie Bishop's youngest daughter and the Girdham kids. Clarrie hoped that Georgie and Phillip Deekin would soon come over to him as he was taking special care to avoid the girls. He was not going to become the butt of everyone's jokes, teased about wanting to dance with the girls. Perish the thought! Even if Mrs Yvonne Bishop, Don's wife, tried to coax him into dancing, he was already planning how he could escape.

Yvonne Bishop's goal was to encourage all the young people of Melrose to dance. She ran ballroom dancing classes, to which Clarrie had been occasionally. He had come to the decision to attend because of the dilemma he found himself in: his mother had given him the choice either to go along to the dance classes with Mrs Bishop, or be babysat by Mrs Greenbank. With the threat of Georgie's mother coming around to his home, while Georgie was himself at the dance classes, he decided to go. At least there would be other boys there, and if he could suffer through having to dance with the girls, he could kick around with the boys afterwards.

But just because he had managed to memorise the steps to the 'Military Two Step' and the 'Canadian Barn Dance' didn't mean he was about to put his skill on show now. He'd already copped a lot of stick from the other boys because he happened to pick up the steps and rhythm more quickly than anyone else. The whole situation was dangerous for an emerging reputation.

Clarrie wondered just how long it would be before someone would take the first step and try out the floor for sliding. Clair Prosser had been very obliging and had spread a thin layer of sawdust and grated candle-wax all over the floor. It came in a specially prepared mixture called 'floor speed', so-called for good reason, as far as Clarrie was concerned, and although it was awful having to explain to his mother just how his trousers had become so dirty at a dance, the sawdust stuff certainly added some speed to a good slide. Even with his arm in plaster, Clarrie was already sizing up just where would be the best place to start. Eventually, it seemed the boys were not going to break away from the girls so he joined in with the school crowd, and began to listen to the talk about the tennis.

"That Oliver Printen thinks he's really good," Phillip Deekin said in the tone of one who thought just the opposite.

"Yeah! I hope he doesn't turn up here tonight and think he's going to be horrible about our dance!" Georgie Greenbank stated firmly, as if the success of the entire night's entertainment rested on this fact.

"I saw your sister making google eyes at him earlier today," Phillip challenged Clarrie in an accusing tone of voice.

"Hey! Don't blame me!" Clarrie put his hands up in a gesture of defence. "I don't have any say in what Sally does."

"He turned his nose up at her anyway," Lynette Clarke said, apparently offended by the slight against one of their own. "I hope Rossy Miller beats him and beats him good in the finals."

"Of course he will!" Neville McCallum said with authority. "Nobody can beat Rossy Miller!"

"Keith Bowman beat him last year!" Lesley Bishop argued. "And that Printen bloke beat Keith today!"

There was a general silence as the group of young tennis fans considered this ominous fact.

"You're in good with the minister, Clarrie," Georgie said hopefully. "Maybe you can ask him to pray for Rossy to win!"

"Do you think we can ask God to intervene in a tennis match?" Merilyn Deekin asked shyly.

"I can't see why not!" Georgie answered.

But before the conversation could progress any further, the group of school children were silenced as they noticed the very subject of their disdain walk through the door. Oliver Printen was very smartly dressed, with his hair slicked back. He was wearing an ultra modern suit, the likes of which was never seen around this country town, and by the look on his face, it was clear to see his opinion of the place – It was obviously 'way beyond the black stump'.

"Tell your sister to steer clear of that bloke!" Georgie hissed under his breath to Clarrie as Oliver passed by.

"You tell her," Clarrie muttered back, quickly relinquishing the responsibility.

"Gentlemen, please take your partner for the Queen's waltz." Mr Clair Prosser had risen on the stage and made the announcement while the younger set were settling their ruffled feelings. Immediately, men all over the room rose and in a reasonably courtly fashion, considering it was 'beyond the black stump', invited ladies to join them on the dance floor. When Clarrie saw Yvonne Bishop heading in their general direction, he decided to make himself scarce. If he was nowhere near the girls, then there was less chance of being forced to dance with them. As he looked back over his shoulder, he chuckled to himself as he saw Georgie Greenbank being encouraged to dance with one of the girls. Some of the other boys had, like himself, beat a hasty retreat, but Georgie hadn't been quick enough. Clarrie was somewhat alarmed at the unbidden criticism that crossed his mind as he watched Georgie's clumsy, uncoordinated attempts to complete one of the simplest dances they had been taught. *Clumsy clot,* Clarrie thought to himself. *I could do it ten times better than that.* Then he pulled himself up in mid-thought and wondered what on earth had possessed him to think such a thing. *Thank goodness nobody can read my thoughts,* he said to himself.

"Reckon you could dance better than that?" Vera Fuller's question startled Clarrie. She had been following his line of vision and had accurately guessed what he was thinking.

Clarrie liked his piano teacher, and wasn't going to lie to her. "I know I could," he said confidently, "but don't tell the other boys!"

"Doesn't fit well with your image?" She laughed. "It's too late, Clarrie," she said. "They already know that you take piano lessons, and that you go to church. What's a little dancing on top of that?"

Clarrie could see her logic, but still wasn't persuaded to race off to the first hopeful wallflower and offer to partner her in a dance.

"Listen, Clarrie," Vera went on saying, "if you want to make yourself unavailable for dancing, I could always use a bit of a hand for a little while."

Clarrie looked at her, failing to conceal his interest.

"Yes!" she said, "I have to set out a whole lot of cups and saucers for cups of tea later. I thought it would be best to get it over and done with now, so that then I can enjoy some dancing with Mr Fuller. Do you mind giving me a hand?"

Clarrie nodded, happy to have an excuse to avoid the dancing. As he followed his piano teacher around the edge of the dancers toward the door at the right hand side of the large stage, he fought his desire to show some of those young people just how the Queen's Waltz ought to be done. When all was said and done, it was not the dancing that he objected to so much as having to dance with girls.

As Vera opened the door at the side of the stage, and Clarrie stood perched above the steep wooden steps that descended into the supper room, again he had to fight the strong urge to slide down the banisters. If it had been just himself and the other boys, there would have been no question, but as it was Mrs Fuller and other proper ladies present, he decided that he had better not try something that was so likely to get him into trouble.

Downstairs was lit brightly, and the normally dingy, cement- floored room was decorated nicely and had many cloth-covered trestles, laden with various delectable supper dishes. Everything looked very attractive, set out nicely on the donors' best china cake dishes and sandwich plates. Vera directed Clarrie to the corner where she was to set out the teacups and saucers.

"You know, when I was a girl, about your age," Vera began, and by her tone, Clarrie knew there was a story coming, "the whole town was dance crazy. This Old Style dancing was at its peak, and we used to have an old style dance every day of the week somewhere about, at Wirrabarra, Wilmington, Booleroo or here. Each night the band would follow through."

"Did you go to all those dances, one after the other?" Clarrie asked, somewhat amazed at the idea.

"No!" she laughed. "I was only young then."

"Did you dance with the boys?"

"Oh, yes!" she said definitely. "But the boys then were a bit like you lads. They were always disappearing just when we wanted someone to dance with."

Clarrie didn't make any comment for fear of incriminating himself.

"You'll grow out of it soon enough, I daresay," Vera added with an amused smile.

"Grow out of what?" Clarrie asked.

"Aversion to girls! I'll give you three or four years and I'd guess you'll take every opportunity you can get to dance with a girl."

"Not me!" Clarrie boasted. "I'm not like my sister, boy crazy all the time!"

"You will be, girl crazy at least, and then you'll find some dark romantic spot to go and be alone and whisper sweet nothings in her ear."

Clarrie was mortified. He couldn't think of anything worse.

"Where do the young people go now to spoon?" Vera asked.

"To what?"

"You know, kiss and cuddle!"

"I don't know," he said, perhaps a little untruthfully, as he knew that Sally often met boys, and they would go somewhere in their car. He guessed it was probably up above the oval at the showgrounds, or up on tank hill; at least that is what some of the kids at school had told him. He hadn't actually been there himself, *thank goodness,* he thought.

"When we went to see the young fellows, we always went to one of the swinging bridges."

"Swinging bridges?" Clarrie hadn't heard of these before.

"I guess there aren't any here now that they've all been washed away. There used to be four swinging bridges across the Mount creek, so that people could cross from one side to the other when the creek was down. There was one just down behind the tennis shed, one up a bit further near the road to the rubbish dump. That was where old Mrs Ey used to live," she added. "Then there was another one across the creek at the showgrounds, and down further at Pride's place. Ey's bridge was the most popular. You could get three or four couples on the bridge sometimes, and of course a swinging bridge doesn't stop still, does it. We'd meet the boys there, and cuddle and swing on the bridge."

"Did you get into trouble?" Clarrie asked, intrigued.

"Only if we didn't get home in time. My father expected us home by ten past nine of a Sunday night, and church didn't let out till eight o'clock, so we had to really be quick to get from the Methodist church down to Ey's to spend a bit of time with our boy."

"I didn't think you'd have been allowed in the old days," Clarrie said, thinking of all the lectures he'd heard that started with, 'when I was your age…'.

"I didn't say we were allowed to meet the boys at the bridge. But we didn't tell our parents, did we. I remember one of my friends; her father was very strict, and she was never allowed to go about with any boys. She asked me if she could tell her mother that she was coming over to see me, when all the time she intended to go off to meet some boy at the bridge."

"And did you let her…tell her mother she was coming to see you, I mean?" Clarrie asked, somewhat puzzled at this rather reckless behaviour from such a dignified, Christian woman.

"I always obeyed my father, if that's what you're getting at, young man, and I practised the piano plenty too."

Clarrie laughed. He could see Mrs Fuller's attempt to change the subject.

"You used to play piano for the dances?" Clarrie said, remembering the stories she'd told him before.

"Oh, yes! My father was very proud of the fact too. At first I just played while the band went to supper. You know that with this small supper room, folks came to eat in shifts, and those that were left in the hall kept on dancing, so I got my debut as a musician taking those shifts. Later on, I formed a band of my own, and we went about playing for dances and balls."

"Do you still play in a band?"

"No! I'm too busy teaching all of you youngsters how to play, and getting up concerts for all of you to perform."

Clarrie wisely decided it was time to change the subject. He had no ambition to perform his choked and stunted version of "Larkspur" to anybody. His dog, Scamp, had already offered a negative opinion on that count.

"I remember when the training farm was going, out at Gumville, they eventually decided that they'd have to shut the dances down for a while." Mrs Fuller went on reminiscing as she placed the last few cups on the remaining saucers.

"Why?" Clarrie asked, alert to a story that involved those elusive soldiers.

"They had a big horse drawn vehicle that they all used to get aboard and come up to the town, especially on a Saturday night. They would play merry, the young men all drinking and carousing around the town. Everybody shut their doors on Saturday nights because the Training Farm would be up. And when they held a dance the organisers said they would never do it again because the training farm boys played up and carried on and destroyed things. They went really silly and Melrose said there would be no more dances on Saturday night while the training farm is here. Yes, I can remember them coming up in that great big long wagon thing, and a lot of them rode their horses up. They had horses out at the training farm of course, and they would go past peoples' places swearing and cursing and cracking their whips. I tell you what, it was a real - I don't know what to say - but they did the town over, that's what they used to say."

"Did you used to know any of the soldiers?" Clarrie had to ask, just in case there was a link he'd missed before.

"Oh no!" Vera said. "I was only eleven years old when they closed the training farm down in 1921. I heard all of this from my mother and father, of course. They kept a close eye on us, especially of a Saturday night."

Vera stood back with a critical eye once the last cup and saucer had been arranged. "Thank you for your help, Clarrie. Now I don't want to keep you from the young ladies upstairs. You'll be wanting to put some of that fancy footwork on show, no doubt."

"Not if I can help it," Clarrie said with a grin. He knew that she was teasing him. "Thanks for the story," he said as he began to mount the stairs that led back into the main hall.

As he walked back into the crowded dance hall, Clarrie was just in time to see some of his school friends executing a particularly good slide along the side of the hall on the other side of the room. He was all admiration until he saw where Georgie Greenbank ended up. If it hadn't been for some quick thinking and the steadying hand of one of the gentlemen, one of the out-of-town ladies would have gone down like a pin in a bowling lane, and Clarrie could just imagine the flurry of fox-fur and tulle petticoats, with high heels kicking in the air. He found it impossible to restrain the laughter that bubbled up. He only wished he had been on the other side of the room with the boys, where he could have done some of the extensive ribbing that they were giving to Georgie. But Clarrie's tune soon changed and the wistful desire turned quickly to relief for a narrow escape when Clair Prosser, the MC, hurried to the group of boys and soundly told them off.

He watched with some interest as the group stood, looking

very sheepish, but as soon as Mr Prosser had turned his back, they had returned to normal, adopting the look of the cool and in charge, and Clarrie accurately guessed that none of them were deeply affected by the reprimand. They would live to slide another day, and most likely later that evening. But for the moment, he could see that they were all heading for the door, and since Mr Prosser was about to announce another dance, he guessed that they were doing the only sensible thing – making themselves scarce. Clarrie decided to follow them.

"Hey, let's go over to Young's Corner for a Coke," Georgie, the newborn hero, suggested confidently.

"Why don't we go a bit further down the road and see who's down there?" This suggestion came from one of the boys in the shadows. Clarrie couldn't quite see who, but he knew what he meant. Everybody knew, even the primary school kids, that with the pub closed by six o'clock, and the law stating that no alcohol is to be consumed within 200 yards of the hall, that at precisely 201 yards away, there would be a gathering of folk with their bottles of beer, having a drink, a yarn and probably a smoke. Clarrie elected to support the one voice that vetoed the idea of joining the dance-hall renegades as he was fairly certain that it would be interpreted, by his mother at least, as getting into mischief. Young's Corner was a safer option, and far easier to explain.

The group of seven boys turned and went all together across the road to Young's Corner. Georgie led the pack and pushed the glass door open, the bell above the doorway starting its continuous ring as the seven lads filed in. Not all of them had money, and those that did were being conservative, since they all knew that they could score supper a bit later on. Two or three of them ordered a Coca Cola, and they watched as Gilbert Young flipped the bottle tops off the small glass bottles with his bottle opener.

"Maybe I should buy a Golden North Giant Twin as well," Georgie suggested, eyeing the glass top of the freezer that displayed the packaged ice-creams and frozen flavoured milk snips.

"There's a lot of good food ready for supper at the dance,"

Clarrie volunteered. "I saw it all when I was helping Mrs Fuller."

"You're always helping somebody, Clarrie Brown," Georgie sneered.

"Yeah! And he always seems to come away with a plate of free food!" Phillip added. He'd seen Clarrie's enterprise, and the rewards, and had considered whether it might not have been worth it in the end.

"Come on. Over here!" One of the other boys was tired of the small talk and decided to take charge, leading the group to the small alcove that ran out from the side of Young's, furnished with several tables and chairs. Each table was covered with either red or yellow laminex, and the stainless steel framed chairs were also brightly coloured. The boys all squashed around one table and began to talk loudly. There were only three cokes, but someone had grabbed a handful of paper straws so that they could share. They kept on in this manner until their attention was arrested by the entrance of Oliver Printen.

"Blimey!" Georgie Greenbank exclaimed. "It's Mr Fancy Pants himself."

The others immediately stopped their chatter and turned their attention to the inner shop. Only Georgie, who was seated in such a way that he could see around the dividing wall and into the shop, could see Oliver Printen at the counter of Young's lighting a cigarette.

"Useless sort of place, this, don't you think?" The tall young city visitor didn't really expect an answer and probably wouldn't have got one in any case, as Mr Young coughed with the cigarette smoke blown in his face. "Don't suppose there's any hope of getting a decent drink here, is there?" Oliver went on nonchalantly.

Mr Young pointed at the blackboard that sat high up on the wall behind the counter. "Got all the usual Trend soft drinks, and Coca Cola, and then we've got the three milkshake flavours. If you want anything stronger, you should've stocked up like everybody else, before the pub shut!"

"This place is full of wowsers!" Oliver sneered

"The law's the same here as anywhere else in the state," Mr Young said firmly, "and we don't usually spend time making those sorts of distinctions. Some of the people drink and some don't! Do you want a milkshake, sir?"

Oliver was in a sour mood, and had been unable to find anybody who would sympathise with his rather uncomplimentary summary of the town. He didn't bother to answer Mr Young, but walked out of the corner store, mumbling something about needing an early night for his game tomorrow.

"Gee, Mr Young," Georgie said openly, once the visitor had gone, "That Oliver Printen is a stuck up cuss."

"He's not the most polite gentleman I've ever met," the older shopkeeper agreed sternly, "But I don't think your mother would approve of you using that sort of language about a stranger in our town."

"Why not?" Georgie argued boldly.

"Because she is a Christian woman, and she would hope that you extend the proper amount of hospitality and courtesy towards strangers."

"He doesn't deserve our courtesy," Georgie was defiant. "What he needs is a good kick up the pants!"

The others laughed at this comment. "Rossy Miller will show him a thing or two when they finally get to play."

"You'd better mind your tongue, boys. You never know who might be listening."

Mr Young's solemn admonition made little impression on the group of school boys, and they continued to crow about how Oliver Printen was going to fall in the tennis finals on Monday.

Beth Brown had gone to great trouble to acquire some chocolate Easter Eggs, the sort covered in the brightly coloured foil. Her two children had grown past the childish stage of Easter Egg hunts and Easter Bunny, but Clarrie was young enough to fully appreciate the gift of chocolate. He'd eaten half of his stash before either his mother or sister had risen from bed.

"Off to the tennis again today?" Beth yawned.

"To church first," Clarrie said easily. "It's Resurrection Sunday, Mum. Are you gonna come with me?"

Beth considered the question seriously. She'd brushed her children off so much lately, and though it was because she was always so worn out, she felt guilty for continually saying no. "I reckon I'll come this one time," she said, trying to sound eager, despite the lack of mental and physical energy.

Clarrie felt ten foot high when he walked into church with his mother. He lamented the fact that Sally refused to come with them, but after he'd resigned himself to that, he was tickled pink to actually sit down with his own family in church. Mr Bishop gave him a friendly wink and smile, and Clarrie beamed in return. Proudly and with all the finesse of a regular worshipper, Clarrie guided his mother through the regular customs of standing just when the organ introduction reached a full crescendo, and sitting at the appropriate moment at the end of a hymn. He greeted Reg Arthur at the door, handing the hymnbook back with all ceremony, and was on top of the world showing the rest of the congregation that he wasn't an orphan after all. The Reverend Anderson had spoken very kindly to Beth after the service, and invited her to join them on a regular basis.

"I'm very busy Reverend," Beth had answered politely, "but I know Clarrie loves church. When I can, I'll try and come with him."

Clarrie was thrilled with this response. If there was one thing he longed for it was that sense of family, the kind he saw in the Bishop family and Curyers and Arthurs. He was quite aware that his father was gone and nothing could bring him back, but still, his mother and sister were important, and in his experience nothing seemed to knit a family closer together than going to church all together.

Beth dropped her son down to the tennis after the service. "I enjoyed Reverend Anderson's talk," she admitted to her son. "It's kind of comforting somehow, isn't it?"

Clarrie nodded happily.

"Go on with you then," Beth smiled warmly. "Have a good time, and be sure to be home in time for tea."

Clarrie got out of the family car, and made his way to greet those he knew already preparing food and setting out tables, and doing all the official tennis records.

Sunday turned out just as well as Clarrie had hoped, and when he talked with Phillip and Georgie, they agreed.

Monday was set to be a showdown as, just as they'd hoped, Rossy Miller was to face the self confident Oliver Printen in the men's finals. The talk fairly buzzed around the courtside, and some who would ordinarily have had enough of tennis for one weekend made definite plans to return on the morrow to see the titans clash.

Clarrie sat with his friends on the grassed slope above Court One, under the shade of the massive river red gum. All of them, including Georgie, Phillip, Lyall and Geoff, had come to see this much talked about final.

The mood around the courtside spectators was quite tense. Oliver Printen had pranced out onto the centre court with all the arrogance of a Siamese cat, and had made the first set look as if he was bored and almost insulted to have to play such a poor opponent. Rossy Miller was flustered, and all those who knew him well could see that he was not playing his normal game.

"I don't know what's the matter with him," Mrs Greenbank said so loudly that even the boys seated some ten yards from her could hear. "Goes to show that this Adelaide fellow has some extra class that our country boys just don't have!" she added, around a mouthful of fruitcake.

Nobody around had the courage to say anything in Rossy's defence, as he had indeed been playing like someone from a much lower grade.

"He's just scared, that's all," Kevin said knowingly. "I heard my dad say that this intimation can really put you off your game!"

"Intimidation," Lyall corrected him casually. "We need to start supporting him," he added. "Come on you boys. Let's make some noise and encourage him."

The score was six-love in the first set, and Oliver had already broken serve in the second when the boys' voices rose above the glum atmosphere that had settled on the crowd.

"Come on, Rossy!" Georgie called.

"You're our champ!" Clarrie added. "We know you can do it!"

And they kept on calling until the umpire, seated on the high-posted wrought-iron seat called out just like Wimbledon, "Quiet please!"

But the encouragement worked. In the very next point, Rossy caught Oliver too wide on the right hand side of the court, and drove home a perfect line drive on the left hand side.

The boys were ecstatic, and the rest of the crowd hesitantly increased their enthusiasm.

"Give it to him, Rossy!" Georgie called.

It seemed that this extra good shot was just the tonic needed to help Rossy rise above his own despondency, and from then on the game lifted, with Rossy fighting back with some really excellent shots. The optimism of the crowd lifted, and Oliver Printen's outward confidence appeared to be shaken.

The second set was a mammoth fight, going backwards and forwards between advantage and deuce, but eventually a tiebreaker was required, where Rossy broke through with a set point to level the scores to two sets all. Clarrie and his friends were on their feet cheering and whistling madly. Even Mrs Greenbank showed that she was impressed. "Well, that's better, at least!" she said firmly. "I wonder if he's got what it takes to win this tournament!"

Georgie rolled his eyes at his mother's pessimism, and joined the others in shouting out more positive comments.

The third set started out as the contest to settle the whole weekend of tennis, and now that it was two sets all, the crowd were back into the spirit of competition, and collectively drew in their breath in anticipation.

In the first game, Rossy went down to a quality service match. Oliver put power and accuracy into his serves and Rossy struggled to return them at all.

"We'd better keep encouraging him," Clarrie said, sensing the immediate downturn in the fickle crowd's expectations. With this the group took it upon themselves to lead the others in supporting the local player. But despite the best efforts of spectator involvement, Rossy had taken a backward step, and suddenly served two double faults. Clarrie waited for Mrs Greenbank's expected doom and gloom prophecy, and it came right on cue.

"Well, you couldn't expect him to keep up such a huge effort for three sets," she went on as if she was the final word of authority on the game.

"Come on Rossy," her son yelled over his mother. "You're nearly there!"

Play continued back and forth and the crowd were all set for disappointment with the scores at four-one in the third set.

"It's no use," Phillip said. "He'll never get up from here."

"It's not over till the fat lady sings," Georgie quipped, casting a glance in his mother's direction, "and at this moment, she's still sitting quietly. Come on Rossy. We're still with you!" he yelled.

Clarrie wanted to join Georgie in his persistent optimism, but he was not at all happy with the turn of events. Oliver Printen looked sharp and was playing very well. Rossy looked dispirited as if he'd already lost. Clarrie wished that he could call a time-out, and go down and have a word with Rossy. He felt sure that if he'd only heard the Reverend Anderson's sermon on hoping and believing, even when it looked as if all was lost, that Rossy would be able to summon the will and energy to win the match. But Clarrie knew there was no such opportunity. They didn't have runners onto the tennis court to relay messages from the coach, like they did in the football matches, *and more's the pity,* Clarrie thought. All they could do now was to sit it out as spectators and keep cheering their favourite player.

"Can't give up on him just because we don't like the feeling of disappointment," Lyall said sagely. "We'd better stick with him till the end."

And so the small band of boys adopted this philosophy and continued to make a lot of noise, which almost seemed out of place amongst the rest of the subdued crowd.

The set continued to deteriorate, from the locals' point of view, until it was five-one, and the score thirty-love, with Oliver serving. He stepped up to the service line, quite confident that he was just two points away from tournament champion, and served a ball that fairly shot down the middle of the court, very close to the centre line. Rossy scrambled after it, and though he managed to connect, the ball ricocheted off his racquet and straight up in the air.

"Fault!"

The linesman's call rang around the court and the crowd waited in anticipation of the second serve, but in vain.

"Fault?" Oliver screamed at the linesman. "Open your eyes. That was clean and inside."

The middle-aged official, a man from Port Augusta, shrank visibly, but still maintained the call. Oliver was furious and turned on the match umpire with fiery purpose.

"You'll overrule that call, of course!" he demanded, purple-faced and angry.

"The call stands," the umpire replied.

"What! Are you blind as well as stupid?" Oliver didn't bother to restrain his expression. "It was clearly in!"

"This is your first warning." The umpire said, his face dead-pan.

"First warning! For what? Questioning a wrong decision? You've got to be joking!"

"Your opponent will be awarded the point, if you continue."

"Where on earth did they dig this relic up from?" Oliver addressed the crowd derisively. "Might have expected a no account place like this would get an umpire without a brain!"

"Thirty-fifteen". The umpire said calmly but firmly.

Printen exploded and his language deteriorated even further.

"Thirty-all," the umpire said in calculated retaliation.

Just as Oliver was set to deliver a new mouthful of abuse, Rossy stepped up and spoke firmly. "If you don't mind, I'd prefer to win the game on my own, without being awarded penalty points."

"On your own!" Oliver jeered. "Ha! That's not likely, the way you're playing!"

"All the same," Rossy insisted. "Can we get back to the game?" The umpire nodded his agreement and the two players returned each to his own end of the court, but Rossy's mood had changed, and so had Oliver's. The umpire's ruling stood, and the score remained at thirty-all.

If anyone had said that those two points had won Rossy the game, they would have been wrong, as Rossy had to fight for every point he won from that moment on. Oliver Printen's outburst had been enough to resurrect Rossy from the doldrums, and he now played with a vitally different attitude, the way locals were used to seeing him. In the end, it came to another tiebreaker, and by this time the crowd were awake and involved, till the atmosphere reached fever pitch.

Rossy won, but only on the last point. He couldn't have done it any harder. But that was enough for Clarrie and the other boys. They were on their feet hooting and whistling and jumping up and down.

Extremely upset with the outcome, and unwilling to be acknowledged as runner-up, Oliver Printen immediately left the court, refusing to shake his opponent's hand, not even so much as glancing in the umpire's direction.
"Well, he is a sore loser, I must say," Mrs Greenbank sniffed, drawing attention to his hasty departure.

But the attention and applause was for the tournament champion, the local boy, Rossy Miller.

When Rossy accepted the silver tray trophy, he gave a short speech, and said in finishing, "I'd like to pay special tribute to my band of loyal supporters, who believed in me more than I believed in myself." He lifted up the silver tray in a gesture of triumph, and looked over toward the boys and gave them a smile and a knowing wink.

Clarrie was stoked.

Chapter Six

Despite the stifling heat, Clarrie had taken a couple of minutes to put on the yellow overalls, now smudged with black soot, and the acquired leather boots. The rate the fire was coming, he didn't know if he would be called upon to help defend the town. He rushed down to the fire shed, all the time keeping the oncoming fire in his sights. It was travelling at a fair rate, but Clarrie could not run away from it, despite common sense. He saw cars with women, children and older people leaving the town, and guessed they must be feeling a hundred times what he was feeling. Were they going to be able to save the old town?

He was no longer a nuisance reporter, but one of the honorary locals, and he came boldly into the shed, ready to be given a job. There were only a few women working with the communication, sending and receiving messages. Clarrie had watched as several people had excused themselves to get their children out of town. This left a skeleton crew to work in the shed.

"I'll give you a hand," Clarrie offered. They nodded their thanks, and gave him a pencil and paper to write down anything that was said on radio. Clarrie felt this was within the realm of his own experience.

"You know that fire's headed this way," he commented. They all knew but it was as if they had steeled themselves against panic, refusing to leave their responsibilities while the radios remained operational. There were people scattered all through the foothills and national park, who were dependent upon the vital link of communication that was provided from this very centre.

Still the roar of the oncoming blaze was like a mighty rushing wind. If they hadn't known it was a fire, they might have imagined a tornado was about to blow the roof off the shed. Through the small window that faced the mountain, in the back of the shed, all the operators could see it burning down the mount towards them. Clarrie sat, his whole body tense, but refused to move or run while these courageous women stuck to their posts.

Then he heard Jenny mumble: "How long do you think we should sit here before we should run?"

It was then that Clarrie knew they were fully aware of the dragon at the door. They were fulfilling their duty, not drawing back with fear. But they felt the fear, even as Clarrie felt it. He didn't have an answer to the question. The radio communication continued to go back and forth, various bits of crucial information being passed from one man to another. It took all the will power in the world to attend to the job and not sit and stare into the face of the oncoming monster.

But at one point even that discipline disintegrated. The fire was so close, at a level that from their viewpoint looked to be at the top of the river red gums, lining the creek. All the workers stopped and watched, almost as if they were expecting the creek trees to burst into flames, and then they would run. But it didn't happen. The wall of fire seemed to hit something, and then rolled like a wave, back onto itself. And then it was gone. Just like that. They sat in stunned silence.

"That looked like the hand of God!" Jenny said.

"I think it was," Irene answered.

Clarrie hadn't thought about God in a long time, but for the second time in twenty-four hours, he was beginning to consider him again.

The trouble with the Easter long-weekend is that it must come to an end, and while for four days kids had been having a wonderful time of celebrating, eating chocolate and getting involved in the town's sporting festivals, on Tuesday, school became a cold, hard reality.

Miss Jolly, unlike her name suggested, was anything but jolly. Although she was a devout woman, and had attended to the necessary religious observances, she was certainly a strict, by-the-book disciplinarian. Easter was over and as far as she was concerned there was no place left for any celebratory residue. It was back to work, and Clarrie found himself seated at the wooden desk, on the fold-down plank-like bench that was attached, taking dictation, answering comprehension questions, writing out spelling words and all the usual boring school activities. He tried to maintain some of the holiday spirit, but Miss Jolly's manner soon put a stop to that.

"It's only a week and a half till ANZAC Day," Georgie whispered to Clarrie as they cut the corners from the tetrapak milk cartons. Clarrie and Georgie were milk-monitors for the day, and they were excused from reciting tables five minutes early so that they could retrieve the plastic crate of Golden North milk cartons from the school fridge and snip the triangular corners off with their small, steel school-scissors. Then they hurriedly inserted a paper straw in each one, ready for the rest of the school children to take one for morning recess.

"I hate milk!" Georgie said. "Why do we have to drink milk every recess? Why not Fanta or Coke?"

"I don't know!" Clarrie shrugged. He didn't mind milk that much, although he had to admit it was nicer drinking it from a glass and dunking one of Auntie Ella's ginger biscuits into it. Still, the milk-drinking chore was an obligation, and all the children stood around the galvanized-iron rubbish bin, slurping their way through their tetrapak of milk. Most threw the carton into the bin with a bit of milk left in the bottom. Fortunately, Miss Jolly had no way of determining whose pak was whose, so it was a crime that mostly went unpunished.

As soon as the milk was consumed, the children broke off to get the most out of the remaining recess time. Some went down behind the art shed to the expanse of lawn and began to kick a soccer ball around. The girls mostly went to the sport's shed, set high up on blocks so they had to take a large step up, and chose their skipping ropes. Clarrie always avoided the girls and their skipping games. They were always jumping through the alphabet, trying to work out who they might be going to marry, and when. He didn't want to be anywhere near and give them any ideas.

Recess was only twenty minutes, and with the milk quickly out of the way the boys didn't want to waste a second. The game of 'brandy' had recently been banned by the headmistress. The boys felt it was an over reaction on her part, and still couldn't see the harm in pitching tennis balls at other kids while they tried to avoid being hit.

"It was probably one of those sissy girls telling tales," Georgie grumbled. Still, they had to reconcile themselves to the loss of the sport quickly, as time was ticking away.

The next suggestion was 'Red Rover'. This was a game that involved as many children as possible, and as it was quite popular, the word quickly spread and soccer and skipping were abandoned. Red Rover was a glorified game of 'catch' played within a marked area, in this case the netball court. The runners had to run straight across. They could not go around, and they could not refuse to run if the colour they were wearing was called out. This gave the 'catchers' a good opportunity to tag those who ran through their territory. Clarrie was easily caught and automatically became one of the catchers. He had to admire Georgie's speed and agility, as by the end of recess, he still remained uncaught.

Soon enough, Miss Jolly was standing by the flagpole, her silver whistle in her mouth and blowing sharply. Nobody delayed in responding. They knew what direct acts of defiance meant. Miss Jolly might have looked like a silver-haired old lady, but she could swing a cane, and her aim was true.

After recess, Miss Jolly announced that they would be making an excursion to the monument the next day.

"See, I told you!" Georgie whispered to Clarrie

"Told me what?" Clarrie whispered back, trying to remain as inanimate as possible.

"ANZAC Day is coming up. This trip up to the monument will be because of ANZAC Day."

Clarrie joined with the other kids in feeling that this was preferable to the everyday drudgery of classroom work. He'd climbed the foothill up to the town monument before, of course. Who hadn't? And though he expected that this trip would probably be somewhat more sober, with Miss Jolly in attendance, at least it would be a change from the norm.

"How come the monument is way up on that hill?" Clarrie asked Auntie Ella after school, this time dunking the ginger biscuit into the glass of milk she'd given him.

"Oh! There was some kafuffle after the first World War, when the town talked about having a monument for the boys that went," she said off-handedly. "A lot of towns have monuments to the World War One veterans, you know. You've seen the ones at Wirrabarra and Wilmington?"

"Yeah! They've got a great statue of a soldier, with a gun and everything," Clarrie said wistfully. "Ours looks more like a rocket!"

"And these other towns have their statues in a sensible spot, right outside the town institute," Auntie Ella said.

"Why is ours up on the hill? It's a long way for you old people to walk!"

Clarrie meant no offence, and Auntie Ella took none, although she did add with a smile, "I'm not that old."

Clarrie didn't believe her, despite the fact that she had been the one to climb to the monument with him the first time he had ever gone. It was a steep and rough climbing trail, with thick bush on either side. The first time Clarrie had gone he'd felt sure he would get lost, and was quite thankful that Auntie Ella had gone with him. The track had been strewn with large rocks and tree trunks, and was certainly not easily negotiated. Perhaps, despite Auntie Ella's silver hair and glasses, she was younger than she looked, but then Clarrie knew she'd been born at the turn of the century. She'd told him she was always as old as the year.

She went on to tell Clarrie some yarn about how the town

decided where to put their memorial to the men that had fallen in the Great War. Of course it took a question or two for Clarrie to understand that by fallen, she didn't mean 'come a cropper,' as he had during the recess game of Red Rover, with the resulting skinned elbows and knees. He was much more sober when he understood that these 'old' men had actually died during the war, as had men from all over the country, and that most towns had some sort of monument in their honour.

"I think in the end, it came down to money," Auntie Ella said, beginning to warm to the idea of telling another story. "There were some who wanted it down the street in front of the institute, and others who liked the idea of having it set up on the hill like it is."

"Everyone can see it up on the hill," Clarrie commented.

"From far away," Auntie Ella agreed, "but only the young and fit can make the climb to read the names."

"Miss Jolly's going to climb up there with us tomorrow," Clarrie announced.

"Is she?" Auntie Ella seemed surprised. "Well, I hope you find it interesting. A lot of folk felt for the families of those killed, having it up on the hill where they couldn't reach it."

"So, how come it ended up there?"

"The one who was putting the most money in wanted it there, and that put an end to it!"

Clarrie felt quite knowledgeable by the time he lined up with the rest of the children the next day. All the children from grades four through to seven were set to go, and several of them were surprised when Miss Jolly stood aside and welcomed Mr Frank Arthur.

"As you know," she announced, "Mr Arthur served in the armed forces during World War Two, some twenty years or so ago now."

Clarrie hadn't known this interesting fact, and doubted that any others of his class would have been aware of it either.

With their special guide the group of children set out by taking the route through the school ground, down between the art and sport's shed, down past the outside galvanised-iron toilet sheds, through the small gate at the end of the lawn and down towards the creek. From here they walked up the other side and along the creek bank toward the caravan park, until they came to the beginning of the upward walking trail. The children chattered happily, and with the absence of Miss Jolly there was nothing to disturb this holiday-like atmosphere as they took the path upward to the monument.

"It doesn't look like a rocket when you're up close," remarked one of the younger grade four students.

"It's called an obelisk," Mr Arthur said of the tall, square, tapering column, capped with a pyramid. As the children moved over to the base of the memorial, some of the older ones began to read the names on the plaque.

In Memory of the Fallen – The Great War 1914-1918

"What was so great about the war?" one of the younger children asked.

"They said it was the war to end all wars," Mr Arthur said in a sombre tone. "The conflict that involved armies from nations all over the world, including Australia."

"Did you fight in that war?" another child asked.

Mr Arthur gave a little smile. "No," he said. "I wasn't even born then. I was with the Australian Airforce that served during the Second World War."

"The Great War is what we call the First World War, isn't it?" Clarrie asked.

Mr Arthur nodded.

"When will we have World War Three?" one of the younger girls asked, her eyes wide with the horror of such a thought.

"I heard my mum say that we'll be sending soldiers off to this war in Vietnam," Georgie said confidently. "Do you reckon that will be World War Three?"

"I don't reckon," Mr Arthur said firmly, "but if you're praying people, you should pray for our boys that will be sent."

"Did you know these soldiers?" Clarrie asked, as he continued to read from the honour list.

"Well, they all died during the First World War, and, as I said, I wasn't even born then. But some of the families still live here in this district.

"E.F. Girdham," Georgie read from the list. "I wonder if that's a relative of Kev Girdham's?" he asked. Nobody seemed to have an answer to this rhetorical question.

"Ernest Fred Girdham," Mr Arthur read from the paper list in front of him, "was a private in the 27th Battalion Australian Infantry. He was killed in action in France, and buried there. He was only nineteen when he died."

"Nineteen!" Clarrie gasped in horror.

"Didn't they bring him back home to be buried?" Georgie asked, troubled.

Mr Arthur shook his head sadly.

"None of the boys killed overseas could be brought back home. It would have taken too long to transport them."

"But he was only nineteen," Clarrie said again, deeply shocked. "That's only the same age as your son, Geoff."

Mr Arthur nodded again.

"I always thought these names were of old men, like the ones who come for the ANZAC Day services." Clarrie went on.

"You know the piece they always say at the dawn services, 'they will not grow old, like we who are left grow old'. All the old diggers were only young when they went off to war."

"That's horrible!" Clarrie cried.

"War is a nasty business," Mr Arthur said. "There's very little fun in it when you consider the price these young men paid, and other young fellows I know during the Second World War, who were killed."

"What was the Slee fellow's name?" Georgie asked, "and was he related to the Slees that are still here in Melrose?"

"His name was Francis Charles Henry Slee, and he also died at the age of nineteen, in France."

Clarrie was too troubled to comment.

"Another name you would be familiar with, Willington, Spencer

William, also died in France. It doesn't say how old he was."

"He's probably a relative of Laurie Willington, who works for the council," one of the older children said.

"The Willingtons have been a Melrose family since the first settlement, I understand," Mr Arthur said.

"And what about C.B. Jacka?" Clarrie asked. "There aren't any Jackas here now, but maybe his family owned the Jacka's Brewery."

As if the mention of the famous Melrose landmark prompted them, all the children looked back at the very clear view of the township below, and the tall, five-storied building that kids often referred to as Melrose's own skyscraper. In the past, it had operated as a flourmill and as a brewery for many years, and though it now stood idle and empty, except for Mr Geoff Slee's storage needs, it was still known as Jacka's Brewery.

"Clement Belmore Jacka," Mr Arthur read, "served in Egypt as a trooper with the third Australian Light Horse. He was twenty-nine when he died.; It was only one month before Armistice that he died, 16/10/1918."

"What's Armistice?" one of the younger children asked.

"On November 11th at eleven o'clock, 1918, a treaty was signed that ended the First World War."

All the children looked suitably solemn at this information.

Then Mr Arthur briefly talked about the other men whose names were preserved on the memorial. E.B. Andrews; T.A. Jones; A.W. Davis; J.A McGregor; W.B. Webb. Following this, he retold the story of the infamous Gallipoli landing and following tragedy, and what the significance of April 25th was now to the Australian and New Zealand Army Corps.

The excursion to the monument had been more than just an excuse to get out of the normal schoolroom routine for a couple of hours. The experience, particularly Mr Arthur's careful sharing about the wars, and about the young men who had died there, moved Clarrie deeply. While the other kids quickly forgot, Clarrie couldn't help but feel afraid for his good friends, Lyall and Geoff Arthur, especially Geoff, who had already been selected for National Service. Jim Bishop had told Clarrie about his time in National Service, when he and Malcolm McCallum had spent the allotted time at the barracks at Woodside in the Adelaide Hills, being trained in the disciplines of war and national security. But from Jim's tales, Clarrie had the idea that it had been more of a lark than anything else. The only serious moment seemed to be when Jim had been chosen to stand in the honour guard for Queen Elizabeth II when she had visited Adelaide in 1954. Clarrie had been impressed until Mrs Bishop had told him it was not due to any special gift or talent, rather that all the men of the honour guard had to stand at five foot ten inches to be of uniform height. Jim was five foot ten and a half inches.

But the requirement to do National Service now, with a conflict brewing in Vietnam, meant that there was a strong likelihood that the current Australian servicemen would have to go. Clarrie knew all of this, having gathered bits and pieces of the puzzle from his conversations with Vera Fuller, Auntie Ella, and Frank Arthur, and, most recently, when he'd heard Mrs Greenbank's loud opinion:

"I don't know what business it is of those Yanks, going off to make trouble in such an insignificant country as Vietnam. And now, bless my soul, if our own Prime Minister isn't talking about committing Australian troops. And what for, I ask you? What business is it of ours? Those little Vietcong are no threat to our shores."

Clarrie had become very alert to talk of the Vietnam situation. His intense interest in soldiers had been part of it, but probably even more the fact that Lyall and Geoff were both very vulnerable.

As ANZAC Day approached, there was talk about the town again, about the position of the monument. Other towns had their dawn services assembled around their soldier statue monument, 'sensibly located', as Auntie Ella put it, just outside the town institute. As the years wore on from Armistice day, 1918, it was now not only impossible for the mothers of the lost boys to climb to the obelisk, but also the 'boys' themselves had legs that could no longer cope with such a steep climb. Over the years, other Melrose lads had enlisted and lived through the ordeal, but they too had grown older, and some had passed on. Men such as Roy Clarke, Charlie Abbott, Stuart Giles and Codger Begg. Jack Dickson was one of the older World War One veterans who remained, and climbing up to the monument, no matter how important the occasion, had become impossible.

"There was a fine old ruckus in the pub this evening," Beth said to her two children when she got home from work. "Joe Clucas was in fine form, carrying on about how he could make a road to the monument."

"Do you really think he could?" Clarrie asked, wide-eyed at the thought of the older veterans having a way to be transported up the hill.

"Of course not!" Sally jeered. "Have you seen that slope?"

"Well, it might be possible," Clarrie said hopefully.

"I'm afraid not, son," Beth said. "I heard one of the men say that getting a road up that wooded incline would be impossible."

"Oh!" Clarrie said, crestfallen. "That's bad luck!"

"Who cares anyway?" Sally said thoughtlessly.

"Well, if it's any consolation, someone dared Joe Clucas to make a road, and he swore he would." Beth added.

"Well, he will then, I guess." Clarrie knew Joe's reputation for doing daredevil stunts no one else would ever dream of doing.

"I don't know, Clarrie," Beth smiled patiently," but judging by the amount of laughter that followed, I think you'd be the only person that believes such a thing would be possible."

Clarrie's faith in Joe's ability to perform such a feat was not at all shaken. He'd heard stories told about Joe for years, and had seen first hand one or two crazy things that had Joe Clucas behind them. Lyall had told Clarrie about how, before Joe had the Suzuki, he had already gone up the rocky slope on his motorbike, right up to the monument. Clarrie was in awe of the achievement as he felt that it was hard enough to climb with hands and legs, without trying to urge a motor vehicle over rocks and undergrowth, and on such a steep grade. It was the sort of terrain that should have required a specialized, four-wheel drive army vehicle.

But about the time the sniggering and laughing about the mad proposal should have died down, the town was all in uproar. Suddenly, it was discovered that there was now a road, albeit a very rough, fair-weather road, up to the monument, and no one doubted for an instant that it was Joe Clucas who had put it there.

"Well, I tell you," Mrs Greenbank said in her characteristic loud tone, "I never thought I'd see the day. What next, I ask you! First a road to the monument, and next they'll be talking about flying to the moon!"

Georgie Greenbank was horrified that his mother should speak so loudly when she was so backward thinking. He was convinced that a flight to the moon was not just out of a Jules Verne novel, but quite probable in the near future. And as to the new road, he was of Clarrie's opinion. Joe said he could and there was little room left for argument after that.

Anzac Day came, but despite the newly graded track, the service was held as it always had been, in the Melrose Institute, with plenty of the Second World War veterans in attendance, men such as Frank Arthur, Bob Bessen and Ken McCallum, but only a couple of the original ANZACS still alive and healthy enough to come and recite 'Lest we Forget' and listen to the Last Post being played. Old Jack Dickson and Charlie Abbott stood to their most solemn attention, recalling the years they had spent facing death at the hand of the enemy, and the mates that had been killed before their youth was over.

Later in the day a number of curious patriots determined to try the road out, and made the precarious trip, with roaring engines and tyres spinning in the loose rocky surface, in the effort to gain traction. A number of cars negotiated the steep climb, and the passengers were rewarded with the satisfaction of seeing the view and paying homage without having to use much physical energy to get there. However it would have to be admitted that a lot of mental and emotional energy was spent as cars struggled against gravity and loose surface, and drivers and passengers alike wondered, on the verge of panic, if they had been wise to attempt such a feat.

Such an innocent thing as a track to a war memorial should have passed with little comment, but somehow, rumour and speculation took hold of the idea, and Joe Clucas, for all his mischief and devilry, became the centre of a town legend.

Clarrie heard some of the wild stories himself. While he was waiting for his mother in the lounge of the pub, he heard a couple of locals talking.

"I heard that it was one of Joe's army buddies that started it all," one of the men said. "He came striding into the pub one day, a stranger in town, and took one look at Joe and burst out 'Clucas!' followed by much patting on the back and old army stories. There was some yarn about how Joe was one of a group of soldiers who took a bet to see who could ride their Harley motorbike up this very, very steep hill, and who could get it to the highest point. This bloke reckoned Joe won the bet and held the record, but one day he pushed it at such great speed until the bike stalled. He left it, and it began to tumble back down the hill."

"That'd be Joe Clucas," the other man said with a laugh.

"Yeah, well, some of the other locals didn't believe the story."

"I don't know why. He does everything crazy!"

"Someone dared him to prove it by taking his bike up to the monument, but of course he wasn't to be shamed into a corner, so he boldly turns around and says 'I'll do better than that! I'll drive the grader up there and make a road!'"

Clarrie laughed when he heard this story. He wondered how much truth there was in it. But the tale only got larger whenever it was told. Clarrie heard some women talking as they waited their turn outside the bank, and he stopped nearby to hear the story, as he knew it was another version of "Joe's Road".

"I really don't think we should be making such a hullabaloo about this road up to the monument," one woman was saying, self-righteously. "It'll only encourage the young folk towards alcohol."

"You don't say," her companion said in a shocked tone. "How do you mean?"

"Well, you know that Joe Clucas was drinking when some fool person challenged him to drive the grader up to the monument."

"Drinking!" The other woman sounded scandalised.

"Yes! And he only went out in the fading light, took the grader without the council overseer even knowing, and drove up there in the dark."

"My goodness! What did Roy Albinus have to say about it? He's the overseer isn't he?"

"Well, I'm sure I don't know."

That was all Clarrie stayed to hear. He laughed to himself as he went on down the street. Once again, he wouldn't put it past Joe to pull such a stunt, but on the strength of that sort of gossip, he wasn't ready yet to condemn the man.

"Nah!" Lyall contradicted all the stories when Clarrie asked him what he thought about it. "That wasn't the first time Joe's driven up to the monument. He used to ride his old motorbike up there all the time. I mean someone dared him to do it in the first place. He followed a bit of a rough sheep track up there, and when someone suggested to him that he should put a proper road up there, and someone else pooh-hoohed it, and reckoned he couldn't do it, it was like waving a red rag to a bull. So he just went ahead and did it."

"Do you reckon that's the truth?" Clarrie asked solemnly.

"Yeah! Of course! First he got the bulldozer and backed it up that slope, pushing down the trees that were in the way as he went. Then he drove the grader up past the rubbish dump and along the rifle range which leads down to the monument, and he was able to drive down the hill from there. He did it that way so that he could tip the grader blade, and dig it in on one side. That would've held him back a bit from hurtling down the hill."

"So do you reckon he took the bulldozer and grader without council permission?" Clarrie asked.

"I dunno!" Lyall shrugged his shoulders. "Probably!"

"Do you reckon?" Clarrie asked again, wide-eyed.

"Why don't you go to the council and ask," Lyall suggested.

Clarrie couldn't let it go there. He'd heard so many stories, all of them painting Joe Clucas in a larger-than-life mode, but he was terribly concerned that Joe had done this thing without the proper permission and that he would eventually end up in some serious trouble. He didn't quite have the courage to front up to the offices of the Port Germein District Council, located just across the street from Young's, but every time he was sitting on the veranda at Young's, he wondered, *did Joe really make that road without the proper consent?*

Eventually his question was satisfactorily answered. One Sunday after Sunday school, Clarrie was saying goodbye to Mr Bishop, when one of the other Sunday school teachers came up to talk to the superintendent.

"Hello, Mrs Albinus," Clarrie said politely to the blond-haired teacher.

"Hello there, Clarrie," she answered with a smile, before turning to talk to Jim. Clarrie was going to slip away, as convention demanded, but Mr Bishop's opening remark kept him hovering within earshot.

"So I hear Roy turned a blind eye to the monument road business," Jim said with a chuckle. Clarrie knew that 'Roy' was Mr Albinus, the council overseer.

"Oh, what a lot of nonsense about nothing," Mrs Albinus said. "Joe Clucas had been on at the council for ages about getting a road up to the monument. Nobody seemed to think it worth going in to, or even that it could be done, but Joe kept on about it anyway."

"So, was it a result of a dare, a foolish escapade or a formal council job?"

"Well, by now who would know, with all the gossip about town, and you may be sure that Joe won't tell you the straight story. But from my understanding, Roy said he would let Joe have a go, but the risk was on his own head. But he must have got permission, as they had to go through the bottom end of Ey's paddock, and couldn't have done that without consent."

"So there was no dare in the pub," Jim seemed slightly disappointed.

"Oh, I hear that it was all planned and talked about in the pub, but then, who really knows?"

Clarrie slipped away satisfied. As long as Mr Albinus knew about it, the road was there and no one and nothing was damaged. Clarrie had his favourite version of how it happened, and no matter what anybody said from now on, he was determined that the road to the monument would be called "Joe's Road".

Chapter Seven

What the people in the fire shed hadn't known was that there was a back burn in progress.

Whether it was the hand of God or not, the fact remained; one moment it looked like the whole town would be destroyed by fire, and the next it was as if the flames were swallowed up by a vacuum. It had simply run out of fuel when it hit the already burnt ground.

Jim Bishop and his crew of son and son-in-law had been sent to start the back burn to protect the town. Others had been sent to the north side, but they were told to start up the south end past the Anglican Church, just on the other side of the creek. Jim was driving their four-wheel-drive and Andrew and Simon Malcolm were on the back, holding hoses that came from the large square tank mounted on the tray top. The back burn fire had taken easily, and continued along the creek right up to the area where 'Joe's Road' began, just over the creek from the caravan park. Then they had to patrol that front to make sure it burned upward towards the oncoming bushfire, and not back towards the town.

They were down the Cathedral Rock end, and the flames were as vicious and hot as the main fire. Jim had pulled the vehicle to a stand-still, and the two boys on the back were hosing it, but the intensity of heat had increased dramatically. Andrew stopped hosing the fire, and began to hose himself and his brother-in-law. Simon persisted in hosing the fire. They both thought that Jim would move the unit along to a slightly cooler spot, but he was oblivious to the fact that they were beginning to roast in the intensified heat.

It became so hot, that the water was drying on their skin before Andrew could bring the hose back for another turn, and it became obvious that Jim had not understood the seriousness of their conditions, and therefore had no plans for moving away.

Eventually, Andrew began to yell as he felt they were going to cook. He thumped on the roof to add strength to his words, pleading for his father to move along. Jim heard the thumping, but didn't know what it was about.

"What?" he called out through the sealed cabin.

"Move on!" Andrew called back, becoming desperate.

"What?" Jim called back, deafened by the noise of the water pump, and the roaring fire.

"Move the truck along!" He'd added a colourful expletive in to help communicate his panicked frustration. Eventually, the thumping, the yelling and possibly the expletive, conveyed the message they wanted, and Jim finally pulled back from the fire.

This time the back burn was a success. It saved the town, and though the two boys were a little roasted, no one was seriously injured.

When they inspected the four-wheel-drive later, the paint on the side had peeled off, and the hoses they had been using had begun to melt with the heat.

So far in the four days of fighting this thing, no houses or human lives had been lost. But sadly, the back burn had been lit with the assumption that the paddocks above were clear. Only after it was well ablaze did the fire fighters realise there was a mob of sheep still there, now caught between the two fronts. There was nothing they could do at that point, and they had to accept that the sheep would be burned to death.

Clarrie saw the notice taped to the inside of Prests' window. He sighed inwardly, struggling with the dilemma that always presented itself this time of year.

All those interested in playing Junior Colts football please turn up for training on Tuesday afternoons at 4.30, at the Melrose Oval.

Clarrie already knew about the training sessions; in fact, this notice was four weeks old. Miss Jolly had read the same information out to the class weeks ago, and some of the other fellows had already been. Georgie Greenbank, Lyall and Neville McCallum and some of the other boys had boasted about their skills and abilities with the oblong ball. It wasn't really a question of whether Clarrie wanted to play or not – he already knew he didn't want to play. It was more a question of peer group acceptance. Most of the boys played football as their winter sport while most of the girls played netball. Tennis was the popular summer sport, and Clarrie struggled through the tennis coaching with Mrs Blieschke to achieve some level of success. But with football there was a lot more physical energy needed, and putting of one's body on the line. Clarrie wasn't exactly afraid, but he didn't have a great deal of ball-handling skill, and couldn't find the passion that some of the other boys had. For them, the satisfaction of successful goal kicking, marking and tackling was enough reward for the heavy knocks and being thrown to the ground. Clarrie rarely marked a ball, kicked very badly and never got a goal. He had no such incentive, and absolutely no desire to just go out there and be thrown about for no reason at all. Still, he knew that he would eventually turn up to practice and be bullied about by Mr Greenbank, yelled at by the other boys for dropping the mark, and generally be the subject of a lot of crowd disappointment as he failed to tag his opponent and prevent him from making some marvellous play. But belonging to a team, especially in a small town, was a very powerful motivation, and Clarrie began to steel himself for his inevitable appointment with fate.

If only my whole life didn't depend on being part of the footy-team, Clarrie thought to himself dejectedly as he trudged out of town on the way out to the oval, his football boots dangling by the long laces about his neck. Only a couple of years back, there hadn't been any junior team, and Clarrie had loved the winter Saturday afternoons, assembling about the oval and watching Melrose's A and B grade football teams fight it out against the other towns. Of course there were seven teams from round about, but no games were as exciting as those played against the old archrivals, Booleroo Centre. Off the field you could have civility, and even friendliness, but come the football season, old hostilities flared and fairly bristled amongst the fans from either town. When Clarrie thought about it he wondered if it was something like the age-old war of the Irish against the British. No one really knew what had started the animosity, but each generation seemed more than willing to keep it going.

Clarrie had only just passed the Masonic Lodge and was walking by Mrs Fuller's house when he saw her at the front, watering her sweet peas that grew abundantly along the fence.

"Hello, Clarrie," she called across the road to him.

"Hello!" he replied, without much enthusiasm.

"You off to football practice?" she asked.

Clarrie was in no hurry to begin his humiliation, so he crossed the road and went over to talk to his piano teacher.

"I can see by the look on your face that you are as keen about football practice as you are about piano lessons," she remarked.

"I like piano better," Clarrie admitted. Vera smiled. "I'm hopeless with the football," Clarrie added hurriedly, trying to justify himself. "I never mark it properly, always drop it, can't kick straight to save myself, and you can be sure they always want me to stand the other team's best player."

"That sounds very tiresome for you," Vera said. "But surely you must enjoy it when your team wins?"

"If it wasn't so embarrassing, I would. Especially when we beat the Booleroo team."

"Oh, yes!" Vera agreed. "Now that is sweet victory, isn't it?"

Clarrie laughed with her, and then decided that he might as well be hung for a sheep as for a lamb, so to speak. If he was going to be late for practice, he might even manage to miss it all together.

"Why do we hate the Booleroos so much?" Clarrie asked, hoping to delay his arrival at practice. "And why do they hate us?"

"Well, there, you know I don't suppose I could really say," she said, with a thoughtful look on her face. "But you know, that old rivalry has been going on for as long as I can remember."

Clarrie knew that he had hit the right button to get a story, and he planned to use that as an excuse for why he hadn't made it to football practice. *Mrs Fuller was talking to me, and I didn't want to be rude,* he practised his excuse in his mind.

"You know, years ago," Vera began in her typical singsong, story-telling voice, "the area where the oval is now was called Dorrington Park. The ground was flat, but there was no oval as such, with any fence or trotting track, like there is now. All the football matches were played there, and I remember even back then Booleroo and Melrose were always terrible enemies during the football season. I remember there was one particular Booleroo man who was a terrible sport and my Dad, Mr Tom Slee, used to walk the oval while the match was on barracking for all he was worth. Dad would sing out, going around with his hands in his pockets, round the oval egging our boys on, and this day, when he came around the first turn, this man was standing there barracking for Booleroo. My Dad, of course out of devilment, said 'come on Melrose, you can lick them any time,' and what do you know, but this man came over and jumped on Dad's toes - jumped up and down right on Dad's toes."

Clarrie laughed at the idea

"Well, Dad said, 'Aw, be your age.'" Vera continued. "I remember Dad came back to where we were sitting, and I was only a youngster at the time, and he told Mum about it. Well, she got all up in arms and was all for going and telling him off. But my Dad was placid and saw the funny side of it, so when Mum got up, all set to tell this fellow off Dad said, 'Aw, leave him alone, he's not worth bothering about.' That started up an argument, because Mum said, 'You've got no pride, letting him do that and get away with it.'"

Clarrie laughed at the thought of these two mature men jumping on each other's toes, and all over a football match.

"Yes, but it didn't end there," Vera went on, enjoying her small audience's response. "My dad used to play as well, and some time after the 'toes' episode, Dad came up against this fellow during a match. For some reason, he'd developed a real grudge against Dad. So when Dad was kneeling down to tie his boot laces, this fellow came and gave him a king-hit…"

"A what?" Clarrie interrupted.

"A king-hit, you know, a full-on hip and shoulder bump, when Dad was off balance, and unable to defend himself. The fellow laid Dad out proper, and there was a real uproar between the two towns then. The rivalry got real fierce there for a while."

"But it's not really anything serious, is it?" Clarrie asked, beginning to feel concerned.

"Oh, my word yes!" Vera said. "It's sheep stations or nothing when it comes to playing Booleroo."

Clarrie's face was a study of worry until his music teacher laughed.

"No, Clarrie," she said, greatly relieving his anxiety. "It's only small town rivalry. If it ever comes to times of great trouble or anything, Booleroo people would be the first ones to be here with their hands out to help. Doctor Wheaton is from Booleroo, don't forget."

"That's right!" Clarrie said with a sigh of relief. "It's only over sport and silly things like that, isn't it?"

"Mostly." Vera gave him a pat on the shoulder and a wink. "Now you get along to football practice, or when you come up against Booleroo, they are going to walk all over you, and then how will that look for Melrose?"

By the time Clarrie had got to the oval, the other boys had already done the running and exercising, and now they were having a scratch-match against each other.

"You're late, Clarrie Brown!" George Greenbank bellowed. "Hope you don't expect to get picked in the team with an attitude like that!"

"No, sir!" Clarrie hung his head as if ashamed, but inside he was thinking it might be a good opportunity to get left out of the team, and still save some face with the other boys by showing a bit of bad attitude. But then he wondered what his mother would have to say when Mr Greenbank told her he'd been behaving badly, as he was sure Mr Greenbank would. Or at least Mrs Greenbank would make it her business. Clarrie decided that the ensuing argument would not be worth it.

"Go on," Mr Greenbank broke into his thoughts. "Get yourself out there and practise with the others. You can be on Georgie's team."

Clarrie dawdled onto the oval, trying not to put himself in a position where he would be a target for the other team's enthusiastic tackling, and hoping they wouldn't find any great need to pass the ball to him either.

"Don't like the game much, do you?" Lyall Arthur spoke to Clarrie after practice, as he was tying his own boots ready for the seniors' practice.

"Not much!" Clarrie admitted. "But I've gotta play."

"Why?" Lyall asked.

"Because everyone plays. Only sooks sit about watching."

"Who told you that?" Lyall looked a bit cross. "Tell you the truth, I don't like playing much myself."

"Well, why do you, then?" Clarrie challenged him.

"I don't know. It's a small town, and if we don't all pitch in, we might not always have a team of our own, and then we'd have to join with another town. Perish the thought!"

"Like Booleroo?" Clarrie said, with a bit of a laugh.

"Now wouldn't that be a poke in the eye for us Melrose blokes?"

"Mrs Fuller told me the Melrose/Booleroo rivalry has been going on for years."

"Oh, yeah!" Lyall said knowingly. "I reckon it all started back with my grandfather, when he was a young bloke."

"Your grandfather. How do you reckon?" Clarrie sounded doubtful.

"When the Arthurs first settled in the district, we were a Booleroo family, through and through. Most of the Arthurs are still Booleroo people. Only a handful of us over here at Melrose."

"Are the Melrose Arthurs all related?" Clarrie asked.

"Yeah! All descendants of Wally Arthur, my grandfather. His father bought a new block of land, you know, Willowmere, out behind McCallum's place at Overdale. Well, Wally, as a young fellow, was the son who got to live out at Willowmere, and as it was much closer to Melrose than Booleroo, he changed football teams, and began to play for Melrose. His brothers were real dirty on him. They reckoned he defected to the enemy."

"Sounds like he didn't start the rivalry," Clarrie said. "Seems like it might already have been well and truly there before."

"You're probably right!" Lyall laughed. "And it's still here today, isn't it?"

"Yeah, but it's not sheep stations, or anything, is it?"

"Nah! None of us are that rich to be betting anything like that!"

Clarrie didn't mind hanging around longer, now that the threat to his own personal well-being was over. He sat on the grass on the edge of the oval and watched as Barnie Furrows put the A and B grade players through their paces. Somewhat more professional in his approach, and certainly a lot more enthusiastic, Barnie had the fellows running and going through game exercises. There were some younger, less experienced players like Lyall and his brothers, and the new young clerk from the district council, Robert Moulton.

When Robert, or Bob as most people called him, had first arrived as a clerk in the ES&A bank, he'd caused quite a stir in the district as a new and very eligible bachelor. Clarrie remembered all the girls his sister hung around with would talk about the local boys, and who was the most popular. He noticed that Bob wasn't as popular as he had been since he'd become engaged to Janice McCallum.

A number of Janice's family members were part of the Melrose Football Club, including her uncle Don and her older brother, Jeff, both of whom were out at practice now.

Clarrie was a staunch Melrose supporter. Even though he and his family had only been living in the town for seven years, the parochial one-eyed attitude seemed to have rubbed off quite strongly. The trouble was, Clarrie lamented as he watched the fellows practise, the Melrose team hardly ever won. In fact, last season, Melrose won only the one game for the season, against Orroroo. The occasion had been so memorable, that it had been much talked about, and treated as if they'd won the grand final. Not only had the fans at the game become unreasonably ecstatic, but also the following celebration at the Morchard pub on the way home had caused some rather serious hangovers.

But this was a new season and Clarrie hoped for something better especially in light of his sister's teasing. Sally had shifted her loyalties to the Booleroo team, the result of some infatuation with a Booleroo boy, and she'd made plenty of barbed comments about Melrose's recent football successes, or rather lack of them.

Clarrie watched the team practise for some time more, carefully looking for the kind of talent that was going to bring home the flag, but reluctantly admitting that he probably wasn't the only one who was lacking the 'right stuff'.

Two days later, when all the other boys crowded about the window at Prests' to read the notices, Clarrie looked to see the team that Mr Greenbank had named. Georgie Greenbank, of course, had been put in as one of the forwards. Some of the boys had insinuated that this was a result of his father's favouritism, but Clarrie knew full well that Georgie possessed as much talent and skill as any of the others. Georgie was as likely as anyone to kick plenty of goals.

After the other boys stepped back from reading the notice in the window, Clarrie stepped forward to see what would be expected of him on the following Saturday. He tried not to let his sigh of relief sound audibly as he saw that he'd been placed as third reserve.

"Bad luck!" Georgie said sincerely, as if Clarrie had suffered the worst blow of all time in not being chosen. "I reckon Dad would've given you a guernsey if you'd come to practice regularly."

Clarrie nodded, trying to hide his elation, and also trying to put on that nonchalant expression as if not being picked had no effect on him. He walked a fine line in trying to communicate the right image to his peers.

"You will come out and watch, won't you?" Georgie asked.

"'Course!" Clarrie said confidently. "We're playing Booleroo first match of the season. You don't reckon I'd miss that, do you?"

Saturday wasn't too hard to face, considering that Clarrie was looking forward to the game, and he knew he wouldn't have to play. It really was the best of both worlds.

"For goodness sake, Clarrie," Sally complained, "don't get all dressed up in those red and black colours. Fancy letting all my friends knows that you actually barrack for Melrose."

"Who else would I barrack for?" Clarrie replied defensively, ignoring his sister's jibe about his black and red jumper.

"Not for a team that loses every time, that's for sure!" Sally replied nastily.

"Things'll be different this year, you watch and see!" Clarrie jutted his chin out stubbornly. Sally laughed jeeringly, but Clarrie wouldn't let her see his doubt, not for all the tea in China.

Clarrie was somewhat relieved to see that his own Junior Colts' team managed to win over the Booleroo team, and he credited himself with helping by making sure that he didn't become the weak point in the side.

The senior colts played well enough, but lost by eight points.

The B grade also put on a reasonable show, but the Booleroo side proved to be stronger and more skilled. All Clarrie's hopes lay with the A grade, and he and his mates found a spot around near the coach's area, so that they could hear all that was going on.

The Melrose boys, in their black footy jumpers with the thick red 'v' at the neck, were very obviously struggling to match their opponents right from the first bounce, but Clarrie refused to concede. He continued to hope for a turn in play, and added his voice to those of the others around him, barracking strongly. Of course there were some of the older fans who kept offering words of advice to the man in white, and letting him know just exactly where it was that he was going wrong. Clarrie laughed at some of these comments, especially when they came out of the mouths of some of the respectable folk, who were normally very careful about the way they conducted themselves. It wasn't hard to see that all rules of etiquette and propriety were abandoned the moment you found your preferred spot around the football oval. Clarrie, Georgie and some of the other fellows were sitting on the benches that were placed around the edge of the field, but a lot of other spectators sat in the many cars that were lined up around the oval. It added a lot of strength to the barracking process whenever a goal was kicked, as car horns blew frantically, sounding out the emotion of the spectators sitting inside. However, all of that was wearing a little thin for Clarrie, as so far, it was mainly the players wearing the red and white guernseys that had been kicking the goals. Clarrie knew which car Sally was sitting in with all her Booleroo friends, and they were making extra good use of the car horn. It half crossed his mind to go around to them and give them a good punch on the nose. But then he pulled himself up short, startled to realise that he was thinking like an incurable football fanatic, where normal good manners and polite behaviour could be abandoned. After hearing Mrs Fuller's story about her father and the crushed toes, he decided that he'd better keep a tighter rein on his emotions.

"Look! Second Time's got the ball!" Georgie yelled. "Now we'll see some action!"

"Come on Second Time!" one of the other boys yelled.

Clarrie joined in with this chorus of support for Col Meaney, the little rover they all called Second Time. "Why do they call Col Meaney 'Second Time'?" Clarrie asked, suddenly curious as to how this nickname had developed.

"I dunno!" Georgie replied, without giving it any thought, and going right back to his barracking.

Col was playing to good effect against the Booleroo defence and his supporters were shouting his nickname loud in their show of approval. The more Clarrie heard it, 'Second Time', the more curious he became, and decided that he would find out.

Second Time did a brilliant job of roving through the centre of the ground, dodging and weaving his way through the

Booleroo defenders, and as he emerged within fifty yards of the goal, he kicked a short pass aiming for Don McCallum, one of the taller forwards. The spectators watched with anticipation, but the ball fell some feet short of Don, and he went after it fiercely intent, his head down. Clarrie could see what was going to happen, and he rose on his feet, like the other spectators, as one of the large Booleroo backmen also put his head down, and went after the ball. Both were totally focussed on the ball, and neither paid any heed to the obvious danger.

"'Struth!" Georgie yelled, as the two players collided, head on. "That's gonna hurt!" he added, and Clarrie had to agree as both players' heads flung back, and both hit the ground, looking for all the world as if they were out cold.

Trainers appeared on the ground without so much as a by your leave, and ran across to the two players. The Booleroo man got up, shaking his head as if to say, 'It's all right. I'm all right!' But to Clarrie's dismay, Don appeared to be knocked out. The two Melrose trainers came up to him, and lifted him into a sitting position.

"Crikey!" Georgie exclaimed. "There's blood everywhere!" Clarrie could see that Don's face was covered in blood, and was concerned, although somewhat relieved to see that he was showing signs of consciousness.

Then there was a general 'Ooh!' from the spectators as they watched with amused interest. One of the Melrose trainers, Laurie Willington, collapsed in a dead faint on the ground. Second Time, and some of the other fellows came over, and the whole game halted while the remaining trainer ushered Don McCallum from the ground, his broken nose gushing blood, and the Melrose players worked to revive Laurie and take him from the ground.

"Don't reckon I'm very good with the sight of blood!" the boys heard Laurie mutter, as he was assisted to the coach's bench.

The incident remained the highlight of the match, as the Melrose players were not so good in the first place, and without one of their best forwards, they deteriorated further. Clarrie was frustrated, knowing he would have to face Sally's smug taunts, but he was not yet prepared to give up on his team. Melrose would win the flag one day, of that he was convinced.

Clarrie hung around the oval for as long as he could. He loved the general after match talk, and wondered if, after all, he should not just become a coach or trainer. He loved the game, but he didn't like getting hurt, and having watched Don McCallum today was just another confirmation that football was for watching, not for playing.

"G'day, young Clarrie!"

Clarrie turned to see Second Time walking towards him, his bag of footy gear slung over his shoulder.

"Hello, Col," Clarrie answered. "You played well!"

"Mm!" Col didn't seem prepared to commit himself on that score.

"Why does everyone call you 'Second Time'?" Clarrie asked, immediately making the most of the opportunity to satisfy his curiosity.

Col laughed outright. "Do you need a ride home, Clarrie?" At Clarrie's nod, he continued. "I'll tell you the story on the way home."

Clarrie climbed into Col's FJ Holden sedan, in eager anticipation. Col Meaney was a good yarn spinner.

"We were playing Orroroo one Saturday afternoon, and were having a pretty good day of it for a change."

"You always play well," Clarrie observed.

"Mm," once again Col's modesty showed. "Anyway, I'd taken rather a good mark right in front of the goal, and was all measured up to kick, and suddenly, I found my mouth full of prickles, my face in the dirt. The rotten Orroroo fullback had come and fairly thumped me in the back, and I'd gone face first into the turf."

"How'd you feel about that?" Clarrie asked, chuckling because Col had actually made it sound really funny.

"I jumped up full of fury. I was set to turn around and give him what for."

"And did you?"

"I began to turn around, ready to put the mits up and trounce the fella. I said 'You do that again and…' and then I stopped. I came face to face, or should I say, face to chest with this great hairy fellow, whose arms were as thick as my legs. 'And what?' he said to me. The man was a huge tree trunk of a fellow and I thought better of giving him his just deserts. 'And….and….and it will be the second time.' I answered."

Clarrie couldn't help laughing at Col's description of the confrontation.

"So ever since then, whenever we've played them, he's always called me 'Second Time'. It's as good a nickname as you'll ever get, don't you reckon?"

"But you are a good player, Col, I reckon." Clarrie said.

"I'm too scared not to be," Col answered. "That Barnie Furrows, he's some coach. He's not out there to see us lose. Trouble is we always seem to lose anyway."

"I try to get out of practice when I can, because I don't like playing football much," Clarrie admitted.

"You won't want to make the senior teams, mate," Col confided. "Our coach has us out two times a week, and one of those nights he makes us run all the way to White Well and back."

"White Well!" Clarrie cried. "That'd be three miles out there and three miles back."

"Something like that!" Col returned.

"Do you make it?"

"Well, I'll tell you a secret, but don't you let on to anyone, promise?"

"Sure!" said Clarrie, wide-eyed.

"Coach is sure that we're all going to be as fit as he is, so he runs out front. Some of us drop back a ways, and when we pass the cemetery, we stop, and hide amongst the trees, until the fellas are on their way back, and then we join in behind them."

"Doesn't the coach get angry with you?"

"He doesn't know, and I hope you won't tell him!"

"No way," Clarrie said firmly, completely empathising with the lagging runners. He knew that he'd be struggling just to make it all the way to the cemetery if Mr Greenbank got such a crazy idea.

"No! Barnie's a ferocious coach, and make no mistake," Col went on. "He's nice enough when you meet him in the street, but something happens when he's got that coach's hat on."

"How do you mean?" Clarry asked.

"Well, you know I'm a plumber?" Col asked. Clarrie nodded. "Well, I was doing some work for one of the blokes over at Booleroo. Now, he's one of the nicest blokes, and a fair football player too, and I haven't got anything against him, but the trouble is he's a good six inches taller than me, and when we're up against each other, I can never take a mark over him, ever. So Coach yells out to me, 'Thump him! Thump him! Thump him!' and I think to myself, it's all right for you. He's bigger than me, and I've got to ask him to pay for the job I've done for him next week."

Col had pulled his FJ up outside Clarrie's house, but Clarrie couldn't stop laughing at Col's stories. "Is that true?" he asked, a little sceptically.

"Of course!" Col said. "You work your way up through the juniors, and you'll find out!"

"I don't think so," Clarrie shook his head as he got out of the car. "I reckon I'm gonna become the coach!"

Chapter Eight

Now that the immediate threat to the town was over, Clarrie stayed near the shed waiting to be given a job to do. There was a team due to go out along the Survey Road and in through Kev Mount's property to try and establish a break through there. A man was due in soon with a bulldozer, and the shift supervisor asked if Clarrie would be willing to go with him and a local guide to drive the extra vehicle with fuel and spare parts. Clarrie agreed, knowing that there was nothing else urgent for him to do at the moment.

While he waited for the dozer driver to arrive, Clarrie couldn't help but remember Joe Clucas, and he asked if this driver was Joe. Clarrie remembered Joe only too well, and the dare-devil things he was well known for. This kind of dangerous work would have been right down his alley.

But it appeared that Joe had already gone from Melrose. Died some years earlier. It was a weird sensation for Clarrie to find himself confronting so many images and people from his childhood, and he always felt a renewed grief every time he heard that one of the old-timers had passed on, and he had not been here to grieve the loss with the rest of the town.

He saw Col Meaney and Clair Prosser, and their sons, whom he remembered as little kids at school. They came in and reported for duty along with the rest. The McCallum men came in periodically, and it probably seemed more often than others, but that was probably because there were so many McCallums.

But what caused Clarrie to reflect more than anything else was the amount of families that he saw. They weren't all in the shed at the same time, of course. Fathers and brothers would come in and join crews to go out to the front, and women would either be taking the various communication responsibilities, or else offering help with anything from food to first aid.

Clarrie couldn't help but think of his own family. How would he feel if Sue were here with the other women, a part of a strong network of community-minded people? And if he'd been a responsible, caring family man, who took his community obligations to the point of laying one's life on the line, like so many others were doing at this moment?

What had he ever laid on the line for anybody? It was an awful question to ask oneself. Clarrie knew the answer only too well. When it came to Sue and the kids, his own passion for gambling and alcohol got first preference. There was very little left over after that.

Then Clarrie asked himself how on earth he'd ever got to that point of such utter selfishness. Seeing this town and these people made him remember the boy he used to be. He remembered the way he used to help at the tennis tournament, and how he would stop and talk to older folks in the town for hours. Now an adult, he could see just how much they must have enjoyed his youthful company. But where had he lost that easy free spirit? What excuse could he now offer? And yet here, in this almost surreal world of community crisis, no one knew about Clarrie's vices, or about his tattered relationships. What he would give to be a part of this kind of world again. A world where he was loving and loved.

Much to Clarrie's chagrin, the football season didn't seem to improve. Only the Junior Colts showed some promise, and then Clarrie rarely had to play. Thankfully, there were plenty of juniors who wanted to play, and that made it easy for Clarrie to be left out of the side. He was very much a part of the team though, as a staunch supporter, and made sure that he cheered loudly on their behalf. Georgie seemed to think that Clarrie suffered a terrible disadvantage in not being chosen for his side, and it was a tricky thing for Clarrie trying to keep Georgie from begging his father to include Clarrie, without showing that he was much happier being left out.

The winter arrived and as the temperatures dropped the farmers stopped complaining about the lack of rain as various cold fronts moved through the mid north region, bringing with it the wet weather that was so much the life force of the farming areas.

The school year progressed with its usual drudgery, and Clarrie looked forward to each weekend for his entertainment. He loved the football, even in the wet weather, and he continued to love going to Sunday School and church. His sister persisted in persecuting him for his "fanatical religious" ways, but his mother seemed to think that Clarrie's commitment to church was a positive thing in the life of a fatherless boy, especially since he was finding father figures there such as Jim Bishop and the minister.

And then, just when the boys from school thought they would die of boredom, something happened that provided them with a story to tell for weeks, and the opportunity to embellish it a little with each retelling.

It was a sunny winter's day, and Clarrie was in school wondering how on earth learning grammar would ever be of any use to him. Suddenly, the quiet classroom was disturbed by the sound of the fire siren setting up its mournful wail. During the summer, it was common to hear the fire siren from the EFS shed, as they regularly tested it. Summer was the grave fire-danger season, and the EFS volunteer workers made very certain that all the emergency fire equipment was ready for use.

But to have it tear through the still winter's day, and to know that it was a genuine emergency, since it was one long wail and not several short bursts of the siren, caused total distraction to the children. Miss Jolly, of course, had the unrealistic expectation that the children would use their self-control and remain undisturbed and indifferent to what was going on outside.

Despite her sharp reprimands, most of the children whispered behind their hands speculating as to what the emergency might be.

"It's only five minutes to lunch time," Georgie whispered to Clarrie. "I reckon I'll go home for lunch today."

"Me too," Clarrie agreed, carefully ignoring the grease-proof paper wrapped sandwiches that sat in the plastic container at the bottom of his school satchel.

The long hand had hardly reached the six on the schoolroom clock and the children were fidgeting in anticipation of being released from the classroom. Miss Jolly seemed to sense this, and true to her nature, and contrary to her name, she decided to make them sweat it out a full two minutes past the usual lunchtime.

"We'll have missed all the action by now," Georgie lamented as the two boys hurried off down the street. "They'll have got the fire truck going and off to the fire before we even get there to find out what's going on."

"Well, we didn't hear the truck come past the school, so maybe the fire is out the other way, south of the town."

But the two boys were only just outside the old blacksmith shop and they could see as well as hear some commotion going on, and their excitement increased when they saw smoke billowing up into the sky right here in Melrose.

Clarrie knew that he shouldn't be pleased to see the smoke, but he was. The crisis was here in the town, and there was a good chance that if they kept out of everybody's way, they would get a ringside view.

"It's the pub!" Georgie yelled as he began to run.

Clarrie suddenly knew a moment's anxiety as he realised his mother was at work in the pub, and his vivid imagination easily saw the kitchen up in flames, and his mother caught in the middle of it. Pain tore through his side as the stitch took hold, and his breath came in ragged gasps. He had run at full speed past the old cemetery, the pool hall, and to the Mt Remarkable Pub, and had a moment's relief to see that it was not the hotel on fire at all, but next door at Sloan's Garage.

Locals ran everywhere. There was a bit of a bucket brigade from the hotel, trying to douse flames with a few buckets of water, and he saw Clair Prosser standing on the roof of Sloan's small house, which abutted both the pub and their garage next door. He held an ordinary garden hose in his hand, with an insignificant stream of water running out, and was obviously trying to save the small house from burning. Clarrie looked across and saw Lorrie Lello on the other side of the garage, another garden hose in his hand, spraying the eaves of the ES&A bank right next door to the garage on the further side.

"Where's the fire truck?" Georgie asked. There were plenty of townspeople there, most of the adults doing something to get water to the flames, but not much could be done without a decent sort of hose.

Then there was a shout, and a few colourful expletives floated through the air as several men came flying out of the front office of the garage. "The petrol tanks are under the office," one of them yelled. "If they go up, it'll wipe the whole lot of us off the map!"

There was a general murmur of confused panic, and a lot of the improvised fire brigade took twenty steps backward.

"Where's the flamin' fire truck?" someone yelled.

"They can't get her started," came the reply above the general hubbub.

Clarrie saw Lyall running across the road to the fire shed. If it hadn't been so serious, it would have been laughable. The EFS shed was only twenty yards up the street from the garage, and twenty minutes into the crisis, the only sign of help from that quarter was the old Blitz, which totally defied its name, slowly emerging from the fire shed on the end of a tow rope. Clarrie couldn't believe his eyes. He almost expected the Keystone Cops to come hurtling around the corner next. But much to his chagrin, it wasn't the Keystone Cops, but rather the Booleroo Centre EFS truck, all hands on deck, their truck running proudly and capably to the crisis.

"Clarrie! Why aren't you at school?" Clarrie turned at the sound of his mother's voice and experienced a wild clash of emotions.

On the one hand he was relieved to see his mother safe and sound, and on the other, he was distressed at having been caught out. He didn't bother to make any excuses, as he guessed they wouldn't be of much use in this instance.

"Georgie and I wanted to see what was going on," he answered his mother.

"And Miss Jolly gave you permission to come?" Beth asked pointedly, knowing full well that was highly unlikely. She didn't bother to wait for his response. "Go on, Clarrie. You and Georgie get back to school before Miss Jolly is on to you."

Clarrie and Georgie returned to school in time for the last few minutes of their break, so they had plenty of opportunity to share their eyewitness accounts of the drama at Sloan's Garage, and despite the fact that they didn't quite know how it all ended, they didn't allow that fact to get in the way of a good story.

"So the Booleroo Brigade got to the fire quicker than the Melrose truck, is that right?" Sally enjoyed provoking her little brother. "Seems like their fire truck is a little bit like their football team, hey, Clarrie?"

Clarrie was not amused, nor was he in the mood to be taunted. "All the Booleroo truck did was just finish off what the Melrose volunteers had been doing all the long while it took for them to get here!" Clarrie answered.

"Yes, but if their own fire truck, the Blitz – is that what they call it – had been working, there wouldn't have been anything for them to do at all."

Clarrie couldn't dispute this rather unfortunate fact. The truth was, as Lyall had so carefully put it, the old khaki coloured army truck that had been converted to the Melrose fire truck had a bad reputation of not starting at the necessary times. The fact that some of the Melrose fellows had pushed and pulled the stubborn old vehicle, and even then failed to get her to start, was something that Clarrie didn't want to elaborate on. At least they had a fire brigade, and every last fellow of them was dedicated and alert at the first sign of emergency.

"So how did the fire start in the first place?" Sally asked her mother, abandoning her taunts.

"They say that the petrol man was filling Sloan's storage tanks. The opening for the tanks is in, or should I say, was in, the office of Sloan's Garage. Apparently the tank had overflowed some, and there was a radiator switched on in the office. They reckon he could see what was going to happen, rolled up his hose and took off."

"It was lucky the tanks didn't explode," Clarrie observed. "Even Booleroo EFS couldn't have done anything about that." He felt as if he'd had the final word.

"Yes! It was lucky, or perhaps the minister might say that God had had a part to play in it. It could have been a lot worse," Beth said in a tone that surprised Clarrie. He wouldn't have thought that his mother would have considered God, but apparently the threat of death had come a little too close for comfort, and maybe she had been thinking beyond the here and now.

Clarrie had looked over the fire scene thoroughly, once they had been released from school for the day. Sloan's garage had been totally gutted, and he felt a little sad to realise that the business would now be closed, though Lyall reckoned that it would only be temporary. Mr Prosser claimed that he and George Puddy had probably saved the house by squirting the roof with their garden hoses. If there hadn't been some quick thinking and action, they might even have lost the bank and the hotel as well, but as it was, it was only Sloan's Garage that lay in charred ruins.

When the emergency was over and Doug Sloan was left to assess the loss, many people laughed about the affair. After so much danger with so much tension, a laugh when it was all over was one way to bring relief to overstretched emotions.

Whether Mr Arthur was quite able to laugh with the others or not, was a debatable point. He'd only just brought his new International tractor into Sloan's, somewhat quietly, after he'd had to fish it out of their dam when it escaped from his son and plunged into the muddy waters. But instead of getting repaired and having all the waterlogged parts replaced, it was burnt up with the garage.

The talk of the fire fuelled schoolyard gossip for a couple of weeks, some new fact or aspect emerging every now and then, to give the teller fifteen minutes of fame.

Clarrie had avoided discussing it with his sister, on account of the fun she would make comparing the two fire brigades. But then Phillip Deekin found out from one of his cousins, who'd heard it from Robbie Robinson's mouth, another angle. It was obviously classified information that should have been kept in the Booleroo camp, but it leaked out, and it changed Sally's tune when Clarrie repeated it to her.

"So, the Booleroo fire truck was lucky to make it at all," Clarrie taunted.

"What do you mean?" Sally reacted instantly.

"The way I heard it, they got the old girl out the shed and the siren wouldn't work."

"That's nothing," Sally retorted. "It's not as if there was heaps of traffic to contend with!"

"And the radio didn't work. They weren't even sure where the fire was, the way I heard it!" Clarrie was enjoying himself.

"How do you know?" Sally asked.

"I have my sources," Clarrie grinned. "And when they were twenty minutes across, and then only half way, one of them remembered they'd forgotten to check if there was water in the tank."

"I don't believe you," Sally accused. "You're just making that up."

"I am not!" Clarrie defended. "By the time the old Airforce Austin chugged around the corner, the fire was all but out."

"Yes, dear," Beth put in with just a touch of a smile on her face. "The Austin and the Blitz were level pegging it at the finish to see who could take the longest to get there."

All three laughed. It was a rotten piece of luck for Sloan's of course, but it was a funny thing in retrospect.

Eventually all talk of the fire and who got there first, died away, and school settled back into its dull routine. If Clarrie had known what was about to happen, he wouldn't have wished for more excitement, as when the news first came to him, his stomach sunk with the feeling of despair.

"Did ya hear?" Georgie came rushing up to Clarrie first thing Friday morning. "Mum was talking to Mrs Arthur. Geoff is going to the war!"

Chapter Nine

Clarrie saw Geoff Arthur again just before the bulldozer finally arrived. Geoff was one of the officers in charge, and Clarrie noticed how he issued orders and gave direction in such a manner that spoke of calm even in the midst of storm. This observation was a confirmation of what Clarrie had seen earlier when they'd been staring death right in the face. Everybody, including himself, had been on the verge of panic. Only Geoff's voice remained steady and even as it came across the airwaves. Clarrie put it down to the leadership qualities that Geoff obviously possessed; a calculated mind that had a plan and knew what must be done to achieve the goal.

Clarrie recalled the time when he'd first heard Geoff had been drafted to go to Vietnam. He'd been a lively young fellow at the time, in as much mischief as all the rest of the lads about town. He couldn't be sure, but Clarrie wondered if this quieter, more ordered Geoff was a result of his time in Vietnam. Clarrie had read enough and interviewed enough veterans to know that it had been a hell of a war, and that few came away without some horrific memory to haunt their later years.

But Geoff hadn't fallen apart, or at least he didn't seem to have, from Clarrie's observations. But those recriminations kept coming back to trouble Clarrie. What war had he been forced to fight? What excuse did he have for all his character flaws?

Perhaps he could lay the blame at his mother's feet. Maybe if she'd left him here to finish his growing up years, instead of tearing him away from the security of friends and a loving community. Would it do to blame his mother for those torturous years of high school, when Clarrie would have done anything to escape the derisive jokes and the very blatant rejection from his peers. There was no such thing as changing schools. They lived in a housing commission home in a low-income area. His mother wasn't the only single mother struggling to support a number of children in the street. The local High School certainly wasn't known for its high level of education. Sadly it was more famous for its level of criminal activity in drug dealing and violence.

But Clarrie pulled himself up short. He wasn't about to blame his mother, or his sister either. It was just one of those things. Other blokes had suffered similar years of disillusionment in high school, and still made something decent of themselves. And there were those blokes like Geoff, who, by no choice of their own, had been dragged off to a war to fight an enemy they had no particular grudge against.

Clarrie steeled his thoughts again. If Geoff can become a useful member of a community, then why can't I?

It was more than a rhetorical question. It was more a motivational statement. Something changed in Clarrie's heart.

"But why does Geoff have to go?" Clarrie asked Lyall, afraid and somewhat upset by the news. For years Clarrie had been fascinated with soldiers and wars, and had read every war story he could get his hands on. But of recent times, a combination of news broadcasts and Mrs Greenbank's much publicised opinions had begun to tarnish Clarrie's view of the 'glory of war'.

The Vietnam conflict was not popular in Australia, and there was always some new story emerging of protests and angry rallies, where hippies and TV personalities alike risked prosecution and gaol for refusing to submit to the drafting process. And according to Mrs Greenbank, the Australian government had no business meddling in the affairs of some insignificant Asian country.

Clarrie didn't know quite what to think. Mrs Greenbank seemed intent on highlighting the horrors of war, the lost limbs, the shell-shock that left men without their proper mental faculties, the lost lives. "And all for nothing," she maintained very loudly.

When war had been the shooting and bombing of the Germans or Japs, in Clarrie's mind that had been excitement and heroism. Now his vivid imagination put Geoff out there on the battlefield, facing mines and snipers, and suddenly it hit home, perhaps this wasn't a game.

Lyall's answer to Clarrie was slow and subdued. He was obviously upset by the news himself. "It was just the wrong time," Lyall said, frustrated. "They chose them by their birth date. Can you believe that?"

Clarrie's face showed his dismay, and he waited for his older friend to continue. "Every six months those who turn twenty in the following six months have to register for National Service and from those a ballot is conducted on birth dates. If the date of your birthday comes out you have to go into National Service. I mean, there is a one in five chance that any of us turning twenty will have to do National Service. I'll be twenty in a couple of years. It could happen to me too. But not all of those chosen have to go to Vietnam. Only about one in three. We'd all accepted the fact that Geoff had to serve his two year National Service term, but to be chosen for this as well…"

"But how did they choose him?" Clarrie wasn't satisfied with the answer.

"When his birth date came up, he was posted to the Battalion that was already preparing to go." Though Lyall was trying to sound held together, Clarrie could tell by his tone and expression that he was shaken by the prospect of his brother going off to war, and he watched him get in his ute and leave without so much as a goodbye.

Clarrie followed the talk of the war closely, now that he had a friend who would be going. He was much relieved to find out that Geoff wouldn't be leaving straight away. He'd already been training and preparing for some months, but there was some time needed for further preparation. Clarrie determined that he would pray daily that the war in Vietnam would end before Geoff's battalion had to go.

Meanwhile the winter wore on. Football games were played, and occasionally, Clarrie was forced to put on one of the jumpers, as team mates came down with the flu and there was simply no one else to fill the spot. Farmers talked about their growing crops as they gathered at the monthly stock sales and the ensuing afternoon tea served at the Institute. Clarrie continued to be a part of every possible occasion, but there was an edge of anxiety that lay just below the surface. Lyall reverted to his former jovial self, teasing and provoking Clarrie whenever the opportunity arose, but neither of them spoke of Geoff as he prepared to leave for overseas.

Clarrie saw Mrs Arthur at church every Sunday, and he watched her furtively, certain that she was praying fervently for an end to the Vietnam conflict. He didn't quite have the courage to broach the subject with her, as the general Melrose way was to go about your business without showing your emotions to all and sundry.

Then one Sunday morning, a rare event occurred to distract everyone from the troubles of the rest of the world.

"What do you think of the snow?" Jim asked Clarrie, the moment he opened the EH Holden's passenger door.

"Snow!" Clarrie exclaimed in surprise. "Where?"

"On the mount!" Jim grinned broadly. "It's the biggest fall I've ever seen."

Clarrie immediately lifted his eyes in the direction of the looming mountain, surprised that he hadn't noticed it when he'd first opened the door to come outside. Sure enough, the huge, tree-covered landmark was covered in snow from the top to about halfway down her slopes. The pristine white showed through most clearly on the large rocky screes where no vegetation was growing.

"What a beauty. I've never seen snow before!" Clarrie exclaimed in wonder.

"That's not surprising," Jim answered. "It only snows here once in a blue moon."

"Do you think we could climb up and touch it?" Clarrie asked, not once taking his eyes from the wonderful sight of fresh white scattered amongst the blue vegetation.

"Well, you could," Jim replied, "if you can find an adult to go up with you." Clarrie tore his eyes away from the scene for a brief hopeful glance in his Sunday school teacher's direction. "I can't!" Jim said, who immediately understood his look. "I've volunteered to collect for the Salvos today. Red Shield day, you know."

"Oh!" Clarrie's disappointment was quite evident.

"I know," Jim said. "I've already had to go through this with my daughters. Luckily, they are young enough to be distracted by a promise of a ride in the car."

"I wonder who else might be going to climb up," Clarrie said wistfully, as they pulled up at the front of the Methodist church.

"Oh, there'll be plenty of people making the effort to go up. You'll be able to find someone who'd be willing to have you tag along."

Clarrie wanted to go and investigate the possibilities right there and then, but was restrained by the knowledge that Sunday school was due to start. He didn't feel that he could just get up and walk out, now that Mr Bishop had gone to the trouble of picking him up. But despite the fact that he stayed, he had a lot of trouble remembering his memory verse, and was more distracted by the fact that other regulars were absent, and he was all but certain that they'd already begun the trek up to the snow.

As soon as Sunday school was over, Clarrie made a quick survey of who was going in for the main church service, just to see if there were any promising prospects for hiking guides. But other than Auntie Ella, whom Clarrie knew was a great sport, but unlikely at her age to tackle the mammoth task of the full mountain climb, and Mr Bishop who had already told him he wouldn't be able to go, there didn't seem to be anyone else. So Clarrie made a quick decision to skip the main service and go down to the main street to see if there were any people gathering who had a mind to climb.

From the talk of the morning, Clarrie already understood that this was a unique snowfall. On the other rare occasions of snowfall, it had usually melted away by mid morning, but the locals were saying that this time they wouldn't be surprised if the cover lasted for at least the whole day or longer.

By early afternoon Clarrie had reached the snowline but despite the wonder he felt at seeing the snow, there was a nagging disquiet which spoiled the satisfaction of his achievement. From the time he'd made the decision to make the climb on his own, till the point where he had first seen the snow some yards ahead of him, he had been convinced that he would eventually run into another group of climbers. The people he had talked to in the town had said that heaps of people had set out, with plenty of kids in tow. When he'd left his home, he'd told his mother that he would be with other people, but had omitted to inform her that it was other people he was hoping to meet on the way.

Now, the joy of picking up a handful of snow was somewhat lost on the lone climber. The mountain air was freezing, which Clarrie had prepared for to some degree by putting on an extra jumper, a waterproof parka, beanie and gloves. But it was the stillness and quiet that began to raise Clarrie's anxiety. It seemed as if the bush birds were huddled away from the frosty day somewhere, too cold to be bothered with singing. And the sky had begun to cloud over again. When Clarrie had started out the sky had been blue and clear, and the sun had been shining, despite the temperature, but it appeared that heavy clouds were moving in from the west again, dark and ominous.

Clarrie quickly decided that it must be time to start back down to the town, but as he turned back in the direction he'd come, he was hit with an awful realisation. He'd left the trail he'd been originally following some time back, feeling sure that it must be a simple matter finding it by just going down. But what he saw in the immediate vicinity surrounding him were two downward directions. From the plain, Mount Remarkable looked like one great big solid mountain. What many climbers before Clarrie had already discovered was that it was in fact made up of many large rises and gullies. There was no simple downward direction, and quite suddenly, Clarrie wasn't even sure which direction he had come from. To add to this dilemma, even when his logical mind started to work, he realised that the sun was now blocked by the fast moving cloud bank, and he wasn't even sure which direction was which.

Panic was not far below the surface, but before yielding to it, Clarrie decided to think more deeply about the situation. Before his father had died, he'd taken his young son out into the Wirrabarra forest, and Clarrie recalled some of the survival tips his dad had tried to impress upon him as a five-year-old. "Don't panic" was at the top of the list, he remembered very clearly, but the others took more time to recall. Mr Brown had told him that it was best not to wander if he were lost, because that made it harder for rescuers to make a methodical search. But Clarrie decided that he needed to find a better spot to wait than here, as it was open and the ground was covered in snow, which he had just discovered was actually quite wet. Despite the fact that seeing snow had been his object, Clarrie wisely chose to move back in the direction he was almost sure he'd come from, where the ground was not quite so wet, and he began to look for some trees that would provide some sort of shelter from what now appeared to be a certain storm.

Pushing the thoughts of anxiety away, Clarrie began to use his initiative and look for smallish fallen eucalypt branches that had some dried leaves on them, placing them on the top of a large bush. He hoped this would give him extra protection from any more snow or rain that was likely to fall. The constant temptation to give in to the nagging fear was coming at Clarrie like a pesky fly, and it took all his courage, as well as reciting a number of Sunday school verses, to keep panic at bay. While he worked at making a shelter, Clarrie became more and more aware of his surroundings. He saw that the clouds now had almost swallowed up the blue, and those still coming were black with threatening moisture. Clarrie wondered whether it would be more snow or more rain. Either way, if it wasn't for the vigorous exercise of collecting bits and pieces for a shelter, Clarrie thought he probably would have frozen solid. He thought many times of how handy a box of matches would have been right about now. He could imagine setting a small campfire, and deriving some warmth from it, but he hadn't considered that he would be doing anything other than playing in the snow, with other kids, so he hadn't thought to bring anything useful like a box of matches.

The more he thought about the fire that he couldn't light, the more his senses sharpened, till he felt sure he could smell smoke. He shook his head in an attempt to dispel the illusion, worried that his brain was freezing into silliness. But shaking his head didn't do any good. The smell of eucalyptus leaves burning only increased until Clarrie decided to check the surrounding area for visible signs of smoke. He was all but scolding himself for letting hallucinations get the better of him when he noticed grey smoke curling up above the trees. Clarrie blinked twice to make sure that his eyes hadn't joined in the deception, but as the smoke continued to rise into the chilly air, Clarrie had to assume that there was a fire burning, and not very far away. The first fear of bushfire was easily dismissed, as the ground was damp and the air freezing. But with the heavily burdened clouds apparently ready to open upon them, Clarrie hoped that this fire, however it had come into being, would survive the downpour.

Without further thought of his rather inadequate attempt at building a shelter, Clarrie began to pick his way over rocks and logs, pushing bushes aside and ducking under low hanging branches, all the time keeping the smoke in his line of vision. He decided not to 'cooee' call before finding out just whom it was that he was approaching, because surely there must have been somebody there to light the fire. The closer he got, the more evident it became that there was someone else out here in the threatening storm. He heard voices, and eventually, through the trees he saw the bright orange of a tent that had been pitched on a bit of flat ground.

He was only ten feet away, but was shielded by the thick growth, and Clarrie decided to let the two boys know that he was close.

"Hello!" he called out.

Two youths stopped their busy activity of stoking their campfire and looked eagerly in Clarrie's direction, and when Clarrie became visible as he broke through the bush they fairly beamed at him.

"Thank goodness!" the taller youth spoke out. "We thought we were going to have to spend the night out here."

"Yeah! Thank goodness you found us. I was beginning to get scared," the other added.

Clarrie's confusion told on his face. If he hadn't known better, he would have assumed that they were taking him for their rescuer, instead of the other way round.

"Where's your dad?" the first boy asked.

"He's dead!" Clarrie said automatically, but when the look of horror crossed their faces, he hurried to explain. "I mean, he died about seven years ago."

"Oh!" They both gave a nervous laugh. "But you have an older brother or adult with you, don't you?" the second one asked tentatively.

"Actually, no!" Clarrie admitted shamefacedly. "Actually, I'm lost!"

Both the older boys' faces showed their disappointment at this news and for a moment the three of them stared at each other in misery.

"Actually, we're lost too!" the taller boy admitted. "What a thing to have to say, when we're out here doing our orientation badge for scouts."

"You're scouts?" said Clarrie, somewhat cheered. "Then at least you'll have come prepared." By this time he had walked over as close to the fire as he could get, and began to absorb the warmth that it offered, despite the fact that it was smoking badly as the result of partly green eucalyptus leaves. Clarrie noted that as the twigs and sticks were drying out, they were beginning to crackle, and he hoped that the boys would be able to get a roaring blaze going before the rain hit.

"My name's Clarrie Brown," he offered. "I climbed up to look at the snow, but didn't wait for an adult, and didn't figure I'd get lost – but I did."

"I'm Mike, and this is George," the taller boy replied, "and we were supposed to be following a plotted course, following our compass and map, but we lost our compass some time back, and seem to have got ourselves more and more lost."

"Reckon it's gonna rain," Clarrie stated the obvious. "Do you mind if I share your shelter?"

"'Course not!" Mike said. "We've been trying to get this fire going for a while now, ever since the clouds first started coming over. We hoped that the smoke would attract somebody."

"It did! Me! But I'm not much use to you."

"Well, let's see if we can get this blaze going before the rain hits, because after that, we are going to have to sit in the tent until the weather clears."

Intent upon this purpose, George went about collecting more sticks, a bit larger than those already burning, and Clarrie followed his lead. At least he now had some sort of shelter when the rain came, and he had company.

By the time twilight fell, Beth Brown was calling people all over the town, asking if any of them had taken Clarrie with them. She had tried Jim Bishop first, as he was the obvious choice, and then Lyall Arthur, and after drawing a blank with them, she was met with one climber after another saying they hadn't seen Clarrie all day. Finally it was dark and Beth was beside herself. She called the policeman in Booleroo, who in turn alerted the Melrose EFS. By seven o'clock that night two things had become obvious. Not only were Clarrie Brown and two visiting scouts reported lost on the mount, but no rescue team would be able to do a thing about it at night. The heavens had opened and rain had begun to bucket down. What rescuers hoped would be a passing shower seemed set to turn into an all night downpour. On any other night, locals would probably have sat in front of their fires and hummed happily to the sound of rain drumming on their iron roofs. But tonight the whole town was only too aware that three boys, an eleven-year-old and two sixteen-year-olds, were out there in freezing wet conditions. The scoutmaster offered the one consolation that at least his boys had a tent and two sleeping bags, but Beth had no such promise to comfort her during the long, wet night. By two o'clock in the morning, she had called the minister at his manse in Booleroo. She had lost her husband just about seven years ago, and the terror of losing a son had driven her to the point that she wanted either to curse God or to beg for His intervention.

Morning emerged reluctantly as the rain continued to fall. The skies were dull and folks on the plain couldn't even see the mount for all the rain cloud that covered her. Many townsfolk had begun to pray. The conditions were not good for survival, especially for a boy with nothing but a parka and beanie. As soon as the grey dawn afforded sufficient light, the rescue teams assembled in the fire shed and studied maps, and talked about plans of search and rescue. They cursed the rain as it really compromised the safety of the searchers. Trekking would be slow and dangerous, visibility poor, and it increased all sorts of other possible problems, the first of which became obvious when they decided to set out in spite of the continuing bad weather.

The search and rescue captain decided that they would send up two teams, one from the monument, and one from the rubbish dump. They were the two most likely paths that Clarrie would have taken, and the scoutmaster confirmed that his boys had indeed gone up from the rubbish dump route. But when they came down to the Mount Creek that separated the town from the mount, the water had swollen into a fast flowing torrent.

The day before there had been a slight flow of water, not more than two or three inches deep, but the Monday morning light revealed that only a four-wheel drive would make it across, and even then there was some concern.

Joe Clucas immediately offered his Suzuki for the job, but it was decided that it was too small and light to hold against the current. Peter Axford eventually offered his larger Toyota Land Cruiser, and he, along with Malcolm McCallum and Don Bishop, got in the front to begin the drive across the creek. The vehicle moved forward into the muddy, froth-covered water, and those watching from the bank saw just how deep the water was as the Land Cruiser began to sink deeper and deeper, until the water flowed above the door line almost up to the window level. There was a general gasp from onlookers as the vehicle lost traction and began to be pulled sideways by the current, and they watched as the three men scrambled out of the now flooded cabin, their engine completely stalled, and climbed onto the roof.

Without anyone saying anything, someone had gone back to the fire shed and started up the Blitz, which, for a change, had decided to cooperate. Eventually a winch cable was thrown out to the stranded vehicle, which every moment looked as if it was going to be washed completely down the creek, but in the nick of time was connected to the Blitz, and slowly dragged back to the town side bank.

From that moment on, the plight of the lost boys took on a serious new dimension. They were not only lost, but their search and rescue team was stranded on the other side of the creek.

Beth had Ella Bishop and Jean McCallum and others join with her, and they prayed the whole morning for the safe return of the boys.

Chapter
Ten

A call had come into the communications shed, relayed from a CB unit somewhere out along the survey road. Carol Bamman had taken the message from Glen Malcolm, who had been pressed into service manning the CB radio in the shed.

Jenny could see that the blood had drained from Carol's face as soon as she'd read the message, and she had begun to tremble.

"What is it?" Jenny asked, immediately concerned.

"I think I'd better go," Carol said in a shaky voice.

"Yes. Go," Jenny said. "Irene and I will manage."

It was quite obvious that Carol was overwhelmed with anxiety, but it wasn't until she had gone that Jenny asked Glen what the message was that had so shocked her.

"Her husband is trapped somewhere, and the fire is closing in on them. They can't see any way to get out."

"You mean Peter Bamman?" Irene asked, alarmed. "He's with the bulldozer crew, isn't he?"

"Yes, I think so. They left here about two hours ago. Three of them."

"And there was that other fella with them too." Irene said.

"What other fella?" Jenny asked.

"That journalist chap, from Adelaide," Glen replied.

Now Jenny was struck dumb. Clarrie Brown was a city slicker. A tenderfoot when it came to fire fighting, and he was trapped, along with two others.

There was no more communication coming in from them. The mood in the shed became very sombre as they considered this situation in which everybody was helpless. They didn't even know exactly where they were trapped, even if there was anything they could have done to save them.

"It's lucky you knew where to find this cave, Clarrie," Mike remarked as they dragged their sodden tent and rucksacks into the relatively dry, dark enclosure.

"I didn't know where to find it," Clarrie immediately admitted. "I only ever heard about there being a cave, and a bit of a story that went along with it."

The three boys were wet through, and shivered from the cold, despite the fact that they were at last out of the rain and the biting wind.

"Let's hope our matches are dry enough to try and start a fire in here," George said, as he shrugged off his wet overcoat.

Within the hour, the three boys had worked very hard to gather wood from the immediate vicinity, but they were frustrated in their efforts to get a fire going. Even with some paper they had to use as dry kindling, they found that the wood was just too wet. They had shed most of their wet clothes, and draped them over rocks inside the cave, but held little hope of them drying in the damp, cold atmosphere. At least they realised that the two sleeping bags, though a little damp, were dry enough to provide warmth for the immediate time at least.

Sitting huddled together, using each other's body warmth, the three began to talk about being lost, about what plans they would make if they could ever dry the wood out enough to start a fire, and what they would do if it ever stopped raining.

"I reckon the creek would have come down for sure," Clarrie said with certainty.

"So do you think they will send someone up here to try and find us?" Mike asked, a bit nervously.

"They'll send someone, for sure, but in this rain, I don't know how far they'll get. It's a good job we did stumble across this cave."

"What sort of story went along with this cave?" George asked, referring to Clarrie's earlier comment.

"Well, I heard that this cave was haunted."

"Haunted!" the other two exclaimed both alarmed at the idea.

"Yeah! And that's why I'm glad I didn't find it all on my own."

"Who told you that story?" George asked, disbelievingly.

"Oh, my friend. His name's George too, or Georgie. He reckons that some bushrangers used to hide up here in this cave, and go out every now and then to rob the miners."

"Miners?"

"Yeah! There used to be copper mines out behind the mount, and apparently the town was full of miners. I reckon the bushrangers were probably hoping the miners would strike gold sooner or later."

"Is that true?" George asked, clearly sceptical.

"Well, I don't know," Clarrie answered. "That's just what Georgie told me."

"So the cave is supposed to be haunted by the bushrangers' ghost, is that it?"

"Oh, no!" Clarrie said seriously. "No! That's not what I heard. Georgie reckoned it was the ghost of that little child that was killed out here all those years ago."

Neither scout said anything. Clarrie had them totally enthralled.

"There were a few families that used to live out back of the mountain. The Grays were one family, and I heard that their children used to have to climb up and down into the town whenever they came into school. But that was years ago."

"So was it their little kid that was killed."

"No! It was another family. Don't know their names. A number of loggers used to live out here in tents, some with families. Apparently the men used to do a lot of tree felling, cutting railway sleepers for the line between Quorn and Hawker. They'd roll the logs down the hill where they would eventually attach them to a timber jinker and transport them out."

"So, what happened?"

"They were rolling logs one day and one went wild, and before they could stop it, it had rolled over one of the tents. There was a little child asleep in the tent at the time and she was killed."

"Is that it?" Mike asked, somewhat relieved.

"Yes and no," Clarrie replied. "The little grave is still out here, I understand."

"Did your mate Georgie tell you that?" George asked.

"No! It was my piano teacher, Mrs Fuller, and she wouldn't lie to me. There really is a fair dinkum grave out here, of the little kid that was killed."

"And the ghost of the cave?"

"Well, they say that the two bushrangers came into the town one day and got as drunk as drunk, on the good Jacka's beer that used to be brewed here, and they confessed to all of their robberies, and when the troopers asked them why they'd come in and confessed, they said that this little white ghostly child had come to their cave in the middle of the night and told them to take their wickedness away."

For a moment, there was a heavy silence in the dark cave as each of the boys considered the gravity of the story.

"I don't reckon that's true," George eventually said.

"Me either," Mike said, releasing the breath that he'd been unconsciously holding.

"Me either," Clarrie laughed, "but my friend Georgie sure can get the girls at school going whenever he tells it."

"So there wasn't really any bushrangers or woodcutters or ghosts." It seemed like Mike just wanted to be certain.

"I don't know about the bushrangers or ghost, but there really was a family whose little child was killed by rolling logs. That part I know is true. Mrs Fuller wouldn't lie to me."

The older boys were quiet for a while. Their imaginations had been stirred by the story, and knowing that there was a lonely little grave out here somewhere added just an edge of thrill to their plight.

Several locals, including Jim and Don Bishop and Malcolm and Don McCallum, had driven down to the showgrounds and crossed over the swollen creek on the small bridge there. By the time their vehicle was over, the water was already up and flowing over the top of that bridge. And before anybody else had been able to cross, they noticed that the bridge was looking decidedly weak under the strain of the fast rushing water. With a lot of shouting back and forth over the noise of the water, it was decided that they wouldn't be able to send any others across safely. So it was only the four men that proceeded with the original plan.

It had been decided that a rescue team would have to hike through the scrub, back along the creek from the showgrounds to the rubbish dump road, where they would begin the search as they climbed the rain-sodden mountain. Everybody knew that it was going to be difficult with slippery slopes and cold and wind and wet, but something had to be done. The men who had reached the other side of the creek had pulled on the oil-skinned raincoats, hats and strong leather boots. They carried with them backpacks that contained every conceivable thing they thought they might need.

And so began one of the most dangerous climbs any of them had ever attempted, despite the fact that they were all familiar with the tracks and surrounding areas.

The Christian ladies of the town gathered together in the CWA hall and prayed some more.

It was approaching dark again on the second day, and the boys were trying to keep their spirits up, considering they had not been able to start a fire, their clothes were still quite wet, and they had consumed all the food that the scouts had along with them. They had decided that they simply couldn't try to find their way down while it was still raining, and now that the light was gone, even if it did stop raining, it was too dark. Though they didn't say much to each other, they all knew that they faced another long, cold night, huddling together to try and keep warm.

"I reckon the minister would be praying for us," Clarrie said at one point. "I reckon we should pray too, don't you?"

"I don't ever go to church," Mike said quickly.

"Me neither," George added. "Don't suppose even if there was a God that he'd listen to me pray."

"I don't think it makes any difference," Clarrie said, hoping that he was right. "My Sunday school teacher told us that God loves us even if we don't go to church."

"Well, why do you bother going then, if you don't need to?" Mike asked the obvious.

Clarrie thought about it for a bit and then answered slowly. "I guess, because I like going. Anyway, at least I know how to pray, and it can't do any harm can it?"

"S'pose not!" George agreed. "So long as you don't think God will be upset having to rescue a couple of heathens like us."

Clarrie grinned and set out to pray the way he'd seen Mr Bishop and the minister pray. He wasn't quite sure whether it would measure up to the prayer book standard, but at least he'd offered up some sort of plea for help, and in his mind, he was certain that God wouldn't mind whether it was the right words or not.

"Do you really believe that God answers prayers?" Mike asked, not unkindly, but with more of a genuine hope.

"I don't know," Clarrie answered honestly. "He didn't save my dad from being killed in that forest accident, but there are other things I've prayed for that have come true."

"Probably just coincidence," George put in.

"Maybe!" Clarrie shrugged. "But just in case, I'm glad I prayed."

The three fell silent each to ponder on their own faith, or lack of it. The cave was pitch dark now, and there wasn't much any of them could do to better their situation.

They didn't have any idea what time it was when the rain stopped. Because they were trapped, the time seemed to go on forever. But with the quietness of the night, the outside sounds seemed to sharpen, and the ghost story told earlier was destined to come back and provoke their imaginations.

"What was that?" Mike asked, his eyes wide with fright. If he thought either of his companions would answer, he was sorely mistaken, and if he'd had the courage to switch his torch on to see their faces, he would have seen an equal amount of fear etched in their features. The sounds outside the cave had been rain and wind up to this point, but now there were sounds of somebody approaching, and low voices. The three boys froze with dread. None of them said a word when the "ghosts" of four bushrangers came trundling into their safe haven, but when one of the "ghosts" shone a torch in their direction, pandemonium broke out in the cave.

Even though rescuers and boys alike had spent a relatively comfortable night in the cave, they all knew that they would have to make some attempt at getting back down to the safety of the town. They spent some last minutes warming themselves in front of the fire that Don had finally been able to get going, and that had burned all night. With their clothes now dry, and with extra raincoats the men had brought, the three boys felt set to try the descent. Though it had not begun to rain again, the morning skies were still overcast and sulky.

The best part about the descent was that all four men knew exactly which way to go to get back to the trail. The McKenzie's Cave was well known to them. Thank God they had all ended up in the same cave.

The only worry now before them was whether the flood water had gone down or not.

"It's probably gone down some," Don said.

"Yeah, but that water level was pretty high yesterday. I still don't know just how we're going to get back across," Malcolm said sounding truly worried.

"I guess we'll cross that bridge when we come to it!"

They all laughed at the pun, which released some pent-up anxieties.

It took much longer than it would normally have taken had the weather been dry, but the seven walkers eventually came to the creek crossing on the rubbish dump road. Just as Malcolm had predicted, it was certainly impossible to cross on foot, and all four adults doubted that one of their vehicles would make it across either. They knew that the Showground Bridge had now been rendered unsafe, and so unless they wanted to hike another two miles through scrub to the main road bridge up near Coonatto Road, they would have no other way of crossing. There was no one actually at the other side of this particular crossing, but old Mrs Ey's house was on their side of the creek. They decided to go and see if they could raise the EFS team by calling from her house.

Within half an hour there was quite a crowd gathered on the other side of the creek. Clarrie saw his mother with Auntie Ella, looking half-pleased, half-cross. Suddenly being rescued took on a whole new meaning. Once he was safely back at home he was going to have to face the fact that he had attempted the climb on his own in the first place. Momentarily he wondered just how angry his mother would be. Still, he wasn't across the creek yet.

The Booleroo ambulance was on hand with two of their volunteer St John's officers. The local policeman was there, and it looked as if there were a couple of newspaper reporters, whom the policeman was trying to convince to get out of the way. It didn't look as if he was having much luck as they snapped away at shots of the fast flowing creek and the small group of stragglers stranded on the other side.

There looked to be some kind of heated discussion going on

between a few of the EFS volunteers, with fingers being pointed at a four-wheel-drive, and then at the water. The shaking of heads and looks of concern probably told the story.

"I don't think they'd make it across in that," Clarrie spoke for them all.

"They wouldn't," Jim confirmed. "We already tried it yesterday, and the water was lower than it is now."

"We'll probably have to sit it out at Mrs Ey's house," Malcolm was saying, before they were interrupted by a loud cheer from the crowd on the other side.

Everybody smiled, even the waiting-to-be-rescued group. The council grader was turning off the main bitumen road and descending toward the crossing. As it began to plough slowly through the raging torrent, making a bit-by-bit crossing, more than one person said, "Only Joe Clucas!"

Chapter
Eleven

Clarrie could see that they were in trouble. The creek-bed was full of reeds and undergrowth, not to mention the dry fallen branches and all the trees that grew thickly along the banks. With the fire rushing their way, it was like sitting on a powder keg. If only there had been water in the creek. As it was, it was the middle of summer, the temperatures soaring into the forties, and there was no water anywhere near that would save them from the inferno that was threatening.

He was with Peter Bamman, and the bulldozer driver. They were out the back of the mountain, Peter trying to guide the process of grading a firebreak and Clarrie was along as an extra driver. This break was another attempt to contain the fire within the National Park, and not allow it to burn south into the foothills where there were farms and grazing land.

But they had been caught. Clarrie could hear the rush of flames whooshing through leafy branches, jumping from tree to tree, coming more quickly than even he had imagined. They were virtually stranded in the bottom of this dry creek-bed, surrounded by tinder-dry fuel. The bank they'd descended was far too steep to try and get back out that way, and there was only a steep hill in front of them. It was not a good option, considering the propensity of fire to burn up hill rapidly, but it seemed to be their only one.

They decided to try it, but it quickly became obvious that Peter's ute was not going to be able to make the steep grade.

"I'll grade a track up to that flat spot up there," the dozer driver yelled above the roar. Clarrie stood with Peter knowing that all they could

do was stand and watch, monitoring the billowing smoke and the approaching flames. With a rough track graded the dozer returned to the bottom. "Now, I'll have to give the ute a bit a of nudge up the hill." It was like these volunteers to speak calmly, even in the face of danger.

A bit of a nudge was not as easy as it sounded. The traction was almost none, and even the dozer, bearing the weight of the utility, had its tracks spinning around and round until it hit rock and took grip. Still nothing was being achieved. The tension rising with each passing second, Peter decided to start the engine of his vehicle to give that extra horsepower to the exercise. What followed was a series of small advances, followed by the ute rolling back into the blade of the dozer. When they connected, it pushed the back of the ute in, making a noise like a rear-end collision. Clarrie who was riding with Peter could almost feel the vehicle getting shorter by inches but even though he felt for Peter, having his vehicle so badly damaged it was easily dismissed as a minor concern when compared to what was coming.

Eventually, they made the small piece of flat ground.

"We'll go back and get the other bus," Peter yelled. Clarrie didn't object. Though it was the vehicle that he'd been driving, he knew that he didn't have the experience of negotiating such difficult conditions that these men had. He waited with the ute already on the level rise.

But when he saw that the fire was now well over the top of the nearby hill and well on its destructive way toward them he felt a rise of panic in his stomach. He realised that Peter had seen it too as he heard Peter's voice calling from the other truck at the bottom of the hill, coming over the CB radio in this ute.

"Melrose Base, this is Melrose 2-1, over." Clarrie heard Peter make the call several times with no response. They were out the back of the hills and the communication often had to be relayed back to the main base. Peter's call came again, and this time got a response from another CB unit not far away.

"We're trapped," he called into the mike. "The fire's surrounded us now. I can't see a way out. Over."

Clarrie wondered what really could be achieved by communicating this piece of news. The situation seemed hopeless now. He'd seen the bits of burning debris carried by the wind from off the mountain, fall and start spot fires, as if it had its own murderous intent to surround and attack. Below he watched as his companions wrestled with the other four-wheel-drive. They had made small progress when he saw the ute slip from the dozer blade and roll back to the bottom of the hill. There isn't time, *he thought to himself.* Just leave it! *But they returned to start the slow process all over again. Meanwhile the fire raged forward, the roaring of the flames increasing with every yard it moved closer.*

Desperately, Clarrie considered starting a back-burn to leave ground around himself free from fuel, but he knew he couldn't do that until the others were with him. Come on! Come on! *He mentally urged them along. It seemed like an age before they were finally on the small flat. Clarrie thought of a thousand things to say, but none of them seemed useful in the face of the oncoming menace. What advice was there to offer in such a situation? The driver didn't comment, but simply began to grade a break. But it was only one blade thick and the way the fire was approaching with such ferocity, Clarrie doubted it would stop a thing.*

There was no time left. The dozer-driver left his vehicle and jumped into the cab of the ute with Peter and Clarrie. The door was scarcely closed and they saw a twenty-foot wall of fire burst up in fury, right in front of them.

"God!" the driver exclaimed.

Clarrie couldn't think of any words to use. "We're finished!" he muttered under his breath.

The roaring blaze seemed to come right over the vehicles to consume them. The heat and the smoke was so intense, it was unbearable. It seemed that this would be the last few moments of their lives.

For the next fifty or sixty seconds, the beast raged over the top of the parked vehicles, the men inside scarcely able to breathe for the oxygen had been replaced by smoke and heat. This huge struggle for life seemed to go on forever, then suddenly it passed. Not the heat, but the flames.

For a few moments they sat in shocked silence, until finally Peter went to get out of the ute. "I've got to get out of here," he said. Clarrie totally agreed, as he felt like he'd been placed to roast in an oven. It wasn't just the unbearable heat inside the cab, but also feelings of claustrophobia. As they got out onto the blackened ground Clarrie noticed that it was only fractionally less hot than it had been inside, but at least the oxygen had returned. He'd burned his hand as he'd unconsciously touched the door to close it and found the metal was blistering hot. For a few moments they just stood speechless and watched the angry monster as it burned its destructive path.

Then they did a strange thing. They turned and shook hands with each other.

It had been said more than once, someone must have been praying. There were too many close shaves going on for it to be complete coincidence.

Kevyn Mount had gone out in response to the radio call for help, and after finding them, he guided them all back in along a route that only a man who knew the country well could find.

The moment they got back to the shed, Peter took off home to find Carol. Suddenly Clarrie longed for his own wife. After having such a close brush with death, he longed for the reassurance of family; times they'd shared when they'd first married, before things had started to fall apart. He wished that he could have her here with him now, and that he could go to her and just hold her. He wanted to let her know that he loved her, and he wanted to know that she loved him.

What with the snow, the rescue and the flood, there was quite a bit of sensation about the town for a number of weeks that provoked lively discussion. Joe Clucas had been duly applauded for his dare-devil drive across the creek, only this time it was being called heroic, as he deposited all the climbers safe and sound on the other side. The boys had been duly whisked off by the St John's people, and just because Clarrie had suggested it might be a good idea, they had turned their noisy siren and lights on to warn all the traffic to get out of their way – which would have been helpful if there had been any traffic, and if there had been a real emergency. Still, Clarrie felt that if he had to ride in an ambulance, he had better have the full benefit of the ride. All three boys endured a bit of poking and prodding from Dr Wheaton and the nursing staff – observation, they called it - just to make sure that they weren't suffering from hypothermia or any other dreaded ailment as a result of their two-day ordeal.

Meanwhile, the countryside remained sodden as not only the Willochra but also the Wild Dog and Whim creeks came flooding down, bursting banks and causing all sorts of delays and damage. Old timers sat in front of their fires and talked about the floods of '21 and '46 and decided that this one paled in comparison to those truly terrible deluges.

Clarrie heard more than one tale from older residents such as Herbie Ey, who said that he'd sat on the steps behind the Institute and dangled his feet in the floodwater of 1921. Clarrie found that hard to believe, as it would have meant that all the tennis courts and bowling green would have been under water – only they weren't there in 1921. Still, the old timers insisted that it was so.

Vera Fuller was eager to tell Clarrie about the time when she and Frank had lived out on the farm on the plain, and the floodwaters from the Wild Dog creek had covered all the paddocks.

"I can remember on the farm when there were flood waters lapping our veranda and we couldn't get out." Vera said in her story telling voice.

"How did you get out?" Clarrie asked, wide eyed.

"Well, we were marooned," she answered. "We couldn't get into the town, so we just had to make do with what we had."

"Was it scary, being stuck out there in your house?" He asked.

"We'd look out our window and could see all this brown water, like we were in the middle of a brown sea, and it got very frightening because we were watching the water rising higher and higher. Two days it was up and then it gradually subsided, but it left everything looking terrible; the fences were down and it had left all gerky things hanging on lone posts."

Clarrie could easily imagine the 'gerky' things as she called them. He'd seen first hand the bits of debris that lay strewn over paddocks as the floodwaters receded.

But his imagination was captured by the tales of the terrible '21 flood. Every time he heard one of the long time locals tell about it, he came to realise that the flood they'd just been through was only an infant in comparison.

When Malcolm McCallum came in to visit Clarrie, to see how he was recovering from his mountain experience, he told the eager listener a tale that his father had told him.

"Fred Slee rode his horse through the flood waters of three creeks, ten to twelve miles from his place near the Gregory School, to see how his sister, Mrs Carter, was faring. When he arrived at the Carter place, he found them sitting on the roof of their house, the water running through their windows. There wasn't a thing he could do from the back of his horse, so he swam it back to his place again. Wasn't like today," he added. "There wasn't anybody he could phone. No big graders or helicopters, like we read about in the paper, to come and rescue them."

"Did they ever get rescued?" Clarrie asked.

"Well, they lived through it, so I suppose they must have got out somehow, once the water went down. But I heard it destroyed a terrible lot of things – land, stock, fences and homes. Those were tragic times for folks then."

Clarrie was intrigued by the sheer size and power of this flood, and asked his visitor more about it.

"Can't say anything more about the flood of '21," Malcolm said with a smile. "I wasn't even born then, but I do remember the big one in 1946. The Whim creek seemed to have covered the whole countryside. You know our farm at Overdale was a good mile and a half from the creek, and yet the flood water was right up to our veranda, and when we looked out, we could see the water coming like in waves."

"Do you think we'll ever have another flood like those?"

Clarrie asked, not quite sure if the excitement of such a disaster would be worth the devastation caused.

"Not now, I don't reckon," Malcolm said thoughtfully. "There are all these new ideas being put about concerning soil conservation and what not. Have you heard about it at school?"

Clarrie nodded. "Yeah! They've planned a special 'Conservation Day' where we have to talk about looking after the trees and being careful about water and things."

"When my father and grandfather were taking up land out here, the general idea was that rain followed the plough, so the settlers tore up a lot of vegetation that was there, and then they had this notion they should put as much stock as they possibly could on the land. When they had a dry year or two, the stock would eat what little vegetation there was left down to the dirt, and so when the rains did finally come, there was nothing to hold the soil together, and the water just ran rampant throughout the country side."

There was no doubt in Clarrie's mind about all the excitement caused by a flood, both past and present. Being the deep thinker he was, he felt as if he should write down some of the things he had learned and felt during the past week. Writing about the snow and being lost, the flood and even about the tales he'd heard from locals of floods past seemed to be an easy thing for him. He only mentioned his diary-like recordings to Georgie once. His friend hooted with laughter, quite unable to understand why Clarrie should spend time writing when Miss Jolly had not ordered him to, and why he hadn't taken the opportunity to come and practise football instead. At this response, Clarrie secretly decided that if he were to continue writing, he wouldn't make it public knowledge. But to himself, he admitted that he quite liked the way things formed on paper, when he set his imagination to it.

And it was to his newly formed decision to record in a journal that he turned the next week when word reached him that a date had been set for Geoff Arthur's battalion to embark on their tour of duty to Vietnam. Clarrie poured all of his distressed feelings out on paper, and found his diary to be a competent listener, though of course it didn't have anything comforting to say in return. None the less, it did help the eleven-year-old work through some of his misgivings before having to face Geoff's brother, Lyall.

Lyall's response to the news was subdued. He was quiet, and though he never said anything much, Clarrie wondered if he was afraid for his brother.

Geoff's cousin, Carol, organised a send-off party for him from all the young people in the district. It was not something that Beth was going to allow Clarrie to go to. But there was to be an official town send-off that was open to anyone, and though not many other children went, Clarrie made certain that it was a high priority.

At the Melrose institute most families were represented. Frank and Sybil Arthur looked proud of the fact that their son was going to serve the Australian Armed Forces. Of course, Frank himself had been with the Australian Air force in the Second World War, and so understood a great deal about patriotism and service for one's nation.

Lyall had told Clarrie that his mother had been understandably upset when she'd first got the news, fearful, as only a mother can be, for her son who was about to be thrust into the front of battle, especially since she'd already been through the years of having a husband at the front. And Frank also had not cheered at the news, but rather accepted it with the appropriate amount of dignity, forcing his own misgivings to the back of his mind. But now they stood with their neighbours and relatives to honour their boy. The nonsense that had gone on around the rest of the country had not made its presence felt in Melrose yet, and most locals hoped that it wouldn't.

"Fancy putting all that guilt on a young boy who has no say about whether he goes or not," Auntie Ella whispered to Beth in Clarrie's hearing. "Thank goodness our people have more sense than that!"

Mr Dick Bishop, as representative of the council, gave a

speech of well wishes on behalf of the community. As tears stung the back of Clarrie's eyes, he wondered if others were as emotional about it as he was, but when he dared to glance across the room, he saw that he was not the only one who felt deeply about Geoff's leaving.

The minister, Ian Anderson, satisfied all the Christian mothers by saying a few words of encouragement, and then leading the gathering in prayer for the town's representative in the overseas' conflict. To end the formal ceremony, Geoff was presented with a card that everybody had signed, and they had a few more speeches and then some dancing. Everyone put on a cheery face, but Clarrie's imagination couldn't let it go, and he ended up going home rather than staying, and there he poured out his emotions on paper. Now that he had discovered this diversion, his notebook was becoming filled with his thoughts, responses and feelings to many different situations.

From the moment that Geoff left Australia, Clarrie couldn't feel totally at ease. While others apparently got on with their lives, the soldier's young friend wondered constantly just how he was faring in the jungles of Vietnam. The nightly news broadcasts on the ABC nearly always had some report relevant to the business of Vietnam, and most of the time it was portrayed in a decidedly negative way. The way some reporters told it, Clarrie might have accepted that the Australian troops were unwelcome in the conflict, and therefore should not be there, and he might even have developed a prejudice against Australian service men. But because Clarrie knew Geoff, and knew him to be a good friend, he could not accept some of the biased opinions that he heard spoken about constantly.

Clarrie's other friends, including Georgie Greenbank, didn't seem to have any further thoughts about Geoff Arthur, Vietnam, or any other political matter two days after the town send-off. They poured themselves into the normal routine of school, football, and any other activities that presented themselves as desirable.

One attraction that had taken the attention of most of the

town's young people was the Gladstone Drive-In theatre. Since it had become operational in the late 1950's, the local picture shows that used to be held in the institute had dwindled until they had been forced to close down. And despite the fact that Auntie Ella couldn't understand why a young person would waste so much petrol to go flitting forty miles to Gladstone, just to watch some moving picture on the big screen, the young people seemed to find it quite an exciting diversion to everyday life. Clarrie had heard about it, of course, as Sally had plenty of eager boys wanting to take her to the drive-in. But Clarrie could only wistfully dream about such an excursion, as even if his mother had been able to afford it, she was most certainly not going to allow her eleven-year-old to jump in the back of a car with a load of rambunctious teenagers. She had enough misgivings about allowing Sally to go. But it was the age where parents were beginning to feel the full effect of the Freudian philosophy; where teenagers were encouraged to forcefully express their emotional demands, and parents could only stutter and splutter in mild protest.

Mrs Greenbank had plenty to say on that score, naturally, and said that Beth Brown had better mind her daughter, and not be letting her run about with goodness-knows-who, just as she pleased. Even Clarrie knew that was easier said than done.

But Mrs Greenbank didn't know that her own son, Georgie, had been engineering a daring plan of his own. He was not without his contacts, and wasn't above manipulating the truth, tailoring it to fit exactly what he knew his mother wanted to hear.

"I'm going to the drive-in Saturday night," Georgie boasted. "Do you want to come with me?"

Clarrie's eyes widened with surprise at the idea. He would have liked nothing better of course. The way that Sally's friends talked about the drive-in, he was ready to believe that it was hallowed ground.

"How come your mother's letting you go?" Clarrie asked. "Mine never would."

"Don't be daft!" Georgie cried. "Of course she isn't letting me go. She thinks I'm going over to Phillip Deekin's place to stay the night."

"But what *are* you doing?" Clarrie asked, wide eyed.

"Oh, I'm going to Phillip's place, but his parents are going to Adelaide for the weekend, and so his older brother has said that he'll take us to the drive-in."

Clarrie was tongue-tied. He couldn't have said anything if he'd tried.

"We're going to see the new James Bond movie, 'You Only Live Twice', you know, with Sean Connery in it."

"James Bond!" Clarrie suddenly found his tongue again. "You can't watch that sort of film!"

"Why not?" Georgie wanted to know.

"Because, I heard your mother say it is disgusting."

"She'd say that anything other than church is disgusting," Georgie dismissed the concern.

"I don't think you should, Georgie." Clarrie sounded quite alarmed.

"Don't be a prude!" Georgie reprimanded his friend. "There's nothing wrong with the drive-in."

"It's not the drive-in," Clarrie stuttered, "It's the movie!"

"What! I suppose you thought I was going off to see 'Mary Poppins'."

In fact, that was what Clarrie had thought. He'd not sat faithfully through Sunday School lessons, heeding all the warnings about the wrongs and rights of society, to think that James Bond had suddenly become an example of morality. Even at his age he was sure he knew the difference. The small demon that sat on his shoulder, whispering all sorts of fascinating temptations, was quickly vanquished by the angel on his other shoulder, who had quite a case to present. Clarrie could not yield to the desire to consider just how exciting it would be to watch a James Bond adventure on the big screen. Even if he could have got away with it, he was sure his face would advertise his sin the very next time he sat in church, and he would eventually confess it all. He could not even imagine what his mother would say if he practised such a huge deception. Though he could easily imagine what Mrs Greenbank would say when she found out how Georgie had spent his weekend. Clarrie was nearly sick with worry for his friend.

The disturbing interview with Georgie was followed by Clarrie's scheduled piano lesson, and with the idea so fresh in his mind, Clarrie couldn't contain his thoughts.

"What do you think about the drive-in?" Clarrie blurted to Vera, before she had the chance to give her first directive for a scale.

"Oh, I don't know," she evaded. "I've only been there twice since we lost the pictures from town."

"Oh!" Clarrie sounded troubled, and her sensitive nature could detect it.

"What's on your mind, Clarrie Brown?" she asked with a smile.

"Nothing!" he answered too quickly, but when he saw her putting on that 'motherly' I'm-going-to-get-this-out-of-you-any-way look, he pressed on.

"Georgie's going to the drive-in, and he asked me to come, but I know that Mum won't let me go."

"Does your mother have a problem with movies?" Vera asked.

"No!" Clarrie answered. "She won't let me go with all those teenagers, and she can't afford it anyway."

"Well, if you want to go," she smiled, "I'd be happy to take you along. Mr Fuller and I are going to see 'The Sound of Music' on Saturday night. You can probably meet up with Georgie there."

"'The Sound of Music!" Clarrie said, startled.

"Yes! I've heard it is a beautiful story, and has some wonderful music. I'm sure your mother would think it suitable for you to see."

Clarrie was confused, especially considering Georgie had told him it was to be the new James Bond picture. Still, it was more likely that Mrs Fuller would be correct, and if she felt it was all right to go, then he wasn't so afraid for his friend's virtue as he had been.

"You know, when the moving pictures first came out, I used to play the piano for them, down at the institute."

A double bonus, Clarrie thought. She's offered to take me to the movies, and she's off on another of her stories!

"How come you had to play the piano?" Clarrie asked, trying to look the picture of innocence, when really he was trying to prolong the diversion.

"The movies were silent, Clarrie, you know like those Charlie Chaplain and Laurel and Hardy movies."

"There's music for them on the TV," Clarrie said, just a tad argumentatively.

"Yes, they've recorded music for it now, but when they first came out, Lester's Pictures used to bring movies up for us to watch every Saturday night, but there was no sound at all. They paid me to sit up at the piano on the side of the hall and play the music for it."

Clarrie looked suitably impressed. "What sort of music did you play?" he asked.

"Oh, I had to play according to the film. There were words written at the bottom of the screen, so that I could follow what was happening. I had my music in stacks, like for galloping and fires and sad music, and I had it all marked. I had piles of music for comedy and danger, and all sorts of things."

"That must have been difficult, sorting through your music for the right piece, as the movie was playing. You must have known what was going to happen already!"

"No! I'd never seen the picture before. But Mr Fuller used to stand up there with me, and I would call out to him which music I wanted, and he would fetch it from the right pile and put it up in front of me."

"Mr Fuller?" Clarrie tried to reconcile the image of the quiet elderly gentleman helping out in this way.

"Oh, we were just young then. It was when we were just engaged and he used to sit there, but how he put up with me I don't know. I'd have to work out what was coming, and I'd say 'Sad! Sad!' and he'd grab the right piece and put the music down for me; 'Racing! Racing!' I'd go, and he'd provide the music again. Then I might say, 'Funeral, dying' and he'd say, 'Oh, sad!' I got him really well trained."

Clarrie chuckled at the thought.

"I did feel sorry for him though. He didn't see much of the picture at all because he was so busy getting the music for me."

"Did you ever play the wrong music?" Clarrie asked.

"I remember the one time I said 'waterfalls' as I wanted some really tinkly music, but he put the wrong music up. I growled at him and played some trills and arpeggios up and down the keyboard. Afterwards we argued about it, as he got what he thought was waterfall music, because I'd said 'waterfall', and I said to him that I didn't even have any waterfall music picked out! But afterward, I felt rather sorry as I got paid for sitting up there at the piano, and he did it just to help me."

"Were there a lot of people who used to go to the pictures here in the town?" Clarrie asked.

"Oh yes," Vera seemed to be reminiscing about her youth. "They had sixpenny seats. They were on the long stools. And there were the other seats, I think they cost one shilling and nine pence. I always remember Vida Jones when she was only about twelve or thirteen. She always used to cause a fabulous scene. She got so involved with what ever was happening on screen. She would scream out loud whenever there was a chase or anything terribly exciting. And she would cry and carry on if anything sad happened. There was one time when one of the characters died, and of course Vida was very upset. But the next week, the same actor played another character, but Vida had taken the whole thing as reality. She got up from her seat, marched up to the screen and cried out, 'that's not right! You died last time! That's not right!' All the rest of the crowd called out to her, 'Sit down, Vida! Sit down!'"

"Did she really believe that the actor had died," Clarrie asked incredulously, "and risen up again?"

"The moving pictures were such a new thing to us back then, Clarrie," Vera explained, "and Vida was only young. It's so common now, you young people even know who the actors are, and what story they will be starring in next."

"Yeah! Like Sean Connery in the new James Bond movie!" Clarrie let it slip out.

"Well, I hope you never get to see such a disgraceful picture!" the music teacher exclaimed. "It's a shame the way that the movie makers have allowed such terrible things to be shown on the screen for all and sundry to watch! What in the world will be next?"

Clarrie didn't answer, as he didn't want to incriminate himself, and it was he who suggested they'd better get back to the new piece of music she had picked out for him to learn.

But the offer to go to the drive-in was summarily made formal by a phone call to Clarrie's mother and being as Mr and Mrs Fuller were a respectable couple, and they had offered to pay for her son, Beth agreed to allow him to go. Clarrie was ecstatic, but didn't tell Georgie about it. He was still uncertain about the mix-up regarding what picture was showing.

And so, they arrived at the Gladstone drive-in, stocked up with homemade toffees and cakes, and a thermos flask of Milo, to see 'The Sound of Music'. When they'd pulled into their place and had attached the speaker from the stand to their car window, Clarrie was relieved to see Julie Andrews dancing across the Austrian Alps with her guitar case in her hand. He would have hated for Mrs Fuller to have been wrong; to have discovered the mistake at the last minute, and have to turn around to go home.

But Clarrie did laugh when he met Georgie in the kiosk. Frank had given Clarrie twenty cents to spend during interval, and he was just making a thoughtful selection when he saw his two school friends, neither looking particularly impressed.

"Does you mother know you came?" Clarrie asked Georgie.

"No!" he answered sullenly. "And to think I'm going to get in to all this trouble, and all I got to see was 'The Sound of Music'."

Clarrie was glad in the end. He was enthralled with the whole drive-in experience, and was even gratified to notice there were some tense moments with German soldiers near the end of the movie. He enjoyed all this with a perfectly clear conscience. Poor Georgie was sure to be discovered in his deception, and even though it was a respectable movie, he was going to get into a lot of trouble for lying to his mother.

"Poor Georgie!" Clarrie thought, and then leaned back to finish watching the lively story.

Chapter Twelve

The fire had not been contained on National Parks land. It had beaten all the attempted firebreaks, both graded and burned, and now was burning in all directions. However, it seemed that Melrose was now considered safe. That was one back burn that had deterred the wall of flames. Now Wilmington stood as the next vulnerable town, but there were many houses and farm buildings lying in the path both to the north and south of the mountain. The local fire fighters were worn ragged. Many of them worked eighteen-hour shifts, with a few restless hours of sleep in between. There were crews of reinforcements now on hand, having come in from all over the state.

Clarrie made notes of all these facts and made sure it all got back to the paper. Some little bits and pieces were printed, but in Clarrie's mind, it didn't reflect the enormity of what was happening. But then in more sober moments, he knew that the rest of the state and nation could not possibly be feeling what he was feeling. He was a local. The permanent residents of the district might have looked upon him as an out-of-town reporter, but in his heart, Clarrie was a local. He felt the strain and alarm of the people he knew. He offered whatever help he could in fighting this horror. Writing his reports became a secondary thing, but what did become clearer in his mind was his sense of family and home. Quite suddenly he felt he wanted to fight for his marriage.

He decided to call home. He had his words all rehearsed in his mind, an apology ready, some sincere promises already committed in his heart.

But the phone rang out. He waited until later in the evening, when he was sure Sue would be home. She always put the kids to bed before this, and she would have to be there. But once again, the phone rang out. Suddenly he felt cold panic clutch his heart. Had Sue left him? *He decided to call her mother. That seemed like an obvious alternative. When he heard his mother-in-law's voice, he suddenly lost courage. But he asked her anyway.*

"I just tried to ring home," he said in a somewhat shaky voice. "Sue's not there? Do you know where she is?"

"This is the first time you've called in four days!" she accused.

"I know," Clarrie said regretfully as he realised his neglect. "I've been…"

"I'm not particularly interested in where you've been, Clarrie," Mrs Houston cut him off. "Sue is here, with the kids, and we are helping to pay the bills that you've let run way overdue."

"Can I speak to her?" Clarrie asked. He didn't have the nerve to try to defend himself. He knew he was guilty on every count.

"I don't think she wants to speak to you," his mother-in-law answered. "I think the less she hears from you the better."

Clarrie came away from the phone call crushed. He couldn't be angry with Sue or her mother. He knew he deserved their blame. He just didn't have the money to make things right. Maybe there had been a time when he'd had the opportunity to make good, but that was long gone. Now all he had was a life of debt and bad credit; emotionally as well as financially.

In late September, Clarrie welcomed his twelfth birthday, especially as it yielded not only some great presents, but also Beth offered a few treats that probably wouldn't have been allowed on a normal everyday occasion.

Unlike other boys of his age, he very much understood the sacrifice his mother had made to buy him the bike he'd so much wanted. Even though it wasn't the Raleigh with three gears on it, like Georgie had, it was still a bike, and it was red, like he'd hoped for, and had the standard bell and carry rack. He knew that he would spend hours riding around the town and out into the country every opportunity he got. This was one present he knew he would treasure with great pride.

Some of his school friends, including Georgie, Kevin and Phillip, came over after school for a party. Beth organised some sausage rolls and fairy bread, which hardly hit the sides as it was consumed quickly, and she ended up sending them up the street to Young's for a milkshake to try and satisfy the ravenous appetites.

But it was the Saturday following his birthday that was the highlight of the annual celebration. Jim Bishop had agreed that Clarrie and Georgie could come out to Gumville and camp down by the creek, and he had organised for Lyall to come along as well, to oversee the two young boys. Lyall, being much older, was to make sure that all camp fires were properly watched, and that no other mischief was entered into. Mrs Greenbank was of the opinion that it might be a little like asking the fox to mind the henhouse, but Lyall assured the other adults that he would be extremely responsible.

The three campers had borrowed a tent, and some old saucepans and a billy to use on their campfire, and Clarrie had the time of his life for the two nights he was allowed to sleep out under a massive starry heaven.

During the day, Jim asked the boys if they wanted to help him with some jobs around the farm. As it was Clarrie's birthday, he was allowed to make the decision, and he immediately accepted. Jim let him sit in the driver's seat of his Holden ute, and gave him some tips and pointers about the use of the clutch and the column gear shift. Clarrie wasn't too quick at managing a smooth take off but eventually handled it without doing, what Jim aptly referred to, as kangaroo hops.

"Show Day next Saturday," Jim said to the boys as they drove about looking at the maturing crops.

"Yeah!" Georgie answered quickly. "My dad says he'll give me two dollars to spend on the sideshows."

Clarrie was quiet. He had about one dollar fifty, and that was an accumulation of saving and a little birthday money that had been taped inside a birthday card from his grandmother in Melbourne. He knew the rides at the show were about twenty cents a go, and he also knew that Beth would never be able to afford extra money, now that she had so extended herself on the new bike. Clarrie carefully calculated his dollar fifty, taking into account the cost of getting into the show, money for fairy floss and a hotdog, and what would be left to spend on the side-shows. There were some rides he simply had to experience. Hamilton's Bucking Horses had been at the show ever since he could remember, and now they had other rides too, like the dodge-em cars.

"Are you going to put any entries in?" Jim asked the boys.

"Miss Jolly will probably want us to display a page of our dictation or spelling book," Georgie said with undisguised disgust.

"Yes, but are you going to enter something for a prize?" Jim persisted.

"Like what?" Clarrie asked. He hadn't, in the past, taken much interest in the competitions that went on in the pavilions.

"What about some art? Or perhaps you could enter Scamp in the Pet Section."

"I think the show is a whole lot of tom-foolery," Lyall piped up.

"What!"

"What do you mean?" Both Georgie and Clarrie were alert at this comment. Counting down days til the show was something only rivalled by preparing for Christmas, in their minds.

"You always go to the show," Jim observed. "Never noticed you being dragged there."

"Ah, it all started when I was a kid," Lyall began. "Geoff was supposed to be looking after me, but wasn't watching close enough, and I got lost."

"Lost! At the Melrose show?" Georgie scoffed.

"It's all right for you blokes now," Lyall defended. "You're both half grown up, but back then I was only knee high to a grasshop-per, and I'd never seen so many people in my whole life."

"The show's the only time you're likely to see two or three thousand people at Melrose at one time," Jim commented, adding credence to Lyall's story.

"Too right!" Lyall added. "We never see more than a hundred or so at anything other than the show. And I can tell you, with all the cars and strangers about, I wasn't too happy."

"So that put you off the show for life, did it?" Jim asked, half amused.

"Well it would you too," Lyall maintained. "I mean, I wandered out on to the oval on my own, where you weren't supposed to be, and there were all these horses, about twenty foot tall, and I eventually found Vic Blieschke. He was MC on the microphone. When I told him I was lost, he made an announcement, and called my dad to come out onto the oval. But when Dad got there, he towed me off the oval like you wouldn't believe, and was real wild with me, and I was wild with Geoff, because he'd lost me, and then Geoff was wild with everybody because he got told off for losing me. Haven't cared for the show since."

The three listeners chuckled at the story, but Clarrie could hardly believe that this childhood trauma would be enough to put anyone off going to the show. The side-show alley was enough to have all the school kids abuzz with excitement, especially the couple of days before the show, when they would see the big trucks and caravans roar past the school, the merry-go-rounds and dodgem cars on the back.

"I reckon I'm gonna have a go at the boxing," Georgie boasted.

"Don't reckon you will," Lyall said quickly. "You're too young and too small for starters."

"They'd let us go in a junior competition, wouldn't they?" he pushed.

"Probably, if you had enough money to pay."

"Yeah, but your mother wouldn't let you," Jim added wryly.

"I wouldn't tell her," Georgie brushed that worry off.

"Yeah, but I would!" Jim's firm comment put a stop to Georgie's wild audacious claims.

"Geoff got involved in a fight last year," Lyall said, perhaps a little forlornly. They didn't often talk about Geoff, but when his name came up, none of them could help feeling apprehensive for his sake.

"So Geoff entered the competition in the boxing tent?" Jim asked, breaking the reflective moment.

"Oh no! There's more fighting outside the tent than in," Lyall said. "All the young blokes watch the proper fights inside, and then get all fired up and the smallest word or look and there's a brawl outside."

"What happened with Geoff?" Clarrie asked, intrigued.

"Well, I wasn't there, but he told me about it in a letter he sent from Puckapunyal, a while back. Apparently, he and a few of his mates were hanging around the side-shows and a bit of a fight broke out. Geoff was a bit slow on the uptake and some bloke from Pt Augusta hit him fair in the face and took a great lump out from under his eye with a ring he had on his finger."

"Crikey!" Georgie said, showing his amazement.

"Well he went down, and the fighting continued over the top of him, and it was all over by the time he got up again. Then his mates stood apart from the other blokes and eyed each other for a while, and then drifted away."

"So why'd he write to you about that?" Clarrie asked, trying to piece it all together.

"You wouldn't believe, when they were assigned to their huts at Puckapunyal, he walked in the door and came face to face with this bloke he thought he recognised. They looked at each other for a bit, and then Geoff asked him if he'd been at the Melrose show last year, and it turned out it was the bloke who'd taken the chunk out from under his eye."

"Bet that went down well," Jim commented.

"Did they fight again?" Georgie asked, eager for action.

"Nah! The other bloke made some comment about how slow Geoff was that day, they laughed about it, and have got on pretty well since, so Geoff said in his letter."

The boys continued to talk about the show, and all of the

possible attractions, listening to Jim as he talked about what his family had always done for the show in the past. Clarrie was interested to hear how 'Gumville' used to be a Hereford stud farm, and each year they would enter the pure-bred cattle in the competition. Auntie Ella used to spend time washing cattle, and Jim and Don would help their father lead the bulls and cows about the judge's ring. That was before they had married. Now they still put some animals in the show, but not as many as before. Jenny Bishop used to ride horses in the show ring competition, but hadn't done so for a number of years.

"This year, we're going to let our oldest girl ride her pony in the show," Jim said.

"She's too small for that!" Lyall said quickly.

"She's six and a fairly good rider too." Jim said with pride.

"What about Erica Jones," Georgie said. "I heard she'd won some state and national competitions. She must be pretty good."

"She's a good rider all right," Jim confirmed. "She makes us all look a bit shabby in the ring."

"I heard someone say they thought she'd make the Olympics one day, the way she is going," Lyall said enthusiastically.

"I wouldn't be surprised," Jim answered.

"Wow! Wouldn't that be great?" Clarrie said, his imagination running wild. "Imagine a local Melrose girl riding for Australia in the Olympics."

"Yeah, well she rode here first," Georgie said, firmly.

Following the time spent at 'Gumville', especially since all the talk about the show, Clarrie decided that he might look into the business of entering something into the show for a prize. He talked with Auntie Ella about it. She suggested cooking, but Clarrie felt that was something open to a great deal of ridicule for a boy, and decided to avoid it. She didn't bother to suggest needlework or flower arranging, he noticed. She spoke about woodwork, but didn't make a fuss about it when Clarrie said that his dad used to have woodworking tools, but his mum had got rid of them.

At the end of the discussion, it was decided that Clarrie would enter his dog, Scamp, into the Pet Section. He was not likely to be considered a serious entry in the Dog Section owing to his questionable pedigree. Along with this, Auntie Ella offered to donate her best eggs of the week for Clarrie to enter into the produce section. They weren't really his own chooks, but he decided that it would be fun to see if he could win any money. First prize was twenty cents, and if he should win in one or both sections, it would mean a couple of extra rides on the sideshows. Clarrie decided that it was a good idea.

Show day dawned with a magnificent sunrise that Clarrie saw first hand. Normally he wouldn't have seen the light of day until the sun had been an hour or so above the horizon, but this day Clarrie had accepted the invitation to stay overnight at the Bishops' house so that he could help Jim with the loading of the animals first thing in the morning. Besides the Shetland pony that Jim's daughter was to ride in the ring events, Jim had entered several cattle, and a couple of pet lambs for his other daughter. Clarrie was up at five thirty and out in the paddocks walking behind a small herd of cattle, urging them toward the cattle yards. Just as the golden rays of sun were breaking over the eastern horizon, Clarrie was clapping his hands and making odd noises, trying to get the last of the show cattle into the yards. It took some time loading them onto the back of the maroon-coloured Bedford truck, but eventually they were all on board. It was the first of several trips that Clarrie made with Jim as they took the stock, pets and other entries into the show.

By nine thirty, the whole family was ready to go into the showgrounds for the day of carnival activity. Clarrie was in the back of the Bishops' green EH Holden, and when they pulled up at the showground gate, Jim wound down his window to speak to Malcolm McCallum, leather ticket pouch hanging about his neck, on duty to collect money from the show goers. Clarrie had his handful of coins ready in his hand to pay for his entry, but before he'd had a chance to pay, Malcolm had waved the carload through.

"I didn't pay," Clarrie eventually confessed as they drove around the southern end of the oval.

"Don't worry," Jenny said easily. "Mr Bishop is a member of the show society, and he gets free tickets every year."

Clarrie wondered if he should object to this generosity, and insist upon paying, but when he considered that he had probably saved himself twenty cents, and that this represented another opportunity to experience a thrilling sideshow ride, he decided to quietly accept.

Jim parked the EH amongst the many other cars that had already found a spot on the hillside sloping up from the western side of the oval.

"Thanks for your help this morning, Clarrie," Jim said, as he pulled the park brake on. "Come around to the Cattle Section a bit later on and see if we've won any prizes."

"Thank you for the free ticket," Clarrie returned as he began to get out. "I'll go and make sure that Mum has brought Scamp in. I need to brush him and make sure he's ready for the judging."

Clarrie had already bathed Scamp the day before, and had given strict instructions to his mother not to let him outside for fear that the little black dog would go and find something smelly and dirty to roll in before he'd had his appointment with the judges.

By ten o'clock the judging began, and Clarrie was shut outside the pavilions where he'd left Scamp on a leash to impress the judges alone, and his eggs were set amongst the other produce. While Clarrie had been sure that Auntie Ella's donated eggs looked like real beauties, he wasn't really sure what it was that the judges were looking for that would set his eggs apart from any of the other entries.

None of the competitors were allowed back into the pavilions until twelve o'clock, and so Clarrie knew that standing about anxiously for two hours to see whether he'd won a prize or not was a poor use of his time. He began to walk over toward the north end of the oval, where all the sideshows were set up, to see if he could find any of his friends.

It didn't take long to find Georgie, Philip and some of the

other kids. They were already lining up to purchase tickets at some of the sideshows.

"Come on, Clarrie," Georgie urged. "I've already had a go on the bucking horses. I'll go again with you!"

Clarrie's mind was busily calculating the cost of the rides and measuring it against the handful of silver coins he had jingling in his pocket. There was no doubt that he wanted to ride the bucking horses, and to feel the thrill of flying through the air, swinging in and out as he went, but he didn't want to part with his savings too quickly. He was aware that there was the whole day, and he wanted to make the supply last.

"Come on Clarrie! We haven't got all day!" Georgie was insistent, and Clarrie instantly decided that he would indulge this once and worry about the rest of the day later.

By the time they'd finished the ride, Clarrie was tempted to buy another ticket immediately. Georgie had mounted his painted wooden horse and had fairly made the animal soar, using his legs to fling the horse out sideways so that he almost rode parallel to the ground. Clarrie had seen Georgie's antics from behind, and had admired the confidence and skill, but had only gingerly begun to experiment in a similar manner when the ride finished. His economic caution was momentarily thrown to the wind and he joined the queue for the second time.

Even after the carnival operator called the riders off for the second time, Clarrie was itching to try again. The thrill of aerobatics had taken hold of him. But as Clarrie watched Georgie and a couple of the others line up in the dodgem queue seemingly without a financial care in the world, he was jolted back to the reality that he had only so much and no more. He steeled his mind against the urge to join them and said he would watch this time. This decision, of course, was met with cries of opposition, but Clarrie's mind remained firm.

When the dodgem ride was over, Clarrie decided to assert himself. "Let's go and have a look at the horses in the show ring," he suggested, using his most confident tone.

"Horses!" Georgie hooted. "What for?"

"Because…why not?" Clarrie defended, losing some of his edge.

"Because they're boring," one of the other kids said easily.

"Yeah, but it doesn't cost any money to watch, and we can save what we have for later in the day."

"If you run out of money, you can go and ask your mum for more," Georgie said, perhaps a little insensitively.

Clarrie didn't want to make any more argument. He felt very awkward about his mother's financial situation, and didn't want to admit it to his friends. He wandered around the sideshow area with the group of kids for a while longer, watching as each one enjoyed different attractions. Clarrie was just about to allow himself to be talked into trying to shoot the moving metal ducks in the shooting gallery when he heard someone shout, "They're warming up for the trots!"

That immediately sealed it for Clarrie. Whether the others joined him or not, he was going to go up to the ringside of the oval to watch the first trotting event of the day. Clarrie had seen Spen Fuller many times training his trotter out on the roads around Melrose. He'd also heard the butcher, Sid Arthur, talk about his horses and the races he'd driven in. There were quite a number of local chaps who were registered with the South Australian Trotting Association, who raced at the country shows.

Clarrie found that the other kids were too intent on spending their 'endless supply' at the sideshows to be bothered coming with him, so he walked around to the eastern side of the oval on his own, but it wasn't long before he saw someone he knew. Vera and Frank Fuller were sitting on their foldout picnic chairs right up near the oval fence, watching the action in the show ring.

"Hello, Clarrie," Vera called to him, and waved him over. "You on your own?"

"I was with the others over at the sideshows, but I wanted to see the trots," he explained.

"Well you'd better hurry," she said. "They've nearly finished the preliminary warm up."

Clarrie came and stood next to the Fullers, leaning on the fence.

They weren't far from the start, and could easily see the half dozen horses and trotting carts lining up behind the elastic barrier that was stretched taut across the trotting track. There was a new voice coming over the public address system, a man from Jamestown who followed the trotting events around the countryside especially to commentate the races. Unlike the easy laid-back tone of Vic Blieschke as he called the other events of the day, the trotting commentator had a more nasally tone, with an urgent ring in his voice.

"And they're racing," he said as the elastic barrier was let go and it sprang back across the track. The horses lurched forward, and the drivers sat up, urging their animals along with some quick flicks of their long whips. They quickly approached the place where Clarrie stood and he watched the group move past, the horses pounding hooves thundering an even pattern over the hard-packed crushed limestone, and the thin rubber-tyred cart wheels whizzing past, carrying their burden.

Clarrie gathered bits of information from Frank and Vera about the various drivers. There were three locals, each one easily recognised by their distinctive brightly coloured driver's uniform.

"They each register their colours with the Trotting Association," Frank explained to Clarrie as they watched the horses round the far turn. "My brother, Spen, wears the plain blue jacket with the white cap, and Sid Arthur wears the blue and white diamond-patterned jacket with the blue cap."

"Mr Arthur is coming second," Clarrie observed. "Who's that driving in first place?"

"That'll be Gordon Pearce," Vera answered over the sound of the horses thundering past.

The racers were on the last lap, so the commentator informed them in his rushed commentary. Clarrie watched with heightened enthusiasm. He didn't really know Gordon Pearce, but he knew the butcher really well, from all the times he'd helped rescue Scamp, so Clarrie decided to barrack for Sid Arthur.

"He's throwing everything at it," the commentator said of the leader, Gordon Pearce. "He's thrown himself out!"

This second comment was accompanied by a collective gasp from the crowd gathered around the oval as they watched the mishap unfold before their eyes. Gordon Pearce had been throwing everything at it, leaning right forward, really urging his horse toward an almost certain victory, but his foot slipped out of the stirrup on the last turn, he lost his balance and tumbled out of his cart onto the track. Luckily, he was on the inside, out front, and he had the quickness of mind to immediately roll onto the grassed oval, out of the path of the oncoming pacers. His horse seemed to lose direction and urgency and Sid Arthur, who had been running a close second, simply moved around the outside of the now driverless horse, and went on to win. By the time Sid had crossed between the finish posts, most of the crowd had begun to breath again, relieved to see that Gordon Pearce was standing on his feet, brushing dust and grass from his uniform.

"My goodness!" Vera exclaimed. "That was extremely lucky. Thank goodness he wasn't hurt!"

"That's one reason I'm glad I don't drive anymore," Frank commented.

"Did you use to race trotters?" Clarrie asked.

"Oh, yes!" Vera answered for her husband. "All the Fullers were horse mad."

"Except me," Frank threw in. "My brother Spen is still, as you can see."

"And of course, Jim was killed, thrown from a horse, years ago." Vera added.

"I'm sorry to hear that," Clarrie said soberly, easily remembering the pain of loss from his own father's accident.

"Still, they don't have many accidents with the trots. Nothing real serious anyway," Frank said. "Not that that fact is likely to induce me to drive again. Not really my cup of tea."

"But they are exciting to watch, aren't they?" Clarrie said.

"My word!" Vera said plainly. "Most everybody leaves what they're doing to come across and watch the trots. Even the blokes at the booth put down their schooners for twenty minutes."

Frank laughed at his wife's comment. "Do you want to sit down for a while, Clarrie?" he asked. "Have a cup of tea?"

"An eleven-year-old is not likely to be wanting to sit down to a cup of tea with a pair of oldies like us," Vera said clearly.

"I turned twelve, last week," Clarrie wanted that point clarified.

"But you would prefer a coke or a lemonade, wouldn't you?" Vera said.

Clarrie didn't want to appear rude, but he nodded the affirmative anyway.

"Tell you what," Frank said. "If you go over to the tank and buy us a billy of boiling water for our tea, I'll give you ten cents to go and buy yourself a lemonade."

Clarrie smiled and easily agreed. It was an easy way to earn a cool fizzy drink. He took the Fullers' billy and the ten cents to pay for the water, and walked back toward the main pavilion. Out the back of the pavilion was a huge square tank, the sort they used on the back of a ute to fight fires. It was mounted on a small brick wall so that it was up off the ground and had a good hot fire going underneath. Rex Deekin was nearby, making sure the fire was hot enough to keep the water on the boil, and he was taking the money. Clarrie was careful not to spill the scalding liquid as he took the billy from Rex and carefully made his way up the bank to where the Fullers were sitting.

"Now you go and buy yourself that drink," Vera directed, "and then go and find your friends. But before you go, you'd better take a little cake with you." She opened her picnic basket and the cake tin inside, and offered Clarrie a little chocolate butterfly cupcake with jam and cream inside. Clarrie knew what Georgie would say if he saw what Clarrie had been given, so he decided to polish off the cupcake and the drink before he found his friends again.

By the time Clarrie found Georgie and the gang, and then spent money on another three sideshows, it was nearing midday. He'd told the others about the excitement of the spill at the trots, and they'd all agreed that they should have come with him to watch. Clarrie assured them that there would be another race directly following the official opening at midday, so this time all of the young friends made their way up to the oval and watched as the President of the Mt Remarkable Show Society, Ken McCallum, was escorted to the microphone to the accompaniment of the Port Augusta Pipe Band. Clarrie had to agree with his friends that he wasn't particularly partial to the droning sound of bagpipes, but they certainly looked a well turned-out company in their kilts and busbies. The president had with him some important member of parliament who was to officially open the show. The kids remained respectful as the speeches were made, and watched as the official party left the oval again.

"They'll go to the main pavilion for the official luncheon now," Clarrie said knowledgeably.

"How do you know?" Georgie asked.

"Everybody knows," Lorretta Young spoke for Clarrie. "My parents cater for the official luncheon."

"Is it open for anybody?" Georgie asked.

"No!" Clarrie said. "It's only for the members of the Show Society. They all sit down to a table set with linen, and they have some more speeches and stuff."

"You seem to know a lot about it," Georgie said, slightly miffed that he wasn't the one with all the information.

"Auntie Ella and Mr Bishop both go. She told me all about it." At that point, the Jamestown caller began to announce the next trotting race and all talk about the official party was forgotten in the face of a far more exciting prospect.

Clarrie's friends were somewhat disappointed that no great fall occurred to colour the race, but it was none the less a spectacle to see.

They moved from there to the hotdog stand and each purchased something to cure their hunger pangs. Clarrie looked at the change he had left and saw he was down to his last thirty cents. Rather than make an issue of it, he excused himself and decided to go and see if he'd won any prizes in the pavilions.

Scamp wagged his tail happily when he saw his master coming, and Clarrie couldn't resist the doggie smile that was cast his way. He had to pat his dog affectionately, even though he'd only won a third prize. The money for third was all of five cents. Still, it would be enough to buy sticky, pink fairy floss before he went home for the day.

He wandered into the pavilion that displayed the produce, and searched among the various dishes of eggs for his entry. Once again he was only slightly mollified to see he'd taken another third prize. For the life of him, he couldn't see the difference between one dish of eggs and the next, and was glad that he hadn't been called upon to talk about the virtues of his particular entry.

Then he discovered that he couldn't collect his prize money until four o'clock in any case, and so he had to accept the fact that he would have to amuse himself looking at the various displays and entries rather than go back to the sideshows.

The cookery section looked tantalising with the many plates of cakes, biscuits and scones displayed. Certain women seemed to have their names displayed on prize cards quite frequently. Marj Thompson, Mollie McCallum and even Auntie Ella scored a few prizes.

The far end pavilion also housed the flowers, and the smell of spring blooms was totally overwhelming as he walked around and admired the various arrangements. The sweet peas and roses and various daisies were truly magnificent.

True to his word, Clarrie eventually wandered over to the Cattle Section and saw Jim's cattle securely tied in their stalls. He was pleased to see that he'd won two or three ribbons. Earlier, he'd seen Jim's daughter riding her small Shetland pony in the ring event. He still couldn't get over the fact that she was so small, but she did hold herself confidently, and wasn't the only young child in the ring. She'd come away with a green ribbon, signifying third place, and Clarrie felt proud on Jim's behalf.

During the afternoon, Clarrie had seen his sister Sally walking about with her friends. All the girls were done up to the nines, dressed in what looked to be brand new outfits. Clarrie knew that Sally had been saving her birthday money for a new dress to wear to the show. He couldn't quite understand it. They had high-heeled shoes on, which he felt was totally impractical.

"Have you seen Mum?" Clarrie asked his sister before she went past.

"She didn't come." Sally said off handedly.

"Why not?" Clarrie asked, surprised.

Sally took him a little away from her group of friends and spoke softly to her brother. "You know that she's tight for money, Clarrie. She could hardly afford to let us come, let alone come herself." Clarrie nodded sombrely. He knew the truth of it, but always hoped that something would one day turn in their favour, and that they would have plenty to be able to do with just as they pleased.

He watched as the group of high school students walked away talking and laughing. He guessed that Sally had probably spent all her savings on her dress, and that she probably wouldn't have had any left for sideshows. An idea quickly came to him, and he jogged quickly after them.

"Sal!" he called. She stopped and turned back to look at him. "I've got some spare money if you want, for the sideshows." As he held out his last precious thirty cents he thought he saw a sheen of tears in her eyes. She looked at him almost hopefully. "Are you sure, Clarrie?" she asked.

Clarrie nodded, bravely fighting back the desire to pocket the money and run.

"You really are a good brother," she said. "You're sure you've had some rides and things?" she asked again.

"Really, Sally. I want you to have at least one turn."

She smiled in a manner Clarrie didn't often see – loving and caring – and took the money as if it was really something quite precious. And it was.

"Thanks, Clarrie," she said before turning away. "I'll make it up to you some time."

With no money left to spend, Clarrie found wandering around with his friends a bit trying. They had gone back to their parents and had come away with more, but Clarrie had no such luxury. He found himself standing alone watching the others enjoying the rides and games of skill, like the darts and shooting. He knew it was nearly time for another trotting race and mentioned this to his friends. They all went together, but when they saw that it was only show jumping for another twenty minutes, they chose to return to the sideshows. Clarrie decided to stay and watch the horses in action. Erica Jones was jumping and as Clarrie watched her direct her mount over the carefully laid course of jumps, he had to agree that she was something pretty special in the way of a rider. He didn't know a lot about equestrian events, but even he felt that her riding stood out from other riders. He wasn't too surprised to see her awarded the blue first prize ribbon at the end of the jumping event.

"Hello, Clarrie!" Clarrie turned to see Lyall Arthur coming to sit on the plank next to him. "Have you been having a good time?" he asked.

"Yeah!" Clarrie answered enthusiastically. "I thought you didn't like the show." He reminded his older friend of the story he'd told last week.

"Oh yeah, but it is the big social event of the year. I could hardly stay at home sulking because of one bad childhood experience, could I?"

Clarrie laughed. "You haven't bought a new suit for the occasion," Clarrie pointed out.

"Not on your life!" Lyall said. "That's the sort of thing my cousin, Carol, would be into. I remember on show day a few years back, when she was still in high school, she had this new outfit and high-heeled shoes. Auntie Lorna advised her not to wear it as it was a wet cold day, but you know what girls are. She insisted. Not only did she freeze, but she kept getting bogged in her high-heeled shoes."

"Does she know that you tell that story about her?" Clarrie asked, thinking what Sally would do to him if he dared repeat such a thing.

"She'd tell you the story herself, if you asked her," Lyall maintained.

"Anyway, it's a beautiful day for the show today," Clarrie remarked. "It's a good job it hasn't rained or anything."

"Well, I remember a few years back when the show was on, there were bus loads of people from Port Pirie and Port Augusta and cars all over the hillside, like today, and a terrible rain storm blew up and drowned the show out. In the finish, Laurie Bishop had to bring in his tractor to pull out all the bogged cars and buses."

"That would have been a bit messy," Clarrie remarked. "Mrs Fuller told me that the train used to run from Gladstone and brought heaps of people, dropped them off just over where the railway line runs near the showgrounds, then went up to Wilmington and brought more people down from there. The train wouldn't have got bogged!"

"No, but I suppose the people might have got fairly muddy tramping around in the wet."

Just then the trotters were back on the track and doing the three-minute warm up.

"I heard my Uncle Sid won a race earlier today," Lyall remarked.

"Didn't you see it?" Clarrie asked.

"Dad told me about it, so I thought I'd better do the right thing and watch at least one race for the day."

Clarrie was glad of Lyall's company as they eventually stood to watch the race. As the pacers broke from the starting barrier a great cloud blocked the sun and the oval went into shade. This didn't make any difference to the spectators, but what happened a bit later in the race when the cloud suddenly cleared certainly made a difference to one horse and driver.

Sid Arthur was in the lead again, and was holding to the inside of the track. Lyall and Clarrie were barracking for him seeing that he was Lyall's uncle. But when the sun broke through again, quite suddenly a long shadow from the football floodlight appeared starkly across the inside of the track. Sid's horse responded as if it was a log on the track and attempted to jump it.

But because the horse was hoppled with long straps that tied front and back legs together, a technique that ensured the horse paced rather than galloped, it couldn't effect a jump properly. It succeeded in tangling its legs and ended up crashing down on its head. A mass of confusion followed, drivers and horses being turned off the track, and the downed horse thrashing about in its harness and shaft of the lightweight cart. Clarrie and Lyall's eyes were glued to the sight, and like most spectators, couldn't have spoken if they'd tried. The race was abandoned. This time, the driver simply didn't stand up. St John's officers raced from their tent and out onto the track. Dr Wheaton was called away from the official luncheon, and there were some very tense moments while those watching wondered just how badly Sid was injured.

Clarrie didn't move from his spot, and wouldn't until he was assured that the town butcher, Lyall's uncle, was perfectly all right. Eventually Sid was moved from the track on a stretcher, and taken by ambulance to the Booleroo Centre Hospital. He had been kicked in the head, and so there was some concern for concussion, and it appeared he might have injured his back in some way.

The incident managed to take some of the shine off the afternoon's events. And when Georgie and the others found Clarrie, they were chagrined to know they had missed the whole thing again. Clarrie told them what had happened, but until he was assured that Mr Arthur was out of any possible danger, he simply could not glory in the fact that he'd been an eyewitness.

Chapter Thirteen

Despite his personal problems, the fire was the subject that took first place in Clarrie's mind. He knew he couldn't do anything about home, and so he chose to stay on in the town and do what he could.

Before long, Clarrie had been assigned as part of Jim Bishop's small crew. This time they were headed south out along the survey road and into an area behind the Mount known as the Saddle. Clarrie heard the instructions, and though he didn't fully understand the routine, knew that they were supposed to be holding a certain front. When they arrived, it became apparent that they were responsible for watching about a hundred metres in area. They were in a depression that rose on three sides. One side of the valley had already suffered from the raging fire, and their job now was to watch for loose burning debris that could easily roll down the hill and set the rest of the valley alight.

They were down there for some time, each man in his bright yellow overalls, knapsack on his back, watching for any possibility of a flare-up. The temperature was still high, and the wind had picked up again, but still the men held their ground. Then there was a call on the radio telling the crews to get out as they'd lost control of the fire further along. Clarrie couldn't see anything as they were so low, but he followed the rest of the men as they began to walk up the unburnt slope towards the parked vehicles.

"This grass would burn in an instant," he commented to Simon, Jim's son-in-law, as they made their way through the knee high dry undergrowth. It was not a pleasant thought and perhaps made them hurry just that bit faster. The vehicles were parked along the track

that led to the top of the Mount. One side of the track had already been burned, and the other sloped down and was still thick with dry grass and bush. The men were three quarters of the way up this slope when one of them yelled out.

"It's coming up behind us!"

Clarrie turned quickly, and to his horror, saw that the fire had appeared, seemingly from nowhere, and was burning up that slope at an alarming rate. The flames were eating up the dry grass, and as they burned straight up, caught the ground in front quickly and easily. By this time all the men were running frantically up the hill. Clarrie found his breath coming in hard painful gasps but knew that he couldn't stop to rest. His calf muscles throbbed in pain, quite unused to this kind of punishment, but Clarrie instinctively knew that being burned alive would be a far worse agony. He kept on until he reached the first vehicle. Andrew had reached it before him by seconds, and left the door open for him to get in as well. Simon went straight for the second vehicle in the line and just got inside with another fellow. Clarrie watched in horror the scene behind him. The whole slope that had sat peacefully some moments before was alive with flames, leaping and licking the sky. Less than a metre in front of this orange demon ran Jim. Clarrie urged him on in his mind. The flames were literally reaching out to touch his back. "Dear God, save him," Clarrie said out loud.

They hadn't thought to leave the door open for him, but it was too late in any case. The flames all but had him. Then Clarrie watched in amazement as Jim did what would have been a perfect swan-dive, only it wasn't a nice clear pool, but the hard metal tray top of the four-wheel-drive that he landed on. The roar and the crackle of fire were right on them, accompanied by the choking smoke. Clarrie couldn't breath, even as he tugged his overall up to cover his mouth and nose. The oxygen was gone, and in its place was the asphyxiating smoke.

For the second time in as many days Clarrie stared death in the face. His own mortality was never more apparent than now.

Then, as if somebody had peeled back the lid and let the air in, a wave of oxygen came to soothe his tortured lungs.

"Thank God," Clarrie said, and then got out of the ute to see if Jim was all right. Men emerged from the vehicles slowly. The fire had consumed that hill right up to the road and then found nothing else to destroy and died right there. Jim got up from his face-down position on the back of the ute.

"I thought I was gonna be cooked," he said. "That was hellishly hot."

Clarrie looked at the others, the look of shock and fear evident on their faces. He knew later he would laugh about this, but now he had to cry.

The show day had been an eventful day, but it was not until later that evening that Clarrie could relax and enjoy his experiences.

He had told his mother about the accident and held on to his concern until in the early evening she suggested Clarrie ring Lyall and find out how his uncle was.

"He's going to be all right," Lyall said. "He is a bit shaken up, and has done some damage to his back which might take a few weeks to sort out, but he'll live."

Clarrie was very relieved to hear this. "I had terrible visions," he confessed. "You know my dad was killed in an accident – not at the trots of course."

"We were all concerned," Lyall stated. "My grandfather, Wally Arthur, was killed in an accident a number of years back, and Sid was the one who was there at the time. We all had terrible thoughts remembering what happened then."

Clarrie wanted very much to ask what had happened, but didn't feel it was polite, and so his curiosity was assuaged when Lyall decided to volunteer the story anyway.

"Wally, my grandfather, had responded to a council decision to begin to clear box-thorns from the area by making a start on those on his place out at Willowmere. He had his dray hooked up with one horse in the shafts and two leaders chained to the dray by their collars. He had ropes and chains around the boxthorns and was pulling them out one by one. Sid was out there helping him.

Wally was standing on the back of the dray and urging the horses forward, but the two front pullers turned a bit quickly, instead of pulling straight, one side wheel dug in and the dray tipped with him on top. Sid said he saw it go over on top of him, and tried to lift the dray, but he simply couldn't. But what he saw told him that it was no use. There was a stream of blood running out from underneath. He raced to the house and called the McCallums at Overdale. They helped him, but it was a gruesome sight. Apparently my grandfather's head was crushed."

Clarrie was silent with the grimness of the tale. No wonder the Arthurs were deeply concerned this afternoon, with that dreadful thing having happened not so many years back.

When he came from the phone he was relieved for Mr Arthur's sake, despite being troubled by the sad story of his father. He decided to sit down and tell his mother about the day's events.

"Sally told me you gave her some of your own money to spend," Beth said. "That was a very kind thing to do."

Clarrie smiled and ducked his head, as if to avoid embarrassment.

"Well it was," Beth insisted.

"Maybe," Clarrie responded. "The thing is, a bit later on, Mr Lolly McCallum…"

"Who?" Beth interrupted.

"You know, Mr Ken McCallum, the one who always gives kids a black and white peppermint when he says hello." Beth nodded. "He saw me taking a last look at the sideshows and asked if I had money for a ride. By that time I didn't, and he took twenty cents from his pocket and gave it to me. I told him that I'd had plenty of rides during the day, but he said it didn't matter, and hoped I'd have fun."

"That was very kind of him," Beth commented. Clarrie agreed, of course. Ken McCallum always had a friendly word, and a welcoming smile. "Actually, after the accident, I didn't feel much like riding the sideshows, so I went to one of the stalls and bought you something." Clarrie retrieved a brightly coloured scarf from his pocket and handed it over to his mother.

"Oh, Clarrie," she said. "That is really lovely. I can hardly believe it only cost you twenty cents."

Clarrie smiled. He didn't bother to tell her that with the ten cents prize money, and ten extra cents that Sally contributed back to the present, it actually cost forty cents, but he was pleased none the less with his mother's obvious gratitude.

The show day and accompanying excitement soon merged into the realms of the past and the school children settled back for the final term of grammar, spelling and arithmetic. Miss Jolly seemed to be in a high temper, frowning a lot more than usual, and waving her ominous looking cane about threateningly.

November approached, and Clarrie listened to the farmers talk about the ripening crops and the estimates of how many bags to the acre would be reaped, and when the reaping would begin. There was a lot of talk about ordering parts for tractors and headers and trucks. All seemed to be getting ready for the wondrous ritual of bringing the crop in from the paddock.

Auntie Ella told Clarrie how they used to reap the grain with horse drawn headers. She told how they would winnow it in a separate process, then bag the grain, sewing each bag up by hand and loading them onto the back of a bullock dray. "In those days," she said, as all old timers do, "they used to take a couple of days to cart the bags down through the Gorge to Port Germein. The windjammers would sail through and the grain would go by sea to Adelaide."

Clarrie was always intrigued with the stories of times gone by. He could see the wistfulness in the eyes of the older people like Auntie Ella and Mrs Fuller, as they talked about a life that was so vastly different from the modern age where the train and telephone had replaced the bullock dray and letter. Even though the television set had found its way into the homes of many of the older generation, their talk still revealed how they felt about the burst of technological advancement.

"And what do you think about this satellite business, Clarrie?" Auntie Ella had asked him in the same conversation. "Imagine, now Australia has gone and launched a satellite from Woomera into the heavens. What on earth will be next?"

"I think they'll try and send a rocket to the moon," Clarrie answered confidently, having followed the 'space race' news carefully. "I hope they send it up from here in Australia. That would be something else, wouldn't it?"

"Good heavens!" Auntie Ella exclaimed. "What call have we got to be wandering about the stars, I wonder. It's bad enough we send our boys off to Vietnam of all places, let alone to the moon!"

Clarrie always laughed at this type of conversation. He decided that when he grew older he would have a television in every room, and if by then it was possible, a telephone too. He was not going to be the sort of old fuddy-duddy that pooh-hoohed every new innovation.

But rockets and satellites aside, there was still grade six to contend with, and along with it the upcoming annual Strawberry Fete. Now if it had just been going along to a lively community event to eat the delicious strawberries dusted with icing sugar and served with cream and ice-cream, then that would have been perfectly all right. But as it was, there was to be an evening full of entertainment. That would have been all right too, but it was well known that Mrs Fuller's piano students were strongly encouraged to perform to the town audience. Of course Clarrie was still taking lessons, he enjoyed Mrs Fuller's company too much to give it up. But his achievement with his piece, 'Larkspur', hadn't progressed nearly as well as it should have. And yet that is what Mrs Fuller had put him down to play at the Strawberry Fete.

Clarrie was all of a dither over the prospect. First of all, the other boys would have first hand confirmation that he'd been taking lessons, and second, everybody in the town would then know just how bad he really was.

"You will play it beautifully, if you spend the next two weeks in earnest practice," Vera encouraged. "Now I don't want you to be shying away from this, Clarrie," she said firmly. "You are quite a lot better at music than you will admit. Your only downfall is that you don't practise nearly enough."

The bell had tolled, so to speak. His mother's sacrifice in paying for lessons was quite understood by him, and the fact that it was one of his deceased father's hopes that he should reach some level of accomplishment as a musician was the clinching factor.

Of course, Clarrie and his teacher were great friends, and when he'd heard tales of another piano teacher who lived out along the Survey Road, of whom it was said that most students came away from lessons in tears, Clarrie elected to stay with Mrs Fuller.

Now, with the threat of a performance looming, he supposed that he had better apply himself. One way or the other, he was going to be found out, so he decided that if he had to be mocked by his school friends, at least he had better get what applause he could from the encouraging adults. 'Larkspur' was about to become a masterpiece under his hands.

Beth didn't know a lot about music, but she was pleased to hear her son practising at his father's old piano, and as far as she could tell, he was doing a wonderful job.

When the night of the Strawberry Fete came round, Clarrie decided that he would confess to Georgie ahead of time.

"You know I'm going to be playing the piano tonight," Clarrie said to his friend, already bracing himself for the onslaught of ridicule that was sure to come his way.

"I figured you would be," Georgie said, without any emotion at all.

Clarrie was slightly taken aback. "What do you mean, 'figured I would be'? How could you know that?"

"All Mrs Fuller's students perform," Georgie said logically.

"Yes, but how did you know I was taking lessons?" Clarrie asked. He was sure that he'd been very careful not to mention it at school.

"My mother told me," Georgie said, unimpressed.

"And you don't think it's sissy?" Clarrie asked tentatively, not really wanting to be made fun of, but having to clear the air completely on this topic.

"Course I think it's sissy!" Georgie retorted. Clarrie's heart sank in disappointment, and he was about to say something in defence but was interrupted. "But what can I say about it when my mother makes me go out to old Mr Fierce to take singing lessons."

"Singing lessons!" Clarrie would have liked very much to laugh out loud, but restrained himself admirably.

"And don't you be going about making fun of it either, Clarrie Brown!" Georgie said furiously. "I haven't said a word about your piano lessons!"

"No, you haven't," Clarrie said gratefully. "Do you have to perform at the Strawberry Fete?" he asked, trying to defuse the tension.

"No! Thank goodness," Georgie said. "He might be a cranky old bean, but at least he doesn't make us perform!"

Clarrie left it at that. He felt certain that he had the best of it. Mrs Fuller did make them perform in public, but she was anything but a 'cranky old bean'. In fact, she was a real good sport.

The two boys joined their other friends outside the institute, neither of them making any comment about music or performance. Instead, they joined in with the general excitement at the news there was to be a shooting gallery at this year's fete.

"They've set up in the ladies' cloak room at the front of the Institute," Phillip informed the others. "And only ten cents for ten shots."

There was no doubt that this was a major consolation for other troubles. Clarrie decided that he would endure what he must on stage, and hopefully, all his mates would be occupied in the front room, shooting at tin ducks, when it was his turn to perform.

Vera found Clarrie when he was buying a saucer full of strawberries and cream.

"Now don't go too far away, Clarrie," she instructed. "The concert will be starting soon, and I need to have you nearby. You'll be on to perform straight after Mrs Meaney."

Clarrie nodded obediently. He knew Mrs Meaney well enough. Second Time's wife. She played the piano accordion and often used to perform at town functions.

He decided not to go back with the other boys to watch more shooting, but to find a place to sit and quietly enjoy his strawberries.

The hall was beautifully decorated with the various stalls around the outside. There was a cake stall, drinks and ice-cream stand, a produce table full of jams, pickles, eggs, fruit and jars of fresh cream, a handicraft stall, which held all manner of knitted, crocheted, and hand-stitched items. There were the tea and coffee tables, two lucky dip barrels, one for the boys and one for the girls, and a white-elephant stall.

Each table had a big frame built over it that was wonderfully decorated with colourful crepe paper, flowers and balloons. It made the hall look very festive. There was also the pine Christmas tree in the corner, and Clarrie knew that Father Christmas would make an appearance before the night was over. He made a quick calculation as to whether, at twelve, he was still young enough to line up with the other children to receive a present. The urge for the present was strong, but so too was the thought of peer pressure. He decided to wait and see which way the wind blew with the other boys.

Clarrie had only just finished the last mouthful of delicious strawberries and ice-cream when the general hubbub of conversation and talk of trade was interrupted by loud cries from behind the heavy stage curtains. No one was really alarmed, most people knowing that it was the beginning of the concert, and that it was most likely the slapstick antics of Clair Prosser. Clair might have been a suave and debonair MC at the dances, but given the opportunity at any concert, he would don his clown attire and cause hilarious uproar. Clarrie went to school with a couple of Clair's sons, and they'd told him that their father used to work as a clown with the Sole Brothers circus for a time, and had taken to the stage with other performers such as Tex Morton and Buddy Williams.

Clarrie watched as the golden velvet curtains began to be ruffled as if somebody was trying to fight their way from behind, and eventually Clair the clown broke through to face the audience. By this time the crowd had ceased their chatter, and there was only the low murmur of people trying to find seats.

Clair, his face painted with bold exaggerated colours, began to tell some woeful tale of trouble about his brother who'd done some grievous thing to him, and was part way through when said brother, Neil, also dressed in colourful, overlarge clothing, burst on stage from the wings, protesting loudly that in fact he was the injured party. The audience responded well to their antics, laughing at the appropriate moments, the children especially amused by the way the two clowns fell over one another. Finally, Clair managed to calm himself and his brother enough to introduce the first serious item. Clarrie was tense with nerves, but relaxed slightly to see that it wasn't Shirley Meaney, whose performance would mark his cue, but rather it was young Janice McCallum.

Clarrie really liked Janice. She was Ken McCallum's daughter and, like her father, was cheerful and friendly and always had a smile. And Clarrie had heard that she and Robert Moulton were to be married in January. This was a wonderful thing in his mind. Of course he wouldn't be invited to the wedding. He'd heard Mrs Greenbank say that the wedding was to be in Adelaide, and that the townspeople would be deprived of the usual popping down to the church to see the bride as she arrived. Janice was a popular girl, and it wasn't just because she sang like a nightingale, but more so because she was such a loving and caring person.

Janice came on stage and performed a spellbinding version of 'Somewhere My Love', the theme song from the movie 'Dr Zhivago'. The audience were entranced and responded accordingly. This item was followed by the first of Mrs Fuller's students, and Clarrie was relieved to hear two or three mistakes in this performance by an older student. It took the pressure from him just a little.

Each item was punctuated by some silly joke or act by the Prosser brothers, until eventually Shirley Meaney was announced as being the next to take the stage. Suddenly, Clarrie's mouth went dry and his hands clammy. It was his cue to move quietly along the side of the hall, down the supper room steps and to the back stage entrance. As he reached the door that led to the steep back stage stairs, he was quite flustered and suddenly couldn't remember where he'd put his sheet music. But thankfully, Mrs Fuller appeared, an angel of confidence, and assured him that it was placed carefully on the top of the piano.

"Don't worry, Clarrie," she said evenly. "You will play beautifully, and do your father proud."

Those were the magic words. Obviously his mother had told Mrs Fuller all about his father's hope of a musical family. If nothing else, he would do his best for the sake of his father's memory.

The steps leading up to the back stage were very steep and the cavity was very dark, with no light to show the way. Feeling his way carefully upward, Clarrie warded off the memory of ghostly stories that he and his school friends had told one another about this secret passageway. After their night in McKenzie's cave, and having scared themselves witless, he had made a decision to stop making up these ghastly stories, but unfortunately, the story that had been told of the dark back-stage entrance had been well and truly established before this resolution had been made. With Clarrie's imagination working overtime, it took some sorting through thoughts to put his performance above the idea of a dark hooded creature at the top of the stairs. Mrs Fuller's cheerful 'good luck' call from below aided in dispelling the phantom.

Having eventually reached the dimly lit backstage unmolested by any spirit, Clarrie stood and waited as he listened to the merry strains of accordion music as Shirley finished her second piece. The audience applauded and Clarrie heard Clair go out and begin his next short routine. Shirley came back behind the side curtain. "Good luck," she said and smiled at Clarrie.

By this time, Clarrie's stomach was in knots, his heart hammering at an alarming rate, his mouth dry and his hands shaking. He wondered how on earth he was ever going to remember where middle 'C' was. And then he heard his name being announced, and what seemed like thunderous applause that followed. For an instant, Clarrie froze, but then the giant curtains were being hauled back by one of the back stage helpers, and he found himself face to face with the anticipating audience.

Where is the piano? He thought for one awful second. And then he heard a helpful stage whisper from the wing.

"Over here, mate," someone said. Relief washed over Clarrie as he saw the old upright piano right on the edge of the stage, not out in the middle. Taking a deep breath for courage, he walked over, pulled out the two wooden chairs stacked one on top of the other to add height, and sat down. Then he remembered to get his music from on top of the piano. It was all very nerve racking, but eventually he managed to collect his thoughts enough to begin, and once started, the automatic pilot of one well practiced took over, and Clarrie was hardly aware that he had finished. It wasn't until the curtains were closed, and he could hear the clowning going on that he realised the ordeal was over.

"Well done, Clarrie," Vera beamed as he made his way down the now exorcised stairwell. "I knew you could do it. Now I don't ever want to hear about how you are no good at music again. Do you hear?"

Clarrie received this praise, but felt just a little sorry that he had now lost his best excuse for getting out of music lessons – that of not being very good.

Afterward, when he went out into the hall he was chagrined to realise his friends had been forced to sit and listen to his whole performance. The shooting gallery was closed while the concert was on. Still, his mates weren't too cruel, as without Georgie's support, which surprised most of the others, there wasn't much to sustain the ridicule.

Clarrie sat with the rest of his friends trying to appear restless and bored for their sakes, while in an ambivalent effort to seem attentive and respectful for both those appearing on stage and those watching. It was difficult work. And he was glad he'd made the extra effort when he saw Jim Bishop after the concert, as his wife, Jenny, had also sung a solo, and he felt he needed to make a suitable comment in exchange for the praise given him for his performance.

Finally, Father Christmas made his appearance, courtesy of the Buff Lodge, and in the end Clarrie's friends agreed that while they were technically still eligible, they would put aside their adopted maturity long enough to receive a gift. But as one, they refused to sit on the jolly gentleman's lap. That was going too far.

Chapter
Fourteen

Driving back out from the Saddle, already shocked by their narrow escape, the men muttered amongst themselves at what lay before them. When they had driven in, hours earlier, the country side was covered in dry vegetation, but what they had not known while they were watching the front in the valley, was that the fire had got away behind them and had consumed everything in its path. All that was left was charred ground and black trees, left naked after they'd been stripped of their vegetation. Nobody said much, but Clarrie could sense that emotions were high.

The orders had been given for their next job. The fire was way beyond the National Park, and every available unit was being called to the farms that lay in its path. Jim's crew went to the first farm where they met with some twenty other units, and there they set themselves to protect the buildings, making breaks and having their hoses at the ready. They tensed as they watched the monster approach. Then as it made an attempt to take each building, the volunteers would fight with all they had until the roaring beast passed by. Then within minutes there would be one unit left to mop up the burning posts and trees nearby, and the rest of the fire crews drove at full speed to defend the next house.

Clarrie didn't know whether to rejoice at each property saved or to weep at the devastation of the surrounding land. They were all so tired.

But when the reports came of sheep that were caught and burned to death, it was an easy choice. Clarrie wept.

Clarrie was very aware of the fact that the paddocks outlying from town had turned a beautiful golden brown colour, and he revelled in the thought of it. The way the community spirits had lifted because the season had gone without disaster was infectious. The talk outside the bank amongst farmers and their wives was positive and full of anticipation for what the actual yield would be. The rain had fallen at the right times during the year, the frosts hadn't been too bad, the fear of locusts had come to nothing, no rust had appeared on the stalks of grain and so far there had been no fires. Clarrie heard plenty about the Bishops' and Arthurs' crops, and showed a remarkable interest, being the son of a logger.

When the conditions were just right, the farmers mounted their tractors, towing the large grain gathering headers behind. A number of boys were chaffing to be out in the paddock with their fathers, but, alas, school hadn't finished yet. There were still two or three weeks of Miss Jolly's rigorous routine yet to be endured.

Then one day, two weeks before school was due to break up, the children arrived in the big classroom to find what appeared to be a massive pudding hanging from the schoolroom rafter. It was wrapped in a calico cloth, but was probably four times the size of a normal Christmas pudding. There was plenty of speculation as to what it might be, but Miss Jolly calmly put a stop to this wondering by stating plainly that it was her Christmas pudding, and she'd hung it up to prove.

Not one of the children believed this explanation. They all knew she was a spinster and lived alone, and even a normal sized pudding would have been too much for a single person. One day she walked quietly into the classroom to find the children making other guesses as to what it might be. Instead of calling the class to immediate attention, she stopped and listened for a while before coming around to her desk. When the children suddenly became aware that she was actually in the room, they stopped their chatter in mid sentence, waiting for the expected whisking of the cane through the air and sharp sound as it hit the front desk. But much to their surprise, no such action occurred. This tack couldn't have been more effective in making the student body come to attention, as it was so unusual and out of character for the strict school ma'am.

"Actually, children," she finally broke the tense atmosphere, "I have heard that it could actually be a bomb!"

Two or three children tittered nervously, the rest didn't quite know whether to take the suggestion as a joke or not, nor did they have the courage to turn to their neighbour and make comment. Then Clarrie saw the corner of her mouth turn up in a smile, and he thought he saw a twinkle in her eye, as if she was having a great deal of fun.

Miss Jolly might have a sense of humour after all, Clarrie thought to himself.

That strange event added further mystery to the object hanging overhead, and stories began to flow thick and fast from their fertile imaginations, to the point where the girls sitting directly beneath the 'pudding' became quite frightened that they might be caught in an explosion. One child was certain that she had heard it ticking.

The last day of school finally arrived. Clarrie had finished grade six and would now be promoted to grade seven. They were all aware that some of their friends in grade seven had now completed primary school, and would no longer come to Melrose but instead, next year, they would take the train across to the Booleroo Centre High School. Phillip Deekin was one of those students, and his leaving added sadness to an otherwise wonderful day of celebration. The final day was filled with cleaning-up activity. All the Christmas decorations that the children had made during Mrs Cordon's craft classes were duly taken down and distributed to their rightful owners.

All the books were taken from beneath the desks, textbooks returned to the cupboard along the side of the classroom and workbooks put inside school cases. Clarrie and Georgie got the job of taking all the blackboard dusters outside and giving them a thorough banging on the bitumen, and then making sure all the blackboards were spotlessly clean, ready for the new school year.

About two thirty, all that remained was the 'pudding' suspended from the rafters, and the children somehow sensed that the mystery would be solved before they were sent home on holidays.

Sure enough, two of the grade seven boys were instructed to loosen the string that was tied to one of the window hooks, and to let the 'pudding' down slowly. Clarrie watched Miss Jolly and confirmed his earlier suspicions. She really is enjoying this, he thought to himself, as he saw her eyes almost sparkle with merriment.

Miss Jolly directed everybody outside and onto the lawn behind the art-shed, and they waited for Miss Both to bring the younger children out to join them. Then to everyone's great amazement, Miss Jolly opened the 'pudding' and it revealed a huge pile of lollies in colourful wrappers. Then she took great delight in throwing them all over the lawn handful by handful, until they were all lying about on the grass.

"Now children, when I say 'go' you may each run and get some, but be sure you let the little ones have their share as well."

Afterward Clarrie expressed his newly formed opinion of the headmistress to his friends.

"Sure was odd behaviour for her," Georgie agreed. "Still, I don't reckon it will make any difference next year when we have to sit down and do grammar and tables again."

Clarrie acknowledged that this was probably true. However, it pleased him to know that Miss Jolly was not all prickles and stings, and that there was a side to her that was merry and kind.

So the school broke up with a week and a half until Christmas. Clarrie knew that he couldn't expect too much from Christmas day as his mother's finances had been stretched to capacity on his wonderful new bike, so he tried not to think about it too much. His mother's parents lived in Melbourne, and his grandparents on his father's side had both passed away some years ago. Clarrie wasn't expecting much in the way of a family Christmas at all.

While Georgie was getting ready to go off to Adelaide with his parents for Christmas, Clarrie was left at a loose end. Most of the other boys were out with their fathers either sitting on the tractor with them, or sitting in the front of the truck, carting the grain into the silo. Clarrie desperately wanted to be part of helping with the harvest, and when he saw Jim at church on Sunday, he came straight out and asked if he might be allowed to come out and help.

"Help!" Jim laughed kindly. "Well, I dare say we could use some help, Clarrie, but it would be more helpful if you had a truck licence."

Clarrie's face fell in obvious disappointment.

"You can come, if you like," Jim was quick to pick up on the slump of spirits. "I guess you can keep us company while we go round and round the paddock."

Beth wanted to know that it was safe, and that her son wasn't going to be vulnerable to one of those tractor accidents that she'd heard enough about over the years. Despite Jim's reassurance, she was not happy with the idea. Having had a husband lost in a machinery accident brought too many fears to the surface. In the end they compromised and Clarrie was allowed to come and ride in the truck, to and from the silos.

As it turned out, it was never the same driver in the truck. Sometimes it was Dick Bishop, sometimes it was Jenny and sometimes it was Jim himself, when it was too cool to reap.

But on this day, it was Jenny who was driving, and Clarrie rode up front in the passenger seat, trying to amuse the two little girls, who by necessity were forced to come along as well. The baby stayed with Auntie Ella on the occasions when Jenny was needed to drive.

They waited in the paddock while the grain was transferred

from the header bin into the great big bin on the back of the truck. Chaff and dust were everywhere in the air as the golden grain poured from the orga funnel, but while Clarrie's eyes watered and his nose itched, he would not have admitted for the world that he was suffering from the dreaded hay fever. He wanted to be a part of this operation and no allergy was going to put him off. Finally they had a full load and Jenny bundled the two girls into the truck cabin. Clarrie climbed in after them, feeling quite old and responsible, making sure that the door was shut properly, and that little feet were clear of the large floor-column gear shift. Jenny started the truck and it rumbled into life, lurching forward with its heavy load. They crossed the paddock to the gate and out onto the road near the old Gregory school, and then began the steady journey down the Coonato Road back towards town. It was a good six miles to travel over dusty dirt roads. Clarrie had the window down to let the air blow in. It was hot air, but was better than the stifling still heat of a closed cabin. When they finally came to the bitumen road and travelled the last couple of miles to the railway station, they came upon a long line of trucks, queued ready for their turn to unload. Jenny sighed in frustration. By the look of it they would have to wait in line for at least a couple of hours.

"It looks like Mrs Clarke is in the truck ahead of us," Clarrie commented to the driver.

"At least we can have a bit of a chat while we're waiting," Jenny remarked. "She'll most likely have a thermos of tea with her, and I've got some cake left over from lunch."

There was a little cake, left over. When they'd all sat down in the shade of the truck to eat the picnic lunch, appetites had been enormous. Even the little girls seemed extra hungry. But at least there was plenty of iced water, which Clarrie thought might have served even better than coke in this hot, dusty weather.

"How are you, Jenny?" Avis Clarke said, as she climbed down from her truck, closing the door behind her.

"Hot and a bit bothered," Jenny confessed. "Jim's father was supposed to be carting for us today, but Don's driver couldn't make it after all."

"Yes, and you know what it's like when the weather is right."

"Make hay while the sun shines!" Jenny laughed. "Or at least get that crop into the silos while the sun shines!"

Clarrie wasn't really interested in the women's talk of the Mothers' and Babies' Health Association or the Kindergarten or School Welfare group, so he took the two little girls for a walk down the track, crossed the main road and went straight over to the creek in the show grounds. There wasn't any water in the creek at this time of year. The round rocks and boulders were covered in the dry slime and other mineral deposits that had remained once the water evaporated. He talked the girls into collecting small stones, and then he used sharp rocks to draw pictures on the smooth surfaces. They were reasonably amused at this game for nearly an hour, and then they decided to go back up to the line to see how far their truck had progressed. There were only three trucks left in front. Clarrie accepted the offer of cake and water. He supposed that the two ladies had probably had a cup of tea and a good afternoon visit, and felt glad that they hadn't been forced to sit in the long line with absolutely nothing to do.

Finally, Avis had only one truck in front of her before it would be her turn to unload the grain. She drove up behind the truck in front while it was standing at the testing shed, and got out to undo the ropes that tied the tarpaulin in place. Before she could let the grain out from the side chutes, she would have to allow the silo workers time to test her load for moisture and weeds. Clarrie had come across to help, at Jenny's suggestion, but before he had been able to loosen one knot, he was arrested by Avis mumbling to herself

"That's the way I tie the knots," she said, observing the ropes that secured the tarp cover over the load. "Only I tie the knots that way. But I didn't put the tarp on," she said.

Clarrie didn't know what she was talking about, but could tell that she was bothered. Then he saw her lift her hand to knock on the side of the bin. When the sound returned the echo of a hollow cavity, even he could tell that it was empty.

"I've brought the wrong truck," she said, her utter frustration written all over her face.

The silo workers laughed at the scene, and eventually Avis gave a chuckle as well. "You'll get your turn quicker than you thought," she said to Jenny.

Even though everyone could see the funny side of Avis's dilemma, they all knew just how annoying and frustrating it must have been for her to drive seven or eight miles and then sit in the heat for two hours, waiting to unload the truck, only to find that she'd left the load behind and now had to start all over again!

Clarrie gave the Bishops' bin a quick knock on the side just to make sure that they hadn't made the same mistake, and was vastly relieved to hear the dull thud of a full bin. That would have been too much, and he could just have imagined the look on Jim's face if he'd gone to fill an empty bin and found it already full, and an empty truck gone. He'd only been part of the harvesting ritual for a short time, but even he knew that it wasn't good to commit such a time-consuming sin. If those farmers could reap in the dark, it was almost certain they would. And for those men who took the Sabbath as a serious commandment, to stay away from the machinery for a day and sing hymns in church instead, showed a true depth of commitment and self-control.

But in the end, all the grain was harvested and duly transported into the silos, ready for the wheat trains to carry away to market. The only slight mishap was when Peter Abbott drove down the road past the Gregory School; his car engine backfired badly several times, and started three small grass fires along the side of the road that quickly spread into the stubble of the adjoining paddock. Luckily two farmers reaping nearby saw it happen, and were quick to take their knapsacks and descend upon the flames, managing to put out the fire before it could spread to their unreaped crop.

Jim and Don Bishop got their crop into the silos two days before Christmas, and to Clarrie's mind it was just in time. The Melrose Methodist Church had been planning their usual carolling venture, but it was somewhat reliant on the availability of a truck, and most trucks in the district were pressed into the important grain carting service at this time. Now the Bishop truck was free, the bin was winched off and put back on its stand ready for next year, and it was made ready for Christmas Eve.

Clarrie's one great anticipation for Christmas was the local community activities on Christmas Eve. The Catholic Church would hold the obligatory midnight mass. This sounded like fun to Clarrie, but he wasn't Catholic and supposed he had better stick to the protestant services. Both the Anglican and Methodist churches held a Christmas Eve service that began about seven o'clock. Even Sally agreed to come with Beth, and Clarrie was almost distracted with the magic of Christmas Eve expectation. Auntie Ella played several favourite carols on the old pump organ, and Reverend Anderson gave the Christmas story in a manner that roused the twelve-year-old's imagination. He loved the idea of the baby in the manger, with the animals round about, the brilliant star in the sky and of course the shepherds and kings. It was a familiar story, but it never failed to rouse feelings of nostalgia and joy.

"Are you going to come carol singing with us?" Clarrie asked his mother, once the service was over.

"No, I think I'll just go home with Sally," Beth said tiredly. "I've some things I want to get done so I can take the whole day off tomorrow."

Clarrie was just a tad disappointed, but he wasn't going to miss this experience for the world. The Bishops' truck was pulled up outside the Methodist church. It now had Auntie Ella's pump organ on the back, butted up against the headboard of the truck. There was some tinsel woven in and out of the securing bars. As church people began to climb aboard the flat-top back, it began to look very festive. Some of the ladies from the Ladies' Fellowship Guild loaded several large baskets of small

Christmas puddings, wrapped in colourful Christmas cellophane. These were to be distributed to some of the elderly folk in the town who'd not been able to get out to the service. With a number of people aboard and Auntie Ella seated on the organ stool ready to play, the truck moved slowly forward, Mr Bishop driving, ready to take the carollers around the town.

Many times they pulled up in the front of a house, to send one of the younger ones inside with the small gift. As the pudding was being delivered, the people still on the truck would strike up a rousing carol, singing with great gusto and enthusiasm. Mostly, the folks inside would come to the front porch and stand and listen to renditions of 'Joy to the World' and 'Hark the Herald Angels Sing'.

But when the truck pulled up in front of Clarrie's own house he was surprised. Most of the places they had been to were elderly people.

"We'd like to give a little something to some of the families that do it a bit hard, Clarrie," Audrey Albinus whispered in his ear. "You can take the gift in this time."

Clarrie was really pleased that they had thought of his mother, and waited to be given the small offering to take inside. But instead of a little Christmas pudding, he was handed a box, brightly covered in Christmas wrapping paper.

"Just something to help you enjoy Christmas," Audrey said. "Take it in to your mother, Clarrie."

Clarrie didn't know what was inside, but just the thought of it brought tears to his eyes. It was so good to know that somebody actually cared about his mother enough to give them a big gift like this at Christmas.

"What's this, Clarrie?" Beth asked as she opened the door to his knock.

"A present from the Ladies' Fellowship," Clarrie answered to the accompaniment of the strains of 'Silent Night' coming from the back of the truck.

"What's in it?" Beth asked, her own eyes misting over.

Clarrie couldn't answer for the lump in his throat, and just shook his head. While the rest of the carollers sang, Clarrie watched as his mother opened the box of goodies. Inside was a wrapped Christmas pudding, just like all the others, but so much more. A small ham, a cold cooked chicken carefully wrapped to keep it cool, a jar of preserved peaches, four striped candy canes and a box of Cadbury Chocolates.

"This is beautiful, Clarrie," Beth said, quite moved by the gift. "Please thank the ladies for me."

Clarrie nodded with a smile, and turned to rejoin the others on the back of the truck.

"My mother says to thank you very much," he said to Audrey as he climbed back aboard. "That was really nice of you to do that."

"It's our pleasure, Clarrie," she said with a smile. "Have a Merry Christmas."

They finished carolling, dropping off two or three more hampers and puddings, and then took the truck back up to the Methodist church.

"Will you be coming down to see Father Christmas at Prests'?" Jim asked Clarrie just before they left.

"Do you think it will still be open?" Clarrie asked.

"I think they were going to stay open until nine o'clock tonight. It's nearly nine now, but if we hurry, we might make it just in time."

Clarrie accepted a ride down to the main street, and decided to see if anyone was still hanging about the grocery store. In fact there were still quite a number of people with children about Clarrie's age. Some were from the Catholic families who would still be awake at midnight, and a few others who'd not gone with the carollers around the town.

Phillip Deekin saw Clarrie and came up to him. "Where've you been?" he asked immediately.

"I went with the truck to sing carols around town," Clarrie said at once, proud of the fact.

"I'm surprised Georgie's not with you," Phillip said, perhaps a little mockingly. "What with him taking singing lessons and all."

Clarrie was shocked speechless. "How did you know he was taking singing lessons?" he asked Phillip eventually.

"His mother told my mother, and then my mother tried to make me take music lessons. As if I would! Can you imagine?"

Clarrie didn't make a comment, especially on the grounds he might incriminate himself. But then Phillip knew he played the piano. He'd seen him perform at the Strawberry Fete.

"Does Georgie know that you know?" Clarrie asked.

"Yeah!" Phillip screwed up his nose. "I made fun of him as soon as I heard."

"What'd he say?" Clarrie asked.

"He punched me in the nose and said I wasn't to mention it again." Clarrie laughed.

"Hey," Phillip changed the subject. "Have you been in to get an ice-cream from Father Christmas?" he asked. "You'd better hurry, 'cause I think they're gonna close the shop soon."

Clarrie didn't need any more encouragement to go inside Prests' shop. Phillip decided to come with him to see if Father Christmas might have forgotten he'd already been through once. But as it turned out, Father Christmas seemed to know Phillip's name, and hoped that he'd enjoyed the Golden North Giant Twin ice-cream he'd received earlier. Clarrie grinned as he received his Giant Twin. Father Christmas knew his name too, and there seemed to be something strikingly familiar about Father Christmas's face under that white beard.

Clarrie had only just started to take off the purple and yellow wrapper when Yvonne Bishop made an announcement.

"Well Father Christmas has to get along now," she said for the benefit of all the wide-eyed children who remained out the front of the shop. "Perhaps we need to cheer him on his way by singing 'Jingle Bells'."

As the group of smaller children began to sing 'dashing through the snow…' on top note, and Father Christmas began to 'ho ho ho' his way out of the shop, Clarrie asked Phillip a question:

"Are they still telling everyone that Father Christmas has left his reindeer over the other side of Mount Remarkable?"

"Yeah!" Phillip nodded. "And he still comes and goes on the back of a ute."

"I reckon one of these days they'll figure out whose face it is behind that beard," Clarrie surmised.

"Do you mean to say you haven't yet?" Phillip chuckled.

"I've figured it out," Clarrie said quickly, but didn't admit that he'd only just made the discovery. He wondered how it was that he'd lived under that marvellous illusion for so long. But then he thought to himself that it was probably because he wanted to believe in a magical, generous Santa Claus. He wasn't too disillusioned by the discovery though. It was still fun to pretend that Father Christmas was out there somewhere, tracking down his reindeer, ready to fly all over the world in one night, making sure that he stopped by his own house as he went past, of course.

Chapter
Fifteen

When the crews came in from the Survey Road they were able to report saving every house. But there was no celebration. Livestock had been lost, and a couple of outbuildings, but worse than this, the fire still raged on. These teams of men had only returned because of sheer exhaustion, Clarrie along with them. It was agreed that they would try and rest for four or five hours, and then they would return to the fight. Clarrie crawled wearily into his hotel bed, hardly thinking of anything before he fell into a fatigued sleep. But even in sleep he could hear the roar of flames and the yell of men under threat. He could see the whole bushland blackened and charred. And in it all, he knew it was a picture of his own life. Desolate, uncovered and despairing. He woke up half an hour before the alarm. His dreams wouldn't allow him any more time to sleep.

But by the time he got back to the shed, he found that the others had slept even less than he, and had already left to go north this time. They were sent to patrol a fire front up near Spring Creek. For a moment Clarrie felt bereft, left without purpose and direction. But then he remembered the real reason he was supposed to be here in the first place, and decided to write up the account of the day.

He hadn't been long, using one of the tables in the communication shed as a desk, when his attention was captured by a change of shifts. He saw Glen Malcolm come in wearing a blue paramedic uniform.

"You're a paramedic?" Clarrie asked the obvious.

"Retired just recently," Glen answered. "But in a crisis like this, it

doesn't hurt to have something that identifies the sort of job you can do. I've just been promoted from radio operator to fireman. I'm supposed to go out with the next crew."

Clarrie gave a chuckle under his breath. He was a newspaper reporter, and in several short days he'd found himself raised to the ranks of fireman, placed on the front lines of battle.

"Just had the most interesting assignment," Glen commented by way of conversation. "I was ordered to patrol the Bishop farm while they slept."

"Was it under threat?" Clarrie asked, alarmed.

"Not really, but those folk are so tired, and knowing that someone was alert and ready to raise the alarm should the wind play some terrible trick gave them enough peace of mind to rest easy."

"Not much action in that job, then?" Clarrie commented.

"I felt a bit like Dad's Army, pacing around a quiet area, no enemy in sight, a knapsack on my back, and wondering how on earth I would fight a fire on my own if it should turn that way."

"I guess I'll go out with the next crew," Clarrie said. "I can't just sit around here waiting to hear what happens."

It wasn't long before a relatively fresh group of men arrived, ready to be given directions, and Glen and Clarrie prepared to go with them. But before anybody had left, an urgent call came over the radio.

"Hold on, Glen!" Jenny called. "You stay here. There's a bunch of men with bee stings on their way in. Can you help treat them?"

"Bee stings?" Clarrie raised his eyebrows. "How on earth do you get a whole lot of bee stings in a bushfire?"

"They didn't say," Jenny answered, "but I guess we will find out when they get here."

Glen immediately responded, readying his first aid kit, and Clarrie decided that he would stay to see if he could help as well. He had passed his first aid certificate some years earlier and knew he could take directions if the more experienced paramedic gave them.

"We'd better get the Booleroo ambulance over here," Jenny said. "Sounds like it could be bad."

Clarrie asked just a couple of relevant questions and went about summoning the ambulance.

"*Seems strange to be dealing with bee stings when you'd be expecting burns or smoke inhalation.*" *Clarrie said, once they were prepared and waiting for their arrival.*

"*It does seem rather strange. I hope there're no serious allergies,*" *Glen replied, "But I guess we'll find out when they get here.*"

It wasn't too long before the ambulance arrived, followed shortly by a convoy of vehicles coming in from the north. It was a flurry of activity. A number of men were suffering from bee stings, but one in particular had taken a sting to the throat, and by the way it was swelling, it looked as if he may have been allergic. He was immediately ushered to the waiting St John's people for emergency treatment, and it wasn't long before the ambulance left with sirens blaring.

The remaining victims were left to the ministrations of the volunteer medicos; thankfully Glen remained with them to add his years of experience. But there were no more life threatening cases, and they worked quietly and methodically to help those who suffered from the awful swelling and pain of multiple bee stings.

Clarrie watched as one of the younger men stepped up for treatment and it was Simon, Glen's own son. As the father cleaned the various sting sites, and added soothing lotions he talked to his son. "How did all this come about?" he asked.

"*We were gathered, talking about what to do next, as we'd lost the front, when a beekeeper drove past, his truck loaded with bee hives. I guess he was trying to get them away from the fire, but he obviously didn't take time to lull them to sleep, or whatever it is that they do. The hives were open, and the bees were angry. I don't know whether they were his bees or a wild swarm that was following him, but when they spotted us they came after us as if we'd caused all the trouble.*"

Clarrie watched as the storyteller winced under the touch of his father on a particularly tender spot.

"*We'd all been standing about, then suddenly everyone was running madly for their trucks. I was a little slow moving off and the bees took to my head. Andrew had already reached our ute and had shut the doors against the swarm, and I was left standing. Jim*

Willoughby got out of his truck, took a hold of me in a rugby tackle, threw me in the nearest cabin, slammed the door and then rolled under the nearest truck."

"That was a fairly brave thing to do," Clarrie commented, wondering if he would have put his own skin on the line.

"Well, you know Jim," Simon said. "He has worked as a stunt man for various movies. It was probably rehearsed."

Glen laughed. It was good to hear a bit of humour in the midst of all this trouble.

"Are you Ok?" Clarrie asked Simon, once Glen had moved along to the next patient.

"I have to be honest, I feel pretty light-headed, but whether that is the bee stings or the smoke or whether I'm just tired, I don't know!"

Clarrie imagined it was probably a combination of all three, and didn't trouble Simon further with questions, but instead offered to drive him home to rest. Simon accepted gladly.

"I guess it's pretty funny when you think about it," Simon said once they were in the car. "Though it didn't feel real funny at the time!"

Christmas day had not been the non-event that Clarrie had expected. With the gift of food given by the church ladies, Beth had been able to arrange quite a nice traditional Christmas dinner, with roast vegetables and gravy, and custard with the Christmas pudding for sweets. The food by itself was a fine treat, but it was the company that Clarrie was glad of. Most of his usual friends had their own family gathering, and so Beth suggested to her two children that they ask somebody else who didn't have family to share Christmas with. Both Sally and Clarrie nearly choked when Beth suggested Miss Jolly. Neither of them had ever thought of her in terms other than the stern faced, humourless schoolmistress who usually caused her students more grief than joy.

"Miss Jolly doesn't have any family of her own," Beth pointed out.

"But she's so cross and harsh all the time," Sally complained.

"She is a strict teacher," Beth agreed, "But perhaps she is harsh because she doesn't have any friends or family."

Clarrie had very much wanted to argue, but his sensitive nature could easily see the point his mother was trying to make, and in the end, he simply couldn't put up any further objection to the idea. Miss Jolly accepted the invitation to Christmas dinner, and so did old Norman Smythe. Sally had made some loud protests to this proposal as well.

"Norman Smythe is a dim-wit," she had complained.

"Now Sally," Beth spoke sternly, "he is a returned serviceman, and they say he suffered from shell shock. I know he seems confused and quiet all the time, but he is on his own, and I can't see why we shouldn't share the kindness that has been shown to us."

Sally had not been able to refute this line of argument. She knew that the church folk had been kind to them, and her mother's idea to invite these two lonely people to dinner was an obvious act of compassion. Under normal circumstances, the Brown family wouldn't have had such a good Christmas dinner themselves. Neither she nor Clarrie could refuse to share their blessing with someone even less fortunate than themselves. And that was how they saw it. They might have struggled for money, and they might have lost their father, but they had each other, and with their mother they had some kind of family at least.

Clarrie was surprised at both Miss Jolly and Mr Smythe. Neither seemed to be what they were supposed to be. Miss Jolly seemed glad to be there, and though she didn't speak often, what she did say showed a depth of gratitude at having been included.

Mr Smythe, generally known for being bewildered and confused, seemed to take great delight in telling stories of the good-old-days when he was young, and how his mother had cooked the Christmas goose in the old wood stove. Afterward, Clarrie noted in his diary that he thought Mr Smythe was happier living in his childhood. The present, and even the harsh past of the war, seemed more than he was able to deal with.

When the three Browns sat down together after Christmas day, they all agreed that they felt good at having shared themselves and their gifts with these two single souls.

———————————————

By the time New Year's Eve came, Georgie and his family had returned from their stay with Georgie's sister in Adelaide, and he came to talk New Year's Eve over with Clarrie.

"There'll be the dance, of course," Clarrie said.

"Oh, yeah," Georgie brushed that aside as unimportant. "What we need to decide is what sort of jokes we can play."

"What do you mean?" Clarrie asked, immediately disturbed.

"Jokes! You know. Some pranks we can play while everybody else is dancing in the Institute." Even when he said it, Georgie could see that Clarrie was going to be hard to convince. "Crikey, Clarrie! You were the one who went and dumped rubbish in the Bishops' ramp on April Fool's."

Clarrie was about to straighten out the facts of that incident, but Georgie charged on. "You were the one who told me about painting Norman Smythe's white cow black, and pinching Lorna Arthur's garden gnome."

"Yeah, but I didn't actually do them."

"Course not! But it gives us some good ideas for our pranks, doesn't it?"

Clarrie hadn't really considered that it would soon be his responsibility for playing the tricks on the unsuspecting townsfolk, but as Georgie promoted the idea, he supposed that with Geoff away, Lyall couldn't be expected to support all the town shenanigans on his own. Besides, he supposed there would come a time when Lyall would get too old and sensible for such things.

"I heard Spen Fuller telling me about the pranks they used to play when they were young," Clarrie admitted, beginning to mull the idea over seriously.

"'Yeah? What did those old blokes used to do?" Georgie asked, sceptically.

"They were young once," Clarrie corrected, his imagination far more able to grasp that concept than his friend's.

"Yeah, yeah! What sort of thing did they get up to?"

"I heard him say they used to pick on the town drunk a bit."

"How?" Georgie pushed.

"They'd unhitch his horse from the jinker and put him in backwards, so when he'd come out of the pub, he'd find his horse facing him. They reckon the poor old bloke could never quite figure out what was going on!"

Georgie laughed, but quickly sobered. "What good is a joke like that for us," he asked. "Nobody drives a horse and cart anymore."

"And then they used to unhitch the horse, take it around a fence, and hitch it with the cart one side of the fence and the horse the other."

"Let's come back to the 1960's, Clarrie!" Georgie said, disgusted. "No horse jokes are going to work for us!"

"No!" Clarrie reluctantly agreed. "I wouldn't know how to unhitch a horse, let alone hitch it up again."

Georgie was intent on coming up with a good joke to play, and he stayed around at Clarrie's for some time, trying for all he was worth to come up with something that would astound and possibly infuriate the poor victim. By the time Georgie was forced to leave, the two boys had come no closer to deciding on the trouble they would inflict on some poor soul, but Georgie was adamant that he would have something, and that Clarrie had better be in a frame of mind to help.

Clarrie didn't worry too much about it, as he felt sure that none of the jokes he'd ever heard about would be possible for two or three primary school boys.

The New Year's Eve dance was in full swing by the time Georgie made his appearance. Clarrie had been with Phillip and some of the other boys, doing their level best to keep clear of Yvonne Bishop and any unattended girls.

"Come on," Georgie hissed under his breath.

Clarrie knew what it was about, and pulled Phillip to come

with them. If there was going to be trouble, he decided that there were better odds of escape if more were involved.

"So what is your great plan?" Clarrie asked, patiently humouring the would-be hooligan.

"We're going to go into the public toilets, behind the hall, and get as much toilet paper as we can, and then we're gonna thread it through some of the fences in the main street."

"Whose fence?" Clarrie asked, not really sold on the idea.

"I dunno. Does it matter?"

"Guess not!" Phillip shrugged his shoulders. "Come on!"

So the three boys walked down behind the hall, the cheerful piano and saxophone music filtering through the high windows as they passed beneath. The old cement walled toilet block behind the institute was dark. There weren't any electric lights outside, and patrons had to use a good deal of night vision to find their way. The three pranksters waited quietly to be sure the toilets weren't currently occupied before they burst in to pilfer the paper supplies. It became obvious that there was indeed a lone patron, so the boys waited until the gentleman came out, and began to go back toward the lighted hall. He didn't see the three hiding in the shadows, or he might have suspected that something fishy was going on.

"Can't see a bloomin' thing," Phillip complained. "Did you bring a torch, Georgie?"

"Stop ya whinging!" Georgie retorted. "There's not much furniture to bump into. Just feel your way around."

Each boy took one of the three cubicles and felt for the toilet roll that should have been hanging from the wall.

"It's not here," Phillip's voiced emerged from the dark. "Only some square metal box on the wall."

"Same here," Clarrie said back. "I reckon it's one of those modern paper holders, like you see in the city railway station loos." After some minutes of Braille investigation, it was confirmed that it was one of those modern dispensers that yielded a single folded sheet of toilet paper at a time. Georgie was frustrated almost to the point of swearing. "Can't very well decorate fences with little bits of paper like this, can we?" he asked of his two bewildered companions. "What use is that sort of loo paper?"

There was some serious discussion at the short-sightedness of the local council in having thoughtlessly introduced such an inconvenient innovation, without a thought for the likes of these three who'd relied upon a roll of paper for their mischief.

Having emerged paperless from the gloomy darkness of the toilet block the three boys walked behind the hall, across behind the EFS shed to the playground. There were some other kids hanging about in the dimly lit area, the large fluorescent lights from Main Street throwing some light their way. A couple of other boys joined them, and more brainstorming began as to what plan they could come up with and successfully execute before the stroke of midnight.

Clarrie wasn't sure whether the resurgence of memory was a stroke of genius or a fit of madness, but when he recalled something he'd heard from a conversation with Jim Bishop, the others took to it like ducks to water.

Removing hubcaps, filling them with handfuls of gravel, and replacing them became a feverish sport that the now expanded group of five took to with relish.

Re-entering the hall an hour later, forever looking like the cat that had eaten the canary, the five boys decided to join in with the last couple of dances as if they'd been there all along. It did not occur to them that such an act of compliance in gentlemanly behaviour would actually be more likely to raise suspicions than if they'd hung about the walls in a disinterested manner. Still, there was only the Canadian Barn Dance, with its ever changing partners routine, and the Queen's Waltz to contend with before Clair Prosser took the stage and announced that it was two minutes to midnight. Everyone stood about in small clusters of friends and partners, and waited for their jovial MC to start the countdown that would see the end of one year and the beginning of the next. Streamers had been handed out to a number of people on the floor and at the stroke of midnight, when the band struck up a rendition of 'Auld Lang Syne', they threw them out in a colourful tangle amongst the crowd.

Clarrie enjoyed the sentimentality of the event, and watched as a number of men kissed wives or girlfriends. But he was somewhat alarmed when an unexpected pair of female lips smacked against his. He was all of a dither at the uncalled for attention, especially since his friends had seen the romantic assailant, and were hooting with glee. Clarrie would possibly have liked the superiority that could have been his had he looked more suave and confident about being kissed, but as it was, he was nothing but confused.

"Come on Casanova," Georgie urged tugging at his arm, at once alert to the new possibilities of having their hard work discovered. "Don't want to miss the action when it happens."

The boys surged out of the hall. There was no doubt that some people would stay on and dance to the wee small hours, but there were also a number of family people who would see the necessity of taking the children home to bed.

The boys went around to the side of the hall and stood a distance away from the cars that they had meddled with, waiting for the owners to come along.

"There's Jim Bishop," Georgie whispered. "His is the EH Holden, isn't it? We put stones in his hubcaps, didn't we?"

Clarrie silently acknowledged that they had, and felt a little guilty at having inspired the whole idea from a story that Jim had told him in the first place.

But Jim didn't get into his car. He opened the back of the station wagon and put a box of things inside, then turned around and went back into the hall.

The next person to appear was Georgie's mother. "We did your car too, didn't we?" Clarrie asked.

"You better not have," Georgie replied, casting a withering glare in his direction. "I'd get such a hiding I won't be able to sit for a week."

"You should have told us before," Phillip said, somewhat nervously. "I thought we were doing all the cars along the side of the hall."

"You didn't!" Georgie looked horrified.

"Well, they won't know it was us," Phillip tried to look confident in the midst of collapsing support.

"Well, I guess we'll see, won't we," Clarrie said as he saw Mr Greenbank emerge from the hall and come around to his Ford sedan.

They heard his parents wondering aloud where he could be, at which point Georgie felt it prudent to quickly come forth in a hopeful attempt at deflecting guilt from himself. As Mr Greenbank backed the car away from the hall, the two remaining boys could hear the gravel rattling in the hubcap, but it wasn't until he'd put the car into first gear and had started forward that it really began to echo around the area. Quickly Mr Greenbank stopped the car and got out. His wife wasted no time in opening the passenger door and getting out as well.

"What on earth is that infernal racket?" she asked loudly. Clarrie noticed that Georgie remained in the car, trying to look bored and disinterested.

Mr Greenbank wasted no time in levering the hubcap from the front wheel, and emptying the stones out onto the ground.

"What's all this?" his wife asked, annoyed.

"Some New Year pranksters," George Greenbank replied angrily. "I'd like to catch the little blighters…"

"What sort of parents let their children roam about at night doing whatever they please? If they'd disciplined the children properly when they were young, they would never think of such ideas."

Clarrie and Phillip nearly hyperventilated trying not to laugh at Mrs Greenbank's outraged comments. Her loud remonstrations drew the attention of other revellers and soon a small crowd of observers stood about, discussing the inconvenience and thoughtlessness of the unknown vandals.

"If I were you," Mrs Greenbank said loudly, "I'd be checking your own wheels. I don't imagine for one minute that this was an isolated attack!"

This seemed to be a sensible idea, and several people broke away from the discussion to check their own tyres. As most found a similar joke had been played on them there were varying responses. Some were cross and breathing threats of reprisal, but others just laughed and began to talk about the times past when they'd been party to a similar activity.

When Clarrie saw Lyall Arthur join the assembly, he decided to go and talk with him.

"Didn't have anything to do with you, did it?" Jim asked Lyall as he emptied out gravel from his back hubcaps.

"Why does everyone immediately suspect me of foul play?" Lyall asked, feigning hurt at the offence.

"Possibly because you usually have a hand in most pranks that go on around the town," Jim said with a laugh. "Come on," he urged. "Admit it. You've done your share of practical jokes."

"Seems to me I'm being unnecessarily persecuted in this instance," Lyall replied. "I can honestly say that I had nothing to do with the placing of gravel in your hubcaps. Honest before God."

"Did you swipe Perc Blieschke's sunflower again?" Jim asked, a twinkle of merriment in his eye.

"Oh, well, of course," Lyall said defensively. "That's tradition."

"How about when he tears across to your father to tell him all about his missing sunflower?"

Lyall laughed. "I couldn't believe it when he rolled up, and Geoff and I were standing there with Dad, and Perc is going for all he's worth about the little so and so's who've nicked off with his metal sunflower from his gate entrance. Then he told dad how some hooligans had torn about in his paddock, doing wheelies and ripping up all the ground. Course, Geoff and I stood there listening, trying to put on one of those sympathetic faces, and acting all outraged along with him."

"And your father doesn't know that you two were the culprits?"

"Well, you know there were others involved along with us.

We weren't the only ones! I resent being accused of every trouble around town." Lyall was obviously not serious about his complaints.

"Well you know what they say, where there's smoke there's usually fire!" Jim had finished fixing the wheels, and stood up ready to go inside and get Jenny to go home.

Lyall stood with Clarrie and Phillip for a while, watching Jim go inside. "So, do you know who fixed all these cars up?" he asked the two younger boys.

"Possibly," Clarrie said, trying to evade the truth.

"And possibly, you'll never tell either, will you?"

"Probably."

While they were standing about, Jim and Jenny got into their Holden station wagon, and Jim started the engine. But instead of the car engaging in gear and moving backwards, there was an almighty roar of the engine, and nothing at all happened.

The three observers rushed up to the car laughing. Jim got out and let out a few words of frustration. "Little horrors," he said. "Look what they've done, and I didn't notice it before."

In the dim light outside the hall, Jim had not seen that his car had been jacked up and left sitting on some wooden blocks, so that when he put it into gear, his wheels spun wildly in the air, just an inch from the ground.

The three youthful observers laughed loudly. They knew that Jim was a good sport, and Clarrie knew from many conversations that this was the very sort of joke that Jim himself would have played on some of his friends when he was single.

As they were standing about watching Jim go to the trouble of jacking his car up again, and removing the blocks, some of the locals stood about and talked about pranks of the past.

"Like the time we young fellows decided to hold up the train."

"Hold up the train!" Lyall directed this comment towards Lorrie Lello, who'd made the bold claim. "That sounds a bit criminal, doesn't it?"

Lorrie laughed. "Oh we weren't much older than Clarrie at the time, back in the thirties. A group of us had been to see one of

Lester's pictures that used to come of a Saturday night here to the hall. It was a western, and some outlaws had held up a train by heaping rocks on the railway line. So we decided that we'd do the same. It was show day, and the train brought a whole lot of people up from Pirie for the day, and used to pull up near the showground to let people off. We spent quite a while collecting rocks and stones from the creek, carrying them up the bank, and stacking them across the railway line. Then one of the other lads had a toy gun he'd got for his birthday, and we put tea towels over our faces, like they had in the movie, and hid in the bushes ready to hold the train up. Well, luckily for us, the train was going quite slowly, getting ready to stop to let the passengers out, and the train driver saw the rocks and came quickly to a stop. The men were out of the train in a hurry and took after us. When we saw the jig was up we took off as fast as we could but too late, as they caught us and we were given a good wigging by the driver."

"Wow!" Clarrie was taken by the story.

"Don't even mention it to Georgie," Phillip said.

"Don't even think of it at all," Lyall said. "Trust me. I know where to draw the line, and I've had enough 'wiggings' in my time to know that holding up the train is not a good idea."

Despite Lyall's fine words of wisdom it was not two weeks into the New Year before Clarrie heard more hilarious news of exploits that had got both Lyall and Jim into more trouble than either of them was worth.

Clarrie was with Lyall again and they had responded to a request from Auntie Ella to pick up some grocery items from Prests' and deliver them down to the showground for her. Auntie Ella was one of a team of women from the C.W.A. who made themselves available to cater for the aboriginal children's camp. The children were brought down to Melrose from Umewarra Mission, an Aboriginal community just east of Port Augusta. The children stayed at the showgrounds, camping in the pavilions and joining in the activities organised especially for them by the two camp directors, Miss Candle and Miss Bright. The Melrose women helped out with the program by working in the kitchen and preparing all the meals. Along with this very much-needed support, they made one special day to host a party just for the children. During this party, any child who had a birthday during January would receive a cake especially for them. Mollie McCallum, who was well known for her beautiful decorated cakes, supplied them for the birthday children. There had been some whisper among the kitchen workers that there were an unusually large number of birthdays registered for one month, but nobody felt like making an issue of it. Working hard didn't seem to bother them, especially since they could see first hand the delight on the faces of the children.

When Lyall pulled up outside the main pavilion, the box of groceries in the back of his ute, he was very much concerned to see Mavis Greenbank charging his way, a ferocious look on her face.

"Now I don't want any of your shenanigans down here this year, Lyall Arthur. Do you hear me? We had quite enough of that last year, do you remember?"

"I'm just delivering some stuff for Mrs Bishop," Lyall defended himself, looking forever the picture of innocence.

"Well see that you put the things inside carefully, and don't be driving madly around like you did last time!"

Clarrie could see that Lyall was set to argue the point, so grabbed the box and lifted it as if to hand it to him, in an effort to distract him from the provocation.

Mrs Greenbank appeared to be done with her accusations, and had turned to go back into the large kitchen at the back of the main pavilion.

"What was that all about?" Clarrie asked, glad that his friend hadn't pushed over the line of politeness.

"If Geoff weren't in Vietnam, I'd be having words with him right now," Lyall said, sounding half serious.

"Why?" Clarrie pushed.

"I'll tell you later." The conversation was deferred til a more appropriate time, and Clarrie carried the second box of fruit and vegetables up the large stone steps into the kitchen area. Auntie Ella was there and welcomed them both with a friendly smile.

"Thank you, boys. I appreciate your help. Would you like a drink and piece of cake before you get along?"

Clarrie couldn't think of any reason why he shouldn't accept, and encouraged Lyall to join him. They were invited to sit down at one of the long trestle tables, each with a large slice of fruitcake and a cup of cordial. Jean and Mollie McCallum and several other ladies were busy helping with food preparation, and the tables were already set for lunch.

The two didn't sit about after having finished their refreshment. For one thing, Lyall had the fidgets, and secondly, the dinner bell had rung, and already several children had formed a line just inside the far side door. There weren't any aboriginal families in the Melrose district, and Clarrie took just a few moments to observe the beauty of their large brown eyes and white gleaming teeth contrasting against their dark skin as they laughed together. In some ways they made the white children look almost insipid and washed out with their pale skin and freckles.

Finally, Clarrie and Lyall were back in the cabin of the ute, and driving back into town.

"So what was Mrs Greenbank having a go at you for?" Clarrie asked, quite unable to let the scene go in his mind.

"Well it was a bloomin' disaster in the end," he said, "but really it wasn't my fault. Not to start with, anyway."

"What wasn't your fault?" Clarrie asked, intrigued, and more so because of Mrs Greenbank's aggressive approach.

"It's quite a long story, Clarrie. Are you up for it?"

There was no going back now. Clarrie's interest was aroused and he wouldn't rest until he'd heard the worst of it.

"It was Geoff who set the whole thing going, last May when there was a church camp down here at the showgrounds." Clarrie nodded.

"Geoff and a couple of his mates had just been to the lodge ball and decided to get up a bit of excitement for themselves by going down to the showgrounds to do some wheelies. When they saw that there were people camping there they decided to give them a bit of a razz, and so after doing a couple of wild laps around the trotting track, they came tearing through the gates, with the intention of locking up their brakes, spinning their wheels just outside the pavilion, and then disappearing into the night. The trouble was, they didn't know that there were some people sleeping on camp stretchers outside where they'd planned their fancy wheelwork, and when they saw them, almost too late, they had to tighten things up a lot, and little stones went everywhere. They hot tailed it out of there real fast, leaving a hornet's nest behind them."

"So what's that got to do with you and Mrs Greenbank?" Clarrie asked.

"It just so happened that I was with a couple of other fellows up on the hill side of the oval, all very innocent like, parked there for a while, and then we decided to do a bit of a lap around the oval. We were driving very sedately, nothing danger-ous at all, but we'd hardly done a full turn and five cars descend-ed upon us. One was Mavis Greenbank, and she took to me, probably because I was closer to her than the others. My mates all cleared off without a thought for their fallen comrade, leav-ing me to face the posse on my own. She said to me, 'I'm very dis-appointed in you.' Of course she thought we'd been the ones to cause all the trouble earlier and had returned to the scene of the crime, but I didn't know any of this."

"Didn't Geoff tell you what he'd done earlier?"

"He didn't confess to that crime for a long time after, and so I went around wondering what on earth she'd got so upset about. I was a bit put out about it, so made up my mind I'd go, hat in hand, and apologise."

"So she still thought you were the one who'd nearly run those outside kids over?"

"Oh yes. And I still didn't know what she was mad about. But it got a whole lot worse from there. I said sorry and asked if there was anything we could do to make up for it. She was quick to respond, and asked if I'd help pick up the Sunday school organ from the showgrounds and bring it back to the church. So I got Geoff and we went with her to load up the organ. I'd already decided to drive very quietly, so didn't think it was necessary to tie the heavy old thing on. Geoff refused to ride up back because he said it was too cold, so the two of us, with Mrs Greenbank, squeezed into the cab of the ute, and I took off."

"What happened?" Clarrie asked, already beginning to anticipate the worst.

"Well we were going along very nicely, over the rough stuff, up onto the main road, about a quarter of a mile. I was grinding through the gears a bit, you know how they make a bit of a business changing, and the bus lurches. I don't know what happened, but Geoff was the first to wake up and he says, 'Lyall, she's gone! She's left us!' I came to a halt very quickly, and we got out and looked rather sadly at the organ that used to be about three foot six inches high, and was now about three chain long and six inches high. It was utterly splintered. It'd just fallen out the back and rolled on itself. Mrs Greenbank was distraught, utterly distraught. By this time, Geoff had gone back along the road to look at the mess, and he was not laughing, but he was guffawing. I could have brained him! When I looked back at the ute, Mrs Greenbank was actually praying, 'God, spare these boys. I think they meant no harm!'"

"Oh, Lyall!" Clarrie said trying to sound grave, but wanting very much to guffaw as well. "No wonder she was upset with you today."

"But it doesn't finish there. It gets worse. There we were and right into the middle of this circus the Sunday School superintendent pulls up."

"Mr Bishop! And it's the Sunday School organ!"

"Yes, and he gets out of his bus and says in a bright and breezy voice, 'What have we got here boys?' I couldn't see anything for it but to say it straight, so I said, 'We've wrecked your organ!'

I thought he would stop and help us pick it up, but no, he slammed his FC into gear and he was gone. Probably thought, I'm not getting caught up in this, especially since he'd been the one to give permission for them to take the organ in the first place. Anyway it took us three quarters of an hour to pick all the bits and pieces up. There she stood, two foot deep of chips and pieces. This time Geoff stood on the back to hold it all in."

"Wasn't a lot of point in that now, was there?" Clarrie asked.

"He probably didn't want to get in the front with Mrs Greenbank," Lyall said. "As we came around Young's corner I asked her if she wanted us to put it back in the church, and it was at that point that she really lost it. She'd been relatively calm up until then. We ended up putting it all in her shed.

"I remember driving home that night thinking how on earth was I going to explain this to people, and how was I going to tell Mum and Dad, especially Mum, her being so dedicated to church and all. I knew I'd have to tell them as I couldn't let the grapevine get hold of it and it get back to them some other way. I thought attack was the best method, so next morning at the breakfast table, Geoff and I were sitting one either side of Dad, looking at our porridge, and I came right out and announced that I'd smashed up the Sunday School organ, just like that."

"What did your dad say?" Clarrie asked.

"Nothing!" Lyall replied.

"Nothing?"

"No! He had his pipe in his mouth and just let it go from one side of his mouth to the other, back and forth. Then he got up from the table and went outside and sorted himself out. Then he came back in and said, 'I think you'd better tell your mother.' I'll never forget that. She was still in bed, and Mum, normally known for her calmness, really lost it. You know, I found out that the organ didn't belong to the Sunday School in the first place. It was a family heirloom of Mrs Schiller's, and she'd loaned it to the church for their use."

"No wonder Mr Bishop took off like that. Imagine having to

go to Mrs Schiller and tell her the family organ has been smashed to bits!"

"Now they've put up a sign at the showgrounds saying 'Vandals will be prosecuted'."

"I think we'd better drive very quietly, Lyall," Clarrie said, realising that he was keeping company with a marked man, and also knowing that there was such a thing as guilt by association. He didn't want that hubcap fiasco to come home to roost like a tired chicken needing a place to land.

Chapter
Sixteen

Clarrie heard from his editor. It was time for him to come back home. The major crisis was over, despite the fire burning on fronts spanning a distance of over fifty kilometres. Clarrie didn't want to leave. His heart was still in this thing. People he'd known years ago were still working round the clock to bring this crisis to a close, not to mention all the people he'd met in the past week. It was as though he'd become a part of the town again, belonging to a community that worked together for a common goal.

And all the memories that had come surging back had renewed feelings of happiness and security.

But the editor had said to wind it up, to write a final piece and come home. He had other things he wanted Clarrie to concentrate on and the fire in the Mount Remarkable National Park was old news.

Clarrie had no choice but to comply. But the worst of it was that he had no chance to say good-bye. The locals were still too busy, and any moment they had free from work they used to try to recuperate. He waited down at the shed for some time, hoping to see those that had been particularly special in the past, but in the hour or so that he was allowed, none of them showed up. As the deadline approached, he jotted a quick note of 'good-bye' and pinned it on one of the notice boards in the shed.

Driving away from the town he felt awful, empty, bereft and friendless. It wasn't even as if he could look forward to going home. His couple of attempts at calling home had told him quite plainly that his wife had taken the children, and that she had no intention of returning home. But then he had to admit that if he took a minute to look into his financial affairs he had probably lost the home anyway. The mortgage repayments were months overdue and he had no way of ever making them up.

As he passed the cemetery he stopped the car and got out. He turned back to face the mountain, now black, scarred and naked. As if all the memories of his childhood had culminated at one point, he closed his eyes and prayed. After all, that was what he had done many times as a child, but somehow had got out of the habit as he grew older. He couldn't quite remember the Sunday School lessons, but he remembered somehow that when there was nothing else left, there was God.

Harvest was finally over. The excitement of Christmas and New Year had settled, and the reminders that school was due to start came from just about every quarter. Every well meaning adult Clarrie saw in the street would ask him if he was looking forward to school. What sort of reply they expected Clarrie couldn't guess. What boy in his right mind would long for the holidays to be over? He always answered as politely as he could, but felt somewhat of a hypocrite. After all, he figured they'd want him to answer that he couldn't wait to get back to the classroom, the books and routine of lessons.

So when the first day of school dawned, Clarrie took his school case, sandwiches wrapped in greaseproof paper, and drink bottle filled with cordial. He met Georgie as he walked to school, and when Mr Briggs drove the blue school bus past, they almost expected Phillip Deekin to hang out the window and wave. But the Morris bus passed by with no such greeting and they were reminded that Phillip had graduated from primary school, and was probably already at the Booleroo Centre High School, ready for his first day in First Year.

Clarrie recalled that this would be the first year that Sally wouldn't be at the local high school. She was going to do her matriculation, but this course was not offered at Booleroo. If she wanted to pass this twelfth year of schooling, she was going to have to attend Gladstone High School. There had been some argument at home over this. Sally had wanted to quit school and find a job. Beth had asked her what sort of job she intended getting, and Sally had suggested working in the pub, like her mother.

Beth had vetoed this idea outright. Clarrie had listened to the two argue, his mother stating that there was no future or glamour in working in the pub, and Sally saying that she was sick and tired of studying subjects that meant nothing to her. In the end, Beth's argument prevailed, and Sally was enrolled at Gladstone High School. During the week Beth had arranged for Sally to stay with some friends from Wirrabarra. The Gladstone school bus ran from there, and Sally could catch it in to school each day. Then each Friday afternoon, she was to catch the train back to Melrose for the weekend.

Already Clarrie missed his sister, and wondered how on earth that could happen. They didn't have much to say to each other when she was here, other than to bicker and blame one another.

So the school year began. Nothing much was different for Clarrie and Georgie, other than they now sat in the Grade Seven row that was the row farthest from the door. There was a new group of Grade Fours, who had been in the junior room the year before, and they occupied the smaller desks closest to the door, and ranking in order of grade and size were the Grade Five and Six rows in between.

Miss Jolly was back, as stern and as strict as ever, and Clarrie could barely remember the small glimpses of softness he'd seen over the Christmas period. That didn't matter, as he wasn't really at school to make friends with the teacher. That sort of exercise was just the thing that would invite derision from his mates.

The first few weeks went along without mishap. The routine was just as it had been last year, only the spelling words were harder, and the grammar more meaningless than it had ever been.

Sally came home at weekends, but even if his mother hadn't noticed, Clarrie could see that she was unhappy. Only a few of her former classmates had gone along to continue at Gladstone, none of them her particular friend, and certainly no boys. Sally had always been more popular with the boys than the girls. Clarrie didn't venture to ask the cause of her obvious misery, and hoped that his mother would get to the bottom of it.

Little things happened about town that caused happy gossip. Robert and Janice Moulton returned from their honeymoon to set up house in their new place out from town, in the old Mt Remarkable Estate lodge house. This sort of romantic happening was always a pleasant diversion to normal faultfinding gossip. And right on the heels of that cheery piece of news came the announcement of the birth of Jim and Jenny's fourth baby, another little girl.

But even happy distractions like this couldn't hide from Clarrie the underlying tension that existed between Sally and their mother.

Then the bombshell dropped one afternoon when Clarrie arrived home from school.

Clarrie was surprised to see Sally home as it was only a Wednesday. She and Beth were sitting at the kitchen table having obviously been talking. Beth looked up at her son, a weary look in her eyes.

"We're going to have to move, son," she said without fanfare.

"Move!" Clarrie exclaimed. "Where?" He tried to remember the last time they'd moved from Wirrabarra, after his father had died. That had been nearly seven years ago, when he was about five. He knew he'd been miserable, but then he couldn't determine whether that was due to the move from one town to the next, or more so because they'd had to bury his father. "Where are we going?" Clarrie asked, imagining that perhaps his mother had decided they'd better move closer to Gladstone for Sally's sake, and not really liking the idea.

But when she announced where, the bottom seemed to fall out of Clarrie's world.

"We're going to have to go to the city," Beth said quietly. "It's no good, Clarrie," she hurried on, seeing his crestfallen look. "I'm not really making ends meet here, and Sally wants to get a job. You know there's not much out here to offer a young person in the way of a career."

"Why can't she go to the city on her own?" Clarrie cried selfishly, not really concerned about his sister's future, only that his own was crumbling around him.

"Clarrie!" Beth had spoken sternly. "That is not very kind of you."

"Well what about me? I don't want to go to the city. What about my friends and my school and my piano lessons?" Why on earth he suddenly felt a great affinity to his education was a mystery even to him. All he knew was that he was familiar with it, and as far as schooling went, there was no real cause for complaint.

"I'm sorry, son," Beth, tried to speak, but Clarrie hadn't finished.

"I can't go while Geoff is still in Vietnam!" Clarrie cried as a last ditch effort.

"The decision is made, Clarrie," Beth spoke as firmly as her tired mind would allow. We will go to Adelaide as a family. We need to be together to help one another."

"But what about Geoff?" he shouted. "Don't you care about him?"

"What is there that you can do?" Beth said with raised voice. "There isn't anything, Clarrie. It won't make any difference where you are."

Clarrie turned and ran out of the house, slamming the door behind him. He didn't want to hear her logical reasoning or even why it was that he should comply unselfishly. This was his home. The only memories he had of Wirrabarra were those that contained his father, and while they in themselves had been happy memories, he knew his father was gone and was not coming back. Since being at Melrose he had a network of friends and family. The friends weren't all kids his age, and the family weren't blood related, but that didn't matter. They were to him what his father might have been if he'd lived, and what his grand-parents and aunts and uncles could have been if they had lived in the same state, and if they had cared enough to be involved.

The next few days were a blur. Clarrie didn't say anything to Georgie or any of the others. He somehow hoped that his mother might just have been having a bad day, and that he would eventually go home and she would say that she'd decided to stay after all. But by the weekend, he knew that it was true.

Sunday morning, Jim came by to pick him up for Sunday school, and the first thing he said was: "I hear that you'll be leaving us soon." Clarrie couldn't deny it any longer, but that didn't mean that he had any words to answer his Sunday School teacher.

"Your mum tells me you're a bit upset about it," Jim went on. "I guess it will be hard at first, but you'll soon find some new friends. And there will be more opportunities to find jobs for Sally and your mother. It's probably the best thing."

"Probably!" Clarrie suddenly found his tongue. "Shouldn't they know for sure before they do something so big?"

"It's too uncertain, Clarrie," Jim spoke on Beth's behalf, and Clarrie began to guess that he'd been commissioned for the job. "One thing is for certain, there isn't any future here for Sally, and there won't be any for you either, when in four or five years you'll be looking to find work too."

"What about you?" Clarrie argued. "You live and work here."

"But I'm a farmer. My father was a farmer, and his father and grandfather were farmers. It's just the way it is."

"Couldn't I be a farmer too?" Clarrie asked, on the verge of tears.

"I thought you told me a while back that you wanted to be a writer."

Clarrie was silenced by this comment. He had divulged that secret ambition in a moment of confidence, and while he still wasn't prepared to shout it from the rooftops, his journal had become his closest companion of recent times, especially since Beth had made this horrible announcement.

"It's never easy making such dramatic changes, Clarrie," Jim went on, "but if you give it time, you will see that it's for the best in the long run. Things will work out better for you. You'll see."

Clarrie couldn't see it. He didn't want to see it.

"And if you send me your address when you get settled, I'll write and let you know how Geoff is getting on." Jim's kind offer broke down the last line of defence. It was settled. There was nothing he could do to stop it. Clarrie would be moving with his mother to the city.

They'd all told him it would be better in the long run, but as Clarrie drove back into the metropolitan area he had to wonder if they had been right.

The memories of that move rushed back at him all over again. Would it be all right? Was there anything that he could possibly do to make it right?

Clarrie closed his eyes in thought while he waited at the lights. He had to try.

Epilogue

2003

Clarrie's heart beat furiously as adrenaline coursed through his veins. He'd only just managed to slam on the brakes in time, his car's tyres screeching in such a manner that one would have anticipated the awful sound of breaking glass and folding metal. But as it was, Clarrie *had* stopped in time, and now that the swearing had passed, he thanked the Lord that his late model Commodore had disc brakes.

He was of half a mind to get out of his company vehicle and give these blokes a piece of his mind. But before he'd had a chance to even unbuckle his seat belt, the two Toyota Land Cruisers had restarted their diesel engines and gone on their merry way. At first, Clarrie was furious, but then he broke into a smile. Of all his early years in the country he had forgotten this strange habit of the locals – that of two approaching vehicles stopping directly adjacent to one another, so that the local drivers, usually farmers, could hang out their windows and yarn about all those things pertaining to life on the land. As he had rounded the bend in the road, he had to shamefacedly admit to himself, if he'd not been travelling at the unlawful speed of 140 kilometres per hour he probably would have seen them in plenty of time, and there would have been no near accident. As it was, the two men in these dilapidated work vehicles had waved to each other, and then to him, before continuing on their way at the approximate speed of 65 kilometres per hour.

Clarrie continued to smile as he started along the final leg of his journey. If his childhood memory served him correctly, he estimated that he was only a few kilometres from his destination. This he confirmed as he saw the grand old mountain – unchanged in the last thirty years.

She doesn't look any different from when I was a kid, he mentally noted. How many times had he been a passenger riding this straight piece of road that looked as if it would go straight into the side of Mount Remarkable? He'd heard it said plenty of times in the past, and he recalled it now - just like the Pied Piper, if you didn't know better, you'd half expect the mountain to open up at the base and swallow all travellers whole.

But Clarrie did know better. He'd lived in this little town for about seven years, from the time his mother had first moved there from Wirrabarra, shortly after his dad had been killed in a forest accident. Mrs Beth Brown, her daughter Sally and five year old son, Clarrie, had come to Melrose in 1960, to pick up the pieces of their lives following the tragic death of their husband and father. And there they had stayed until circumstances had forced the Brown family to move to the city in search of better work opportunities.

Clarrie Brown had received his tertiary education, and had done well for himself. He now worked as a journalist for a popular national magazine. In all those years since he'd left this town, he'd only returned the once, in 1988, during the time of some of the worst bushfires in history. He'd been here to write up a story then, and now he was back on a similar errand.

He made a mental note that the mountain had recovered from the dreadful ordeal, and looked as blue and full of vegetation as it always had, though when he'd left those fifteen years ago, he'd almost cried to see her charred black, naked and scarred from the ravaging fires.

But he wasn't here to report on disasters this time. The town – Melrose – had reached a milestone, and the local community was all abuzz with plans for celebration. One hundred and fifty years since the first European pioneers had settled to make a town-community.

First thing I'm gonna do, Clarrie thought to himself, is stop in at 'Young's Corner' and get myself one of those milkshakes. Don't s'pose old Mr and Mrs Young would still be there. Crikey, they'd most likely be dead and gone by now.

Even as Clarrie was musing about the fate of the proprietors of the small business formerly known as 'Young's Corner' he drove into the town proper, and past all the houses – some familiar friends of yesteryear, and some stark new strangers. As he continued along Nott Street, he saw that the old butcher's shop was now empty and in a sad state of disrepair, and Christianson's General store was, of all things, now an antique shop. At least it was in good nick. And then Clarrie's heart fell. He remembered now, when he'd been here reporting on the fires, that Young's Corner was no longer the thriving, bustling café that it had been in the 60's.

He pulled the Commodore around the corner and parked in front of the newly renovated council chambers. Half a thought crossed his mind about the look of that place, now re-named the Mount Remarkable District Council. Clarrie thought to himself that it now made more sense than the previous name of District Council of Port Germein, seeing the building nestled at the foot of the great Mount Remarkable and was many miles away from the seaside town of Port Germein.

But it was Young's that drew him. He walked across Stuart Street and onto the veranda area. How many days had he spent sitting on this veranda, watching the activity of the town's people, and those who came in from the farms? It used to be one of his favourite pastimes, just sitting and watching. He went to the glass door that was set at an angle to come in from both Nott and Stuart Street. A corner door for a corner store. He peered in through the glass into the darkened interior, and could almost hear the laughing and joking of the young people who used to come in to buy icecreams and milkshakes, and sit about socialising at the tables in the little alcove. But despite the echoes of his own memory, there was no life or activity inside. There was evidence of some occupation, Clarrie judged a craft group of some sort. There were spinning wheels, and hand-made woollen garments stacked about. The hand written notice on the door caught his attention then, and he realised he was staring into the meeting place of the Flinders Hand Spinners' and Weavers' Guild.

Clarrie was not particularly impressed, more so because of the sadness he felt at witnessing change. He was one of those strange sorts of blokes who could live life on a wave of activity, going from one technological advance to the next in terms of cars and computers, but he'd always held those few important growing up years in Melrose as a foundation – a point of reference. In his mind, Melrose was just what it had been in the 60's. To see all these changes in the town – faces that he didn't recognise, and names on buildings that were unfamiliar, like Serendipity, where Prests' should have been - caused an unsettling feeling.

He walked on down Stuart Street toward the school, trying to capture those memories of that time so long ago. Thirty years is a long time to abandon a friend – and Melrose had been his friend. The whole town and community had been that shaping, guiding parent in the absence of his father, and Clarrie felt it deeply to realise that not just the outside world had experienced change. So had his little town.

But there was one change that he was pleased to see. The old Blacksmith shop. When he'd been a kid, he'd often walked past the old stone building, and wondered what was inside. All the kids from the school had developed their own stories, of course, which ranged from anything that involved ghosts, to stories of an imprisoned family. Of course, Auntie Ella had told him that it was just closed up, and was used to store old stuff. Clarrie wasn't sure that he liked this simple and uneventful explanation.

But now, here it was, open for business. Oh, not as a blacksmith shop anymore, though it used its former history as a tourist theme. But it had been renovated and restored, with all the blacksmith paraphernalia, and was now a happy, busy little coffee shop that served cappuccinos and other continental fare.

Even way out here in the country that multi-cultural flavour is trying to make its mark. Not quite a Rundle Street café, Clarrie decided as he drank his short black, *but it's not Australian rural like it was.*

Clarrie was glad that the old blacksmith shop was open and busy. All the mystery of yesteryear was completely dispelled. But other businesses in the town were closed and fallen apart. This undeniable fact caused Clarrie to really think about things. The nostalgia began to get at him, and he decided to go for a drive out to the cemetery.

When he arrived, he began to walk up and down the rows of graves, paying tribute to old friends who now lay at rest. Auntie Ella and Mr Bishop, Frank and Sybil Arthur, Vic and Claire Blieschke, Ken and Jean McCallum; all lay side by side. Clarrie couldn't help but shed a few tears. They had all given so much of themselves to him as a child. But when he found the grave of Frank Fuller, Clarrie became alarmed. *Where was Mrs Fuller?* She was one woman he would never forget for all that she had done for him. *Surely they wouldn't have buried her anywhere but next to her husband. Perhaps she was still alive.*

This thought intrigued Clarrie, and he did a quick mental calculation. She must be well into her nineties, if she was still alive.

The afternoon shadows grew long and Clarrie knew he would have to return to town. Tomorrow was the Melrose Show, and one of the central celebrations of this 150th year. He needed to book one of the holiday cabins for the weekend, as he was expecting others to join him tomorrow. Even Sally and her kids were going to come and celebrate.

The show day dawned, and Clarrie couldn't help thinking about the many shows he'd gone to as a kid. He wondered if Mr Bishop was up early, rounding up cows to bring in for competition. By ten o'clock, the rest of the family arrived, and they took half an hour for a cup of tea before freshening up to go to the show.

It was like old times, and yet it was so different. Thirty odd years does things to people. Clarrie recognised faces, but they were different. But then he spent a lot of time having to remind people of who he was. At forty-seven, the years had told in his appearance as well.

Well into the afternoon, Clarrie was talking to a group of organisers for the Melrose Community Development, taking notes and generally trying to formulate a story for his magazine. Then he heard a voice from the past that made him stop and listen carefully.

"Who's that lady talking over there?" he asked the man he was interviewing.

"Oh, that is one of Melrose's former citizens. She used to teach piano here for years and years, so I understand."

"Mrs Fuller?" Clarrie asked.

"Yes. Do you know her?"

But Clarrie didn't answer. He got up from his chair and walked over to the gracious little old lady who sat chatting and laughing with some other people. Even as he approached he could see it was the same woman who'd sat so patiently with him, week after week, trying to encourage him to play well. Once he was standing right next to the group, they stopped talking and looked expectantly at him.

"Mrs Fuller," he addressed her. "Do you remember me? You used to try and teach me the piano. I always gave you a lot of trouble with 'Larkspur'."

"Clarrie Brown?" she asked, a hesitant look of recognition in her eyes.

He smiled as something of the past crossed between them.

"It's so good to see you after so many years," he said.

"Yes!" She laughed. "A lot of water has passed under the bridge since last we met, I dare say. What have you made of yourself?"

"I'm a journalist," he said proudly.

"And family?" She probed.

"My mother and sister are here this weekend. You remember them, don't you?"

"Yes," she smiled. "What about family of your own?"

"I have two daughters, in their twenties now. That makes me sound old, doesn't it?"

"Don't talk to me about old, young man," Mrs Fuller joked. "And what about your wife?"

Clarrie looked across the room, his brow furrowed for a moment. Then he replied: "There she is over there. Let me get her for you. I'd love you to meet my wife, Sue."

Local
Yarns

In the course of putting this book together many local people sat and told our interviewers accounts of things they could remember from years of living in Melrose. Some of these yarns have been worked into the main story, but not all of them could fit into 'One Remarkable Year'. We have included a few extra stories – real memories from the mouths of real people – for you to enjoy.

SCHOOL DAYS

Don Bishop

When I went to school, I used to ride the bike to the corner to meet Geoff Clarke on his horse. It was a pretty big horse and he used to carry a bamboo stick about three feet long. The main road in those days was a floating surface. Arty Nadar used to grade the road with his two horses and the grader and he would make a windrow one day then leave it in the middle of the road over night, and come back the next day to finish it.

One day there was a head wind and I'd met up with Geoff on his horse and me on my bike, so he held his bamboo stick out for me to grab hold of and he gave me a tow. Just before we got to the railway line, I got caught in one of Arty Nadar's grader rows while steering with one hand and holding the stick with the other. I got a bit of a speed wobble and the policeman came putt, putt, putting down the road. He didn't think that was quite the proper behaviour, us taking up half the road and doing speed wobbles, so he stopped and gave us a big lecture. We didn't do it again for about six months. It scared us.

Trevor McCallum

Talking about pranks, the girls' toilets at school had bucket toilets with a trap door on the back. One of the older boys used to undo this trap door and tickle the girls' bottoms with a stick and then run off. One day he did it and didn't look to see how big the bottom was. It was one of the teachers.

Lorrie Lello

The Teacher gave us an English history lesson on the barons and the lords, at the time when they raided a castle and captured it. So for a practical demonstration, he picked about eight of us to be lords and told us Monument Hill was our castle. We had to defend it while all the other kids were the robber barons coming to take the castle. There must have been about fifty kids charging up the hill. We found it a bit difficult to defend so we started rolling rocks down the hill as fast as we could. The rocks were bouncing about eight to ten feet in the air amongst all these children. We couldn't understand why the teacher was hollering and shouting and jumping up and down. We never hit a kid, never got one.

Audrey Albinus

When we played basketball (it's called net ball now) the older girls would put us younger ones up in the ring and we'd sit in it. One day it broke, I think it was with Val Curyer, and she fell. Ooh, there was strife over that.

Geoff Arthur

Mr Keith Fuller started the bus run, picking up kids with an old dual cab chev ute. Later, when Mr Briggs took over the run, he had an old ford truck that he got from his brother. We sat on loose forms on the back of the truck, no windows to look out of either. He'd made a canopy out of masonite to keep the wind and rain off, and there was a little ladder that we all climbed up. A decent wind came up and that masonite monstrosity blew away and smashed itself. I only got one go in the thing because it blew away in the holidays and next thing, Briggsy turned up with this little blue Morris commercial van.

WAR TIME AND SERVICE

Clair Prosser and Peter Abbott

During the war years rabbits were in plague proportions here so no one was short of meat. The main work was with a farmer; you'd get 5/- to 10/- a week plus your keep, and in a lot of cases a half sheep to take home to your parents. Although we were on ration tickets, here in Melrose, the butchers always gave a little bit extra. You'd pay for what you bought but only give ration tickets for what you asked for. My mum, Sis Prosser, and Dick Cope had the milk rounds, and Mum wasn't allowed to sell butter or cream because that was rationed. Practically everyone had a garden of some sort and they used their bath and wash-up water on it. Then we swapped what we had. Anyone with a horse and cart could get water from the council well in the creek for yourself and your neighbours. Clothing was our big trouble. Everyone wore patched clothing,

Peter: My parents always said that tea was the worst thing because you could grow your vegetables and your meat but you couldn't grow tea.

Clair: Yes, it was all tea, no coffee, and tea was often kept from meal to meal, on the side of the stove to keep it warm and then you'd just add to it.

Doll & Ralph Girdham

Doll: During the war we had to black out the windows so there would be no candlelight or lamplight showing.

Ralph: They had just strips across the headlights on the cars.

I helped with the digging of the air-raid shelters over at the high school but we didn't have any on the farms.

Doll: They used to have fundraiser concerts for the war effort, and the Air force came from Pirie as a feature plus local talent. Mum made pyjamas and knitted socks for the soldiers.

Ralph: The family had a car but they used a horse and jinker to go into the town. There was petrol rationing and it was four gallons a month and the old cars used to do about twenty miles to the gallon. Most of that petrol was used for going to church.

Vera Fuller

On Armistice Day, 1918, everybody flocked to the churches. We had the three churches then, Church of England, Methodist and Catholic, and the churches were packed with people. People were going to each other's doors and saying, "Isn't it wonderful," and they were knocking on doors and everybody sort of became as one. Although I was only young I remember the feelings that swept the town at the end of the war.

In the second war I remember we were doing something patriotic. We burned an effigy of Hitler down at the reserve. We all dressed up and they had a procession. A lot dressed up as soldiers and nurses, or anything to do with the war. The men played the women at football but the men had dressed up as ladies and we dressed up as men. That was ridiculous because the men had long skirts on. But of course we were all right because we were in pants, weren't we? Of course they could play football and we couldn't, so there you are.

HOME COMING FROM VIETNAM

Geoff Arthur

We got off the ship in Sydney in the morning and marched down the streets of Sydney before going by bus to the airport and flying back to Adelaide. Mum, Dad, Lyall and Brian were at the airport to meet me. Mum cried. They were horrified at how skinny I was and the sores on my arms. They were scratches that became infected because of the poor hygiene. There were no facilities for keeping yourself clean. In the dry season we got ten litres of water a day while we were in camp and the cook took half of it, so it didn't leave a lot for looking after yourself. Of course when we were in the bush we got nothing.

It was a great shock the first night home. I stayed with Grandma and they had gone to an enormous amount of trouble to organize a bed for me, but I was unused to sleeping in a bed and I felt I was suffocating so I got out and slept on the floor. It was weeks before I could sleep in a bed again. I had to spend a little bit of time each night until I got used to it. Everyone had moved on and I had come back thinking everything was going to be the same. I had to make new friends and I had to learn to drive again. The freedom was just wonderful, being able to go anywhere and not have to worry about anyone doing you harm. And yet a lot of people didn't even know I'd been away. That was a bit of a shock too.

THE DEPRESSION

Shirley Meaney
In the depression Dad used to go out behind the Mount trapping rabbits and he'd bring back a wheat bag full of rabbits. Mum could make everything out of rabbits. We'd have roman rabbit pudding, and crumbed rabbit; there'd be stewed rabbit, curried rabbit and roast rabbit. That was our staple diet.

Audrey Albinus
Things were very hard in those days. I remember people didn't have water because they couldn't afford to buy a tank. I remember carting water from Yates well, which is just down where Mount's shearing shed is. They had beautiful water in that well. Jack Hunt had an old draught horse and it must have gone for water, fell down the well and drowned.
Jennette: What would be the worse, losing your horse or having a horse down your well?

BUSHFIRES

Clair Prosser

Lloyd Arthur was the one who had the idea of having a fire brigade in Melrose. Lloyd and Frank Arthur were semi partners at that stage and they had a truck between them. That truck was used to load the water from the platform that we put up at the sale yards. We had a shed underneath the stand to put the engine pump in, and two big square tanks up on top. The first Melrose Fire brigade was Lloyd Arthur, Col Frazer, Gordon Prosser and myself and we used to race there as soon as the siren went, and load these tanks. I'm not going to tell you how many black toes or fingers we got, but the whole four of us were often lame or sore handed for days. That was our fire brigade before we got the big old blitz that was kept at the Council Chambers.

The first fire I can remember was when I'd just started school and it was when Will Jacka was running the brewery. My dad, Stewy Prosser, was head bottler there. This day they were working overtime, and Mum, Gordon and I went there. Will Jacka had a quick temper. On this particular day one of the Crofts driving two horses in a tip dray had come back with a dray of empty kegs, to report to Will. When he got on the dray the lead horse refused to move. It just stopped dead in its tracks and wouldn't move. Will, in his quick temper, grabbed an arm full of hay, put it under the horse and set it alight. Well the horse moved on and it moved on just far enough to put the dray right over the fire. No laid on water in those years so the bucket job went into gear, but it didn't save too much of the dray or the kegs, but the horses were OK.

MEMORIES OF DROUGHT

Ralph & Doll Girdham

Ralph: The worst drought was in 1945. Going to Port Augusta you'd have a sand hill on one side of the road going up and on the way back it would have drifted onto the other side of the road, reaching half way up those old netting fences.

Doll: I remember we had a cement fence around the house and the sand would just build up until eventually we just had to cart it away with a horse and dray. It was shocking! The pattern on the lino would be covered so you couldn't see it. But of course these days they haven't got all the horses or cows that used to cut everything up like they did in those days. There are better farming practices now.

Lyall Arthur

I remember Mum telling stories about those fearful drought years. They were in one classroom at Willowie and the dust was so bad that they couldn't see across the room, and they all had to wear handkerchiefs across their faces to keep the dust out. That must have been incredible

I reckon my experience of drought is the opposite. The wet drought. I can remember on a couple of occasions having to use two tractors to seed, just trying to get through this almighty mess, and in those years we virtually grew nothing because it was too wet.

MEMORIES OF FLOODS

Ralph Girdham

One night my older brother could hear water running at the end of the cellar and he walked around to see what was going on. That was a nasty shock for him because the floodwater was running into the cellar, and he found out that the end of the cellar had collapsed when he shot down this hole into the floodwaters in his pyjamas. He scrambled out, but it was a nasty experience in the dark.

MOUSE PLAGUE

Vera Fuller

During the mouse plague, I had very long thick hair, and while I was sleeping the mice chewed all the ends of it. I remember my Mum crying over it when she brushed my hair to plait it. So she singed all the ends of my hair to get the mousy smell off it. I would have been about seven or eight at the time. It was just before the war ended because I can remember my Mum saying "The Bible has said that there will be wars and rumours of wars and plagues". She was alluding to the mouse plague.

Lots of babies got bitten on the face and they developed what we called mouse plague sores. They were really nasty sores. A lot of little children and babies were bitten by the mice. You'd go out in the yard at night, and I remember my Dad holding a lantern up and the ground would be moving with mice. And everything smelt mousy. I suppose we all smelt mousy. I know everything around us smelt mousy.

MELROSE BUSINESSES

Don Bishop
In the early 1900's in the bakehouse, above the mixing trough there was a nice flat slate windowsill where a big black cat slept. Sometimes, when they tipped the bags of flour in to mix up, there was a mouse in it. The cat that was seemingly asleep would pounce into the flour after the mouse. It would go in black and come out white with a mouse in its paw.

Lorrie Lello
One of the employments in Melrose was wattle barking. This was a process by which the bark was completely stripped from the wattle trees, thus killing it. The landowners used this as a way of clearing the wattle. The bark was then sent to tanneries in Adelaide for processing.

Audrey Albinus
Bennetts had a shop next to the North Star Hotel, and the house next door belonged to Miss Williams. At that time, there were shops right up to the corner. Miss Williams had an orchard at the back of her house and we used to sell her fruit for

her. On the other side of the North Star was Mr. Lewis's general store. Matthews' emporium from Peterborough used to come and sell their wares from the billiard room in the hotel.

Where the General Store is now, there was a billiard room owned by Mr Thomas. He did haircuts and sold lollies.

When the McKenzies owned the shop they used to make iceblocks with fruit for us to buy.

YOUTHFUL MEMORIES

Shirley Meaney

We had big cracker nights when we bought crackers for a penny each. I'd get a penny a day for doing all Mrs Nugent's messages and getting her paper. We'd save our money to buy a heap of crackers from Mr Christianson's shop. We didn't have the power on at the cottage in those days. We were going to have a really big cracker night. All the kids from the town had come around. My brother Col had bought a lot of crackers and put them in a shoebox and he wasn't going to use these until last, thinking he'd let everybody do all theirs first and save his till last. Anyway the others were urging him to get his crackers, but he wouldn't and wouldn't even tell us where they were. So we continued to let off everybody else's crackers and the last one was one of those jumping jacks. Now, Col's crackers were hidden around the side of the old corrugated iron shed, and this jumping jack went jumping all over the place and around the corner and into his box of crackers. There was a terrific explosion, just about blew the roof off the shed, and he lost the lot. Old Mr Willington said, "Oh, it looks as though Ozzie's got the power on at last!"

Still on the subject of crackers: Grandpa Keogh used to accumulate quite a lot of logs for the wood fires. One day he realized that the woodpile was going down and he thought someone must be taking it. So he thought he'd have to get into this, and decided that he'd get hold of some of those crackers, you know the fire works. He put these two-penny bombs in this load of logs. Then one night he got invited to some friend's place where they often used to play cards. When they thought they'd stoke up the fire and the wood blew up, it was embarrassing, but he knew where his wood had gone.

Lorrie Lello

Eddie's after school job was to bring Mrs Slee's cows home to milk every night. If you wanted a bull you watched the calves and if you got a nice one you would keep him for a bull. They had one picked out for a bull, he wasn't a bad calf either, and we'd go down every night and ride him. We had a little race down there and he could buck too. Anyway he'd be staggering by the time we finished and Mrs Slee couldn't understand why he wouldn't grow.

Eventually we got a bit game and we got Jim Stutley's saddle, a beautiful little riding saddle, and we stuck it on this bull calf, and did he buck with that on. But we broke the tree of the saddle doing it. Quietly, we hung it up back in the shed and it must have been five or six years before they took it down to use it and found the tree broken, and do you know they had the cheek to accuse Eddie and me of doing it!

MELROSE SHOW

Malcolm and Jessie McCallum

Malcolm: Melrose Show –One year it rained so much, the water went over the bridge.

Jessie: yes the bridge was washed away or at least the sides of the bridge were. Herb Walter had built a little bridge across the creek for the kids to walk across and I was there to meet Debbie from the school bus. She was coming across the bridge and had just handed me her case when the bridge just went "swish" down the creek. She had just stepped off it.

Carol Bamman

My first year as Secretary of the Melrose Show the official luncheon was in the old luncheon pavilion and Marj Thomson was to receive her life membership. Just as everything was about to happen somebody told me this policeman was after me. I got to the door and he gave me a kiss. It was the longest walk I'd ever had to take right around the room. It was Peter's cousin who was coming back from some trek up bush.

A very wet show that I remember, was the first year I had bras and high-heeled shoes.

Lyall: what have the bras got to do with it?

Carol: Well we always had new clothes for the show and I had my first bras and my first high heels and got all decked out. Mum had advised me not to wear the high heels, because it was too wet. But I did and I ruined them because I kept getting bogged in them. The thing was, that was the start of spring. You all had your new spring outfit for the Melrose Show and you had to wear it, no matter what.

SPORT

Keith Fuller

In the paddock behind the Mt. Remarkable hotel they had race meetings. They formed a Jockey Club called the Frome Jockey Club. Later the Jockey Club shifted down to the oval where they had picnic races. The Frome Jockey Club also had two or three meetings down at the Laura Race Course but when the depression came the Frome Jockey Club folded.

TRANSPORT

May Crittenden

When I drove the horse and cart through the scrub there was a stretch that had magpies. When they were nesting they used to swoop down and peck the horse on the head. The horse knew this stretch and he used to take off and wouldn't stop till he got to the end. One day I had people with me and he took off. They were almost hysterical but I said, "He'll stop in a minute", and he did.

Vera Fuller

My Dad had the second car in Melrose. Dad was a very careful driver, and 25 miles per hour was very fast. But Dad was extra careful and he just crawled along. Old Mr. Mount was the butcher, and he was a very careful driver too. Well they only met in a head-on collision in the back lane. Everybody laughed about it. Tom Slee and Tom Mount they've had a crash in Petticoat lane. Everybody in town knew that they were such slow drivers, and it tickled everybody's fancy to think they'd had a crash in Petticoat Lane.

When we got the car I remember thinking, "Oh yes, we've got a car," and when we went anywhere I would sit up and look around and hope that everybody was looking at me in the car.

THE UNUSUAL AND THE DIFFERENT

Doll & Ralph Girdham

One of the peculiarities of Melrose was that when we went to the bank, customers went into the bank one at a time. We all lined up outside. This was so no one knew the other's business. Strangers to the town would go straight into the room and we would all give them a dark look and say, "Who was that? Well fancy pushing in like that, what authority did they have to do that?" In the cold weather we used to squash into the little porch to wait our turn.

Shirley Meaney

Now about the ghost at the top pub: Well, the publican's wife told us these visitors were leaning on the bar. They hadn't had anything to drink. When they looked up the passage they said to her, "Oh, there must be a fancy dress ball here tonight."

She looked surprised and said, "No I don't think so."

"Oh!" they said, "look at those two people up there that have just come down from the passage, all dressed up."

She asked "What do you mean all dressed up?"

"Well, one is dressed like some sort of a king and the other one is dressed in a long robe." When they looked they couldn't see anything. The woman who spoke seemed quite sensible but the publican's wife said when they looked there was just nothing there. Then on another occasion the publican's little daughter used to call out to her mother in the night, saying, "There's a little girl in my room, Mum." They thought she was dreaming but she kept this up each night. So they took her to the doctor. But then one day the school was visiting the museum and they were looking at an old book. The child pointed to the photo and said "Mummy, that's the girl who comes into my room." When they looked, it was old Gran Jacka as a child.

Jim Bishop

One time a crook was going through Melrose, and someone rang the policeman to let him know. The crook had stolen a modern car that just flew past the policeman as he just tootled along in his old Rugby 1928 model. He would have had a top speed of about 40 miles an hour. The crook went through the ford in the creek that was here before the road was built, and the water in the creek splashed the distributor and his car stalled. So the policeman came along and he caught him anyway.

Gweneth McCallum

On the pageant train to Adelaide: We'd been to the John Martin's Christmas Pageant in Adelaide once and Trev said "Well that's it, there's no way I'm going to take you down to the pageant again."

I said, "All right, I'll organize a train."

So I wrote to the Chairman of the Railways and he wrote and said "Not a hope". But I also wrote to the minister for transport and there was an election soon and he decided that it would be a good vote winner. So he asked how many people would go if they put one on. I canvassed Wilmington, Melrose, Booleroo, Quorn, Gladstone, and Wirrabara. People even came from Baroota. Some people, I found out afterwards, replied that they were coming because they thought it was a good cause, but it did snowball when they put some publicity in the Flinders' News. We had to get up very early and go to Gladstone to catch the train. When we got there they'd brought a beautiful historic steam train up with leather bound seats and individual compartments. Some railway buffs came up with it, and rode back in the afternoon on our return trip as well. We got home really late.

Lorrie Lello

On Sundays the pubs were closed, so someone would go out to a nearby hill and fire a shotgun. The policeman would go out looking for him, and when the gunman saw the policeman coming, he moved to the next hill and fired again. While the policeman was out, all the other men went to the pub. Then the next week it would be someone else's turn to fire the gun.

LIFE'S LIKE THAT

Carol Bamman

We used to have a baby parade in my day. We would get dressed up and go into town. Once we'd parked the car, we'd get the pram out with all the pretty pram cover and rattles and then we would walk up to Prosser's, across the street and then back down to the post office to show everybody our baby. The men used to go to the pub and the Council blokes all went after work. The wives would be doing the shopping, showing off the baby, cleaning up the afternoon tea and then when the pub shut at 6pm they all went home.

www.ingramcontent.com/pod-product-compliance
Lightning Source LLC
Chambersburg PA
CBHW070548120726
47909CB00007B/2280